ALSO BY CLIFFORD GARSTANG

IN AN UNCHARTED COUNTRY

WHAT THE ZHANG BOYS KNOW

The Shaman of Turtle Valley

For Natalie,
I hope you enjoy!

ScBA 19

THE **SHAMAN** OF **TURTLE VALLEY**

a novel

CLIFFORD GARSTANG

BRADDOCK AVENUE BOOKS

UNCOMMON BOOKS · UNCOMMON READERS

Printed in the United States of America
10 9 8 7 6 5 4 3 2 1

FIRST EDITION, May 2019

ISBN 10: 1-7328956-6-9
ISBN 13: 978-1-7328956-6-9

Book design by Savannah Adams
Cover design by Savannah Adams & Adeeba Arastu
Cover photo by Fabrizio Conti, Unsplash

Braddock Avenue Books
P.O. Box 502
Braddock, PA 15104

www.braddockavenuebooks.com

Braddock Avenue Books is distributed by Small Press Distribution.

MOUNTAIN SHRINE

A sudden gust washes over the mountain,
clouds hide the sun, and parched boughs cry for rain.
As the hermit scrambles between singing stones,
the ancient crane sails above the vanishing peak.
The mountain god descends like a meandering stream,
calling to the trees and deer as he flows past.
His breath is swallowed by the thirsty earth,
but the bamboo knows when he will return.
Yi Ku-yong

THE **SHAMAN** OF **TURTLE VALLEY**

a novel

PROLOGUE

The stones have been here forever, and they will outlast everyone. The mountain streams have always flowed and always will, reaching out for fertile lands in an endless, welcoming grasp.

When the first white settlers arrived in this corner of the Great Valley of Virginia in the years before and shortly after the American War of Independence, they must have found the twin humps of Brother Mountain comforting and familiar. Covered with native chestnut and hemlock, black pine and walnut, laurel and rhododendron, the lush peaks promised abundance and beauty, sustenance and shelter. The newcomers stopped, taking the soaring hawk and plodding turtle as signs that their journey had ended. They cleared the bottomlands, put down roots, and made their homes.

Dermot Alexander, an Ulster Scot, was among them. For his farm, he chose land nestled in a broad hollow not far from Stillwater, a new settlement growing on the banks of the winding Turtle River, and he built his cabin so that when he rose each morning he would see the early light spread across Brother Mountain like wildfire.

A head taller than most of his acquaintances, with a flowing white beard, Dermot toiled in his rocky fields from dawn to dusk while his wife, Margaret, tended their livestock—and their children. It was a life of hardship—two of their girls died in infancy, and a son, the youngest boy, nearly perished when a wave of influenza swept the Valley—but also one filled with beauty. Dermot took the time in spring to savor the flowering of the hillsides: the dogwoods that looked like drifts of snow among the evergreens; the redbuds, with their rivers of pink light flowing through the understory; the blossoms of the black locust that smelled, to him, like butter. And in the fall, with the harvest behind him, he paused to behold God's glory in the leafy flames that seemed to leap from tree to tree until the entire landscape was consumed by shades of red and gold.

Margaret, who sometimes longed for her childhood home in County Donegal, had little time to notice the grandeur of the Valley. If her eyes rose from her labor to the peaks of the twin mountains, it was because she detected on a breeze the dull scent of a spring shower or heard the rumble of a summer storm. She saw her husband gaze dreamily toward the hills, but she had no time for such nonsense. There were animals to feed, bread to bake, trousers to mend. And yet, she wasn't oblivious to the land. Over time, she grew skilled at reading nature's portents—it was she who foretold the blizzard of 1806—as if the earth itself had divulged to her its secrets. After the sickness that took her babes, she learned about native cures from an old Blackfoot medicine man who lived on the mountain—the sumac leaves that, when brewed into a tea, would cure asthma, the poultice of goose blood and sassafras bark that would speed the mending of broken bones—and her reputation as a healer spread.

Born in the shadow of Brother Mountain, the children of Dermot and Margaret found their own solace in the natural world that harbored them, in the bog that muddied their bare feet, and in the forest that fed their imaginations. Elizabeth, the baby, freed from the chores that occupied her brothers and sisters, explored the farthest in her quest for the glittering rocks she admired. She searched for them in the rushing stream, tracing it up the mountain, filling her pockets with smooth stones, until she discovered, hidden behind dense bramble and sweet hawthorn bushes, a narrow cave. Dark, and ripe with smells she associated with her mother's animals, it was the perfect hiding place for her treasures, to which she would return again and again.

When Elizabeth was still a girl, Dermot's brother Elias arrived from Pennsylvania, where he had made his home after the brothers left Ulster. Like Dermot, he was drawn to the game-filled hollows and the enchanted crags of the twin peaks. If her husband was late for supper, Margaret knew he had wandered off with Elias, searching after a tune only they seemed to hear, a scent only they could smell. A childless widower, Elias looked to start again in Turtle Valley and, or so it seemed to Margaret, had his eye on young Elizabeth. At Margaret's urging, Dermot confronted his brother on one of their sojourns in the hills, and, during the struggle that ensued, Elias fell into a rocky gorge. Dermot managed to carry his brother back to the house, but, despite her skill, Margaret could not—or would not—heal his wounds. They buried him next to the tiny graves of their girls.

By the time Stonewall Jackson marched through the Valley in 1862, the Alexander house had been enlarged—wings, a cellar, a second story, a wrap-around porch—to accommodate the ever-expanding broods of Dermot and Margaret's eldest child, Archibald, and Archibald's eldest, Jeremiah.

Now, more than two centuries after Dermot felled the first trees for lumber, the log core of the homeplace is invisible from the outside. Subsequent generations replaced Dermot's spartan barn with one that rivaled the house in size. They needed a shed for logging operations in the hills and built that. The privy was demolished when bathrooms were added to the farmhouse. And over the years, through wars and disappointments, death and distant attractions, the Alexander clan, having reached its peak at the turn of the last century, gradually diminished, until the dwindling lands and sprawling house, one of the oldest in Turtle Valley, came into the possession of stolid Henry Alexander, his wife, Ruth, their only surviving son, Aiken, and the ghosts of their ancestors.

TURTLE VALLEY, VIRGINIA

MAY 1996

1

The front door booms shut, rooting Aiken to the driveway. Half expecting the wobbly shutters to fall, he shields his eyes against the fierce sun and squints at the tiny cottage. Now the door swings open, and Soon-hee dumps another armload of his underwear and socks on the stoop.

"Take things away," she shouts. His wife's crazy English sounds even thicker, wetter, when she's angry. "Away!" The door slams again.

"Jesus," he says, twisting to check for the snooping eyes of gossips, like that George McCormack across the street, who would surely turn this latest quarrel into something more sinister than it is. None of the nearly identical houses on Pioneer Drive sits more than a coffin's length from its neighbor, but if there are witnesses to Soon-hee's insanity, they're invisible. Or hidden behind drawn curtains.

All couples go through this, don't they? Not his parents, he suspects, who've lived in bliss their whole lives, but everyone else. Kelly and her husband? Sure. Cousin Jake and his wife? No question. Everyone. Aiken hurries to the door, bends, and scoops up the jumble of clothes. As he straightens, pain shoots up his back, like fire ripping through dry leaves, and he has to lean against the siding to keep from dropping the bundle.

"Soonie, don't be like that," he says softly, his face next to the door. He knows she can hear his voice. They're only inches apart. He feels her presence the way he feels the stifling heat, the way this new pain has filled him. "I know we agreed, I know what the lawyer said, but this is silly. Can't we talk?"

Except there's nothing to talk about. He's said it over and over and in a dozen different ways. That she shouldn't listen to Tammy's crazy notions. That his cousin doesn't know what she's talking about. That he hasn't cheated on her, not now, not ever. That he wants to stay. For little Henry. For all three of them. That he'll do anything she asks. That he's sorry for whatever it is she thinks he's done. For whatever he's actually done.

"Go," she shouts from inside, the door barely muting her voice. To Aiken, familiar by now with Soon-hee's moods and inflections, it sounds final. And so there's no point in staying.

He'd told his parents they were separating—God, how he'd hated making that call—and with nowhere else to go had accepted their invitation to move out to the farm. "Temporarily," he'd insisted. "We'll see," his mother had said, as if she'd been expecting this outcome all along.

But he hadn't realized how much debris he'd accumulated in only a few years: T-shirts and jeans and boots; a carton of grease-stained work clothes; the cracked lamp he's been meaning for months to mend; a footlocker crammed with musty Army gear; a box of his favorite books; the orange crate of record albums he'd salvaged from his brother's room after he died, afraid that his parents would discard Hank's only legacy.

Even late in the afternoon, the sun is relentless, the hottest day of the year so far and summer just getting started. Not like Kuwait during the war, but the hottest Turtle Valley day he can remember. It's the sort of day folks will talk about for years, maybe generations, growing hotter with each retelling: the day the highways melted, the lake boiled dry, insects sizzled in the burned grass.

He lifts his T-shirt to wipe the sweat from his forehead and gazes again at the cottage. Henry is peering through the picture window, and their eyes meet. The boy's shoulders droop, his stomach pooches out, hands and forehead pressed against the glass. He's a handsome child, with his mother's flat nose and broad cheeks, Aiken's blunt chin, even a hint of his Grandma Alexander's mischievous eyes. Aiken heaves a cardboard box of shoes and work boots into the truck, moaning as his spine burns, and waves for Henry to come outside. He doesn't move.

Aiken has explained to his son what's happening, why he's leaving, and where he's going. He's promised to visit often. He's promised to take him out to the farm, where Henry loves to explore in the fields and the wooded hills. He's promised that nothing will change. But the boy's blank eyes stare back at him, and the tears that roll down his cheeks make Aiken's own eyes fill.

Just yesterday he'd taken Henry to the park in Stillwater where they strolled around the duck pond, watching massive carp rise to the surface and sink again like submarines. At the water's edge, they tore bread into pieces and fed a family of mallards, Henry tossing a crust to the smallest of the birds and squealing when it grabbed the bread with its bill. Aiken held his son's hand as they investigated the petting zoo where

Henry bounced from lamb to calf to piglet, his delight with the baby animals uncontainable.

"Daddy, can we take a lamb home with us?"

Henry struggled with the word "lamb" and Aiken couldn't stifle a laugh. "No, buddy, we can't do that. We've got Ralph, though, right?"

Henry shook his head. "Ralph's just a dog," he said. "It's not the same thing." But he didn't persist, and Aiken saw both longing and understanding in his son's eyes.

Aiken considers going back into the house now. He'll grab Henry and go. It's not right to separate a boy from his father, and it's not right to leave him with a deranged Korean woman, even if she happens to be his mother. It's not safe, not when she's behaving erratically. To hell with his stuff and to hell with Soon-hee. She can't stop him. He'll take the boy, and he won't tell anyone where they're going. They'll get in the truck, head out, start a new life in a new place, father and son. A team, just the two of them. Leave all this misery behind. A new life and a new story. They'll build a new home, one that doesn't involve a crazy Korean woman with crazy ideas.

And then Soon-hee pulls Henry away from the window. Aiken holds his gaze steady, as if he can summon the boy's return. But a minute passes. Two. The dead yard darkens in cloud-shadow, and then the searing light is back. He shields his eyes. Sweat seeps into his T-shirt. He smells smoke on the air, searches the horizon for a distant fire, but sees nothing. He recalls the incessant fires in Kuwait, the oily, black smoke that followed him everywhere, and braces for another attack, another explosion. But no, there is nothing, and again he wipes the sweat from his face.

Of course he can't just take Henry from his mother. He knows that. And this mess is at least partly his own fault. While he worries about leaving his son with Soon-hee, worries about being apart from Henry for even a day, there isn't a damn thing he can do about it. She's not crazy. She's just unhappy. She loves the boy and she's a good mother, in her way. But Aiken hates the feeling of powerlessness, and the only option left to him now is to watch from a distance, do what he can to stay in his son's life, and come when he's needed.

Facing the stacks of boxes that flank the driveway, he estimates what more will fit in the truck. Piles of lumber sit in the carport still, plus the old TV Soon-hee has said he can take. She'll keep the 27-inch Sony with the built-in VCR they dragged home from Wal-Mart to celebrate their first reconciliation, when Henry was still in diapers and Soon-hee had accepted, belatedly and temporarily, his protestations of innocence. Tammy was behind that eruption, too, he's sure. But the truck is full enough. No point putting it off any longer. His folks are waiting.

He whistles for the dog. Ralph gallops around the corner of the house and jumps into the cab of the pickup, a gift from his father when Aiken got out of the Army. He coaxes the rusty heap into gear, backs out of the short driveway, hesitates when he hears the load shift and resettle, and watches the house recede in the mirror.

Henry can't see him, he knows, but Aiken waves anyway. This habit, this waving at every departure, no matter how mundane, is an Alexander family tradition, or maybe a Turtle Valley tradition. He remembers standing on the porch with his brother Hank, both of them returning their father's wave as he drove off in this very truck. He remembers waving at

Hank's school bus, too, and sobbing because Hank didn't wave back. He always waves for Henry.

George McCormack must think the gesture is meant for him, because he salutes as he plops into the rocker on his front porch. The Campbell kids chase their mutt through the drooping chokeberry at the corner. Ralph stands on the seat and barks. A kid on a motorbike roars out of nowhere, and Aiken hits the brakes to let the boy pass. The jolt sends a box thudding to the truck bed. Aiken's heart pounds, his back hurts, and he's even more aware now of the fucking heat, the collapse of his marriage, the pain of leaving Henry behind, the humiliation. Only failures move home. He's moving home.

As he turns out of the neighborhood, stiffening in the seat to fight the ache in his back, he smells smoke again. It wasn't his imagination after all, a joke the war played on him from time to time. He picks up speed, then heads into the hills toward Brother Mountain.

2

I pray to Sansin, the Mountain God.

In this small house in America, *Mi-Gook*, the Beautiful Country, I make a shrine to Sansin. On a knee-high, lacquer table, in a corner, I make offerings of rice and fruit. I bow, I kneel. I pray to Sansin to keep demons away. I write his name on scraps of yellow paper. In red, like blood, I write his name and carry this *pujok* in my pockets, I paste *pujok* to walls for protection, I burn the yellow paper and crumble ashes into our soup.

I bow, I kneel. I pray to keep demons away. I pray for wealth to come to my son, my Ha-neul, my Sky, and also to my father at home in Pae-tu whom I shamed. I pray for spirits to guide us. I pray for justice. I pray for the spirits of my mother and my baby sister. I pray to keep this tiny money I save from what Ay-ken gives. For my son, Ha-neul.

The *mudang* in my village, the shaman, she teaches me about Sansin, the Mountain God. In my country it is the women who are *mudang* and have the power to call the Mountain God. The spirits teach me.

12

* * *

Ta-mee visits. Ta-mee is like a sister, and she makes me think of my sister who died. She watches me pray before the shrine of the Mountain God. I bow, I kneel. I pray for my family. I pray to keep demons away.

At first, I think Ay-ken is kind. In Seoul he is gentle, generous. I am pulled by his yellow hair and broad shoulders, by his bright eyes, like two moons. Is it *his* art, or mine, that draws us together? He is not like other Americans, so rough and loud. With him, I feel safe.

He brings me to the Beautiful Country. I am afraid, but he speaks softly to me, and I see the warmth in his gaze when he holds Ha-neul in his arms. Still, I am alone all day when he works, and sometimes also at night. I fear the power that binds us cannot last, is not meant to last. Sansin tells me this. Ta-mee tells me.

It is hard in a strange country, and Ta-mee helps me.

"We're the same," she says. "We're both victims."

"My sister," I say, because I want to tell her about my little sister who died.

"Sure," she says. "Sisters. You and me."

I am a victim, Ta-mee tells me. We sit in my kitchen and we drink tea. Sometimes she sings and plays her guitar and I listen to her sweet voice, the stories her songs tell. She says I am ripped from my home. I am a child with a child. I am made to do what I do not want to do by my father and by Ay-ken. This *man*. All *men*.

Ta-mee teaches me. My sister.

* * *

"Soonie," Ay-ken calls me, like a dog. "Wife," I tell him, or "Soon-hee," but he does not listen. He does not listen, and he does not hear.

Ta-mee teaches me English. It is not like the school in Seoul where we repeat and repeat. My name is Lee Soon-hee, my name is Lee Soon-hee, my name is Lee Soon-hee. She talks and I listen. I hear. And then I talk. She tells me about her school and boys she knew, a man. In a whisper, she tells me about a baby, but Ta-mee does not have a baby. She tells me about her husband who strikes her, but Ta-mee does not have a husband. She tells me there is a new man for her, but does not tell me his name. I tell her about our life in Seoul, about meeting Ay-ken. I tell her that he is gentle and kind, and I tell her about my dreams for Ha-neul.

"You can't trust men," she says. "You don't know him." She tells me she sees Ay-ken with other women in the wine house. I think of the wine house where I met Ay-ken. I think of my father and his new wife, how she took him from me, betrayed me. I think of Ay-ken.

"They're all alike," she says. "Tomorrow, the next day, a year from now. He'll be gone. Trust me."

And so I wonder. Ay-ken will leave? If he leaves, what can I do? If he leaves, I must not let him take Ha-neul. With the help of Sansin, I will fight to keep Ha-neul.

At the shrine in our house, I bow, I kneel. Sansin comes to me, comes into me, speaks through me. He tells the man to go away, to leave Ha-neul with me. Tells Ay-ken to go away. In me there is shouting I cannot control, dancing, whirling music, voices. He comes in dreams, at first, and then always he is present in my mind. When Ay-ken goes, Sansin rests.

Two kinds *mudang*: the vision is passed from mother to daughter to granddaughter, or it comes from pain. My vision is from pain. Ay-ken is the cause of my pain; he rips me from my home and brings me here. Ta-mee helps me see. I pray to Sansin to give Ay-ken pain, like he gives to me.

In our village the drums bang, the drums curved like a woman's body, the cymbals crash, tall banners wave, yellow and red, the healing fires burn. I come with the other children for cakes and candy, but the *kut* is serious, it is not for us, it is for the old man in the house. The *kut* is for him, to make him well.

When Ta-mee teaches me, she tells about the brother of Ay-ken, handsome and strong, and his departed spirit, about all men, the man who hurt her. She tells me about Ay-ken's rich family, that they have too much, the big house, the big land on the mountain. Ta-mee is victim. She wants what belongs to her. Ta-mee is my friend, my sister. I am victim.

I bow, I kneel, and I pray to the Mountain God.

3

She's a child, this wife of my cousin, and reminds me of
what I once was. Pretty. Innocent. Out of place. She doesn't
belong here. He shouldn't have brought her here. My cousin,
thinking with his dick, like all the Alexander men, like his
brother Hank, like their cousin Jake. But she's here, and she
needs to learn. She needs instruction, and she surely won't
get it from Aunt Ruth.

Aiken's up to no good. They all are.

So I sit at her table and drink her lousy tea and explain
to her how things are and try to understand what the hell
she's saying.

In high school, I had the biggest crush on Hank Alexander,
my cousin. My stepcousin. Not that I ever told anyone. I kept
it to myself. I strummed my guitar and wrote songs about
love and heartache, and all the time I was writing about
him. The Alexanders—they had the big house, the farm.
A father who hadn't run off, wasn't falling-down drunk. I
knew they weren't rich. Nobody around here is rich. But I'd
heard stories. My stepfather, Hank's uncle, a Yancey, talked

about money, or gold, or jewels hidden on the property. He scoffed, said it was a foolish notion. But Jake heard the same stories. Jake believed.

Hank and Jake were older than me, but one summer night on the farm we built a fire in the pasture, the three of us, the house hidden from view. We could have been on the moon. Jake and Hank and me, watching the sparks fly up, like they wanted to be stars. I sat between them, sipping the beer Hank gave me, wishing Jake would leave us alone, grateful to be with them. I played the guitar, hummed my song, and listened.

"Where is it, Cousin?" Jake asked. "The treasure. You can tell us. We're family."

Hank shook his head and opened another can. "There's no treasure, man. That's just a story. A dumb legend."

"Even legends have to start somewhere," Jake said. "There's always some truth at the beginning. Right?" Jake wrapped his arm around me and pulled me close. "Am I right, little Cuz?"

"Sure, Jake," I said. I had no clue, of course. What was I then, fifteen? Sixteen? And I didn't move when Jake kissed my neck, or when his arm drifted lower on my back, or when I felt his hand against the skin under my shirt.

But I was watching Hank.

KOREA

1992

4

After Desert Storm, Aiken had orders for Korea. In between, it was home to Virginia.

On his first morning of leave, still feeling Kuwait like rumbling thunder that lingers after the lightning has faded, Aiken thumped down the stairs to join his mother in the kitchen. He drank coffee, listened to her go on and on. Had she always talked this much? He didn't think so, but couldn't be sure. It had been so long. So much had happened.

"You remember the Cochrans?" she asked. "Of course you do. Do you want breakfast? Wasn't their boy Frank in your class at school? Anyway, with all the kids grown, they up and moved to Florida. Scrambled eggs? I could make pancakes. Don't they feed you in the Army? Sold the farm to some people from Connecticut or some such and now they're gone. Just like that."

Aiken had a vague recollection of a boy named Frank, a kid who avoided him, avoided all the jocks, thought he was too good.

"And the Wilsons? Do you remember them?"

On and on, and he listened, and then he ate what she set before him, fried eggs, ham, potatoes, toast, and he listened some more.

He thought he might tell her about the war. About Mitch and Davy and the others he'd lost. About the smell of the fires, the bitter smoke that was everywhere, filling his nose and eyes and mouth. The explosions that sounded like the end of the world. The dust and sand and blood. But even if he knew where to start, no one wanted to hear it, especially not her. They'd seen it on CNN. They'd counted the bodies, heard about the missiles, eyewitness reports, watched the oil wells burn, and thought they knew it all.

As he began, floundering, reaching for words, she dropped a juice glass. They both watched it fall, as if in slow motion, powerless to stop its descent. The glass shattered on the kitchen floor, shards, like shrapnel, peppering his feet.

"Oh, my," she said, as he bent to gather up the fragments. "Sometimes, I swear, an imp just knocks things out of my hands. Either that or there's a curse on this house. Yes, that's what it is. A curse. Be careful, dear. Don't cut yourself."

"You should take a look at the service," his father had said when Aiken was fresh out of high school, jobless, drifting.

But he had Kelly, his girl, and the future lay ahead of them. All he wanted was for his father to tell him how to get there. They never talked, not that Aiken could remember, but there they were, the two of them, repairing a cow-pasture fence on a scorching summer day, pounding posts into the dry, packed dirt, winching barbed wire until it sang.

"No," Aiken said. "We want to get married." They'd been going steady for more than a year, he'd given her his high school ring, the whole bit. He was ready.

"You're young," his father had said. "Wait."

His father had been in the Navy in World War II, saw action in the Pacific. He came home, met Aiken's mother, and married. The Navy hadn't changed his destination, only the path he took to get there. Aiken didn't see the point of the detour if it was going to lead right back to the same place.

"Son, you can't see the future if you don't know what the possibilities are," his father had said. "You can't grow if you don't stretch."

His father gave him brochures, even invited a recruiter to the house, the son of a friend. The man wore a crisp uniform, ribbons decorating his chest, and made promises of travel, training, unlimited opportunity.

And finally Aiken's father wore him down. Hank had given in, too, apparently, and had planned to join up, until his accident intervened. Why should Aiken be any different? There *was* no future for him in Turtle Valley, with or without the Army. His path had to change, one way or another. He had to stretch. Kelly would wait, or come with him.

Except, she didn't.

He listened to his mother go on.

"Have you called Jake? What about Tammy? You were all so close as kids. I'm sure they'd love to see you."

No, they had not been close. Cousin Jake, always trailing after Hank, everything he did meant to impress Hank, lost like everyone else when Hank died. Still struggling, as far as Aiken knew. And Tammy? Constantly looking for shortcuts, tickets out. Dreaming of making it big in Nashville. Another cousin with no compass and no future.

"They've both had a hard time lately, you know."

"You've seen them?"

"Tammy visits sometimes. And Jake calls. They know we're alone here."

Alone because Hank was gone. Alone because Aiken kept his distance. Jake and Tammy. They surely wanted something. And his mother was too trusting. He remembered the salesmen who got the better of her over the years, a vacuum, an insurance policy, a church, a charity.

The war still pounded in his ears, rattling his bones, too recent, not yet a memory. Fog shrouded his horizons, but at least he had the Army to tell him where to go.

Next stop, Seoul.

5

When I am ten, my baby sister is sick with the spots on her body. My mother is already gone. My father's new wife chases her spirit from the house. Little Mother is not interested in my sister, a weak child who can do no work, no sweeping, no washing. And so there is no *kut* to protect her. No gods are called, no ritual. I hold her in my arms to comfort her but it does no good. I do not yet have the power. She moans, the spirits battling inside her, demanding. And then the spirits cease.

Little Mother has a boy baby, a little emperor who is her future, who grows fat with rice and meat that is not shared. I do work in the house and kitchen and in my father's tired fields, and there is no time for school. From morning to night I work. Until one day my father takes me by the hand and walks with me into the village. He is carrying a bundle, a coarse cloth tied at the corners. He speaks nothing.

In the village we stand by the side of the road and wait, and still he speaks nothing. And then we climb into a bus, a red and white water buffalo with hard bench seats. He pushes the bundle into the rack above my head, too high for me to reach, and presses into my hands a purse, no bigger than my fist, made of yellow, green, and red silk, the colors of good fortune, and still he speaks nothing. Coins jangle in the purse. He bows to the bus driver, and then he leaves me as the bus begins to move. I am too astonished to cry, but only wonder at my fate. In the purse, tucked in with folded, soiled notes, is a piece of paper with writing I can barely read, the name of my father's sister, her address in Seoul, a distant place I cannot even imagine, and there is also the yellow *pujok*, the warning to the spirits.

Little Mother does not want me in her house, and my father is powerless against her magic.

I watch our mountain fade into the distance and the green fields of rice wave as we pass. Fields and villages, mountains, streams, temples.

I tremble when the city rises around the bus, like the mouth of a fish that would swallow us. Then there is no sky, buildings block the stars, and I clutch the *pujok*. The bus stops in the middle of a wide lake of buses swimming side by side, like geese, and the driver summons me forward, pushes as I descend, one steep step at a time. I hear my name, called by a shrill voice, a gray woman in gray *hanbok*, her gray hair pulled tight behind her, my aunt. The bus drives away and I remember the bundle, but it is too late, and I do not even know what is inside, what I have lost.

I miss my poor father and our household shrine and the lonely spirit of my sister. I ache for the mountain and the fields and the air that is filled with memories.

But in Seoul there is freedom, there is school. There is learning. I read poetry. I see that the world is wide. The days pass. Years.

In school we study English. We have a pretty teacher with streaming yellow hair who tells us about America. It is difficult not to stare at her long nose and that hair. She speaks slowly and carefully, and I understand what she says, most of the time, unless my mind is elsewhere, like when I imagine the Beautiful Country, America.

My friends and I decide we will go to America, but that is impossible. Instead, we ride the subway to Itaewon, near the American Army base. We walk up and down the street and look for places to practice our English, but we are too afraid. Finally, I see the picture of the white horse and I say to them, "Here." I push the door open and they follow me. It is a wine house, I realize, but I am the leader and cannot turn around. I do not look at the man behind the bar but lead my friends to a table. He does not tell us to leave, and so we stay. We are in America, the Beautiful Country. I gaze at the white horse and wonder what mysteries will come.

6

Compared to Kuwait, Aiken thought Korea was heaven. Boring, beautiful heaven. No one shooting at him, no one dying. This wasn't the Korea of M*A*S*H. He had his work, of course, and didn't mind it. He shuffled papers, mostly, kept track of things in Supply. He was good at it, too—organized, careful. Knew where to find everything, how to procure whatever the bosses wanted. Made sure they always had just enough of whatever was needed. Accepted praise with a grin and a salute.

He even made a little cash on the side, selling a few things the Army would never miss and the locals couldn't seem to get enough of, although in 1992, Korea already a wealthy country, there wasn't much they needed. A can of coffee, a jar of peanut butter. Nothing big, nothing traceable. He followed the "pig rule"—something he'd learned from Sgt. Michalski during Desert Storm: everyone takes what they can get, but no one in the Army gives a damn, no one even notices, unless you make a pig of yourself. He turned it into a game. How far could he go? What was the limit? It helped the days pass, and he tried not to feel guilty.

Outside of work, he spent his time reading—the post library was well-stocked with mysteries and thrillers, even poetry—or roaming the Itaewon district, not far from the base's East Gate. Shops lined the main drag, filled with knock-off Korean antiques, cheap imitations of name-brand sportswear, tacky gewgaws and souvenirs, and the bars—wine houses, the Koreans called them—spilled into the side streets and alleys. He'd visited countless Itaewon nightclubs in the year he'd been stationed at Yongsan Garrison, spent most of his pay, including the income from his sideline, on beer and the company of "hostesses"—the elaborately made-up Korean hookers who urged guests to buy expensive, watered-down drinks—and it had all grown monotonous: bars that reeked of stale beer and cigarette smoke; bars that played scratchy country-and-western tunes; bars that almost—but not quite, with their paired American and Korean flags, with their misspelled and ungrammatical signs and menus—looked like slices of home.

At least it wasn't the desert, but he was more than ready to get out, head back to Turtle Valley, to make plans for whatever was next in his life—school, a trade, a career. He knew it was too late to make things work with Kelly, as much as he still longed for her—his mother had reported in a letter that Kelly was married now and had settled in Roanoke—and exactly what he was destined to do was a blur the beer only made more impenetrable. But once he got home, the picture would clear. He was sure of it.

He missed Kelly, married or not, hopeless or not. Lying in his bunk, he wrote her letters. He described the crowded, noisy streets, the spicy food, the rank smells that hit him the minute he stepped off base. He told her he missed her, that he didn't know what had happened to them. He'd grown up, he said. He was different now. And when he finished a letter, he tore it into shreds.

One day near the end of his tour, he stopped into the White Horse for a quick beer and to see if he could unload a carton of Marlboros he had managed to make disappear from inventory. Although barely distinguishable from half a dozen other bars, this was one of his favorites when he just wanted to kick back, with a cowboy theme and country music on the jukebox, and no hostesses. He hadn't planned to stay. For once, he would make it an early night, maybe get back to the barracks and write his folks an overdue letter, read the latest John Grisham novel from the library. He concluded his business with the bartender, a plump Korean with gold-capped teeth who was fond of American cigarettes, and then noticed a cluster of girls in a booth, wide-eyed and laughing. He shook his head, grinned at the bartender, who grinned back. He'd seen kids in the bars before, amateurs, knew enough to stay away from them. The pros were safer; they weren't real.

But something about one of the girls caught his eye: a cockeyed smile that was a hair more confident than the others', a laugh that was deeper, more genuine. He took his beer to their booth and pulled up a chair, enjoyed the shy giggles and looks of horror on their faces. College girls on a lark, he guessed, not the anti-American kind, the kids who were protesting on campuses in Seoul and Pusan and the bigger provincial capitals, or they wouldn't be in a place like the White Horse. They recovered their composure, practiced their English, experimented with cigarettes he lit for them, shared a Coke. It was all in fun. Harmless.

When an Alan Jackson song came on, he reached out his hand to the girl with the crooked smile. "Dance?" he asked.

She laughed, one girlish hand covering her mouth, and shook her head, letting her black bangs dangle over her eyes. But she allowed him to lead her to the dance floor. He liked this girl, although their conversation was halting and garbled, like the signal from a distant radio station. She wasn't afraid of him. Later, when he'd had too much to drink and her friends had all gone, she took a sip of his beer and then let him buy her one of her own. She came from a small village, she told him. He took her hand in his. She attended college in Seoul, living with an aunt, she said. Enchanted, he couldn't move his eyes from hers.

They danced, and he kissed her.

"My aunt will be very, very angry if I go home late," she whispered.

He kissed her again and pulled her close.

She pushed him away and repeated that her aunt would be angry, but when he wrapped his arms around her she laughed and pressed against him.

The music stopped mid-song. He looked at the bartender, whose hand rested on the volume controls. The bartender shook his head.

"Turn it up," Aiken shouted. "We're dancing here."

The bartender shook his head again, and Aiken gave him the finger.

Aiken looked at the girl, the smooth curve of her cheek, trusting eyes that gazed back at him with questions, questions but no answers. He loosened his grip on her and stepped away.

"I guess the party's over," he said.

She smiled her crooked smile, then stepped toward him with open arms. "Dance?" she asked.

"No. No more dancing." Again he stepped away, retreated toward the door, and stumbled back to the base.

On the job, he thought of her and little else. He'd made a mistake by letting her go. But, no, she was young, he'd done the right thing. It was for the best. Yet, surely he'd made a mistake.

He went back to the White Horse, the bartender eyeing him as he climbed on a stool at the bar. He sipped a beer. He asked if the girl had been back. The bartender lit a cigarette and glared at him.

Every day for a week he went to the bar. Every day was the same.

And then one day she reappeared.

They ate steamed dumplings in an alley shop. The metal chopsticks confounded him, and she laughed. The spicy cubes of pickled radish brought tears to his eyes, and she laughed. He paid for their meal with U.S. dollars, and she laughed at that, too.

They strolled side by side on the streets of Itaewon, stopping to look in store windows, at their own reflections, the American soldier and the Korean girl looking back. In one window, a pair of dolls caught Soon-hee's eye, a boy and a girl dressed in Korean get-ups, the girl in a wide, pink skirt, the boy in gray trousers and a white jacket. Aiken took her hand and led her into the shop. They left clutching the dolls.

Soon-hee smiled broadly, and Aiken was no longer in a hurry to get home to Turtle Valley.

One afternoon, as they meandered through the streets around Dongdaemun Market, dodging sidewalk vendors and armies of tourists, Soon-hee stopped and pointed to a second-storey sign. "Tak-ku," she said, taking his hand and pulling him toward a door and up a flight of stairs.

"Tacos?" he asked, knowing that couldn't be what she'd said. At the top of the stairs they passed through dark curtains and entered a vast open space filled with a dozen or more ping pong tables, most occupied by players who appeared to be taking the game very seriously. The click of the bouncing balls filled the room.

Soon-hee rented paddles and balls for them and found an open table. "Tak-ku," she said again, bouncing a ball on her paddle.

He took up a position at the opposite end of the table. "Ping pong," he said. "We played this in the church basement when I was a kid, but I don't really remember much about it."

"Hit back," she said, tapping the ball with her paddle so that it bounced over the net.

He swung and managed to return the ball, but on the resulting high bounce Soon-hee smashed it past him, laughing as he lunged.

"So, you want to play rough?" he asked after he'd retrieved the ball. He gazed at Soon-hee's grinning face and served, the game coming back to him. He managed to keep the score close, but his rusty skills were no match for hers.

Finally, missing a last smash, he tossed the paddle on the table and held up his hands in surrender. They found chairs along the wall where they could watch the other players and talk.

"I never asked you what you're studying in school," he said. "Your major?"

"Major?" she asked.

"You know. The subject you study."

Her face remained blank.

He tried again. "What do you want to do when you graduate?"

She stared at the paddle she still held in her hand. "Go home," she said. "Teacher?"

"I bet you'll make a good teacher. You listen. Most teachers don't listen."

"Listen," she repeated. "Yes. I listen. And I like children. Like my sister. I teach."

He took the paddle out of her hand and caressed her fingers. "None of my teachers looked like you," he said. "I wish they had."

Now she brushed *his* fingers with hers. "I know your future," she said.

"Oh? And how do you know that?"

"Eyes," she said. "I see in your eyes. You like to build. You will build houses."

At that he laughed. Construction? Not likely. He built model cars as a kid, but that was the extent of it. He couldn't imagine working in construction. "What else do you see?"

"Children," she said. "I see children. You want children?"

"I suppose I do," he said. "Yes. I want children."

7

The American is beautiful, like my teacher, although his yellow hair is cut short. Not as tall as the other *ko-jaengi*, the nose people, or as loud, he does not frighten me. And his pale skin and blue eyes make me laugh. I try to look at him when he is not watching, but he is always watching. So, I cannot see him until he comes to our table and sits down, and then I cannot stop seeing him.

I tell him I am in college. I know if I tell him the truth, that I am in high school, he will be angry.

He is gentle with me in a way I cannot explain. When I see him, I know. I see our future together, and so I do not fear. He takes my hand, we dance, and I know. But the music stops, and we stop, and he is gone.

When he goes, I am relieved. I am empty inside, but I am happy to have had the gift of him for a short time, and also happy I do not have to decide. Dancing with him, kissing, I was a woman. But now, again, I am a girl.

In school, my friends ask about him, and so he is still with me. I think of him. I hear stories of the *ko-jaengi* who left and never returned, as if they had never existed. Or they return as ghosts, summoned like spirits from the dead. And so I pray that he will come back to me. At the shrine in my aunt's apartment I light the incense and I pray that we will meet again.

And when I return to the wine house, he comes, my prayer answered. I hope the spirit of my mother is not angry. With him I grow stronger.

I am rejected by my family, but when I look in Ay-ken's eyes I see America, and then I can see nothing else.

The time goes fast. We are together often, and even when we are apart we are together. I did not know about these feelings, what I feel when Ay-ken touches me.

I have heard of a place called Kanghwa-do. It is like a dream, people say, from our country's history. But it is not a dream. It is a real place that we study in school, and after Ay-ken and I have enjoyed our time together for some weeks I ask him to take me there. It is a mysterious island where giants roamed in ancient days and left their playthings behind to tell their stories. Or it is the home of Buddha and his books. Or it is where silk, one of the great treasures of our land, was born. We climb onto a bus, and I want to tell Ay-ken all these stories, but I do not have the words.

In Kangwha village Ay-ken buys a basket for me—the shopkeepers boast of the famous local weavers—and a bag made of yellow, red, and green silk. It is good luck, our luck, I tell him. We walk and walk, and for once the people do not stare, or maybe they stare but I do not notice. I take Ay-ken's hand and I brush my shoulder against his arm to let him know I am content, that there is nothing to fear.

We walk, and from a hillside pavilion that smells of pine and sweet incense we gaze north toward *Buk-Han*, brother country of my people.

"Brother," I say, in English, but I do not know how to explain about the war. It happened long ago, before I was born.

"Your brother?" he asks.

"No," I say. And then, "Yes." I mean our brothers and sisters in the North. I mean my father's lost brother, about whom my father does not speak. "War," I say, remembering the word at last, and Ay-ken nods.

"Yeah. War. I know about war." His voice trembles and he stops. He rubs his forehead with his fingers. He coughs and looks away. "I had a brother," he says.

I do not understand. But I do not ask.

We walk and walk past fields of ginseng, the *in-sam* I cannot explain, the root shaped like a man. We find a shop where we drink spicy tea made from *in-sam* and Ay-ken nods again. We walk and walk and at the end of the road there is a stone—two times my height, wider than Ay-ken's outstretched arms—the giants' ball, carved with symbols we cannot read. I walk round and round the stone, moving closer with each circle, as if, like the earth, like Ay-ken's eyes, it pulls me near. I reach out to it and feel its warmth, its pulse, the spirit of the stone a living thing, and I feel it enter my body.

My aunt is angry. She knows about the American. She tries to stop me, but I cannot stop. I feel the power inside me. How can I stop becoming who I am?

8

In a tea house so dark Aiken could scarcely see her face, Soon-hee poured for them both. He took one sip of the bitter tea and let his cup grow cold. He looked at her, but she looked away.

He reached for her hand. "Please," he said, almost whispering.

She looked at her feet, at the gleaming Adidas shoes he'd bought for her in one of the Itaewon shops.

"Please," he said again.

At the White Horse, they swayed to Alan Jackson, the bartender surrendering to the inevitable. Soon-hee wore a blue sweatshirt he'd bought her, "U.S.A." emblazoned across her chest. Aiken kissed her. He held her close. He whispered in her ear. "It's time," he said.

He lifted his hand to her chin and turned her face toward his. "Yes?" he asked. They danced.

*   *   *

The entrance to the Yongsan Friendship Hotel was around the corner from the White Horse—a weather-beaten door, steep stairs to registration, rotund clerk, cubbies behind him with keys chained to black plastic diamonds. Having given in to the urge and persuaded Soon-hee, Aiken tapped on the counter in an effort to hurry the formalities along. Soon-hee stood behind him, her arms around his waist, head pressed against his back—hiding, Aiken thought, or in love—while he scrawled a name in the register. Money changed hands, the clerk at last presented a key, and they rushed down a dim hallway to their room.

He could tell she wasn't sure how to be with a man, how to undress with him, how to touch him, how to lie down with him, how to open to him. She cried out, then hummed with the rhythm of their bodies—it was more like a chant, or a prayer—until he had finished and lay by her side. Tears streamed across her cheek, and he brushed them away.

They returned the next night, and the next. He worried that she was too young, although she refused to reveal her age—"no problem" she said when he asked—and he didn't press. He didn't want to know. She was in college, she'd said. He was only a few years out of high school himself, so he figured they were about the same age. All the girls here looked young to him. She reminded him of Kelly—it was the uneven smile, he realized, because otherwise they looked nothing alike—and that made him want her more. He had no idea what notions bubbled inside her head most of the time, couldn't read her face the way she claimed she could read his, or understand her words even when she seemed to be speaking English. Mostly, they communicated with their bodies and hands.

He half expected her to ask for money, the way others had. But, no, he knew she wasn't like them.

Through one of her friends she'd found a cheap place for them to stay in Myong-dong, in the heart of Seoul, not far from the famous cathedral. It was a room in a Korean-style inn, a *yogwan*, furnished only with a thin sleeping mat on the oil-paper floor, a low dressing table and mirror, and a glass vase holding a single plastic rose. He would get away from the base as often as he could, climb in a taxi, and navigate through a labyrinth of lanes and alleys behind the church. He went directly to the room, avoiding the innkeeper's disapproving glare—the same glare that burned on the faces of all Koreans who saw them together—and knocked on the frame of the flimsy rice-paper door. He would hear her laughter, hurry into the tiny room, and be in her arms before the echo of the rattling door latch faded. It scarcely mattered to him that the sound of their lovemaking exploded through the gauzy walls.

One night, lying in his arms in their candle-lit room, she asked, "What does 'Ay-ken' mean?"

"Mean? It doesn't mean anything. It's just a name."

She peered at him, her expression darkening.

"Why?" he asked. "What does 'Soon-hee' mean?"

"My name means 'gentle happiness,'" she said. "My sister's name is—was—'Soon-bok': 'gentle blessing.'"

"Tell me about her," he said.

She struggled with the words. "Like doll," she said finally, pointing to the dolls he'd bought for her that adorned the dressing table. "Small."

He laughed at that, but she shook her head and touched her fingers to his lips, tears forming in her eyes.

"She was sick," she said. "She died."

"I'm so sorry, honey. I didn't know."

"Your family?" she asked. "Your brother?"

"Definitely not small," he said. "He was big and strong. Everyone loved Hank. Even my idiot cousin Jake. Everybody. But he had an accident." Now it was his turn to cry. She brushed a tear from his cheek. "I miss him."

"I, too," she said.

They lay silently for a while, and then she asked, "Mother? Father?"

"Not much to tell, really. Farmers. They work hard. Good people."

"My father farmer, too," she said. She sat up on the mat. "Work hard in fields." In the light of the flickering candle he saw her smile.

"How about that," he said. "We're the same." He pulled her back down into his arms and blew out the candle.

She often played hooky from school, and they explored Seoul and the surrounding countryside together. One afternoon she took him to the South Gate Market where they browsed among the countless stalls selling bolts of bright silk, just as many offering bed mats and quilts, row after row of vegetable and fruit vendors, and a vast, foul-smelling pavilion housing fishmongers and butchers. Just beyond the market they stopped at a nameless shop where Soon-hee ordered two bowls of spicy noodles.

"Korean spaghetti," she said, lifting a steaming clump with her chopsticks. She slurped the noodles into her mouth and he laughed.

When he tried to imitate her, the chopsticks fell from his exasperated fingers, and it was her turn to laugh.

She took him to Gyeongbok Palace, where they strolled through the manicured gardens and gazed at the magnificent imperial residences. They visited Jogye Temple, not far from the palace, where she showed him how to bow and kneel before the massive golden statue of Buddha. She even took him to the Shinsegae Department Store, a multi-story shopping mecca that was just as overwhelming and dazzling for him as it was for her.

Sometimes on these outings she lowered her eyes and hid behind her black bangs or a wide-billed cap, as if, like a child, she believed she couldn't be seen by judgmental strangers as long as she could not see them. *He* could see, though. He saw the stares that greeted them everywhere they went, he saw the pointing fingers, and he didn't need to know the language to understand the muttered curses that followed. But then they returned to their room and lay together in silence until the fury of those encounters dissipated. All they needed was each other. No one else mattered.

The more time he spent with her, the more he wanted to be with her. She made those last months in Korea bearable. Gentle Happiness, indeed.

One day, he knocked on the door of their room at the *yogwan* and heard no giggling from inside. He slid the door open. The bed mat and quilt lay folded in the corner, the hard cylindrical pillows piled on top. His eye was drawn to a torn sheet of notebook paper on the floor, its edges curled like a dry leaf: a note, printed in her awkward hand.

"I go home," it said.

Home? To her aunt's apartment in Seoul, or to the village? When would she be back? *Was* she coming back? They'd argued the day before about nothing important—what to eat, or how to amuse themselves. It had passed, a brief squall, and they'd made up. Was she still angry? Why would she go home now, and why hadn't she told him she was leaving? She'd spoken a little about this village of hers, about her family, a sister, a half-brother, but he wasn't sure he'd understood. Pae-tu? Was that it? A farm near a village called Pae-tu?

How would he find her? Did she want to be found? He *had* to find her.

With the help of the bartender at the White Horse, who overcame his disapproval of Aiken's relationship with Soon-hee at the sight of U.S. dollars, he figured out the probable location of Soon-hee's village, but then he had to find the station, buy tickets, and hope he boarded the right bus. Like most American soldiers, he spoke no Korean. He couldn't read the blocky script with the lines and circles, and the Chinese characters on many of the signs completely baffled him. When he approached Koreans to ask for help, they backed away. Bus station agents yelled at him when he didn't understand what they'd said, and more often than not he yelled back.

He wasn't even sure why he was looking for her, why he was putting himself through this. They'd had a nice fling. She was a nice girl and a lot of fun. The anticipation of being with her had made the days pass. But his tour was almost over, and Korea—the Army—would soon be a memory. Why not leave her tucked in that memory, a story to tell and embellish for the guys back home? But every time he closed his eyes, she filled the darkness. He heard her laughter, saw her smile, and he wanted to be with her. He hadn't felt like that since Kelly. Gentle Happiness.

He boarded a bus, headed God-knows-where. At first he gazed at the passing sprawl of Seoul, and then at the impossibly green rice paddies as the bus sped through the lush countryside. The fierce odors of this strange land, these strange people, the garlic and fish, and the babble of unfamiliar words swirled around him. He closed his eyes to escape the stares of white-bearded farmers and old women and little boys. He fell asleep, head pinned between the seat and the grimy window, and then awoke, aware that the hum and bounce of the road had ceased. He opened his eyes and found himself face to face with the red-jowled bus driver. The man tugged on Aiken's arm, pointed out the window, and shouted. His breath reeked not of garlic, as everyone else's seemed to, but of cigarettes and rotting teeth. Aiken was only too glad to make his way off the bus.

There were shops, a pharmacy, a bakery with its familiar scents of fresh bread and sugary Korean cakes. He asked about a hotel—he remembered the word "yogwan"—and the shopkeeper pointed vaguely down the dusty road. From the stares he attracted as he walked, he figured news would spread that a foreigner had arrived. If he had indeed found her village, it would only be a matter of time before she'd hear that he had come for her, even if no one would tell *him*, this foreigner, how to find Lee Soon-hee. He located the inn, even smaller than the one they had made their home in Seoul, just a few tiny rooms arrayed around a courtyard filled with dwarf trees, a rock garden, and a gurgling fountain.

He waited. He ventured out from time to time to find food—beer and peanuts from the corner grocer, gelatinous pastries from the bakery—or to search for her. In the shops or on the street, he asked: Do you know Lee Soon-hee? When he tired of the blank stares, the pointing and laughing children who trailed after him wherever he went, shouting words he didn't understand, he retreated to the inn. He would sit on the floor of his room, gaze out into the courtyard, drink his beer, and plan.

On one of his forays, he came across a shrine tucked into a narrow lane. Wooden, with a tile roof and colorful eaves, green and red and blue, it was presided over by a massive painting of a bearded old man holding something, a flower or fungus, Aiken couldn't say which. The background was a golden yellow, interrupted by a towering pine tree and a waterfall that reminded him of the mountain at home. At the old man's feet was a ghostly tiger, whose eyes followed Aiken as he moved deeper into the shrine. He lit incense, as he'd seen Soon-hee do in a temple in Seoul, and prayed to her gods to bring her back to him.

After two days, his leave gone, he had to return to the base. He would put her out of his mind. He'd go home to Turtle Valley, take classes at the community college as his mother had urged, really think about the future. He'd improve himself and stop wasting time. As his father had advised, he'd stretch and grow. His parents would be happy. Soon-hee would be rid of him and could finish college, go back to being a normal Korean girl and find a nice Korean boy. Everybody would be happy.

He was sitting on a stone bench in the courtyard, listening to the innkeeper's son, a pudgy boy in short pants, recite the English vocabulary he'd learned in school, when a man entered through the *yogwan's* swinging doors, pulling Soon-hee by her sleeve. Aiken stood and felt his heart race. The man nodded to the innkeeper. He wore baggy gray trousers and a brown felt hat that seemed oddly formal. Soon-hee was in pale yellow, a short jacket over a long, full skirt—a stark contrast with the blue jeans she always wore in Seoul. In her arms she held a bundle, a blue scarf tied together by its four corners and stuffed like a pillow. Her head bowed, she kept her eyes down, her face hidden. She looked like a child. Even more like a child. The little boy squatted in the courtyard and stared up at the old man, then at Aiken.

The man spoke. Aiken saw the words form on his lips, heard them rumble from deep in his throat as he grew louder, angrier.

"What did he say?" he asked Soon-hee, but she didn't answer and kept her eyes fixed on the ground. "What the hell did he say?" he asked the boy.

The boy said something to the man, who spoke again. "He say, 'My daughter,'" translated the boy.

"Ask him how old she is," Aiken said.

The boy asked and the old man answered.

"Ten-seven," said the boy. "Seventeen."

"Jesus." He closed his eyes, not wanting to believe what he'd heard. "I'm dead," he said. "She said she was in college."

The boy looked puzzled. The man spoke again, then shouted.

"What did he say?" Aiken asked.

"He say, 'Baby.'"

The man yanked Soon-hee forward and pushed her roughly at Aiken, bowed abruptly to the watchful innkeeper, and left.

"Jesus," Aiken said.

9

My aunt notices, although Ay-ken does not. She confronts me, and when I admit there is a baby, she says I cannot stay with her in Seoul. There is nowhere for me to go and so she sends me home to Pae-tu. I am frightened but also happy that Ay-ken's baby is growing inside me. I know I cannot tell him. How could this happen? I am sure he would be angry if he knew, so he must not know. He is not from here and cannot stay; this is my home and I cannot leave. So I go back to my father because I have no choice.

But I am not welcome in my father's house. Little Mother spits on my feet. My father says I bring shame upon my ancestors. I know he is right. The price—it is always the price, but I thought for me, my father's only living daughter, it might be different—is banishment. I beg him to let me stay. I promise to work in the fields and put my baby to work, too, but he will not listen.

It is like the day he sent me to my aunt in Seoul. He calls me from the house. We stand in the courtyard while Little Mother watches from the inner rooms. He has gathered my belongings—a few scraps of silk, mementos from my mother—and he hands me the bundle. I remember the bundle, so long ago, that I left behind on the bus, and this one I clutch to my breast. The little emperor, my brother, runs to me, slaps at my legs and runs off again, sent by Little Mother, I am sure, to urge me away. And then it is time. As we leave the courtyard I feel the spirit of my sister fade because she cannot go with me. I say goodbye forever and follow my father. I do not know where we are going.

My eyes watch the ground, the finely swept dirt, the prints of my father's slippers as he marches before me in stiff, angry steps.

Then I hear Ay-ken's voice! He has come for me! But I cannot speak, I cannot look at him, I cannot show him that I am sorry for lying to him, or that I am overjoyed. I am overjoyed, but also I am not overjoyed. What if he will not protect us? We are a burden. What if he does not want us? I cannot look into his eyes, because I am afraid to know what fate holds for us.

10

Soon-hee's father bowed to the innkeeper, glared at Aiken, and left. Soon-hee, tears streaming down her cheeks, dropped her bundle and sank to her knees.

With the innkeeper shouting at them, Aiken ran to Soon-hee's side and knelt with her. He helped her rise and, ignoring the innkeeper's shouts, took her to his room. The innkeeper's son followed with Soon-hee's bundle in his arms, delivering it to her and backing away. He bowed and closed the rice-paper door.

Clutching the bundle, Soon-hee slumped to her knees again.

"Why did you leave?" Aiken asked, his voice gentle, almost a whisper. "Why didn't you tell me about the baby?" He sat close and wrapped his arms around her.

She shook her head, sobbed, and buried her face in the bundle.

"Don't cry," he said. "Please don't cry. Everything will be fine. I promise." There were options, he knew. He wasn't the first soldier in this predicament, and he'd heard about doctors who would make it go away. When they got back to Seoul he could get names.

But, no, that's not what he wanted. He couldn't do that to her. Or to his baby.

"We'll get married," he said without thinking. Did he mean it? Could he really marry her, still a child?

"Married?" she asked. Now she looked at him.

"Yes. Married." Was there another way? "Sure. We'll get married as soon as possible. I'm getting out of the Army in a couple of months and then we'll head back to the States, have the baby there." Really? Was it the only way?

"Married," she said. "Baby." And now there was the faintest trace of a smile on her face.

"Married," he said. "Baby."

On a crowded bus bound for Seoul, he held her hand. Were the other passengers staring? Were they whispering about him? He didn't care. It didn't matter anymore.

All night long, while Soon-hee had slept, he'd been thinking, examining the possibilities, searching for solutions. He imagined what his father might say. There was only one answer, finally, the right thing. His duty. They'd go home to Stillwater, he'd get a job. They'd be a family.

As the bus pulled away from her village, Aiken leaned toward Soon-hee and kissed her cheek.

"What is America like?" Soon-hee asked.

"Big," he said. "Quiet. Compared to Seoul, anyway. You'll like it. At least I think you'll like it. Stillwater is kind of like your village. Not much going on."

"Your family? Big house?"

"Pretty big, yeah. It's just an old farmhouse, nothing special. Plenty of room, though. It's just my folks. They'll be thrilled to have us. They'll love you. You'll love them."

The bus lurched around a corner as it entered the highway to Seoul, pressing Soon-hee into Aiken's shoulder. She laughed, he laughed, and then her laughter became tears.

"What's wrong?"

"Pae-tu," she said. "My village. My family. My home."

"I know. It's hard. I'm sorry. But Stillwater will be your new home. You'll love it. I'm sure. We'll be our own family. The three of us."

TURTLE VALLEY, VIRGINIA

MAY-JUNE 1996

11

The drought has scorched the hills, turning them the color of the desert. Everything looks thirsty and baked, worse than he's ever seen. Even the evergreens that run the ridges are tinged with yellow. And in the middle distance, where the peaks of Brother Mountain nestle shoulder to shoulder like a camel's humps, smoke rises from a fire that's sure to spread. It's what he smelled before, and now he can taste the bitterness.

The load in the truck bed shifts again. In the rear-view mirror, Aiken sees something—a T-shirt, he thinks—flap loose and take flight, settling on the highway behind him. He doesn't stop. He's not far from the farm now.

Aiken's marriage has always been a struggle, as if he and Soon-hee both knew from the beginning that it was a mistake. He'd married her because she was pregnant—the Army chaplain in Seoul said he'd seen it a thousand times—and she married him because her father had commanded it. That was an old story, too.

At the time, Aiken thought their relationship might work out, impulsive or not, mistake or not. Unlike his older brother, who'd always seen gloom in every obstacle, Aiken expected tough knots to unravel, locked doors to open. But he hadn't considered what would be best for Soon-hee. He admits that now, and it weighs on him. When her father brought her to the inn and left her with him, and when Aiken had abandoned the idea of an abortion, he thought of no other option but bringing Soon-hee home to Virginia. It was honorable. But was that the right choice?

They'd lasted this long—four years, going on five—only because of Henry. Henry is everything. Aiken loves being a father, enjoys nothing more than sitting with his son, reading to him or telling him tales, folklore passed down from his own parents, or listening to the boy babble and sing, as if he's telling his own stories. Aiken knows Soon-hee loves Henry, too. She tries her best with him, even if she doesn't always know exactly how to ease a fever or calm an upset stomach. Instead of children's Tylenol and damp, soothing towels, she chants over him, bangs pots and pans, brandishes a knife in the air above his head—until Aiken puts a stop to her nonsense. He tells her it's only superstition, from her backward country, but she doesn't listen.

She doesn't listen and she doesn't even try to adapt. At least, that's how he sees it. Sure, nothing here is like it was for her back home—the food or the appliances or the telephone or the bus or *anything*—but it's all better in America, newer, faster, and he doesn't understand why she can't, or won't, change.

"It's easier here," he'd said to her, not for the first time, when he found her on her knees washing clothes in the bathtub, up to her shoulders in suds. Water sloshed onto the floor and she smelled of bleach. "There's a washing machine in the basement—you don't have to scrub."

"No understand," she'd said, her answer for everything, because that way she didn't have to try, didn't have to learn anything new. And maybe she *didn't* understand. But when people don't understand each other, when they talk and don't listen, eventually they're at each other's throats.

"It's *easier* here," he'd said. He heard his voice grow louder as he repeated himself, as if that would somehow make the words sink in. "We buy food from the supermarket. We wash clothes in a machine. Everybody has a car. Everything is just fucking *easier*." And he'd fled to the dank basement to listen to Hank's old records, the Springsteen and John Cougar, and to dwell on what might have been, what he'd given up for her.

But still she insists on washing clothes by hand. She bought greens from the farmers' market until her own meager garden began producing what she wanted, those thick radishes that never lose their smell of dirt and the tough white cabbages that taste like cardboard. And, instead of learning to cook like an American, as he's begged her to do, she makes the food she remembers, the food of her ancestors, stinking up the house with garlic and red pepper, dried fish and sour pickles.

Making things worse, Soon-hee's English is still raw—even after studying the language in school back home and spending the last four years in the States, practicing almost daily with Tammy. After Henry started talking, picking up both languages, he sometimes translated for them. It was funny at first to watch this toddling go-between, a midget ambassador, but now it seems sad.

She doesn't fit in, is what it comes down to, and he's about given up hope that she ever will.

* * *

Pulling onto the Valley Pike, heading south toward the farm, he remembers those smells that he thought he'd left behind in Korea. *Now* he'll be done with them, once and for all. At least there's that.

He's not happy about moving in with his folks, though. He'd been a kid when he left town one lazy, jobless year after high school—spent in a hungover daze that he's not proud of—but he grew up fast. Not that his mother has noticed. She criticizes the jeans and T-shirts he always wears, the dirt under his nails, the snake tattoo on his forearm, as if he were still seventeen. She complains about his hair, which he's grown long and sometimes wears in a ponytail. She nags about the school janitorial job he settled for instead of enrolling in the community college to train for something better—forgetting that he has to work to support his family. Until now he's mostly only visited the farm to get away from Soon-hee's griping and wild accusations and to give Henry a taste of something other than her rancid *kimchi* and tasteless rice.

His father's not much better. They've never been close, especially since Hank's death, but at least he's solid, dependable. No one's ever accused him of being soft or approachable or talkative. And it's obvious where Hank got his moodiness. The old man has always loved farming and the feel of dirt in his hands; he's most comfortable outside, working the land or tramping the hillside behind the homeplace. Hank had been into all that, too. Not Aiken. He likes small-town life in Stillwater well enough, likes knowing who his neighbors are and doesn't think he'd last long in a real city, like Seoul, or Richmond, or even Roanoke, but sees farming as a dying occupation. At least his father seems to understand what

Aiken's been through. He hasn't once questioned Aiken's choices. He knows that Aiken stopped being a kid the minute he put on a uniform and, if that wasn't enough, really grew up in Desert Storm. After that there was the stint in Korea and taking responsibility for Soon-hee and the baby, and Aiken's father understands that, too. He'd been in the Navy. He's seen it. He knows.

On the way home from Korea, with pregnant Soon-hee at his side, Aiken had imagined their future together. They would stay on the farm with his folks until after the baby was born, until they could afford a place in town. He'd help his father with the chores, and find a paying job somewhere, too. His mother would show Soon-hee how things were done in America, how to shop and cook and clean, and she'd help with the baby. Soon-hee would become part of the family, an American. He'd had it all worked out. He'd explained it all to Soon-hee.

The new life started as he'd hoped. His father met them at the airport in Roanoke and—although Aiken could see shock in his father's face as Soon-hee's tender age registered—he'd wrapped his arms around them both. That surprised Aiken, but made him even more hopeful. Usually reticent, his father chattered on the ride home about what a pretty girl Soon-hee was, how they made a handsome couple, how happy old Ralph was going to be, and how much everyone was looking forward to having a baby around the house. When his mother came onto the front porch to add her welcome, she hesitated only for a moment at the sight of her new daughter-in-law. She took Soon-hee's hand and beamed at her as she would a shy child, asked about the baby, reached to touch Soon-hee's belly. Picture perfect. Better than he'd expected.

But things changed overnight, like the sudden onset of winter. Aiken had no idea what had happened. What had he missed?

"She doesn't belong here, does she, Aiken?" his mother had said to him in hushed tones, glancing toward the kitchen ceiling, toward his old room that he was sharing with Soon-hee. This was after just a week, when so much still bewildered his bride, and she spent long hours in the bedroom, emerging with teary, red eyes, and then only when he insisted. "She's not like us."

"Of course she's not, Ma. Give her time."

"She won't go to church with us."

"Her family's Buddhist, Ma."

"Church is church, Aiken. She should come."

At dinner that same night, Soon-hee stared at the meatloaf on her plate, hands in her lap. He urged her to take a bite, although he knew she'd never seen anything like it, and then watched her fumble with the silverware. She wasn't being stubborn, Aiken knew. She was afraid.

"No, not like that," his mother had snapped, grabbing the knife and fork out of Soon-hee's hands. "Don't they teach girls anything over there?"

She corrected Soon-hee's English, her table manners, even the way she made the bed. Still forgiving, still hoping she'd learn, he'd defended his wife then, explained that it was all new to her, that everything was different where she came from, that they all needed to be patient. But his mother wouldn't listen. Instead, she barked instructions at Soon-hee, barely looking at her, and stormed out of the room.

*   *   *

His mother wasn't the only one in the clan who had trouble accepting Soon-hee.

"What's it like with her, Aiken?" asked his cousin Jake, not long after their arrival from Korea. Jake was Hank's age, a head taller than Aiken and a good deal thicker, with wispy blond hair and a thin moustache. He and Hank had played football together in high school, were constant companions off the field, and Jake had been as broken up as anyone when Hank died, or claimed to be. He'd stayed close to home after school, married a plain girl he mostly ignored, and worked for his brother-in-law as a landscaper. Aiken had noticed Jake leering at Soon-hee at a family barbecue in Stillwater Park, but he hadn't expected Jake to say anything to him, not anything like this.

"What do you mean, Jake?"

"I hear gook girls fuck like rabbits."

Aiken knew his cousin didn't know better, might even be joking, but he slugged him anyway, hard, in the gut.

"Go fuck yourself," Jake had managed to say, still bent over double.

Jake and his wife had kept their distance after that, which was fine with Aiken, and then disappeared altogether—looking for work down in Florida, Aiken had heard.

But not everyone in the family was hostile. When Henry was born, Aiken's cousin Tammy made a point of coming by from time to time. He wasn't sure why she took such an interest—he and Tammy hadn't been close as kids, since her stepfather and Aiken's mother rarely spoke, and he didn't remember her as the helpful sort, more the opposite, in fact—but there she was: cooing over the baby, running interference with Aiken's mother, taking Soon-hee to Wal-Mart to buy little outfits for Henry. Some kind of maternal instinct kicking in, he figured. She didn't have a kid of her own, so she was making do with his.

He couldn't imagine that the two women had much to say to each other, given the language barrier, but when Aiken rented the saltbox cottage, Tammy helped Soon-hee turn the spare room into a nursery, with colorful pictures on the wall, a mobile of sailboats over the crib, even a rummage-sale lamp in the shape of a puppy. Soon-hee was out of the shadow of his mother, out of the big house that frightened her, the baby kept her busy, and in Tammy she'd even found something of a friend.

There had been some good times back then, and Aiken was still hopeful. When he'd heard about a strawberry farm near Stillwater, he took Soon-hee and Henry, just a few months old, and they spread a blanket on the farmer's lawn under a clear blue sky. While she nursed the baby, he picked strawberries, quickly returning to his little family with his bounty. He listened to Soon-hee sing to Henry, a lilting tune with words he didn't understand, and to the baby's gurgled response. He'd never been happier.

He lifted a large ripe berry to her mouth, and she closed her lips around it and bit. Her eyes closed, and a deep moan rose from inside her while juice streamed down her chin.

"Like home," she said. "With you. In Seoul."

"I remember," he said, and licked the strawberry juice from her lips. And then they ate the rich berries until they could eat no more.

In the truck, Aiken glances at Ralph, his golden head stuck out the window into the breeze. Henry will miss Ralph, but there's no way Aiken can leave the dog with Soon-hee. She would turn him loose to roam the streets or forget to feed him. She's never taken to Ralph, and Ralph doesn't seem to think much of her either, so he can't be sure what she might do. Aiken leans across the cab and strokes the old dog's shaggy flank.

Once they're on the Pike, Ralph paces the seat, pokes his head out the window, settles down for a while, then paces again, as if he knows where they're going and is as agitated about it as Aiken.

Except for that plume of smoke, like some indecipherable message swirling on the horizon, the mountains in the distance on both sides of the highway, east and west, are sharp-edged against a cloudless sky. On a day like this, if he remembers the story right, his ancestor Dermot, the first Alexander in Turtle Valley, after building his cabin and raising a trio of feuding sons and one feeble-minded daughter, wandered off into the hills, never to be heard from again. Some said he left because he'd murdered his own brother and couldn't live with the shame. Others said he'd been dispatched by a witch, and still others said that witch was his wife. There were sightings around the Valley off and on for years after, and inexplicable events like disappearing livestock and raging wildfires were sometimes attributed to the old man, but he never returned and the mystery was never solved. When Aiken was a boy, Hank and Jake teased him about old Dermot, frightened him with claims that their ancestor's ghost feasted on little boys who got lost in the hills, and then laughed when Aiken ran, trembling, to the safety of the house.

There's a westerly breeze now, and the scent of new-mown hay replaces the smoke. A pair of red-tailed hawks circles overhead.

He turns off the Pike at Chestnut Road and heads south, winds through Blake's Orchard, and thinks of Kelly, as he almost always does when he passes by this land once owned by her grandparents. He hasn't seen her in years, although he thinks his mother keeps up with *her* mother. Kelly's down in Roanoke, a nurse, and married. That's all he knows. They were inseparable the last couple of years of high school, lovers from the night of the Christmas dance in eleventh grade right up to the morning he left for Basic. By the time he came back for his first leave, eager to take up where they'd left off, she was gone. No explanation, nothing.

The Alexander farm is down McPheeter's Lane, off Chestnut, a gravel road that's worse every time he visits, ruts knifing through worn tracks, barely passable in some places even in the truck. Across the one-lane bridge. Finally he comes to his family's farmhouse, standing with its back to the piney woods and its face open to the broad vistas of the Blue Ridge—a hulking, tottering ghost of a house, stuck in the past.

12

The pot bubbles on the stove. I stir. The herbs churn up and dive again, their escape impossible, like insects trapped in yellow stones. Steam rises, forming a cloud that fills my head with pictures of home, rocks on mountain slopes, pine trees twisting against the wind, the supple *dae-namu* waving like giant leaves of grass, water flowing, carving through earth to the still pond below. I think of my mother, and I wonder if it is my destiny, like her, to be the first wife.

I remember happier days. We ride in the truck, Ay-ken, Ha-neul, and me, visiting the animals in the zoo. The tiger paces in his cage, the bear, the lion. I look in their eyes and we speak. We see each other, trapped. We see snakes, thick ropes coiled behind glass. Ay-ken points to the picture on his arm, the blue snake, and then to the glass, and Ha-neul laughs, looking back from one to the other and then into his father's eyes.

I stir the pot and remember what Ta-mee has said.

When the gods come, there is pain for Ay-ken.

I stir the pot and remember the *kut* for my mother, the black smoke, and the guides to take her into the next world. The banging drums, the singing. My mother lies inside, her spirit still with the flesh, but not for long.

The *mudang* dances in the courtyard, another shaman, her high-pitched wail like a voice from a different world. My sister and I cover our ears with our hands, but we watch, unable to pull our eyes from the spectacle of the *kut*. Fire rages when village women toss oil-soaked rice into the flames. Black smoke rises, first like a finger, then a hand, then a whole being who flies among us. I am afraid the flames are for my mother, that these people intend to burn what little meat is left from her brittle bones.

But, no, the flames are meant for evil spirits who battle for her life, to drive them out. And so the *mudang* calls for household gods to descend, to protect my mother from their evil brethren who would do her harm. When the voice deepens, when the shrieks fall and melt into the dark moans that erupt from the *mudang's* mouth like vomit, I know the end of the fight is near. The battle will be won or lost, but it will be finished. The shroud across my mother's chest is folded into the fire, and now it, too, dances, rising and falling on the currents like a leaf.

I watch the *mudang* and feel her spirit in me. Do the others see?

Ay-ken is gone. I cannot let him stay. Ha-neul watches and cries. But it is what must be done. For Ha-neul. As Ay-ken speaks to us through the door, I wonder. He wants to come back to us. He makes promises, and I do miss his touch. Is it the right thing? Does Ta-mee know? But this is her country, and I am lost here. She is a woman. She understands. I must listen to Ta-mee, and I must do what is best for Ha-neul. But the boy cries, and I cry.

13

When the girl calls to tell me Aiken is gone, I rush over. I can't believe she finally threw his ass out. Who knew she had the guts? I feel kind of bad for the guy. He's my cousin and all, *step*cousin, and he's not the worst of the bunch. But I've seen him at the Turtle, flirting with Jeannette, the old bartender, and any bimbo who comes through the door. I know what he's like.

I tell her she's done the right thing. We drink that tea of hers, and I wish she had something stronger. There's a foul smell in the kitchen, a bubbling pot on the stove despite the heat, and she says something about her gods. But there's no time for that nonsense now.

"Have you thought about what you're going to do?" I ask. Because I know from experience that getting the asshole out of the house is a big step, but it's not the end.

"Do?" she asks.

And I see she hasn't thought this through the way I told her, no matter how many times I warned her it wouldn't be easy. So I tell her again: she has to move, she has to sell what she can because money is going to be tight, she has to stay away from Aiken because he'll pull all kinds of tricks to get her to change her mind. And, here's the kicker, she has to use the kid for leverage.

We drink her bitter tea and I hear the kid crying at the window, asking when his daddy is coming home. Your daddy left, kid. That's what they do. Get over it.

But he won't stop. So I grab my guitar and sit down on the floor next to him. I strum a chord, and he looks at me, the sobs forgotten. I strum again, pick out a melody, and begin to sing: *Dry your eyes, baby boy of mine, there's no need to cry, not this time.* He sits and watches my fingers move across the strings. *Dry your eyes, baby boy of mine, learn to fly, and cry another time.* The crying stops.

Once, I was alone with Hank in the barn out on their farm. I knew he had a girl, someone his own age, but I didn't care. Why should I? He was tinkering on that bike of his and barely knew I was there. I wanted to scream at him to pay attention to me. I'd done my nails in that pink Aunt Ruth said was pretty, and my hair was up and out of my eyes for once.

I went up to him and put my hand on his back.

"What are you doing, Tammy?" He shrugged my hand away. "I'm trying to get this timing right."

I put my hands on his head to turn him toward me, and I kissed his lips. He jerked away, sputtering, wiping his mouth with the back of his hand.

"Jesus, what's gotten into you?"

"I love you, Hank," I said.

"No, you don't," he said, and started putting his tools away. "You're my cousin. We can't do that, even if I wanted to. Which I don't. Besides, you're a kid. And besides *that*, I've got a girl. Remember? Jesus. Get the hell out of here."

"I'm *not* your cousin," I wanted to scream, but the words wouldn't come. I'm *not*. Then the tears started. I wasn't going to let him see me cry, wouldn't give him the satisfaction, so I turned around and I ran out of the barn, kept on running, never stopped running.

I'm stronger, now. I've got my dreams. Soon-hee does, too.

"No more of this stuff," I say, and put my cup down. I grab my purse and pull out a joint. She looks at it like she doesn't know what it is, and maybe she doesn't.

"A different kind of tea," I say.

"Marijuana," she says. "I see on TV."

"I'm impressed. Someone's been paying attention." I light up, take a deep drag and hold it, letting the smoke out slowly. "Like that," I say. "You want some?"

Oh, she's conflicted, I can see that. On the one hand, she's afraid. On the other hand, she's curious and wants to give it a try. She looks over at the kid, who's staring out the window, waiting for his daddy to come home or whatever. I hold the joint out to her, try to look encouraging.

Finally, she nods, wipes her hands on her apron, and pinches the joint with her thumb and forefinger. She places it between her lips, takes a hit, nothing major, but not bad for the first time. She hands it back to me.

"Don't expect to feel anything right away," I say, although the first time I smoked, with Jake and Hank when we were kids, it was like firecrackers going off inside my head right from the start. I take a hit, then she does, and each time we trade she gains confidence.

The kid is standing by the kitchen table—how the hell did he sneak up on us like that?—and says, "Mommy?"

Soon-hee giggles. I don't think I've ever seen her laugh, much less giggle, so I know the pot has done its work. And

I can't help but giggle myself. The joint is spent and that's funny, too. She starts speaking Korean to the kid, and that's just hilarious. I laugh so hard I nearly fall out of my chair. We're all laughing and having a grand time, even Henry, and for a few minutes we forget about everything. About Aiken and Jake and Hank, who I almost never stop thinking about. And for now, at least, we forget about running away.

Whatever it is that she's cooking up on the stove bubbles over with a great splash and hiss. Soon-hee jumps up to attend to the mess, and our spell is broken.

I convince Aunt Ruth to buy me a tape recorder. If I'm going to get to Nashville, I tell her, I need to make a demo tape so the record producers can hear my sound. She looks around the kitchen as if making sure nobody can see and then nods. I jump right out of my chair and give her a big hug. "You won't regret it," I say, beyond excited.

She couldn't go right that minute, but the next day I come back and we go to Wal-Mart. We wander up and down the electronics aisle a dozen times looking at all the different makes and models, but I keep gravitating to a Sony machine that looks like a professional recording studio. It has places for two cassettes and lit-up dials to show sound levels.

"I think this is the one I need," I say.

Aunt Ruth studies it and puts her reading glasses on when she examines the price tag. "It's awfully expensive, Tammy. Are you sure?"

"Those producers expect professional sound quality, you know. That's why this costs so much more than the others. It's perfect."

"But you said it's a 'demo tape.' Isn't that what you called it? It's not like a real recording at all. I don't see why it has to be so fancy." She turns to the opposite shelf and points to a Sanyo recorder, way cheaper than the Sony. She taps the machine. "I think this one will do nicely." And she marches off toward the cashier with the box under her arm.

Back in her kitchen, we take the recorder out of the box, find the right kind of batteries in her junk drawer, plug the microphone into the side, and stick a cassette into the slot.

"Sing something, Tammy," she says. "You've got such a pretty voice."

I'd lost interest in the third-rate machine, I have to say, the wind taken right out of my sails, but maybe it will do. Aunt Ruth is right. It's just a demo. So I turn it on and start to sing a Reba McEntire song I like, and I forget I'm in her kitchen. It's like I'm on stage in Nashville, singing my heart out.

When I'm done, Aunt Ruth starts clapping and I think she even wipes a tear from her eye. "That was beautiful, dear," she says. "Those record people are going to love you."

14

He stops the truck on the gravel drive, between the house and the barn. Ralph leaps past him when the door opens; Aiken stays in the truck.

"Is that you, Aiken?" his mother calls from the porch. The screen door bangs behind her. She's a small woman who has broadened with age, and her hair, once chestnut, is all white, pinned atop her head. She wipes her hands on her apron, then raises them to shield her eyes from the late-day glare as she grips the railing and comes gingerly down the porch steps. Ralph runs to her, sniffs her feet, then trots off when she shoos him away. She looks past Aiken into the cab of the truck.

"Isn't Henry with you?"

"Henry's not coming, Ma. I told you. He's staying with Soon-hee."

"I know," she says, a high-pitched complaint creeping into her voice. Although his mother has never accepted Soon-hee, she adores her grandson. "I thought maybe you'd bring him for a visit."

His father limps out of the barn, followed by a couple of the cats, the big gray that always traipses after him, and the striped tom. Ralph catches sight of the cats and gives chase, torn when they fly in opposite directions, then settles for the attention of the old man. His father used to be tall—Hank had resembled him—but now is stooped. Instead of gaining weight with age, as Aiken's mother has, his father has dwindled, as if his shriveled form is in danger of disappearing altogether.

Aiken drops the truck's tailgate, slides out the first box, and begins building a pile on the porch. His mother finds a few small things she can carry, and these also land on the porch: a black garbage bag of T-shirts and socks, the frayed cushion that serves as Ralph's bed. When his father sags under an over-filled carton, Aiken takes it from his arms.

"There's not that much," he says. "I'll get it."

His father nods. Gratefully, Aiken thinks. While his mother is tanned from working in her garden, his father's face seems ghostly. Both of them drop into rockers on the porch, and Aiken's mother cools her face with the funeral-home fan that has somehow survived for more than a decade. Even on the porch, out of the direct sun, the heat is stifling. Sweat rolls down Aiken's neck and arms as he works.

He hasn't noticed until today how much his folks have aged. He's only twenty-four himself, nearly twenty-five, but he'd been something of a surprise—that's how his parents put it, and it was a running joke in the family—coming when his mother was almost forty and thinking she was done with babies. They'd thought Hank would be it for them—their darling, only child—but along came Aiken to change all that. Now his father is pushing seventy and can't do as much as he used to. Spending more time with the old man could be a good thing.

He climbs the stairs to his childhood room. The banister still wobbles after all these years, despite his father's long-ago promises to fix it. That was before Aiken left for the Gulf. And the stair-runner is loose in at least three places, worn on every step. It's a miracle neither of his parents has tripped and fallen. He resolves to get to some of those chores himself, now that he's here. Or convince them it's time to move somewhere easier to maintain. Fewer steps, fewer burdens. His father is probably ready, despite the Alexander family's centuries-old connection to this land. His mother—probably not.

The room is smaller than he remembers. The last time he'd stayed here was with Soon-hee when they came back from Korea. It's as tight as a tank, the shelves closing in on the bed, and already he's having trouble breathing. How did he ever live here?

One shelf holds model stock cars, now looking fragile and small, the decals he'd painstakingly applied peeling and cracked. Other shelves are lined with ribbons and trophies, little plastic statues of a man at bat, with the year stenciled on the base. Turtle River High School, 1988, says the biggest, one he received for being the most valuable player that year. And a trophy for basketball—his real passion, even though he'd always been told he was too short, a five-eight guard on a team of goliaths—along with a picture of him and the rest of the Terrapin squad. 1987? Must have been. The cars, the trophies, the picture—they're all free of dust.

Aiken sits on the edge of the bed, winces at the squeaking springs. Those springs bring back memories, too.

"My folks are at a church supper," he'd said to Kelly as they came through the front door. "Please, Kel. It's perfect. We've got the place to ourselves. Who knows when we'll get another chance?" He tugged on her fingers and led her to the stairs. The house was dark and quiet, filled with the aroma of the apple pie his mother had baked that afternoon.

"It doesn't seem right," she'd whispered.

"They're not *here*." He went up, and Kelly followed.

And he remembers the joy he'd felt in making those bed springs shout, his own loud pleasure and Kelly's, and then horror at hearing a door bang down the hall. They'd dressed hurriedly, ran down the stairs, and when he returned from taking her home, his parents were waiting for him at the kitchen table.

"Aiken," his mother began, her voice soft but strained, and then retreated to the sink. His father looked away. Aiken waited. "Tell him, Henry." Now her voice was louder, sharper.

His father lectured him on responsibility. It wasn't the last time he and Kelly made love in that bed, but it sure as hell was the last time they got caught.

His mother has added a few touches to the room since then. A framed picture of him in his Army uniform. On a corkboard over the dresser, thumbtacks hold yellowed clippings from the Stillwater Daily Record: "Alexander Completes Basic Training" and "Alexander Deployed to Gulf." There are snapshots he sent back from Kuwait and Korea, but nothing about his wedding.

There's one other clipping, right in the center: a birth announcement—for Henry Dermot Alexander.

The smell of his mother's roast chicken and biscuits drifts upstairs. It's a smell he associates with his childhood, with growing up on the farm, with his whole life up to the time he joined the Army. It is decidedly *not* kimchi and rice and fermented beans. It's far too hot for such a feast, but he knows his mother wants to celebrate his homecoming, even under the awkward circumstances. His father, looking limp and wan, is already seated at the table, steaming bowls of mashed potatoes and candied carrots within easy reach. Sam Carpenter, a family friend who lives on the other side of the mountain, sits at the opposite end of the table. "Uncle Sam," he and Hank used to call him, to everyone's amusement. It never failed to bring forth a chuckle from the old man, and he'd show the gaps in his yellowed teeth in a broad, sloppy grin.

As Aiken enters the dining room, Sam rises with the aid of his hickory walking stick and embraces him.

"It's been a long time, boy," he says.

"Good to see you, Sam," says Aiken.

He remembers fishing with his father and Sam. Hank was still alive, and Aiken was maybe five or six. The four of them were at Sam's cabin on Beaver Lake, up in the gap between the humps of Brother Mountain, a musty, rustic place Sam said he got to as often as he could. That year, though, was the first without his wife, who had died of cancer in the spring. They'd found the disease early, and treated it, even removed a breast when the lump appeared, but it kept coming and kept coming and finally there was nothing more they could do. So Sam was alone, and Aiken's father decided he and the boys would join him on the fishing trip.

Aiken and Hank shared a bed in one corner of the cabin.

"Remember old Dermot Alexander?" Hank whispered in his ear on their first night in the bed. "The ghost who murdered his brother and eats little boys?"

Aiken nodded. He'd been keeping an eye out for Dermot as they hiked up to the cabin.

"Don't you think Uncle Sam looks an awful lot like him? Long white beard, spooky eyes. Right down to the dirty fingernails from burying little-boy bones. Makes you think."

Aiken edged closer to Hank in the bed, never letting him out of his sight on that trip. For years, whenever Sam was around, he wondered what had become of Dermot.

Sam has carved the chicken—a task Aiken's father has always performed—and sets the platter in the center of the table. His mother says grace, and Sam, as if offering his own blessing, praises the meal. They eat in humid silence except for his mother's occasional questions that Aiken struggles to answer between mouthfuls. Is it wise to leave Henry with his mother? Will Henry come to visit soon? Does he think Henry will be okay without his daddy?

No, he doesn't think Henry will be okay. But Aiken can't say this to his mother, or that the separation is killing him. He wants nothing more than to go back into Stillwater to read Henry a story before bed. Henry loves his stories, and Soon-hee always listens, too, leaning against the bedroom wall while he curls up next to Henry with *Goodnight Moon* or *Clifford, the Big Red Dog*. He reads softly, in a deep voice that he imagines soothes the boy, until the eyes droop and the breathing steadies. Then Aiken eases himself off the bed and tucks the sheet around his son, switches the nightlight on, and kisses Henry's forehead. Even on the bad days, when he and Soon-hee had been arguing, the stories brought a smile to her face. But he can't do that now, doesn't know when he'll be able to do it again, and wishes his mother would give it a rest. Once more, the thought of taking Henry away to Texas or California or anyplace far away crosses his mind.

His mother brings out a pecan pie from the kitchen and cuts him a wide slice.

"Your favorite," she says.

He can't remember if it really is his favorite or if this is more family lore that slips by unchallenged.

"It looks great," he says.

His mother serves Sam and cuts a sliver for Aiken's father, which she sets in front of him. "That's all you get, now," she says, patting his arm.

Aiken looks at Sam, thinking he might speak up for his old friend, but Sam merely smiles. Aiken wants to tell his mother that the man isn't a child, that she shouldn't talk to him like that. But she speaks again before he can find the words.

"It's so rich," she says, "he really shouldn't have any at all." The prescription is her own, relying on generations of folk wisdom rather than trusting a doctor. For herself she pours iced tea and takes no pie, content to chip away at the edges of the pan with her fork, ferrying minuscule bites over the safety-net of her cupped hand.

His father eats and says nothing. Sam eats. Aiken feels a breeze through the open window, but it's a short-lived reprieve from the heat. The silence grows heavy. Too heavy for his mother.

"Have you heard from Jake since he got back?" his mother asks finally. She'd given up trying to end the old feud between Aiken's father and Jake's, but she seemed to think there was still hope for this generation.

"Jake's back? What happened to Florida?"

"Maybe you should give him a call."

"He was Hank's friend, Ma. Not mine." Although Jake is his father's nephew, Uncle Archie's boy, Aiken never understood why Hank tolerated him. It was Jake who got them arrested for a joyride in a stolen car. It was Jake who led the way into brawls and brushes with the law. It was always Jake.

"He's family, Aiken," says his mother. "And down on his luck."

"Is he now?" He regrets the sarcasm when his mother purses her lips, which he knows means she's hurt. "I'll give him a call," he says, knowing he most likely won't. He doesn't understand why she gives a damn about Jake, who is no kin to her. She doesn't know him like he does.

Once, when he was a kid, he'd followed Hank and Jake up the mountain. Hank carried their father's shotgun, and Jake had a rifle slung over his shoulder. Aiken kept his distance, undetected, and spied on them from behind a limestone outcropping. In a clearing, the older boys set up beer cans on a log and took turns firing at them, the shots echoing between the hills. When the cans were all down, Hank trotted to the log to inspect the damage and set up more targets, but on the way back stopped in his tracks when Jake raised the rifle and pointed it at him.

"Whoa, Jake, put that down," Hank said.

"Tell me where it is," Jake said.

"Don't be an idiot. Put that down."

"Tell me."

Aiken stood, no longer trying to hide, and trembled as he watched Jake take aim at his brother. He didn't know what they were talking about and strained to hear. He heard Hank shout "No," and then the gun fired, a puff of smoke escaped the barrel, and Aiken jumped, expecting Hank to fall. Instead, one of the cans pinged off the log and bounced in the dirt. Jake burst out laughing and shouldered the rifle, but Hank, his expression grim, grabbed his shotgun and left Jake in the woods. Aiken hurried after him.

*   *   *

After Sam leaves, Aiken's father, who'd nearly nodded off at the dinner table waiting for the dessert, plants himself in front of the television, and Aiken joins him. For a few minutes they watch the Phillies and the Cardinals, until the old man's head rolls onto his shoulder and he begins to snore. Aiken had thought they'd have a chance to talk, so he could hear whatever advice his father has to offer about the mess Aiken's made of his life. Soon-hee's come unglued, and he has no idea what she'll do next. Should he have tried harder to stay home, to help her and protect his son? He wants to talk to someone about these things, can think of no one other than his father who might listen. Not that he ever has before. But it'll wait. Everything will be fine, he hopes. It will all blow over. Soon-hee just needs space. Soon, she'll come to her senses. He'll move home and Henry will be okay. He's doing the right thing. That's what he wants to hear from his father, whose upper lip has curled in his restless sleep.

Aiken goes to his mother in the dining room, helps her clear the last of the dishes. He watches as she runs hot water in the sink, pours in a squirt of green soap, not too much, more is wasteful, she's always said, pulls off her wedding band and heirloom solitaire, passed down from his father's mother and grandmother before her, and sets them on the windowsill. It's what she's always done, as long as Aiken can remember. Keeping the rings safe, lifting a vase from Aiken and Hank's path as they raced through the house, holding Aiken inside when his father and Hank were mowing or chopping or plowing. "Out of harm's way," she'd say. "That's the place to be."

They work as they had eaten, mostly without words. It's all familiar, ritual. The television drones from the living room, the baseball game interrupted by loud commercials for beer and potato chips. When they're done with the dishes, they linger awkwardly in the kitchen. She puts the last of the plates away and stretches to lift glasses to the high shelf in the cabinet. Aiken leans back against the counter.

"He needs to see a doctor, Ma." For as long as Aiken can remember, his parents have avoided doctors. Or, rather, his father expressed no opinion one way or the other, but his mother insisted that she could treat at home whatever ailments the family might develop. And so, as a boy, although he was allowed the inoculations the school district required, his childhood bouts with the flu and chicken pox and such were dealt with at home: wild ginger tea for the fever, a poultice of wild parsley for the boils.

"He's fine. He says he's fine."

"Obviously, he's not fine." He watches her wipe down the counter and waits for her reaction.

"I put fresh linens on your bed," she says. "And towels."

And so the subject is changed. "Got to feed Ralph," Aiken says.

"I'll just see to your father."

Ralph greets Aiken at the door, his sweeping tail the only thing that stirs the hot air, and the two of them locate the sack of kibble among the boxes and bags still piled on the porch. While Ralph inhales his dinner, Aiken watches the sky darken. The barn's floodlight hums as it blinks on. The moon peeks over the sycamores.

Back inside, he steps into the living room. His mother sits at one end of the sofa in the glow of the table lamp, a *Reader's Digest* open in her hands. His father sleeps in his armchair, an occasional wheeze gurgling from his nose. A variety show—one that Aiken thought had gone off the air years before, with that big-mouthed redhead—blares on TV, and he wonders how his father can possibly sleep through it.

"It's been a long day, Ma," he says. "I think I'll turn in."

"Sleep well, honey. Want me to wake you in the morning?"

"I'll be fine."

He climbs the stairs, notes again the wobbling banister, and, as he turns into the dark hallway toward his room, he sees Hank. Just for an instant, and then he's gone.

15

Is this on? Hello? I don't know. Is it working?

This was Tammy's idea, so don't blame me. "Aunt Ruth," she said, "you've got to do this for Aiken and his boy." Said she'd read about it in a magazine, about people who tell their stories into a tape recorder, and then their children and grandchildren can hear them after … after they're gone. But it's plain silly, if you ask me. An old woman talking to herself.

I bought the recorder for *her*, originally, so she could send a tape to some record company, but she turned up her nose, said it wasn't "professional" enough. Finding a reason for me to keep it, that's just her way of saying "thanks, but no thanks." Well, fine, I'll keep it then.

I tried to convince big Henry to do it. He has so much more to tell than I do—the Alexanders have been on this land for such a long time, back before we were a country, almost—but he waved his hand, said, "It's a gol-darn waste of time," said, "Get that thing away from me," when I set the machine on the dining table.

Well, fine, he doesn't want to say his piece, and I guess I've got enough to say for the both of us. Isn't that the way? The man can be as stubborn as a stone, and that's the truth, so help me.

Is this on? It doesn't sound like it's on.

Tammy's a good girl. My only niece in a family of men, and with big dreams, too. Wants to go to Nashville, become a star, like that other Tammy. Plays guitar, a nice voice, too, and a pretty smile. Just had some bad luck is all. That husband of hers. Ex-husband. She comes around and we visit. Gossip, you might say, although I don't like to call it that. If it weren't for her, I might not know anything that goes on in town. She's the one who told me about Hilda at the beauty parlor and her cancer. Poor girl. Henry's no good for things like that.

I had another visitor recently. I was working in the garden, bent over the tomatoes where I'd found one of those nasty-looking hornworms, and a shadow fell across my path. It seemed odd, because there hadn't been a cloud in the sky when I started. Naturally, I looked up. It was a man! And I hadn't heard a sound. But the sun was behind him and I couldn't see his face, all covered in shadow the way it was. So I got to my feet—no easy task for me these days.

"Hello, Aunt Ruth," said the man.

"Jake! You startled me."

"I'm sorry. I didn't mean to." He looked around the yard, and I knew he was keeping an eye out for Henry. Jake's father Archie has been feuding with Henry since . . . it's been a long time. I know Jake doesn't feel welcome here with Hank being gone. They were such good friends. Can't blame the boy.

"Henry went into town," I said. "It's just us." I took his hand then and led him into the house. We settled onto the porch with glasses of lemonade.

"It's so good to see you, Jake. You're back from Florida then? For good?"

"I think so. Things didn't go so good for us down there."

"I'm real sorry to hear that," I said. I'd already heard from Tammy that Jake spent some time in jail down there. All a misunderstanding, I'm sure. We sat quietly for a while and listened to the birds chatter. Then Jake reached into his pocket and pulled out a folded square of paper. He opened it, smoothed it against his leg, and handed it to me.

I probably gasped. It was a pen-and-ink drawing of Hank. So true and clear, almost like a photograph. I looked at Jake. "You did this?"

"I had some time on my hands," he said and stood up. "Anyway, I wanted to give you that. I should be going."

"Thank you, Jake. Come by any time." But I had a feeling I wouldn't be seeing much of him. Not the way things stood with Henry and Jake's father.

How do these quarrels start? Henry was the oldest child in their family, and his brother Archie wasn't cut out for the farming life, not the kind to think about the future for half a second. A handsome devil, he was, and he took full advantage. From what I hear. He let Henry buy his share of the farm for a pittance and off he went gallivanting somewhere, coming back with his hand out when the money'd slipped through his fingers. Henry wouldn't listen, of course, and he was right. A deal's a deal. Still, it's a shame. Henry hasn't spoken his brother's name since, and he can't look at Jake without seeing Archie.

Not that I'm on such good terms with Tammy's stepfather, my own brother. But maybe that's a story for another day.

Speaking of Tammy, on one of her visits, while we sat and rocked on the porch, sipping sweet tea, she started to tell me something about Aiken and a woman he's been seeing on the sly, behind that Korean girl's back. Said she'd seen Aiken down at the tavern where she plays music sometimes. I cut her off.

"Tammy," I said, "don't you talk about Aiken like that, and, besides, I don't believe a word of it."

She got quiet then, but I could see by the shine in her eye that she was itching to say more, and to tell the truth it seemed like something I ought to know. Just didn't feel right, is all. Tammy's a good girl. Like a daughter, you might say.

Anyway, about this recording. I'm supposed to start at the beginning, Tammy says. Before the beginning, even, which I don't really see how that's possible, but I guess I can tell what I heard. God knows people back home were always telling stories. Same here in Turtle Valley.

I was born in a shack. People say they were born in such and such a place and what they mean is they were born in a hospital in the town or the county where their parents lived. Not me. Not my brothers and sister. We were born in a shack, right there in my parents' bed tucked under the loft where the older children slept. I didn't know it was a shack at the time, it was just our house, but that's what it surely was. I haven't been back in nearly forty years, but I can see it plain as I can see the brown spots on the back of my hand. Logs, rough board floors, a stone chimney that was all we had for heat, a porch that ran the length of the cabin. It seemed strong and safe back then. But I do remember two or three poles outside bracing the side walls, and in a storm the roof was like a sieve.

Is that the kind of thing they want to hear? I swear it brings back memories. Reading by a kerosene lamp, doing everything by hand, the laundry and such. Listening to the old folks tell stories. But I don't know what else to say.

Tammy says I should talk about Aiken and his wife, but there isn't much to tell. The girl's a witch. That's all there is to it. Tammy surely did laugh when I told her that. Wanted to know all about it. But I don't think she caught my meaning. All you have to do is look into those black eyes to know. It's a marvel that Aiken can't see it.

Tammy says to talk about secrets, be sure to tell where the skeletons are buried, she says. I don't know about any skeletons, but I might have a secret or two I wouldn't mind getting off my chest. I'll have to think on that some.

My heavens, how do you shut this thing off?

16

Why old Dermot Alexander stopped here in Turtle Valley and how he acquired the farm that once covered many hundreds of acres—now dwindled to just seventy—are mysteries that have never stirred Aiken's blood. His father, though, when Aiken was a boy, frequently spoke of the family history and collected whatever books and documents he could find on the area's earliest settlers. There were colorful dissertations during Sunday dinner on the exploits of old Dermot—one that Aiken remembers involved an encounter with an Indian medicine man who cured Dermot's youngest son of a fever they all thought would kill him—and speculation about the harsh life back in Ireland and Scotland that prompted their forbears to uproot. There were stories about a half-wit daughter who found gold in the streambed, rivalries among Dermot's sons that occasionally erupted into fistfights, and speculation over what really happened to Dermot the day he wandered off into the hills.

"Here's what I think," his father had said during one of those Sunday dinners. "I think old Margaret got tired of Dermot's running off to go fishing or hunting instead of tending to the fields, and she cast a spell on him. But the gol-darn thing backfired and he just disappeared. Poof, in a cloud of smoke."

"You mean she was a witch?" Hank asked. "A real witch?"

"Stuff and nonsense," their mother said.

"That's what they say," their father said, winking at Hank.

"There's no such thing," Aiken said. "That's just a made-up story. There's no such thing as witches."

"Then what happened to Dermot?" Hank asked.

"Probably he got tired of being a farmer in this dump and took off for the big city. Can't say's I blame him."

His father had glared at him. The story—and dinner— came to an end.

Hank had been as passionate as the old man, asking questions about their ancestors and cousins and far-flung relatives, constructing a chart that looked to Aiken less like a family tree than a clump of interconnected bushes strangled by creeping vines. When Hank died, their father packed the books and charts away, and now rarely talks about the past, distant or otherwise. It's as if, for him, the family ghosts, once as alive and real as the rest of them, died along with his namesake.

For Aiken, whose brand of curiosity makes him look forward, not back, the house is and always has been just a place where he was born and grew up. It had stopped feeling like home a long time ago. And now it's simply a place where he's going to sleep until he gets his life turned around.

His mother, he knows, feels differently about the house. As dilapidated as it is, the structure far surpasses her family's cabin in the hills of Southwest Virginia. Her grandfather on one side was a coal miner, on the other, a preacher. Her father, when he had work, was an auto mechanic, and the rest of the time wandered the countryside offering his services as a tinker. Neither one brought in much money. She and her brothers and sisters grew up in a single room and slept dormitory-style in a loft, while their parents occupied the one bed down below. So she takes pride in the big farmhouse. Falling down it might be, but the place is clean, the bathroom is indoors, and the roof doesn't leak.

Aiken has always wondered why his mother didn't reach out to Soon-hee, a girl from a background in many ways similar to her own. Growing up, he often heard his mother's wish that one day Hank would marry and bring his wife home to raise children in the sprawling house. As the first son, that was his duty: to carry on the family tradition and name, to fill the house with laughter and running feet, to produce offspring who would help with the never-ending chores that a farmhouse spawned—scrubbing linoleum, polishing the pine planks in the dining room, washing three stories of windows, doing the canning and the laundry. That's how things were done in her family, and in their neighbors' families, the homeplace with its blessings and burdens passed down from eldest son to eldest son. But Hank was gone, and, when Aiken brought Soon-hee home, he'd expected to take his brother's place in that vision, whether he wanted it or not. His mother would turn this pretty Korean country girl, no stranger to hard work, into the daughter-in-law she'd always talked about. And they'd raise their children here, a new generation of Alexanders.

He's still not sure what happened after the initial warm welcome, but he suspects Tammy had something to do with his mother's change of heart, as if, by dislodging Soon-hee and Aiken, she might find a spot for herself in the family home. Not that she would. It was true that his mother sometimes treated Tammy like the daughter she never had, gossiping over coffee, giving her the occasional gift of a scarf or stockings, sharing produce from her garden, or recipes. But they weren't close. More than once Aiken had listened to his mother criticize Tammy—her smoking, her endlessly changing hair color, her foolish Nashville dreams, her skirts that barely justify the name, the new tattoo that had recently sprouted on her calf—and Aiken couldn't imagine Tammy being any more welcome in the house than Soon-hee.

"You and the girl will be happier in your own place," his mother had said to him only a week after their arrival from Korea. "I'm sure she doesn't want to live out here in the sticks."

"She's from a tiny village, Ma. She hated Seoul. Cities give her the creeps."

"Stillwater's not exactly a city, Aiken. It'll suit her."

End of discussion. She didn't want Soon-hee in her house any longer than necessary. They had to leave.

Which was fine with Soon-hee. She had told him more than once, usually in a whisper even when they were alone, that she was afraid of the farmhouse. Not afraid of his mother, which Aiken would understand, but of the house itself, of its creaking, slope-floored wings and rickety porch, the shutters that banged in a storm, the roof shingles that occasionally flapped loose and landed in the yard with a gut-wrenching slap. "Make noise," she said, maybe speaking of the banging pipes and the hissing radiators, or the moaning walls, or the rattling windows. "Too big," she'd said. "Too tall."

She might have thrived in the country, with more room for her garden. She would have loved roaming the rocky hillsides that reminded her of Korea. But the minute he landed a job—as a janitor at the high school, not exactly his dream, or his parents', but a way to pay the bills—they moved into town, into that little rented cottage, far from his mother, far from the farmhouse.

17

Ha-neul and I both think of Ay-ken. We stand by the window and watch for him to return. A truck passes and Ha-neul waves, waves and waits.

To keep his mind off his father, we play games. In the yard it is hot but we play *kongki noli*, a game from my childhood. I find five pebbles and throw them on the ground. Then I show Ha-neul. I pick one up and toss it in the air, snatch another pebble off the ground, and catch the first one. Then I toss the two pebbles and snatch another. It is a game for girls, but Ha-neul laughs, and it makes me happy to hear him laugh.

Ha-neul is happy with his game, but I think of Ay-ken on his family's farm, in the big, angry house filled with spirits, hungry ghosts. When we came here four years ago I did not want to stay in such a house, but where could I go? I had no other home but with Ay-ken and the family of Ay-ken, my new family. It is my place as the wife, to become daughter to my husband's mother, to work in her house. But the spirits were too strong, too angry.

First time I see the father of Ay-ken, I feel his spirit. He touched me with his hands, his body, and I feel warmth, like my own poor father. I prayed for him, prayed that the god of his mountain would protect him. There is great distance between Ay-ken and the father, but I pray.

When I see the mother of Ay-ken, I cannot look in her eyes. I am afraid she will see me, as I see her. She is not my mother, but I know her. My new mother.

Inside the house, the voices are loud, like never before in my head, like the *mudang* says. They want to speak, but I cannot understand. They are angry, and I cannot stay inside with them. I fly out and run through fields. No rice or millet, like home, but the rocky hills, mountains—they are the same. I feel the same warmth there on the mountain, the same power as at home. The pine trees, they are the same. The streams and the birds—they are the same. I run and run until I find my place to rest. In this dark cave there are rocks, pink with bright spots, and I take them into the sunlight where they glitter and shine. I pile one on top of another. It is my poor gift to the god of this mountain, to ask his blessing for the father of Ay-ken.

I remember poems from my school days, about the shrine on the mountain. The poet Yi Ku-yong sings of my mountain and its power to mend. The sparse clouds swirl above me and I turn with them and close my eyes to hide the sun. The memory takes me home.

The voices here, on the mountain, only whisper, not like in the house. They are peaceful and they welcome me. An old man and a girl, like my sister. They are at rest. I sit on hard, dry land, like stone. From here I see the house, falling roof, chimney that bends, like a young tree in the wind. I feel the baby rumble inside, the baby who will be Ha-neul. I close my eyes to calm my stomach. I hear the footsteps approach.

"Well, hello." It is a man's voice. I open my eyes. His white beard flows to his chest and he carries a thick, gnarled stick that he lifts, as if he means to strike. I duck, but the stick drops to his shoulder, and his deep laughter rolls across the hills like thunder. A big orange cat, striped like a tiger, weaves through his legs.

I stumble to my feet, afraid, and run, downhill, down, tumbling, toward the house, away from this Mountain God.

Now I long to see the Mountain God once more, to guide us, to protect us.

I do not know what to believe. Even after all this time, I do not belong here. Ay-ken and I do not speak, or he does not hear when I speak. I try to teach him about Korea, still my home, but he becomes angry, insists that I should learn new ways, eat new food. He should understand my loneliness, how I miss my home, but he does not. And so I listen to Ta-mee, and I do not know what to believe.

Ha-neul tires of the game of stones. I show him another game.

"Put the stone on the back of your hand," I say, then toss it in the air and catch it with the same hand.

He laughs again, but he cannot catch the stone and this makes him angry. Frustrated. I show him the tiny flecks of color in the stones, but now he wants Ay-ken. He will not sit still. He cries and cries and calls for Ay-ken.

18

He's never known his father to sleep past sunrise, but that's now a daily occurrence. Aiken is out the door and on his way to work, his mother washing the dishes after their silent breakfast or already puttering in her rain-starved garden, and his father is still in bed. One more thing for Aiken to worry about. One more thing to fix.

Although the farm is much farther from the school than the house was, he doesn't mind the extra driving time. In the middle of a stream of pickup trucks and rusty sedans, winding along the Pike into Stillwater, he makes plans: to spend a day with Henry at the duck pond in the town park; or to go away with him for a vacation, maybe a fishing trip to Lake Moomaw if he isn't too young for that; or to get Soon-hee to talk, for the two of them to see a counselor, if she's willing; or, if she's not, to find a way to take Henry from her permanently.

He thinks about what to say to his mother, to get her off his back.

"I'm not living in your house forever," he might say, one more time. "I'm a grown man. It's temporary." Or, "Ma, I'm not Hank."

He thinks about his father, how the old man has faded in the time Aiken's been home from Korea, even in the week he's been back in the house. He's pale, his skin droops like a half-empty sack of feed, and he doesn't walk anywhere so much as shuffle—down the hall to the toilet fifty times a day, from the dining table into the living room to watch TV, back and forth from house to barn, as often as not forgetting to change out of his slippers and into his boots.

Aiken has tried to get his mother to talk about his father's decline, but she clucks and flaps her dishtowel. "Nonsense," she says, and that's the end of it. Or she brews a putrid tea of weeds and wildflowers that she gathers on the mountain, one of her countless home remedies. He urges her to talk to a doctor. The more he pushes, the more distant she gets. What else can he do?

He thinks about Hank. He's dismissed the fleeting apparition in the hallway on that first night as a trick of shadows. But still, Hank has been on his mind. He remembers watching the high-school football games, sitting in the stands with his parents, cheering for Hank and hoping, secretly, that Jake, who teased Aiken endlessly unless Hank was around, would suffer some gruesome injury. He remembers Hank being unhappy all the time, angry, awash in dark moods that affected everyone, especially Aiken's mother. He remembers a girl Hank spent time with, a dark-haired girl. He remembers spying on Hank and Jake as they built a bonfire in the pasture, out of sight of the house. They piled deadfall from the woods, lit a match, and the fire whooshed into life. They laughed and laughed and passed a cigarette between them, and flames leapt into the night sky, as tall as a man.

Passing the VFW Post on the Pike, he thinks about the war. Most of the time he tries to block those memories, but the images creep in: that guy from Brooklyn—Boomer was what they all called him, but Aiken can't remember his real name—incinerated when the SCUD missile hit their barracks; the body of that old Arab at the side of the road as their convoy moved north, half of his face blown away; the Oklahoman who couldn't take it anymore and turned his M16 first on his platoon leader and then himself; the field hospital where Aiken's buddy Mitch lay dying, his shattered torso a bloody slab. When those memories come, it's hard to dismiss them. He struggles to hold back tears and doesn't always succeed.

He thinks about Kelly, whom he lost because of the Army, and he thinks of the nice life they could have had together, in Stillwater, or on the farm, or anywhere she wanted to be. But Kelly's married now, and so is he, and that dream is gone forever.

He thinks about Soon-hee, and how hard her life must be, isolated in a foreign bubble as she is. It hasn't gotten better over time—it's worse, and he can't seem to do anything to help. All he wants is for the three of them, him, Soon-hee, and Henry, to live together as a family. He still wants that.

He thinks of Henry and counts the days until they'll be together.

Aiken finishes work at the school—it's summer, his duties light—and gets in the truck to drive home. It isn't his day to see Henry, according to the deal the lawyers worked out, but he swings by the cottage anyway. He still has no idea how or when Soon-hee managed to hire, much less communicate with, a lawyer—although he guesses that Tammy, who knows her way around divorce court, was involved—and her move had forced Aiken to hire his own. Despite the deal they struck, she might let him take the boy for an ice cream, or a quick trip to the park before dinner, and that would be a fine end to the day, like a glorious sunset. A cure for what ails him.

In front of the house he sits and waits. He wants to say the right things to her. He doesn't want to make her any more upset than she already is.

He could tell her he loves her, but he wonders if there's ever been real love between them. There's been heat. There's been volatility. In Korea he didn't think he could live without her. And in the time they've been married Aiken has grown truly fond of Soon-hee, despite her moodiness, her odd ways. Especially at first, when Henry was still tiny, they enjoyed each other's company.

One evening, they walked down Stillwater's main street together, pushing Henry in his stroller. They attracted stares, just as they did in Seoul, but here people were merely curious, not angry or hate-filled.

When Aiken noticed a star in the darkening sky above the courthouse, he pointed it out to her. "Make a wish," he said. He explained the superstition, something he learned from Hank. "Make a wish on the first star, but don't tell anyone what you wished for or it won't come true."

She squeezed her eyes shut. "I wish," she said, and held a finger to her own lips.

He made his own wish—for Henry to grow up healthy and happy—and took her hand. They nodded and waved to their neighbors as they continued down the street. He leaned into her and kissed her cheek.

There was another night when they sat in the park on a bench, watching boys and girls playing tag in the dusk. When a firefly blinked nearby, Soon-hee gasped.

"What is it?" she asked.

"They don't have lightning bugs in Korea?" he asked.

Now they swarmed, a hundred bulbs flickering just above the heads of the children, and Soon-hee laughed.

"No, I don't think so," she said. "Maybe." And then she began to cry. "I don't remember!"

Aiken slipped his arm around her, felt her trembling shoulders, and they watched the silent show as the darkness grew.

He wishes now he could go back in time, recreate those nights. Maybe he can. He could tell her, for starters, how nice she looks. And it's true. She's even prettier than when they met, in fact, with her smooth, ruddy complexion, like the skin of an apple—not a real apple, with all its flaws, but the idea of an apple—her tiny, flat nose, and her coal-black hair that she's let grow long, so that it cascades to the middle of her back. Her crooked smile.

He used to tell her all the time that she was beautiful. On that first walk through the gardens of Gyeongbok Palace they had stopped to rest. He bought Cokes for them and they sat on a stone bench under a pine tree.

"You're very beautiful," he said. Her face was bright with their exertions, a soft glow on her cheeks.

She lowered her eyes and sipped from her straw.

"I really mean it."

"Thank you," she said, but she still wouldn't look up at him. "You are also very beautiful."

He laughed. "No! You can't say that about a man." Now she looked up, eyes expectant. "A man is 'handsome' or 'good-looking.' Never 'beautiful.'"

She smiled then. "You are very handsome," she said.

Is there any hope for them? Can he somehow make things right? Or is that another pipedream? The truth: they have nothing in common except Henry. That had been enough, until recently. They'd managed to hold the marriage together. He understands, though, when every day is a struggle, when nothing comes easy—not language, or comfort, or peace—that people get tired. They let go. They lash out.

Watching the house, he sees no signs of activity. But Soon-hee could be out back working in her tiny garden, or maybe they're at the little table in the kitchen eating an early dinner. He realizes he should have brought something for Henry. The boy needs to understand that his father still loves him, will still take care of him. Next time, he'll bring a present. Not some expensive trinket he can't afford. Something he can make. His father used to have a wood shop in the barn where he fashioned crude accessories for the house—the shelves in the boys' rooms, the key rack on the kitchen wall. After the accident, when Hank was gone, the shop fell into disuse. Maybe Aiken can bring it back to life. Henry will love anything he makes, whatever it turns out to be.

He gets out of the truck and jogs to the door. He plans to avoid an argument. He's going to visit with his son, he'll say, and won't listen to Soon-hee's protests or any of her accusations. He'll let them float past him like clouds. He won't touch her, won't even look at her, won't let his eyes linger on that perfect skin.

He rings the bell and expects to hear the dog bark, because that's what always happens when the bell rings, but then he remembers that Ralph is out at the farm. There's no barking. He hears nothing at all. He looks in the window and sees no movement, no flickering TV, nothing. She has no car, hasn't learned to drive, rarely goes out. Maybe they've gone for a walk, although it's so hot he thinks that's not likely. Or maybe Tammy has taken them shopping in some air-conditioned mall. He tells himself not to be overly concerned. There are explanations. It's not his day to see Henry. He isn't expected. He checks the backyard, but it's empty, the garden dry and drooping. He returns to the front and rings again. He pounds on the door.

On the drive to the farm he listens to the radio. The Statler Brothers are on again, singing "Flowers on the Wall," always a local-station favorite. Even Soon-hee likes the Statlers and hums along whenever she hears one of their songs. He wishes she were here now, with Henry, so they could all sing together. Where the hell are they?

19

We have no incense, so I burn candles that smell of pine trees
before the photograph of my mother. At home in Pae-tu our
shrine spilled over with fruit and bowls of water, a golden
Buddha, paintings of the gods, a bronze bell, and flowers
brought down from the mountain, our favorite cosmos and
lily. Here, there are no god pictures, but in my mind I see
him, the man I met on the mountain when I first came to
this country, his white beard and staff, the tiger at his feet,
and I place that picture on my shrine. I see him as clearly as
I see the flickering candle, I see him in the smoke that rises
from the flame.

"Please tell me, Lord Sansin," I say, careful to use the
respect for my elders that I have learned from childhood,
"how to survive here in this country, this strange place." My
voice is soft and sweet, and I repeat my plea. There is no
answer. "I cannot stay here. I am not wanted. How can we
go home?" There is still no answer.

I cook rice for Ha-neul and me. I place a small bowl on
the shrine for Sansin. From the garden I shred cabbage, fry

with garlic and red chili. There is no cost. There is no money. We must save the money.

Ta-mee comes. In her car we shop, but there is no money, only the secret money I hide from Ay-ken, which I must save, and we buy little. We drink *cha* in the kitchen and we talk. She sings sad songs and plays her guitar. It is the music Ay-ken likes, I remember from the wine house in Itaewon, about cheating and heartache.

I tell Ta-mee that I can see the future. The *mudang* in the village performed *chom* to conjure visions of what will be, and I say I have this power. It is the power of the *mudang* I am becoming, so I must have this power.

"You're a fortune-teller?" Ta-mee asks. "For real?"

"Yes," I say, although I know nothing of fortune. It is the *chom*. The kitchen is hot, but the spicy tea in my stomach fights against the heat, and my body is cool.

"Can you tell my future?"

I take Ta-mee's hand in mine and let my eyes close. In the darkness I see Sansin, with the white beard and the stick, the smiling cat, the flowing water, but I do not call to him. He is not Ta-mee's god. I hear music, the sound of my own voice, and a yellow glow emerges in the distance. The light spins around and around, like a ball on a string, faster and faster, until I can see nothing, hear nothing, feel nothing. My head slumps forward and the darkness returns.

"Well?" Ta-mee asks.

"The household gods," I say. "They have spoken."

"And? Girl, talking to you is like pulling teeth. What did they say?"

"Teeth?" I ask, and shake my head. "No teeth. They see a man."

"Hell, I could have told you that. There's always a man."

"A man with money."

"Damn, now you're talking," Ta-mee says. "That's the best news I've had all week."

"The man is tall," I say. He looks like the cousin of Ay-ken, angry and shouting. "He is rough. Dangerous."

"Even better," Ta-mee says.

20

When Soon-hee tells me she sees a tall man in my future, I figure she's the real thing. No one knows about me and Jake, but somehow *she* does. That changes everything.

We're sitting there drinking that tea, singing a little, and talking about men and money, my two favorite subjects, and I'm thinking this little girl could be useful. If she can see the future, what else can she do? Find the treasure that Jake is convinced Uncle Henry has hidden out there on the farm? Maybe? Why not? Who's to say? If Aunt Ruth doesn't spill the beans in those tapes she's making, Soon-hee may give us what we want. I can't wait to tell Jake.

Jake. When we were kids, when Hank pushed me away, I took up with Jake. Played around some, even though, like now, he didn't want anyone to know about us. Then Hank died, and Jake seemed to die a little, too. We all did. Shit happened. Jake acted out, ran off and got married. I had my own mess of a marriage.

But one day not long ago I was sitting in my trailer, noodling on the guitar, daydreaming, and there was a knock on my door. Where I live, out by the edge of the hills, nobody just drops in, so I cracked the door open to see who it was, and there he stood, big as life in a white T-shirt and his hair wild and down to his shoulders, looking like some kind of god.

"It's been too long," Jake said. His hands were stuffed in his back pockets, as if he were some shy kid who didn't know how to talk to a girl. "Can I come in?"

I knew it was a bad idea, but I opened the door wide, stepped back, and let him in.

"How've you been, Jake?" I asked. But instead of answering, he wrapped his long arms around me and kissed me. Another bad idea, but I kissed him back.

Soon-hee can see the future, all right. Now, what else does she see?

21

One day, soon after my Ha-neul was born, Ta-mee comes for the first time. There is a knock on the door, so soft I barely hear it, but when I go to look, there she is. The dog runs in circles and jumps on her, but she pushes him down.

"I didn't ring the bell because I didn't want this one to bark and wake the baby up," she says "Can I see him?" She wraps her arms around me, but I don't move. "My God, you're stiff as a statue, girl. Get used to it. I'm a hugger. C'mon, let's try that again."

This time I do as she does, only for a moment.

"Better," she says. "We'll have to work on that." She moves past me into the living room, looking at the furniture, the poster on the wall, the medicine chest Ay-ken bought, and then down the hall toward the nursery.

I follow. "Sleeping," I say.

"I'll be quiet," she says.

We tip-toe into the room and stand over Ha-neul's crib, watching him. Ta-mee reaches toward him. I want to stop her, but he twists in his sleep and she pulls her hand away.

In the kitchen we sit at the table.

"So, here's the thing," she says. "I think we should take Henry—what kind of a name is that for a baby, anyway?—we should take Henry out to see Ruth."

"Ruth?" I ask.

"Aiken's mother, silly. Ruth. I know she'd like to see the baby. Her only grandchild, you know."

"She asked?"

"Well, no. More like hinted. But I could tell. So what do you say?"

"Say?"

"Let's go! Right now. The kid won't know where he is. I'll drive you out there and we'll have a nice visit with the old lady. She'll ooh and ahh and serve us tea and cookies and everyone will be happy."

"The house." I didn't know how to explain to her about the spirits. And I didn't know how to explain that I was ashamed. It is my duty to serve the mother of Ay-ken and I have failed. I cannot go to her.

"I know, the place is a monstrosity." She looks around my kitchen. "But, honestly, it's way better than this dump. No offense."

We bundle Ha-neul into Ta-mee's car and drive out to the farm. The hills, the trees, the air all make me think of home. I close my eyes and I drift to Pae-tu. I long for my mother and my baby sister, my father.

We climb the porch steps. Ta-mee knocks on the door. I hold Ha-neul in my arms and shut out the voices of the spirits. I do not breathe.

When she comes to the door, the mother of Ay-ken is wiping her hands on a towel. At first she smiles at Ta-mee, and then something dark crosses her face when she sees me. But her smile returns when she sees the baby in my arms.

"Oh, look at him," she says, reaching for Ha-neul.

I do not want to let go. I need to protect him from the spirits in this house. But what can I do? I must. And so I let her take my baby from me.

Do not look into her eyes, I want to tell him.

We sit on the porch. The mother of Ay-ken rocks while Ha-neul sleeps in her arms. Ta-mee prepares tea and cookies that she brings to us. I do not eat. I do not drink the tea. I sit and watch my baby.

"You could leave him with me sometimes," says the mother of Ay-ken. "I wouldn't mind."

"Mind? You'd love it and you know it," Ta-mee says. They laugh. The baby sleeps.

"There aren't any other Koreans around here, are there, Tammy?" she asks.

"Not that I know of, but what do I know about Koreans. Soon-hee?"

I shake my head. "No Koreans," I say.

"Must be lonely," says the mother of Ay-ken. "Not having anyone to speak your language to, I mean. None of your own kind."

"She's got Henry, of course."

"Sure, but it's not the same, is it?" She looks at me. "Wouldn't you rather be around people like you? Back home in Korea?"

Two bright red cardinals quarrel in the bushes. I watch as one scolds the other.

"My home is with Ay-ken and Ha-neul," I say.

"Who? You mean Henry?"

I nod.

"But you have to think of yourself, don't you. Isn't that your way?"

"I don't understand."

"I mean, you were thinking of yourself when you got my son to marry you. Cast your spell. What was best for him didn't enter your thinking, did it? You got what you wanted."

"Aunt Ruth, that's not fair," says Ta-mee.

"Well, never mind. It's water over the dam now. But she could make it right and make herself happy at the same time. That's all I'm saying."

I stand up. "Ta-mee," I say, "I would like to go home now, please." I go to the mother of Ay-ken and take Ha-neul from her arms. He is startled and opens his eyes, but then he settles into my arms and closes them again. I take him to Ta-mee's car and we wait.

I am older now, Ha-neul no longer a baby. I understand the dangers. And in these four years I have grown stronger.

22

In the morning, before his parents are up, he calls his own number. The phone rings, but there's no answer. He redials, in case he's made a mistake, although he knows he hasn't. The result is the same. Soon-hee never leaves the house so early. Where would she go? How? He tries not to give in to the idea that something might be wrong, but it won't leave him.

He heads directly to the house instead of going to work. He pulls into the driveway and hops out of the truck, doesn't take the time to close the door. He rings the bell and knocks at the same time, opens the screen door and knocks again. He uses his key, which he has promised Soon-hee he won't do. In his mind he sees horrific images of what he'll find inside—in Kuwait and Iraq, he'd seen it all, and nothing is unimaginable.

The air in the house is stale and hot. The sagging, stained sofa and shabby armchair they'd rented from the house's owner sit where they always have. But Soon-hee's poster of Korea's snow-peaked Mount Sorak is gone from the living room wall. The waist-high Korean chest he'd bought in

Itaewon, a flimsy knock-off of a traditional medicine chest with dozens of narrow drawers, is gone, too. The boy and girl dolls he'd bought her that first week in Seoul, that she kept in their bedroom—gone. In the kitchen, all of Henry's finger-paintings are gone. The cupboards are open and empty. In the bedroom, the bathroom, Henry's room—everything is gone. Where could they go? How?

The heat is suddenly unbearable, and he can't breathe. He runs back to the truck and speeds to work. He's late, but he doesn't care. He slips into the teachers' lounge and picks up the phone there, the one he isn't supposed to use, and calls home. When his mother answers, he asks for Tammy's number. She wants to know why, of course. What can he tell her? He evades the question. But when he calls Tammy, there's no answer, and now he's sure something is wrong. He leaves a message on her machine and hangs up.

The lawyer had said Soon-hee needed permission to leave town with Henry. He has rights. She's supposed to tell him everything. Thinking it through, he's calmer. She can't have gone far. It's not legal and, more comforting, it's not possible. She has no car and no money. He'll find them. There's no phone book in the lounge, and he wishes he'd kept the lawyer's number in his wallet. He considers calling the sheriff, but it's too soon for that, surely.

At lunchtime he leaves the school, something else he isn't supposed to do. He can't find a parking spot on Central Street and drives in circles, each red light tightening his chest as the minutes slip past, and he curses the city planners. Why in a dying town with no traffic are there so many god-damned traffic lights and so few parking spaces? By the time he gets a space two blocks away, up on Maple, squeezed between another pickup and a van, he's afraid he's too late, that

Soon-hee has done something terrible, has found a way to break their deal or chosen to ignore it, that somehow she and Henry are gone for good. He should have called the sheriff, after all. He runs to the lawyer's office and bursts in.

"Where's Roberts?" he asks the receptionist, breathless.

"Mr. Roberts is at lunch," she says. "Can I have him call you?"

She's polite and friendly, but right now she's the enemy, standing between Aiken and his son. He clenches his jaw and leans on the desk with balled fists.

"I need to talk to him now, right this goddamned minute. Where is he?"

Minutes later, when he finds Roberts at Woody's Diner, around the corner and down two more blocks, he's calm again. Soon-hee couldn't have gone far. People don't just disappear. Surely there's an explanation, a message left for him somewhere that he's missed, or that his mother neglected to give him. He slides onto the stool next to Roberts at the counter, nods to the lawyer, and orders coffee. His breath is steady. He explains what he's seen at the house and why he's worried.

"They'll turn up, Aiken. She probably moved to a smaller house."

"You can't get much smaller than that place," Aiken says. "But anyway, she's not allowed to do that. Right?"

"No. But she knows the house is expensive. She probably wants to save you some money, that's all."

Probably this, probably that. Now it's Roberts who stands in his way, and Aiken wants to grab the lawyer, shake him, anything to make him see. Probably isn't good enough, but no one seems to understand that.

He slams his coffee cup on the counter and runs back to his truck. He speeds out to Tammy's place, but as he approaches he sees no car, no sign that Tammy's home. He gets out, knocks on the door, peeks in the window, and assures himself they aren't there. Where the hell can they be?

The weekend comes. There's no word from the lawyer and nothing from Soon-hee, still no answer at Tammy's. He doesn't know what to do. The phone doesn't ring. He paces on the porch, Ralph at his heels. From one end he can see another old farmhouse, not too different from this one, set up on a clearing on the hill. He can even see their neighbor, Mrs. McGrady, hanging laundry on her clothesline up there, despite the blustery wind and skies that threaten to bring the first rain in weeks, and a couple of her grandkids racing between the whipping sheets. He can see his mother, too, who has come out to tend her stunted garden. But when he reaches the other end of the porch, his view is of an earlier time. The Alexanders might as well be the only people in the Valley. From here, not much has changed since the days of old Dermot. Brother Mountain stands perpetually silent, twinned. Dense woods cover the hillside. The parched fields are brown and barren. Aiken sees no houses, no people, not even the road.

What he does see, though, is his father's barn.

A classic Scotch-Irish bank barn, with two stories and a stone foundation tucked into a gentle slope, it's in good shape. The house has fared poorly over the years, but the barn for generations has been the farm's lifeblood and has been carefully maintained. Even now, with the family holdings reduced, no crops planted and no animals to raise but a few chickens, the barn is, for Aiken's father, what makes the place a farm.

Aiken was probably only five or six when he had an argument with his mother; he can't remember now what it was about. Or it might have been with Hank, who seemed to get anything he wanted from their parents, and more than once they fought over some toy or model car or comic book that Aiken coveted. Whatever it was, Aiken had determined to run away. He didn't belong. He wasn't wanted, and so he resolved to leave. He made it as far as the barn, where he hid in one of the stalls, teaching them all a lesson. Night fell and he slept, waking to the sound of Hank's voice calling his name, coming closer and closer, coming to find him in the barn.

Where has Soon-hee run to? Where is Henry?

The dark skies open. Whether it will be enough to end the drought remains to be seen, but for now rain drips off the barn's forebay and splatters into the corral, which hasn't held a horse in years. The roof looks sturdy enough, no gaping holes. And the walls seem straight. The McGradys have a barn of about the same design and age that tilts so far to the right they've had to prop it up with a forest of 4x12s, and even then some neighbors have placed bets on when the building will fall over.

He eyes the solid raft of clouds and the welcome downpour. Soon-hee's disappearance worries him. Has he done all he can? He hopes they're safe and dry, but, for once, his optimism fails, and he's afraid of what he might do if Soon-hee has put Henry in danger. He wonders if there is any point in prayer, if God might come through if he gets down on his knees.

He gazes through the rain, as if looking for an answer, looking for Henry, but there is only the barn. The barn. Had he told Soon-hee that story from his childhood about running away? Could they be hiding in the barn? Thunder cracks above the hills and the rain intensifies. He runs down the porch steps into the torrent, across the drive to the barn door.

23

Ta-mee says we must leave this house before Ay-ken returns, and so we pack. I do not know where we will go, but we must go.

"Are you sure?" I ask. I don't know.

"Of course I'm sure," she says. "You're better off on your own. Trust me."

From Ta-mee I borrow a suitcase and fill it with clothes for Ha-neul and me. On top I lay my *han-bok*, the dress that reminds me of home, my mother, my baby sister. We fill boxes and bags with shoes, toys, clothes. There is not much.

We cannot take the bed, the chairs, the TV, and Ta-mee promises to come back. She'll sell it all, she says. We'll need the money, she says.

We have nowhere to go.

With Ha-neul I come back to the hillside behind the big, noisy house, to my stone shrine, to the place where I saw Sansin, the Mountain God. I show Ha-neul the narrow cave. I show him how to pile rocks. I teach about Sansin, like my mother taught me, how he has the power to heal. I hold a rock in my hand and I tell him about the spirit of the rock.

I speak to the spirit, and ask its blessing, and then we add it to the pile. This is our special place. At home, usually, only women are *mudang*, but there is light in the eyes of Ha-neul, and I wonder what his future holds.

Rocks, pine trees, sun, deer—all mean long life. They bring blessings, along with the heavenly clouds. But now the clouds are dark, and they swirl above us, angry. I bring Ha-neul here to meet the Mountain God, but I am afraid Sansin will not come because of the clouds.

From our shrine on the hill, I watch Ay-ken's house below. It shimmers, alive, as if its ancestor spirits boil inside. The mother of Ay-ken comes out to the garden. Her white hair blows in the wind, like smoke. We are the same, I think. She knows the Mountain God. She knows the spirits. She is like *mudang*. It is why she fears me and chases me from the house. She will not share Sansin with me. The mother of Ay-ken raises her face to the sky.

And then the rain comes, as if the old woman has summoned it. The clouds pour down, we run to the cave, and Ha-neul clings to my skirt among the rocks.

How can we stay here? How can we live like animals on this mountain? Why has Ay-ken done this to us?

We sit together on the damp ground and listen to the rain. There is the smell of earth. The air is still and cool in the cave, like a tomb. I long for my mother, my sister, at home in the dirt. Their memory slips away. Have I abandoned them?

"Your grandmother," I say to Ha-neul. He looks up at me, his eyes drooping. We are both tired. "In Korea."

"Korea," he says, and his eyes close.

"Korea," I say.

We were happy in Korea, Ay-ken and I. But I don't belong here. His mother is right.

24

Inside the barn, Aiken sees no sign of them. He shakes the rain from his hair and listens to the pounding on the roof, the echo filling the cavernous space. He'd been so sure he would find them, just as Hank found him when he was a boy. If not here, where can they be?

He fumbles for the light switch that sits just inside the wide barn door. He knows the switch is there because when he was in high school he helped his father install it, running a cord up the wall and through the rafters to the fixture hanging high overhead. It was Aiken who had climbed the ladder, every step watched by his father.

"Not like that, boy," the old man had shouted when Aiken looped the cord around the rough-hewn beam. "You got to tack that wire down."

He seethed at being corrected but did as he was told, securing the cord along the beam as far as the doorframe and linking it to the line they'd already run from the house, then finally installing the switch they'd discovered in a box of junk in the cellar.

Now, when he throws the switch, the bare bulb casts a dim light: on his father's workbench in the corner, over a tarp-covered mound against the wall, and reaching back toward the vacant barn stalls like an outstretched hand. The dirt floor is rough, abraded in places, straw-covered in the rear, worn hard and smooth near the door. Black shadows fill the corners. The air smells of mice and cats.

The surface of the workbench is barely visible, and not because of the poor light. His father has never been this disorganized. When Aiken was a kid, the household rule had been "a place for everything, everything in its place." The boys complied—their father wouldn't have it any other way—with Hank riding herd on Aiken if he occasionally forgot and left his clothes on the floor or failed to return a book to its shelf. Aiken has always attributed the insistence on order to their Scotch-Irish heritage, and the habit had served him well in the Army, but now it looks as though his father has abandoned the principle, or has been too tired or distracted to live up to it. There's a kerosene lantern, rusty and dented, pushed to the back of the bench. His father's tool chest is on the bench, too, instead of underneath, where it's always been. The lid stands open like a gaping mouth, and a screwdriver, the socket wrench, and a hammer lie scattered nearby. Several empty sacks are balled in the center of the mess: plastic, paper, burlap. A can of Sherwin-Williams paint, seafoam green, the lid not completely closed. A canister of RatRid. Scraps of lumber. A stack of tiles he remembers from the time his father started to renovate the house's only bathroom, stopping mid-job when Aiken's mother turned up her nose at the unnatural shade of pink he'd chosen without her input. The mud-caked blade off a hoe. Dog-eared seed catalogues, a corroded hose nozzle, a chipped vase.

He turns his back on the bench and studies the covered mound. He lifts one edge of the tarp and sees the tread of a flat tire, enough to know it's the Triumph, Hank's motorcycle. He'd forgotten about the bike, and he's surprised that his father has kept it all this time. He wonders if his mother knows it's here. She'd always hated the bike and had begged Hank not to ride it. Aiken remembers being angry with her for being right, for not doing more to stop Hank if she was so sure of the danger. He pulls the tarp off the rest of the way, launching a cloud of dust. It isn't much to look at: front fork smashed, fender shredded, the chrome body scarred and dented where the bike slid along the pavement. He recalls how, months after Hank's accident, they'd loaded it in the back of the truck and brought it home from the sheriff's impound.

When Aiken was about eight, the family went to the county fair. It seemed like paradise, with its seductive midway of carnival games and rides, bright lights, loud music, and sugary treats. His father had wandered off to a display of farm equipment, and Aiken begged his mother to let him ride the Ferris wheel. She said no, it was too dangerous for a little boy. But Hank took his hand, paid the barker out of his own money, and sat with Aiken in the swinging chair as the wheel began to turn. With Hank's arm around his shoulders, his familiar scent so close, Aiken felt no fear, and when the wheel stopped, leaving the boys adrift at the top, he saw distant lights in all directions and the pink glow of the sun beyond Brother Mountain.

Looking at the bike, he feels Hank with him now. His chest tightens, breath labored. Even after all he saw in the war, after the mutilated comrades he held in his arms, after everything that has happened since and the years that have passed, the thought of Hank's death still does this to him, this loss that is so personal, so permanent. And remembering his absent brother makes him think again of his son, whom he could not bear to lose. He's heard of cases where one of the parents disappears with the kids, never to be seen again. Hell, he'd thought about doing that himself. He can't let Soon-hee take Henry. He has to stop her.

He'd forgotten about the bike, but now he's glad to have found it. It's a way of keeping Hank close. He replaces the tarp and watches the dust settle. The downpour has ended, and the barn is eerily silent.

All the rest of the weekend he searches. He goes back to the cottage and looks for a note he might have missed or any indication of where they've gone, but there is only dust upstairs and damp in the basement, where Soon-hee has abandoned his recliner. He crosses the street and knocks on George McCormack's door and paces as he waits for his neighbor to appear.

"You must have seen them move," Aiken says, straining not to show his anger. McCormack is retired from the Dupont plant and spends long days on his porch, watching the traffic on Pioneer Drive, so surely he would have seen a truck or a van parked in front of the house. "Where did they go? When?"

McCormack scratches his gray stubble and shakes his head. "Now that you mention it," he says, "it's been awfully quiet over there."

He claims to have seen nothing, but Aiken doesn't believe him. He doesn't know why George would do it, but the man must be lying, and to avoid shouting at his old neighbor he holds his breath and backs away. He rings the bell at the Wards' house, and the answer is the same, and he hears it again at the Paynes' and the Coffeys'. No one has seen her and no one knows where she's gone. He doesn't believe any of them. Surely there was a truck, and she must have had help. He can't imagine why they're protecting her, but it's not possible that no one saw them go.

He calls the landlord, who badgers him about past-due rent until Aiken hangs up on him. He drives all over Stillwater, calls the parents of Henry's friends and teachers from the pre-school he'd attended for the past year, checks the city parks, the library, the grocery store, the bus station.

He finally gets Tammy on the phone. "Where's Soon-hee?" he asks. "Where's Henry?"

"Haven't got a clue," she says. "Did you check the house?"

"Of course I checked the house. They've disappeared. That's why I'm calling you. Where are they?"

"Told you, Cousin. I don't know."

"If you're lying to me, Tammy, I swear—"

"Cross my heart."

On Monday there's still no sign of Soon-hee and no word from the lawyer. Aiken hasn't slept all weekend, he can't speak to his parents except in unintelligible grunts, can barely speak to the dog. He doesn't know what else to do, so he calls the sheriff to make a missing persons report. Not that he knows what that means, exactly, this term he's heard on bad television dramas. As far as he's concerned, though, his wife and son are missing, he needs someone's help to find them, and so he makes the call.

Deputy Billy Crawford meets Aiken at the cottage, and the two of them walk through each room, as Aiken has already done countless times.

"There's nothing here, Billy. They're gone. I told you."
He knows his frustration is obvious and won't do any good,
but he can't hide it.

"I know you did, Aiken. But I've got to see for myself."
They examine the basement and the bedrooms and the
kitchen. Crawford opens closets and cabinets, finds a single
child's sock that Aiken had overlooked, and a yellow strip of
paper with red marks on it. He shows it to Aiken, who shrugs.
Something Soon-hee made, one of the crazy pictures she'd
stuck on the wall in Henry's room. He's never been able to
make sense of them and got no answer from Soon-hee when
he asked what they were.

He knows that Crawford's had a tough time himself. Not
everyone in Turtle Valley was ready to accept an African
American deputy, even one who grew up there, whose family
had been around as long as anyone's. Then there's a nephew
who manages to find trouble on a regular basis, and Aiken
hears Billy's wife has been sick. Aiken is grateful for his
help, now and always. In fact, Billy was first on the scene of
Hank's accident, and he looked the other way a couple of
times during Aiken's wild post-high-school year, mediating
one or two drunken brawls in which Aiken had been a
willing participant, if not the instigator. He'd stopped by to
thank Aiken for his service when he came home on leave
after Desert Storm. Even called to congratulate him when
Henry was born.

"We'll look for 'em," says Billy, jotting notes as he speaks.
"Can't have gone far. My guess is they're in a motel somewhere
around here, until she figures out what she wants to do next."

"Next?" Aiken asks. "Isn't this kidnapping? Shouldn't we
call the FBI?" He hears the pitch of his voice rise.

"Too soon for that," says the deputy. "Let's wait and see."

* * *

Wait. Nothing good will come of waiting. Not this time. If the deputy can't or won't do anything about finding Soon-hee and Henry, he'll keep looking on his own. He took a sick day to meet Billy, so he'll spend the afternoon checking all the motels he can find, up and down the Pike and out along the Interstate. If she's hiding with Henry in a motel, as Billy seems to think, he'll find them.

He drives north to the county line and pulls into the deserted parking lot of the Valley Budget Motel. The place looks like a prison—gray, barren, shut up tight. Despite the recent rain, dust blows across the gravel lot. Just as he's about to turn back onto the highway, thinking the motel must be closed, another victim of the Valley's dying economy, a light flickers on in the office.

When he pushes inside, a tinny bell above the door rings, and a splotchy, bearded face pokes out from behind a curtain. A window air-conditioner is making a racket but provides little relief from the heat.

"Morning," Aiken says. "I wonder if you can you help me?"

The clerk rubs his eyes, as if he's just climbed out of bed.

"Looking for a young woman," continues Aiken. "A girl, really. Korean? And a little boy. You seen 'em?"

"Buddy, ain't nobody here, and I ain't seen nobody sounds like that." The clerk wipes his mouth on his sleeve.

"You've been here since Friday?"

"Told you. Ain't nobody here. Nobody. You want a room, or what?"

Aiken drives south and repeats the scene a dozen times or more, at the Comfort, the Value, the Regent, the Fairview. Only the clerk at the Days Inn even has to check the records to answer his questions. All the rest can tell for certain that no Korean woman has checked in any time recently, or ever, much less a Korean woman with a child.

When he gets home, his T-shirt damp and stuck to his throbbing back, he finds his mother in the kitchen.

"The school called," she says. It's even hotter inside than out, but she leans over the stove, stirring a bubbling pot.

"And?"

"And they wondered why you weren't here, since you called in sick." She turns to look at him, a dripping spoon in mid-air. "Are you sick?" The tone of her voice, the one that says she knows the truth and is waiting for him to confess to his lie, is nothing new. She won't come right out and say she disapproves; he's supposed to recognize his failings on his own.

"I had some things I needed to do, Ma."

"I'm sure you did." She dips the spoon into the pot and tastes, then adds salt and stirs. "Tom Roberts called, too. He's a lawyer in Stillwater, isn't he?"

"I believe he is."

"He said there was no news. Of course, I didn't ask him what kind of news you were expecting from a lawyer." She looks his way again, just for a moment.

He fills a glass with water at the sink and drinks while he decides what he'll tell her.

"It's nothing," he says. But he knows that won't be the end of it.

She stirs, tastes, adds more salt. She lifts plates and bowls from the cabinet and arranges them on the table.

"There was one other call." She pulls silverware from the drawer next to the sink. He takes the spoons and knives from her, not too abruptly, he hopes.

"Just tell me, Ma."

"Tammy wouldn't say what it was about," his mother says, and sniffs, to let him know that she's hurt, either by his evident impatience or by Tammy's silence. "Don't see why she wouldn't even say. Wants you to call."

He drops the silverware onto the table and heads to the telephone in the living room, dials the number, which by now he knows by heart.

"About time, Cousin," Tammy says.

"Ma only gave me the message a minute ago, Tammy." Although he's in the living room, he senses his mother is standing by the door, just inside the kitchen, listening. He lowers his voice. "Where are they?"

"Got a surprise for you," Tammy says. He hears whispers and static on her end.

"Hello?" Henry's voice is soft, tentative. They've practiced talking on the telephone because Aiken wants the boy to be prepared in an emergency, but he still sounds unsure of himself. Maybe that's stage fright. Or maybe there's something wrong.

"Henry, it's Daddy. Are you okay?"

"Uh-huh." And then silence. Aiken hears the phone changing hands, muffled voices. He feels lighter and cooler now that he knows where Henry is and that he's all right. Even the ache in his back has eased. He pulls his keys from his pocket, ready to go get the boy.

"Talkative little fella," Tammy says. "Make a typical man some day."

"Is he okay? How long have they been there? Why didn't you call sooner?"

"Slow down, Cousin. He's fine. I called, didn't I? He missed his daddy. Soon-hee didn't want you to know, but it seemed like the right thing to do."

"Keep them there, Tammy. I'm coming."

"What's in it for me?"

"Don't let them out of your sight."

"A reward, maybe? I think most men in your situation might be willing to pay a little something to get their sons back."

He closes his eyes. "You want me to pay some kind of ... ransom?"

"It's a joke, Cousin. Lighten up."

He hangs up the phone and calls Billy Crawford, thinking the deputy should hurry over to Tammy's to arrest Soon-hee, and maybe Tammy, too.

"She hasn't done anything, Aiken. She hasn't even left the county, for Pete's sake."

"She disappeared for three days! She's not supposed to do that."

"She's not disappeared now, is she?"

He calls Tom Roberts, who tells him the same thing. Whatever case he might have had is gone. She hasn't left the county, much less the state, and so far hasn't violated any laws.

"She even called you. Better late than never."

"It was Tammy who called, dammit." He knows he's shouting, and he regrets it instantly, but no one seems to be listening to him, and he needs to make himself heard.

"I've got real work to do here, Aiken," Roberts says. "Glad you found your boy." The line goes dead. He turns to see his mother, her head in a questioning tilt.

He races across the county to Tammy's. He has no intention of leaving there without Henry. He doesn't care what some judge said about custody; he isn't going to let Soon-hee have him. She's a danger to his son, and anyone ought to be able to see that. He speeds through Stillwater, cursing at red lights, barely slowing for stop signs. As the land rises near the mountains, and the highway stretches through rolling pastures of dry grass, he grows calmer. He's thinking about their problems with communication, how trying to talk to Soon-hee only makes him angry. He won't need to yell at her now. It's not going to help and will only upset Henry. He won't even talk to her. He'll take the boy and that'll be it. Let the lawyers work out the details.

Tammy's Civic is parked next to her lopsided and dust-covered trailer. She'd been married, briefly, while Aiken was away, and had this to show for it. The guy was long gone—no big loss, she frequently reminded the family—but she had a place to live, free and clear, apparently, so all in all it hadn't been a bad deal. He runs to the door and doesn't knock, yanks it open. Tammy sits at the fold-out table in the trailer's tiny kitchen, her hands wrapped around a coffee cup. Her hair, which was black the last time he saw her, is now an unnatural shade of yellow. Tanya Tucker twangs "If Your Heart Ain't Busy Tonight" on the radio.

"Come on in, Cousin. Oh, that's right, you're already in."

"Where is he, Tammy?"

"Fine thanks, and you?"

"I don't have time."

"Actually, you do," she says. "Because they left right after I talked to you."

"Shit," he says, slapping the closest wall and sending a tremor through the trailer. "You were supposed to keep them here." Now he pounds the wall with a fist.

"You didn't seem very happy to hear from me. And anyway, I couldn't very well tie her up, could I? She knew you were coming, because I told her, so she took the kid and left."

"Where did they go? How?"

"I don't exactly know where. But seeing you now, barging in here like we're all supposed to bow down to the great god Aiken, I've got a pretty good idea of why. Can't say I blame her. As for how—"

"Jesus, Tammy. What the fuck have you done?" But they can't have gone far. He shoves the door open, making the hinges groan, and runs to his truck.

25

She was the loveliest girl. Don't think I didn't see that.
Skin so bright! Darker than us, of course, and that worried
me because of how folks around here can be. Suspicious.
Distrustful. And yet . . . those big brown eyes. The pretty
black braid that ran the length of her back like . . . a snake,
really, but that's not a nice thing to say about a person, is
it? The handsome curve of her belly. So, so young. I could
barely believe my eyes, my Aiken with that poor child. Of
course, not long ago that was the way in our hills, wasn't it?
And was I that much older when I married Henry?

But my word, she didn't belong here. From the moment
she set foot in the house I knew there was something wrong,
like she'd carried with her a disease, some darkness, and it was
going to fall on me to remove it. I tried all I knew. Leavening
the bread with bitter root. Boiling cherry bark until the house
filled with the scent of burned sugar. Peppering my kale soup
with green lichen peeled from our walnut trees. It's the good
medicine passed down through generations in my hollow to

combat the bad, but nothing I tried took the fire out of the girl's eyes, and finally I had to send her away.

"She doesn't belong here," I said to my boy, and I knew I spoke the truth—just not the whole truth.

"Give her time," he said, but he hadn't seen what I had seen. He didn't know what I knew. And how could I tell him that the devil was in that child?

He didn't understand our ways any more than his father understood, didn't notice what went on around him, never thought to ask. That's the way with men. But women in the hills know things, and what we know is gospel. We have ways, and we learn as much from the land as we do from our ancestors, who teach us before they leave this world and then come back to carry on the learning.

I wondered from the start what kind of spell she put on my son. Don't think I don't know what I'm talking about. These things do not happen by accident. Just ask my sister Helen how I took Henry away from her. She'll tell you. But what about Aiken's wife?

That girl and I—we're too much alike. I couldn't let her stay.

Working in the kitchen this morning I heard Aiken's dog barking on the porch, then a knock on the front door. I dried my hands on a dish towel, thinking about who it might be. Tammy, maybe, or Mary McGrady from up on the hill come to borrow something, sugar or butter. That's her way, and I don't mind, really, although, she almost never pays it back. They've got hard times, though, and I'm only too happy to help.

But when I pushed the door open it wasn't Tammy or Mary either one. It was Jake. He held a faded ball cap in his hands, wore a filthy T-shirt with the sleeves ripped off, and sweat poured down his face and arms. He had one skeptical eye on Ralph, who looked just as wary of Jake.

"Morning, Aunt Ruth," he said.

"Gracious, Jake, don't you look hot," I said. "You come on in and I'll fix you a nice cold lemonade."

"Don't have to ask me twice. That sounds mighty good. Say, I didn't see Uncle Henry's truck in the drive. Or Aiken's. Are they here?"

I wondered how Jake knew Aiken had come home.

"I don't rightly know where Aiken's gone. But Henry's off at the cattle auction, I think. Not that he's in the market for livestock. He just likes to shoot the bull with his pals." I was happy to see the smile on Jake's face—whether because he caught my little joke or because of Henry's absence I couldn't say—and he followed me into the kitchen.

I fixed us both a tall glass and we sat at the kitchen table.

"It's nice of you to stop by, Jake," I said. I figured there was a reason for his visit, and he'd tell me in his own time.

"We had a job out this way."

"Still working for Dave, are you?"

"Yes, ma'am."

"Always a need for landscaping," I said.

"Yes, ma'am."

And we went on that way. I asked about his wife. He was noncommittal. Same thing when I asked about his drawing. I remember that sketch he gave me of Hank. Jake just shook his head, but then he pulled another picture from his jeans pocket and unfolded it on the table. It was a drawing of the house, as sharp and clear as could be, the shutters and the chimney and my rocker on the front porch. Must have done it from memory, I suppose.

"It's beautiful," I said. I meant it, too. "You've got a real knack."

"It's nothing," he said.

And then he pushed away from the table and stood. Never did say what was on his mind.

"I need to get back," he said. "Thanks for the lemonade, Aunt Ruth. It sure hit the spot."

He went out the back door, and I watched him circle the house and climb into his truck. He couldn't see me, but I waved.

26

The next day, Aiken misses work again, and then the day after that. He spends the mornings looking for Henry and Soon-hee, calling Tammy to see if she's heard anything, stopping by to see Tom Roberts, leaving messages for Billy Crawford. In the afternoon, when there's nothing else he can do but worry, or shout uselessly at the very people whose help he needs, he goes out to the barn.

He puts his father's tools in the chest where they belong, trashes the ruined can of paint—the color has mottled, the surface is cracked and broken like a dry pond—and returns the pesticides to the cabinet where his father always stored them. He sweeps the moldy straw out of the barn and sets about grading the dirt floor: scraping with the shovel and rake, tamping and checking his work with the spirit level, using the tape measure to get the exact dimensions for the planks he plans to install.

The lighting in the barn is miserable, and the old kerosene lantern that he's filled and lit doesn't help as much as he thought it would, although the smell of the burning oil evokes a memory that he can't quite bring into focus. He's in the barn spying on Hank, who's with a girl. They're kissing and don't know that Aiken is watching. And then the image is gone, the memory with it. He locates his father's ladder in the crawlspace under the house—no place for it, he knows, when there are hooks on the barn wall where the ladder belongs. But maybe they're too high now for his father to reach comfortably, so he lowers them. He runs new wiring along the beams, tacking it down as his father instructed long ago, and hangs a fixture—another rescue from the junk box in the cellar—above the workbench. He replaces the dim bulb in the rafter lamp. Then he tackles the window, caked inside and out with years of mud and dust. He fills a bucket at the pump and scrubs the glass with a rag that he rinses and wrings out until the water runs dung-brown and the barn window sparkles. In the new light, Aiken sees the dust and cobwebs and dirt accumulated everywhere inside—along the window ledge, under the bench, beneath the rafters—and they are next to go.

Work on the barn progresses, slowed from time to time by his feelings of guilt. He should be searching for Henry. But he's run out of places to look, and what else can he do?

In addition to his morning call to Tammy, he also calls each night, after his parents have gone to bed. He listens to the house, its creaks and whispers, and dials Tammy's number.

"Heard anything?" he asks when she picks up.

"Not a damn thing," is her usual reply.

"Are you sure?" Where else can Soon-hee turn, if not to Tammy?

"I told you, Cousin. Not a word."

Night after night it's the same, and he gradually allows himself to think the unthinkable. His interest in cleaning up the barn fades—he realizes he was making a home for him and Henry, so what's the point now?—and, instead of finishing the work, he drinks. Except for that year after high school, before he joined the Army, he's never been a big drinker. But now he sits in the cab of his truck and sweats, and he drinks. The war comes back to him—the unbearable noise pounding in his head, the killing, in his head, too, the shimmering flesh that falls at his feet when the bomb goes off, the certainty that next time it would be him. He's beyond caring what happens, thinks what he might do to Soon-hee if she were to appear suddenly, contemplates what he might do to himself if he can't find Henry. He remembers the days and months after Hank died, the anger he felt, how the house was filled with an emptiness, how it took him the better part of a year to convince himself that Hank was really gone. How can he live without Henry?

There's another memory of Hank, too. He's dressed up, handsome, wearing a suit and tie. A carnation in his lapel. The girl, the one Aiken saw in the barn with Hank, clings to his side in a long flowery dress, a corsage on her wrist. Their smiles beam as Aiken's father snaps picture after picture. Whatever became of those pictures?

One night, after finishing a pint of bourbon, having succeeded only in making himself feel worse, Aiken stumbles into the house when the windows in his parents' bedroom go black. He calls Tammy, gets a wrong number, mumbles his apology to an indignant voice, then dials again, struggling to focus on the blurry numbers.

"Heard anything?" he asks when he hears her voice.

She says, "Maybe."

"Tammy," he says, alert with renewed hope, shaking off the drunkenness, "you better tell me if she called you, because I'm going to come up there and wring your neck if you don't."

"Since you asked so nicely, Cousin," she says, "your lovely wife did call this afternoon."

"Where is she? Is Henry okay?"

"She needs money. Have you been drinking?"

"You tell her—"

"Two grand."

"Jesus, Tammy. She knows I don't have that kind of money. We barely get by as it is."

"Can you borrow from your folks?"

"Why are you taking her side?"

"I'm not taking anybody's side, Cousin. Just trying to help. She needs the money. She wants to go home."

"She can't very well go home now that she's emptied out the damn house and turned the place over to the landlord, can she? And where did all the stuff go, anyway?"

"It's amazing what people will buy at a yard sale. But not that home, smart guy. Korea. She wants to take Henry back to Korea."

"Fuck," he says and slams down the phone. It's late, and he's still drunk, but he calls Billy Crawford to tell him about Soon-hee's plans.

"Now will you do something?" he asks "Before she takes my kid to goddamned Korea?"

"That's a different story, Aiken. We'll look for her."

He calls Tammy back and makes it clear to her—he's shouting, so he's sure she gets the message—that she's not to let Henry out of her sight for one second if they come back. But he can't trust Tammy. She put Soon-hee up to it in the first place. He just doesn't know why.

*   *   *

With the hunt now in Billy's hands, there's nothing else he can do, so in the morning he resumes his efforts to fix up the barn and looks forward to showing it off to his father. The project is a distraction, at least. It occupies his hands and gives him something else to think about, although Henry is always on his mind. He hasn't been to work in a week.

"What should I tell the school when they call?" his mother asks.

"Tell them I'm still sick."

"You can't lie to these people, son," she says. "What if they find out?"

"Then they find out."

When he at last leads his father out to the barn to show him the results of his labor, the old man doesn't ask what it's about. Either he already suspects what Aiken has done, or he has no idea that anything out of the ordinary has happened. Or he doesn't care, just as he hasn't cared about much of anything for years. Aiken turns every couple of paces crossing the drive from the house, impatient for his father to keep up as he rests his hand on the pickups, first his own, then Aiken's, to catch his breath. He doesn't resist when Aiken takes his arm to help him along.

Aiken flings the barn door open. The new light fixtures are ablaze, despite the sunlight streaming through the spotless window. The floor sparkles, the planks Aiken has put down polished to a high sheen.

His father makes his own way to the bench Aiken has built with the leftover lumber, and sits, coughing and wheezing. He barely glances at the tidy workshop, the glittering table saw, the window. He hasn't turned his eyes toward the Triumph, now uncovered and in the early stages of restoration, the tarp *under* the partly disassembled bike instead of hiding it from view.

"What do you think?" Aiken asks. He lifts the lid of the tool chest to show that every screwdriver, every wrench gleams from its designated place. He opens the new cabinet he's built in which he's stored the pesticides and solvents, the paint, the motor oil and lubricants, and demonstrates the lock that will keep it all secure from a certain little boy. He flicks the light switch off and then on again, because his father hasn't looked up to see the bright bulb overhead, or the new fixture over the workbench.

"I think I need to lie down," his father says.

"But there's more to see," Aiken says, backing toward the one stall he's scrubbed and floored.

"It's nice, Aiken."

His father struggles to rise from the bench and heads toward the door.

"I thought you'd love it, Dad." He's afraid there is disappointment in his voice, a tone his mother might take.

"I need to lie down," his father says again.

Aiken, standing in the brilliant new light of the barn, watches his father shuffle across the drive, and then, when the old man stumbles, jogs to his side to take his arm.

There's been no news from Billy Crawford, not a word from Tammy, and no sign of Soon-hee or Henry. He continues to work on the barn, preparing for the boy's homecoming, but the more he thinks about what his wife is doing to his son, the angrier he becomes. He drives across the county and parks his truck along a road that gives him a view of

Tammy's trailer. He returns each day and watches through binoculars, waiting for Soon-hee to appear, ending his stakeout only when Tammy emerges and waves to let him know he's been seen.

One night, Tammy calls.

"She wants to meet," Tammy says.

"Finally," says Aiken, almost shouting. A weight has been lifted. He's still angry, but he's relieved that Soon-hee hasn't left for Korea, that there's a chance to get Henry back. "She could come here anytime she wants."

"Not a good idea."

"What about your place, Tammy? You being so neutral and all."

"Hell, no. I don't want no murders in my living room."

"Her? Or me?"

"Either way," she says.

He has never been to Common Grounds, the coffee shop where Tammy sometimes sings and plays for tips. It's across the street from the Emmett Theater, the town's cavernous movie hall, and a block from the Turtle Tavern. The place is dark, except for spotlights aimed at unframed abstract paintings on the brick walls. A tall, bald man with gold loops in both ears stands behind the counter, flipping through a magazine. Aiken's glance slides over the wild artwork as he sits at a table in the corner without ordering.

A stooped gentleman totters in and settles into a sofa along the wall. Aiken listens to the magazine pages flip, flip, flip, like a dripping faucet. A girl with pink hair comes in and leans on the counter, staring up at the menu, which is scrawled on a smudged chalkboard. She glances over both shoulders, smiles at Aiken, then turns back to the bald man.

The pink-haired girl sits, crosses her leg, bobs her head to a tune Aiken cannot hear, then bounces out of her chair and back outside. The old man follows shortly thereafter.

He feels the pain in his back again, the tightness in his chest. Why is he sitting here? Who are these people? It's all a waste of time. Where the hell is Soon-hee?

The mailman comes in and drops a stack of mail on the counter. He has leathery skin and a ponytail like Aiken's, a shiny stud in one ear. After a quick exchange with the bald counterman—the heat's something, ain't it, any rain in the forecast?—he's out the door again. Then a pair of white-haired women enter, then a blond woman in high heels, a pink suit, and pearls, carrying a shiny black purse, then a bearded man with glasses, a book under his arm. Soon the place is empty again, and Aiken thinks about ordering coffee so he won't feel so naked and ridiculous sitting at the table doing nothing. Or giving up on the whole absurd idea. Or finding Tammy and Soon-hee and throttling them both.

He realizes—and can't believe it hasn't occurred to him before—that Soon-hee would probably bring Henry with her. He's thrilled that he might see his son at any moment, and a picture of the boy fills his thoughts, a picture that loses focus the instant it appears. Is his hair that long? Is the color right? Isn't his nose flatter than that, more like his mother's? He's horrified that his memory of his own son's face has dimmed in this way. His fists and jaw both clench and his aching back stiffens as his anger at Soon-hee—which had been eclipsed by the image of the boy—returns, and he isn't sure he'll be able to contain his fury when she shows up. Unless Henry is with her. Again the thought of his son calms him and he settles back into the chair. But, if Henry is going to come, he should have brought a present for the boy. That's what the work on the barn was all about, initially, but he hasn't yet brought the wood shop to life, and he hasn't made a damn thing. He considers running out now to find a toy or a book, half stands to go, but Soon-hee is already late. She'll be coming through the door any second. He can't be gone when she finally shows up.

He buys a coffee, waits another fifteen minutes, feels the ache seeping up his spine as he watches customers enter, order, and leave the shop. He sips the coffee, which is now cold, and sloshes it into the trash on his way to the payphone next to the restrooms. He calls Tammy, and gets her answering machine.

"I've been waiting here over an hour, you goddamn, lying bitch," he says. "Have a nice fucking day."

27

"Jake," I say, "you'll never believe this." And I tell him about Soon-hee and her powers.

"Bullshit," he says, and rolls on top of me. We're in bed and he's only got one thing on his mind. He doesn't want to hear about Cousin Aiken and his spooky wife, even if she might be the answer to his prayers.

"How else can you explain it? She knows about us. She held my hand, looked into my eyes, and described you exactly."

"Some trick," he says, and then his mouth is on mine and the discussion is over.

Later, when we're lying there smoking a joint, I spell it out for him. I tell him she can help us find that treasure he thinks is buried out at the farm. I see a light go on in his eyes.

"So she's some kind of fortune teller?"

"That's what I've been trying to tell you."

"And you believe that crap?"

"I've seen stranger things around here all my life. Haven't you?"

There was this one time when I could have sworn I saw Hank standing right here in my kitchen. I don't believe in ghosts—not really—but I didn't know how else to explain it. "Hank?" I said, and then whatever it was disappeared. Smoke, I thought. A hangover maybe. I didn't tell Jake I'd seen Hank's ghost because, one, he'd tell me I was nuts. And, two, he'd pull himself inside his shell like a turtle, the same way he always does when someone mentions Hank.

Jake can be a sweet guy. He just doesn't let anyone see that side of him very often. But when he's here he leaves these little drawings around where I'll find them—a sketch of me, or the trailer, or a fawn he's seen grazing on the hillside. Would he do that if he were the tough guy he wants everyone to think he is? I don't always get the message, but that's how he communicates.

"What if we play along," I say, "see if her visions or whatever turn something up?"

"You think there's anything to it?" He takes a last hit on the joint, holds the smoke in his lungs for a long time, and exhales. The smoke drifts around us and he takes me in his arms. "Like visions of sugar-plums," he says. "Sure. Why not?"

28

Ha-neul cries and will not stop. Fire burns in his eyes and cheeks. I brush my hand over his hair and forehead, whisper into his ear. But he will not stop. He asks for Ay-ken. He will not stop. I also long for Ay-ken.

We are on the mountain, our true home, like Pae-tu. The pine trees stand guard over the cave, and the deer visit, as if their immortal spirits know us and protect us. I have nothing to offer them except the withered apples I find in the orchard on the slope below. The deer eat and laugh.

But Ha-neul cries and will not stop, and so I prepare for the *kut*. The ceremony will bring Sansin back to us and will frighten the demons who have invaded my son's body.

I carry Ha-neul from the cave. On the forest floor, in the pine needles, I draw a circle around him where he lies, exhausted from the crying and the fever. I have brought the candle from the shrine in our little house. I pile rocks and balance the candle among them. I remember the *mudang* at home, how she bowed her head and closed her eyes, summoned the Mountain God in her own voice, and when she looked up she was transformed. Her eyes were clouded with new sight. She was the god.

I close my eyes. I breathe deeply and let the sweet pine scent fill my lungs while the hot wind swirls around me. I hold my breath until my head spins, and then I breathe again and again and again, faster and faster. In my mind I hear the drums beat.

I feel him in me. I am not Lee Soon-hee, mother of Ha-neul, sister of the spirit Lee Soon-bok, I am Sansin, protector of the mountain. I rise. I spin. I see Ha-neul's body and the demon spirit hovering above him. Ha-neul moans. The candle's tongue darts into the sky. I spin again. I twist around the shrine of rocks and then around the circle in the pine straw. I spin. I extract the knife from my sash and I chop the air. I spin faster, orbiting the body, stabbing at the demon, shouting at him to leave us. Faster, faster, spinning, shouting, stabbing. Ha-neul moans again. I am Sansin. Leave us, devils, leave the boy to me.

Ha-neul sleeps in my arms, but he is too sick for the cave. We go to stay with Ta-mee. At first she says we cannot stay, that there is no room, but she looks at Ha-neul, caresses his forehead, and lets us in. To pay, I perform the *chom*. I summon Ta-mee's household gods to show us the future. Again I close my eyes, breathe deeply, and let the darkness spin until there is a light shining in the distance. I call out to the gods.

"Ask about that man with money," Ta-mee says.

"He is coming," I say.

"Yes!" Ta-mee says.

We sit at the small table in her trailer, while Ha-neul sleeps on her bed, thrashing and moaning as the fever rages. It is late, and outside the night is black. Ta-mee sips beer from a bottle that shines with sweat. I cool my face with a fan, but the fan only makes the skin burn when I stop.

A noisy truck is outside and we both turn to look at the door. I am sure it is Ay-ken, come to take Ha-neul. I do not know how to fight, but I must. For Ha-neul. I am prepared. I pull the knife from my sash. Footsteps approach. The door rattles.

"You in there, Tammy?"

It is not Ay-ken. It is the voice of another man, the cousin of Ay-ken.

"Jesus, Jake, it's the middle of the night. You 'bout scared us half to death."

And Ta-mee lets the man in. My hand tightens on the handle of the knife.

"Well, lookee here," he says. "If it isn't the chink." He looks around the trailer and spots Ha-neul on the bed. "And the half-breed, too. Y'all having a little slumber party?"

I don't know what he means, but I remember Ay-ken tells him not to say these things to me. I do not talk. I am worried for Ha-neul.

He wraps his arms around Ta-mee and they kiss until Ta-mee looks at me and pushes him away.

"What do you want, Jake?" Ta-mee says.

"That's no way to talk," he says. He pulls her close again. "I missed you, babe."

"I've got company."

"The thing is," he says, "besides just wanting to see my girl, I was wondering if you might have a little green you could lend me. Or maybe some of the sugar your fine, upstanding ex-husband was known to sell?"

Ta-mee looks at me, and her voice gets quiet, but I still hear when she speaks to Jay-ke.

"Get the fuck out of my house," she says. "You're just like him." With both hands she pushes his chest.

"You want to play rough?" He grabs her wrists, and in her twisted face there is pain. He looks at me. "Holding out on me, lover? But maybe you've got something else I want. We could have some fun right here."

"Get out," says Ta-mee, louder.

He steps to me. My hand is on the knife. His hand flows along my arm like oil. I hear Ha-neul stir in the bed. My hand is on the knife.

"Get out," Ta-mee shouts again.

"Think about it," he says, laughing. "You said she could help us find what we're looking for. I don't believe in that mumbo-jumbo, but she could still make herself useful. They don't flash it like some do, but my dad always said Aiken's folks have got bread—buried treasure or not. We've got her and the half-breed. Bargaining chips, girl. Give and take. We all win."

She pushes him again and finally he leaves.

Ta-mee sits at the table and looks at me. "*All* men," she says.

I know now what I must do. I cannot stay here. It is not safe. When my father sees that my child is a boy, he will forgive me, no matter what Little Mother says. He will accept me and Ha-neul, and I will make my living as *mudang* in our village. I will find the money. We cannot stay with Ta-mee. We will go home to Pae-tu.

29

Jake shows up at the trailer when Soon-hee is there with Henry, but I figure it doesn't matter because she already knows about us, right? It's no coincidence that he comes right then, though, and I don't like the way he's looking at her, like he's got something on his mind other than buried treasure, like burying a little treasure of his own. So I throw him out. But I know he'll be back. I hope he'll be back.

When I wake up, Soon-hee and the kid are gone. How the hell did they do that? And where could they go? At least now, when Aiken makes his demands, I can truthfully tell him I don't know where they are. So much for the plan to meet him at Common Grounds.

But Aiken is the least of my worries.

30

At the farm, Aiken's mother has taken a message from Tammy and reads it to him from a notepad on the kitchen counter: "She's sorry, but Soon-hee changed her mind. Maybe another time. They'll be in touch." His mother looks up at him, her eyebrows raised.

"What's it mean, Aiken? You weren't going to talk to her were you? You're not going to bring her here? Does that seem like a good idea to you?"

He lets the screen door slam on his way to the barn. He's through defending Soon-hee to his mother. Admitting that she's been right all along will only make him angrier. Why did Soon-hee want to meet and then back out? It doesn't make any sense, but none of it makes sense. What does she want? And what's in it for Tammy?

Under the bright barn lights, he eyes the last of the leftover lumber and a half sheet of plywood he found in the loft. He sets that up on the workbench, like canvas on an easel, and he looks at it, imagining what he can make for Henry that won't cost money he doesn't have. He stares at the wood and sees nothing.

There's a commotion in the loft, and dust filters through the streaming light. He hasn't managed to chase all the swallows out of the barn, and the truth is he's enjoyed their company when he works. Still, they don't belong in the barn anymore, now that he's made it their home, his and Henry's, and he should get rid of them. The birds will find another spot to build their nests.

Aiken grabs a pencil and a straightedge from the workbench and draws a square on the plywood. He stares at it, pondering whether to continue, whether it might not be foolish to believe he could turn this discarded slab into anything of value. But he applies the pencil and straightedge again and draws a triangle on top of the square. He makes an exact copy next to the original. He hasn't figured out how to use the table saw yet, but he's too impatient for that now. So he removes the handsaw from its wall hook and begins to cut the figures he's drawn, doing his best to keep the lines straight when the brittle veneer chips and cracks. Sawdust fills the air and drifts to the new floor. When he has the pieces cut, he leans them together at the vertex and sees what he needs next. He draws three more squares and cuts those. He finds nails in the tool chest, and fastens two of the square pieces to the third square along their edges, then nails one of the oblong pieces at the end. He doesn't know where his father's drill is—he hadn't come across one as he cleaned the barn—so with the awl and hammer he chips a hole in the triangular segment of the last piece. It's a messy process. When he's able to stick two fingers through the hole, he guesses it's big enough and nails this last side to the others.

He laughs at himself when he realizes that the house needs a roof.

He holds the last of the plywood above the little box and visualizes what he still has to do. He measures and cuts two rectangles. He nails one to the sides of the triangles. He holds the last piece in place, ready to pound the final nails in his creation, when he sees his mistake. He should have beveled the edges of the roof pieces so they'd form an even joint at the peak, although with a handsaw on plywood that would have been next to impossible. Now the roof is going to be a mess, with a gap at the top. But just as he is about to strike, resigned to his house's shortcomings, he sees he can eliminate the gap by moving the second roof piece higher. The eaves of the house won't be the same length on both sides, but will the birds care?

Henry certainly won't. For just a moment, he wonders if Henry will ever see it.

In the cabinet where he's stored the salvageable paint—discontinued samples that his father bought years ago at half price and never discovered a use for—Aiken finds one can of pea green and one of lavender. Puke and purple. Paint is paint, though, and Henry won't care about that, either.

There is a small, stiff paintbrush among the supplies, and Aiken holds that under a stream of water from the pump in the yard, loosening the bristles. When he has dried the brush, he dips it into the paint and in a few strokes has covered the walls of the birdhouse in a deep purple, like the irises in his mother's garden. He paints the roof in that horrible shade of pea green. He realizes too late that he should have waited for the purple to dry, because the house is hard to handle—he's left thumbprints on all sides—and the two colors run together where they meet. But it's done. He sets it on the workbench and steps back to admire his monstrosity, thrilled and amused when a shaft of sunlight strikes the thing, as if it has been blessed despite its deformities.

He puts away the tools and the paint, rinses the brush again and sweeps up the sawdust and scraps. He wipes purple and green drips from the floor and his boots. He rounds up stray nails and stores them in the tool chest. Before he leaves the barn, he takes a last, satisfied look at his creation, wishing Henry were there to see it.

At dinner, after his mother says grace, Aiken spears a chicken breast and a leg from the platter she has set in the center of the table. He slathers two biscuits with butter and honey, ladles a mound of steaming peas onto his plate. He's already ripped into the chicken when his mother picks up his father's plate and, with her fingers, lifts a scrawny leg onto it, a hillock of peas, half a biscuit.

"I was thinking of fixing up the barn," Aiken says. He's still chewing and half expects his mother to scold him for talking with his mouth full.

"You've already done wonders with it," his mother says. "According to your father."

Aiken is surprised he's mentioned the barn to her. He looks at his father, who seems not to have heard and is intent on eating his chicken, and then back at his mother.

"I mean really make it nice. You guys aren't using it for anything but storage. My old room is . . . cramped, and I thought I'd move out there."

"It's a barn, Aiken. You can't live in a barn."

He's lived in far worse conditions in the Army, especially in Kuwait, but he sees no point in repeating what he's told her a dozen times. "There'd be enough room out there for Henry, too, if he came to live with me."

"There's plenty of room right here in the house. More room than we know what to do with."

"I know, Ma. It's just something I want to do. For Henry and me."

"With a perfectly good house to live in?" asks his mother. "What will people think?" She folds her napkin in her lap. His father says nothing.

After dinner, he helps his mother with the dishes. As he's drying a plate, he scans the kitchen: his father's boots by the back door; a broom leaning in a corner; a collection of black and white pictures taped to the refrigerator. He looks more closely at these. They're drawings. One is of Hank and another is of the farmhouse, but it's the third one that grabs his attention. Henry.

"Where'd you get these?" he asks.

"Jake did them. Boy's got talent, don't you think?"

"Jake? When?" He sets the plate aside and pulls the picture of Henry off the door, gazes into his son's eyes. It's not a photograph, but it might as well be. Aiken even recognizes the T-shirt Henry is wearing.

"I don't know when he did them. Don't think he said."

"But how did you get them?" Jake has seen his son?

"Jake brought them by. Why are you shouting, Aiken? I told you he comes by to visit now and then. I'm sure I told you. He should do something with that talent."

"This one," Aiken says, holding up the picture of Henry, "when did he bring this one?"

"This afternoon. Said he had a landscaping job up this way and stopped by. He's working for Dave, you know, although I don't think he cares for it much. Anyway, he gave me the picture of Henry. Isn't it the cutest thing? Now that I think of it, he said to be sure I showed it to you."

So Jake has seen Henry and wants Aiken to know about it. Soon-hee won't let Aiken near his own son, but she lets Jake draw him?

He thrashes in bed, thinking, planning. At first light, he'll drive to Jake's and confront him. He'll find out where Henry is, even if he has to beat it out of his cousin.

In the night, he hears shouting. He thinks it's a dream at first, but then, as his awareness grows, he recognizes his mother's voice, shouting his name. He runs down the hall and pushes into his parents' room.

"Something's wrong with your father," she says.

He jumps to his father's side. The old man stares blankly, gasping for breath, clutching his chest. Aiken knew this day was coming, and he'd thought about what he would do; he's surprised his mother isn't prepared, isn't springing into action. Instead, she's paralyzed, motionless on the bed, watching Aiken, a hand clamped to her open mouth.

He learned in the Gulf that time is critical. He knows he can get to the hospital faster than paramedics can reach the farm, so he runs back to his room and dresses, then carries his father—so light and bony in baggy pajamas, a bundle of sticks—down to the truck. His mother has finally stirred. She opens the door, and Aiken lays his father, still gasping, on the seat. She appears to want to climb in, but the cab is small and she hesitates. She stands with her hand on the door, looking frail and bewildered, her nightgown flapping in the hot night breeze.

"Call the hospital," he tells her. "Let them know we're on our way."

She shakes her head, shuts the door, and backs away from the truck, her trembling hands raised to her ears as if she doesn't want to hear more.

"Call them," he shouts.

With one arm on his father's chest to keep him from rolling off the seat, but also to comfort him, to let him know he's not alone, Aiken races up the Pike to the county hospital. The road passes in a dark blur, black trees rushing beside them, and in a jumble he sees his father atop the old Harvester, commanding his fields like a great general on horseback; he sees him lifting his rifle, taking aim at a buck; he sees him casting into a trout stream on Brother Mountain. He sees his own hand reaching out toward his father, who turns his back. He sees him, ghostly, at Hank's funeral: head bowed, cheeks sunken, eyes red with grief and rage. He sees the future, too, but he can't bear it.

"Everything's fine," he says, glancing at his father, whose eyes are wide. "Don't worry about a thing." Is the sound of his voice reassuring? Or does his father hear the terror and helplessness?

The hospital is relatively new, but Henry was born there and Aiken has been to the emergency room twice with him, the first time when the boy swallowed a dime he'd found on the kitchen table and a second time when he'd fallen off a swing set in the park. There'd been a third visit, when Soon-hee sliced into her hand with a butcher knife, chopping cabbage to make that awful Korean stew she liked. She'd stared at the blood spouting from her palm, the knife still in her grasp, and stiffened while Aiken wrapped her hand in a kitchen towel for the trip to the hospital. That time, he'd waited in the lounge, Henry asleep in his arms, while a doctor sutured Soon-hee's wound. And every minute, transported to the bloody field hospital in Kuwait, he'd wanted to flee.

A man in a white coat approaches Aiken in the waiting room. He holds a red file folder with both hands; a stethoscope dangles from his neck like a talisman. His nametag announces that he's Dr. Patel.

"It could have been a stroke," Dr. Patel says, "or an MI." A heart attack, he explains before Aiken can ask. Patel is young, too young to be a doctor, Aiken thinks, but his expression is calm and serious.

"Will he be all right?" Aiken asks.

The doctor offers no encouragement, no soothing lies, tells him there isn't anything Aiken can do for now, except wait.

But he can't wait. He doesn't want to be there, he doesn't want to see what happens in a place like this. Because he knows. He doesn't want to be there when his father dies. He doesn't want to be the one at his father's side when he wakes up. He doesn't want to comfort him; he doesn't know how. It isn't that he doesn't care what happens to his father. But he's afraid he doesn't care enough—it's Henry who's on his mind—and somehow his father will know. He can't stay there and think about what he can't change. He can't be his father's favorite, he can't suddenly find the warmth that has never existed between them, he can't bring Hank back, he can't care about the family farm, or old Dermot, he can't be someone he's not.

What he wants is to be with *his* son, to live in the future. He wants this battle with Soon-hee to be over. He wants to be asleep on the couch with the TV on, Henry in his arms,

Ralph at his feet, and a warm breeze washing over them through an open window, and he feels guilty for wanting all this while his father lies unconscious.

He knows he should tell someone he's leaving—the young doctor, a nurse, anyone—but he can't. If he speaks to them, they will see the truth, and that will make it all worse. Instead, when his father is surrounded by the people who will take care of him, whose *job* it is to take care of him, he goes out to the truck. He drives back to the farm.

In the morning, with no sleep, he brings his mother to the hospital. At the information desk they learn that his father is in intensive care, third floor, South wing. But when they locate the ward, and find the nurses' station, there seems to be no record for Henry Alexander. Then confusion, worry over what this absence means, then the discovery that his first and last names have been inverted on the chart, and finally they are directed down the hall to his room. The old man is unconscious, no damage assessment yet, nothing they can do, Aiken's mother will wait. Aiken can't do that, and can't look at his mother because he knows her eyes are pleading for him to stay. He takes one last look at his father—it's fleeting, because he can't bear it—before he goes.

He calls Tammy from a payphone in the lounge, but there's no answer and no point in leaving yet another angry message. He drives by the saltbox house, but there's no activity there. He even goes up to the front window and looks inside to be sure that the living room is still bare, as if he might have imagined their disappearance, or Soon-hee might have come to her senses and returned. But it's like peering into a cave—dark, long shadows, nothing else.

He finds Jake's apartment in a shabby development on the outskirts of Stillwater and bangs on the door. There's no response, but he bangs again and, this time, he hears movement inside. Jake's wife Debby opens the door. She's wearing a robe, her eyes half-closed with sleep.

"Where's Jake?" he asks.

"Jesus, Aiken. I work nights, you know."

"Where's Jake?" he asks again, more insistent. "It's important, Debby."

"How should I know? Work, I guess. Hell, I have no idea."

And then it occurs to him that no one had picked up the phone at Tammy's, but that doesn't mean they're not there.

He drives back to the farm first. He thinks of wrapping the birdhouse, to make it look like a real present, but it isn't the boy's birthday, or Christmas. The thing itself is what he wants to give Henry, something he's made, not some hidden surprise. He carries it from the barn, shaking his head again at its sheer ugliness. He anticipates ridicule from his cousin, and he considers leaving the birdhouse behind. But he has no reason to care what she thinks. He settles it onto the seat next to him and drives to Tammy's.

He's sure he'll find them this time. Where else can they be? Tammy's been lying to him all along, he knows it, although he has no idea why, and somehow Jake is in on it. Aiken pulls up behind Tammy's Civic, lifts the birdhouse off the seat and carries it to the front door. He knocks. He thinks he hears voices inside, maybe Henry's.

He hears crying. He knocks louder, nearly dropping the birdhouse, anxious to be with his boy.

"Just a minute. I'm coming." Tammy's voice is loud, but he doesn't care if she's impatient. He's impatient, too. He knocks again.

He hears the toilet flush, then the whole trailer seems to shake as she steps to the door.

"Hello, Cousin," says Tammy. A cigarette drips from her mouth. Her too-blond hair sags in wet waves. Her flowered robe hangs loose, and she pulls the belt tight. She opens the door for him.

There's no one else in the trailer.

"Where are they?" he asks. "I heard voices."

"Nobody but us chickens," she says, nodding to the radio. She pours coffee for herself and sits down. Her cheeks are drawn, and in the dim light of the trailer her skin looks gray. She takes a drag on her cigarette and looks at Aiken as if she's forgotten he's there. She gets up slowly and pours a cup for him. "What's with the ugly birdhouse?"

He was so sure. "Where's Soon-hee?"

"You tell me."

"She's not staying here?"

"She *was*. They came back a couple nights ago. Wouldn't say where they'd been, or how they got here, but I don't think they'd washed in a while, if you know what I mean. They slept out here on the couch, ate up a storm, about wiped me out. Soon-hee made me swear I wouldn't tell you they were here. Then this morning I come out, and they're gone, no note, no nothing."

"Why are you helping her, Tammy?"

She shrugs.

"Seriously. You're sticking your nose where it doesn't belong, and you need to stop."

"Are you threatening me? Because you ain't seen nothing yet."

"What's that supposed to mean? What did I ever do to you?"

"Has to be about you. No other possibilities. Typical." She lights a new cigarette. "Not that you care, but the girl needs help. I'm helping. End of story."

He takes a step toward her. If he says anything else, if *she* says anything else, he'll only get angrier, and so there's no point in talking. His fists are clenched.

"Go ahead, big man, hit me. Will that make you feel good? Make you feel like you're in charge? Well, I've got news for you. You're not. And you have no idea what you've gotten yourself into."

"Just tell me where they are, Tammy."

"I told you before. I don't know."

TURTLE VALLEY, VIRGINIA

JULY-AUGUST 1996

31

Aiken mounts the crude birdhouse on a fencepost between the house and barn. A day later, he's rewarded with the arrival of a pair of finches. He sits on the porch, holding Ralph in check so he won't molest the birds, and watches the couple race into the fields, return with straw clutched in their beaks, slip inside the hole, and come out again to repeat the journey. He wishes Henry were there to see it.

Aiken's mother spends most of her time at the hospital. He visits his father sporadically in the first days, but being there floods him with regret over the gulf that's grown between them. He'd hoped one day to bridge that distance, but now it's apparently too late. His father is too weak to talk, or maybe he's paralyzed. Aiken isn't sure which and doesn't know how to ask the doctor, who volunteers little information. His mother continually wipes tears from her eyes, as if her grief can somehow change what has happened to her husband. Aiken blames her. Couldn't she see it coming? Why did she do nothing? The tears are as useless as her home remedies and good luck charms.

Aiken accepts that his father may never come home, that in fact the old man is for all intents and purposes already dead. His habitual optimism gone, he feels even more guilt for giving up, like the burning ache in his back that is sometimes forgotten yet always present, but in his mind he has said his goodbyes. There's nothing else he can do. Sometimes you have to move on. The war taught him that. He's even beginning to lose hope that he'll find Henry.

He's working in the barn when he hears a truck pull into the drive. He comes out and sees Jake sitting in his pickup, windows down, the engine idling.

"I hear you've been looking for me," Jake says as Aiken approaches.

"Where's my son?" Aiken asks.

"No idea."

"That picture you drew."

"Yeah, what of it?"

"When did you do that?"

"Uncle Henry here?" He nods toward Aiken's father's truck.

"No. When did you draw the picture, Jake?"

"A few days ago. Me and him went out for ice cream. Kid sure likes ice cream. Did you know his favorite is strawberry?"

Aiken lunges at the truck and grabs Jake's shirt. "Bastard. Where the hell is he?"

Jake yanks Aiken's hands away and twists his arm until Aiken has to back off.

"Shit," Aiken says. "Where the fuck is he?"

Jake's truck is moving in reverse now. "He's a cute kid, Cousin. It would be a shame if something happened to him. But I don't know where he is." And then the truck is out on the road, speeding away.

* * *

He goes back inside. He's moved his bed out to the barn and settled in. When Henry comes come—*if* Henry comes home—he'll build a new bed for himself so they can live out there together. For now, he's making a new solitary life for himself. Each morning, he goes over to the house to wash up, although sometimes he makes do with a bucket of water filled at the pump. He had expected his mother to complain about the new sleeping arrangements, and his argument is prepared—he and Henry need space to call their own—but so far she's said nothing.

With his father away and his mother preoccupied, breakfast is cold cereal and milk, and after breakfast Aiken drives her to the hospital. On this day, a Tuesday, he stops at the saltbox cottage on the way home, parking across the street, imagining Henry peering out at him from the picture window. He sketches the house. He's not an artist, with nothing like Jake's skill—he can't remember ever making another drawing, even when he was a child—and his sketch is more than a little rough, but he notes the three windows upstairs across the house's face, the steep roof in the back, the chimney in the center. He doubts that anyone else would recognize what he's drawn, but it's all he needs for his new project—a second birdhouse, made from scraps of lumber he's been collecting, leftovers from the work he's done on the barn, even stray pieces he's scavenged from trash heaps. Leaving his old neighborhood, he goes to a lumberyard to buy sheets of plywood in varying thicknesses. At the hardware store he finds screws, butt hinges, and finishing nails.

* * *

In the evening, he returns to the hospital to pick up his mother. As soon as he enters his father's room, he realizes that something has happened. His mother sits by the bed, her two hands on one of his father's. The old man is awake, his eyes open, following Aiken as he crosses to the opposite side of the bed.

"How're you feeling, Pop?" Aiken is unexpectedly hopeful, seeing him alert like this. His father blinks.

"He can't answer," says his mother. "But he just needs to come home. I think he'll be fine."

Dr. Patel, when he visits, is blunt and tells a different story. The change is illusory. Aiken's father has had a stroke and may never fully recover the use of his left arm and leg, or his ability to speak.

And yet, his eyes are bright, as if he'd just woken from a restful sleep.

"One step at a time," Aiken says, and he means it. Maybe his mother is right. He shouldn't have given up. He hadn't said as much to anyone, but he's afraid they could all see it in his eyes, that even his father knew.

He won't give up on Henry. There's still hope he can find him and bring him home. When he leaves the hospital, he drives slowly through town hoping for a glimpse of Soon-hee. He calls Billy Crawford and Tom Roberts. He calls Tammy. What else can he do?

Aiken draws the pieces he will need for the new birdhouse— the ends, a divider, the floor, front and back, the short side of the roof, and the long slope. Studying his sketch, he realizes he needs a chimney, and finds a scrap pine board that he can cut to fit. By noon, after teaching himself to use the table saw, he has cut out the pieces and swept away the debris of dust and shavings. Ralph, having fled the noisy saw, now returns, only to dash back outside at the sight of Aiken wielding the broom.

Making an entrance hole is the next step, but he knows that punching it out with an awl, as he did on the first house, would be a mistake. He searches again for his father's drill and bits, and this time he locates them in a cellar storage bin, buried under a mound of tangled extension cords. He marks the center of the spot where he wants the hole on one of the end pieces and locks in place the largest bit in the assortment. He remembers that there's a special bit for boring holes, but, if his father has one, he can't find it. Just as he is about to pull the trigger on the drill, he hears Ralph's frantic barking, followed by a knock at the barn door.

In pushes Garth Keeler, assistant principal of Aiken's school, a trim man, no taller than Aiken, with a thick frosting of white hair and a florid, open face.

"Hiya, Aiken," says Keeler.

Keeler's always been friendly with the staff, and Aiken's got nothing against him, even though he has a good idea why the man has stopped by. He's been expecting to hear from him, in fact. Although it's nothing more than he deserves, he's not happy about what's coming.

"Mr. Keeler," he says. He resumes his work, even pressing the bit into the wood, concentrating on boring the perfect hole.

"Haven't seen you around school much," Keeler says. "Guess you've been sick."

"Uh-huh," Aiken says. He pulls the trigger. The drill whines and wood chips fly.

Keeler steps back. "I left messages." He's shouting to be heard over the squeal of the drill.

Aiken releases the trigger and the barn is filled with quiet.

"Look, Aiken, I came here to talk to you."

Aiken blows dust away from the hole. He's comforted by the drill's warmth and the sweet scent of pine.

"Sure," he says, although he's not looking at Keeler. "Go ahead."

"I mean, could I have your attention for a minute? Maybe we could go outside."

He wipes his hands on his jeans as he follows Keeler out of the barn, and the two men cross the drive to the house. On the porch, Aiken directs Keeler to the rocker while he settles onto the swing. Ralph trots over to sniff Keeler's shoes, then nudges Aiken's knee before settling at his feet. Keeler fidgets with his necktie, and patches of sweat darken his pale blue shirt.

"Aiken—"

"You see that birdhouse on the fence post over there?" Aiken points to the board fence around the corral. The gaudy purple and green have already faded, and he realizes now that he used indoor paint that wasn't made to withstand the bright sun. "I built that for my boy." He isn't sure Keeler knows he has a son, but maybe it's in his personnel file, and maybe Keeler took a look at the file to see what kind of trouble there might be when he dropped the bombshell he's here to deliver.

"You got kids, Mr. Keeler?"

"Two girls," he says, nodding.

Dark clouds are swarming in from the west, over the mountains, holding the promise of an end to the dry spell, or at least a respite. He hopes wherever Soon-hee and Henry are they're safe and dry. Soon-hee, who grew up where electrical storms were rare, is afraid of the thunder and has passed her fear of storms along to Henry. Every time one rolls through the Valley she shakes like a rattler, he remembers, and hides in the closet. He wonders where she's hiding now.

"The reason I came out here, Aiken—"

"You ever make a mistake?" Aiken doesn't want Keeler to think he's talking about not coming to work, so he barrels ahead. "I mean in your personal life, like when you were younger?"

"I guess I don't know what you're getting at."

He has both feet on the porch and pushes off in the swing. Keeler rocks a little in response, and Aiken smiles to think of what he set in motion. Cause and effect. It all started a long time ago. When Hank died, maybe. Or before that. Thunder rumbles softly in the distance, still too far away to count on, but there's hope. Keeler grips the arms of his chair, but his expression is blank.

"Say a boy graduates high school and does something he regrets. Never mind what it is. What's he supposed to do then? How does he get past it?"

Keeler's eyes narrow. He leans forward in the rocker and clears his throat. "That's a real hard question to answer. I don't think I'm the right man to do it, to tell you the truth."

There's more thunder, louder, closer, like an explosion, and Aiken thinks about Henry, but he also thinks about Kuwait, Desert Storm.

"We don't do a very good job of preparing kids," Aiken says. "Seems to me a boy gets taught to kill, first squirrels and deer and such. Then men, and you send him off with a gun and a license, basically, 'get as many of the bastards as possible.' And then what?"

"Aiken—"

Lightning interrupts Keeler, with a sharp crack of thunder close behind that makes him jump in his chair. The wind stirs a ball of dandelion fluff at their feet.

"Storm's coming." Aiken stands, setting the swing in motion again.

Keeler stands, too. "Aiken, look, I don't mean to be the bad guy in this, but you know I don't have a choice. We have to let you go. You can't disappear from work like that without an explanation."

He stares into Keeler's eyes, sees how uncomfortable the man is, between the heat and the storm, the silence. He feels sorry for him. Keeler waits, as if he expects Aiken to get angry, or violent, but Aiken's got nothing against him. The man's only doing his job.

"We'll give you a good reference," Keeler says. "Seeing as how your work was good, excellent even, before this . . . trouble." He flaps his hand at the barn as if the farm is the trouble he's talking about. "So there's no problem there."

The clouds are on top of them now, a front overhead, dividing the sky, like a knife, into black and blue. The tall, dry grass beyond the fence rustles in anticipation. Aiken turns away from Keeler and heads down the steps, back to the barn. He looks behind when he gets to the door, expecting to see his visitor climbing into his car now that he's finally said what he came to say, but Keeler has followed and stands close. He has an envelope in his hand. He thrusts it toward Aiken.

"It's a check," Keeler says, smiling. "Last one. Plus a little something."

Aiken doesn't return the smile. The first drops of rain fall noisily onto his truck, and Keeler laughs, a nervous little laugh that gives Aiken some comfort. His visitor backs away while raising his hand in a half wave, and jogs to his Caprice.

When Keeler is gone, Aiken goes inside the barn and tosses the envelope on the workbench. It will come in handy, but it represents a break with the past. And an embarrassment. He's glad it's over. But what's next?

32

I wake, lying next to Ha-neul on the pine needles. He is peaceful, the fever broken, his breath easy. I expect the candle to be extinguished, but it still burns, flickering in the night breeze, protected by Sansin. I did not see him, but I have felt his presence. The storm is over. The moon winks through the pine boughs.

When I gaze down at the house from our hillside, I sense the father of Ay-ken fading. His gentle spirit grows weaker. He was kind to me from the first day, and reminded me of my own father. But even from this distance I can see the light fade. The *mudang* at home said she saw these things, too.

And so I go to the father in the hospital. Nurses do not speak to me as I pass. I am invisible to them. But when I enter his room, his eyes are open and he watches me. I go to the window and close the blinds, bring darkness for the *kut*. In his eyes the fire dims. I bring candles that I light, and now I see the flame. I pull the knife from my sash.

* * *

An elder in the village is dying. A one-armed man, with half his face a blur, melted, he tells stories of the hated invaders from the East who enslaved us, and of the years of nothing, when there was no food, and then the fighting between brothers when the *ko-jaengi* came, tall, godlike, and there was fire. Loud noise and fire, many people dead. Now he is old and dying, asleep in the inner room, and the *kut* begins. The *mudang* beats her drum, and the village women fill the courtyard. Cymbals crash and the *mudang* speaks, take the sickness from this man, cleanse his spirit, let the Mountain God descend and heal our grandfather.

I am a child, watching through the open gate. I see the glint of a knife as she, the powerful and great *mudang*, enters the house.

In the hospital room, I lay the yellow paper on the father's chest, the *pujok*, with the red writing, the names of Sansin and the high officials who will protect the father of Ay-ken. I lift the knife above him. My eyes are closed, but I feel him watching. I whisper, so the nurse will not hear, and call for Sansin to come to take away the sickness. I bring the knife down. The father of Ay-ken moans as the spirit enters him, and there is a woman, the nurse, screaming behind me— me, the *mudang*, casting out the demon. But the *kut* is not finished. The demon's hold is strong.

I kneel before the shrine on the mountain. The stones are damp and thunder fills the sky as I pray to Sansin.

At first I do not like Jay-ke, the cousin of Ay-ken. But he comes to Ta-mee's house when she is away and promises to help us. I see in him some of Ay-ken, a connection. The eyes are the same. He drives. He brings me to the mountain. He buys ice cream for Ha-neul and draws his picture. I do not tell Ta-mee, but Jay-ke says we can get money from Ay-ken, from the mother of Ay-ken. It is his idea, but when I have the money we will return to Pae-tu, Ha-neul and I.

In the truck, Jay-ke puts his hand on my arm.

"We can both get what we want," he says.

I nod and pull away.

"Okay," he says. "It doesn't have to be about that. Strictly business. Probably better that way."

Jay-ke drives, and I hold Ha-neul close. I whisper to him in Korean. "We are on our way home," I say.

33

When Hank died, I thought I would die, too. I'd never given up hope that one day he would see me. And when he saw, he would want me. I couldn't go to the funeral. I just couldn't. Jake—he was a mess, too—picked me up and we drove. Up one side of the mountain and down the other, drinking beer and smoking, not saying a word. I swear, once or twice I saw a tear roll down Jake's scruffy cheek, but he wiped them away. I didn't bother to hide mine.

We came back to Stillwater and drove to the cemetery. From the truck we watched as they put him in the ground.

Later, when we made love, Jake was the opposite of what I expected. He was gentle like never before, as if Hank's death had taken all the fight out of him. I understood that. I felt the same way.

I've told Jake he's not to hurt Soon-hee. She can help us get what we want, and no more. Then he leaves her alone. We're not greedy. We just want what's coming to us. He promises he'll leave his wife when it's done, and we can be together. We'll get far away from here. Nashville, maybe. We'll make a new start. My chance.

34

He cleans the drill bit he'd used and puts it in its sleeve, sets the drill in its case, and stores them both under the workbench. Lightning flashes and thunder rattles the barn window as he works. He sweeps up the last of the sawdust and wipes the surface with a rag. Then he lines up all the pieces he's cut for the new birdhouse and goes over the next steps in his mind. He'll miter the edges of the front and back, glue and clamp the pieces in place, drill pilot holes for screws, reinforce the structure with finishing nails. This time he'll attach the floor with hinges, for future cleaning. It's all ready for tomorrow. If Henry were there, he could help. They'd learn together.

As he drives into Stillwater to pick up his mother, the wind carries the sound of sirens. Ahead of him on the Pike he sees fire engines turn, racing toward the mountains. He rounds a bend near the town limits and spots their destination: fire has engulfed a church. Its white steeple is visible, but so are the orange flames and billowing black smoke that remind him of the burning oil fields of Kuwait, of the senseless death and waste.

At the hospital, he approaches his father's room just as his mother emerges.

"Sleeping," she whispers.

Aiken nods, but moves past her into the room. "I'll just stay a minute," he says, leaving her in the hallway.

The old man's eyes are closed. He's surrounded by beeping machines and tubes. The light is dim. Aiken wishes he were somewhere else, considers backing away, fleeing. He stands at the foot of the bed, hesitates, retraces his steps to the door, ready to leave, his visit pointless. But he doesn't go. He stays and settles into a chair by the window. He's aware of the back pain again, a stinging sensation that he tries to ease by sitting straight and then, when that doesn't work, by slouching. When he sees his father's eyes open for an instant, or thinks that's what he sees, he moves the chair closer to the bed. He must have imagined it, he decides. The lids flutter, but that's all. He takes his father's hand and watches the eyes again. Still nothing. The hand feels light and bony, like a sparrow. The skin is soft and cold, the fingernails gray.

"I wish I could bring Henry to see you, Pop," he says, if only to fill the silence with something other than the machines. He waits to see if there's any reaction. The smallest movement. He tries not to blink, afraid he'll miss it. "But they probably don't let kids in here anyway. Don't want them playing with the buttons or anything." He forces a laugh. Still nothing.

Talking feels good. He needs to talk. He tried with Garth Keeler, but that was a mistake. This will be better, even if he's not getting through. "I don't know what to do, Pop. Soon-hee's been acting crazy. I can't find her anywhere, and she's got Henry with her."

Now he's sure he sees the eyelids flutter, and Aiken wonders what his father might have heard. Is he trying to speak? Does he have something he wants to tell Aiken? Advice? But the eyes don't open, the machines keep up their steady beeps, there's still no warmth in his father's hand.

Aiken's eyes are drawn to something on the nightstand that he recognizes: a yellow square of paper with thick red lines and squiggles, mustard and ketchup, like the mysterious pictures Soon-hee often posted on the walls at home.

"Where'd that come from, Pop? That yellow paper?" Aiken stands to grab the paper, and his eyes scour the room as if he expects to find Soon-hee.

35

Testing, testing. Isn't that what they say?

Poor Henry, all alone in that hospital. I don't suppose we had much choice, but I wish to God we'd not taken him there. What good has it done? And I've about given up hope, I'm ashamed to admit. I sit in that room and hold his hand, and sometimes he looks at me as if he's about to speak. But he never does. Then he's asleep again, and I wonder where he's gone.

This journal isn't supposed to be about that, though, is it? Tammy says to talk about the past, the "good old days" she called them, as if anything that happened a long time ago is somehow scrubbed clean of suffering, relieved of its burdens. I'm supposed to reveal all the secrets, say where the bodies are buried, so to speak.

Maybe she's right, come to think of it. Because I won't be around forever, and even now the memories are like ghosts. I think I can see them, can almost grab hold, but then they vanish. So much smoke and mysteries of light. Makes you wonder. And, to be perfectly honest, I sometimes doubt myself.

There are things I remember that might be my imagination, or stories I heard. But did they really happen?

What I *do* remember, what I *know* is real, is the homeplace in our Valley, the house where my momma and daddy raised me up. I already told about the house I guess. I could talk about family. Haven't said anything about them, yet. I'm sure of it.

My people are Yanceys. But there are Yanceys and then there are Yanceys. The Yanceys who own the mill up in Burketown, those folks are Northern Yanceys, and they're plain different. I don't mean to speak ill of a soul, living or dead, but the rich folks in our Valley were nasty, and those Yanceys were rich. We stayed away from the Burketown Yanceys. The men treated their women like caged animals. That's what I remember. That's what I heard.

We were the Southern Yanceys. You might say our family was the Typton Hollow Yanceys, because we mostly kept to ourselves, and didn't see the cousins all that often. But they were scattered across the mountains, that much I know. And I suppose the Burketown Yanceys were cousins, too, but I couldn't tell you the connection exactly. There was a rift, you see, way back when. We weren't the only ones split apart by that war. Happened to lots of families. Two brothers, one against another.

Momma's people were Boones. They claimed relation to Daniel Boone, and they might very well have been right about that. For all the good it did 'em. But that might just be another story passed down.

It was Momma who taught me the craft. Or Momma and Granny Lyddie, who wasn't really our granny, but that's what everyone called her. Closest thing we had to a doctor up there, although the men called her something else, a word I don't like to use unless it's the only one that will do. She had cures and spells for just about anything. Sometimes I still find myself singing one of those chants she taught me. Don't even think about it, just streams through my lips like it's her own voice. Big on charms and such, too, and ways of grabbing luck, or at least being careful not to lose it. "Never leave a hat on the bed," she'd say, "or evil spirits will rule your marriage." That's one I follow to this day. I know it's true. I've seen it.

There were nine of us in our house. Momma and Daddy, my four older brothers, and me and little Joseph. The oldest was John, who Aiken favors so much, with his solid chin, piercing eyes, the thick blond hair. John's gone. Good heavens, it's been fifty years. More. Then Samuel, and Robert, and Benjamin. Plus my sister, Helen, of course, who was like another mother to us young ones.

I remember when Momma was ripe with Joseph but still working, in the house, in the garden. There was no time to stop and rest for babies, but she made a little high-pitched noise and sat down right in the garden on a row of beans. I laughed and laughed, but Helen's face was stricken with fear.

"Go fetch Granny Lyddie," she said to me.

I knew better than to question her, and I dropped the beans I had picked and took off running down the lane, straight over the ridge to Granny's house. I thought there was something terribly wrong with Momma, but by the time I came back, pulling Granny by the arm to make her go faster, Joseph was already born and resting in Momma's arms.

So long ago, it seems. So long. It wasn't all bad. We had glorious days. I miss ... Now it's simple foolishness to get so sentimental over what's done and gone. But sometimes ...

Until my own boy Hank came along I don't suppose I really understood about babies. Oh, I knew where they came from. I don't mean that. It's just that there's an attachment that can't be explained in books, with pictures and diagrams. He was born right here in this house, in this very room, and when the midwife placed him in my arms, and I saw how much he looked like Henry, I was in love. I gazed into his dark eyes, and it was then I knew. I could see that he was in danger. From that day on I did anything to keep him safe, to change his destiny. It wasn't enough. I'm not proud of everything I've done in this life, but I'd do it all again to have Hank back in my arms. I don't suppose that's possible.

Oh, my goodness. No one wants to listen to an old woman cry, do they? How *do* you shut this thing off?

36

Although there's been no change in his father's condition, the future is certain, if he's reading Dr. Patel right. Aiken had given up prematurely, which he regrets, but really it's just a question of time, and not much time at that.

When she's at home, Aiken's mother spends hours on the telephone, calling friends and relatives, preparing them for the inevitable. He's relieved that she hasn't enlisted him to help, or to make any of the other arrangements she's itemized on the notepad by the phone—the minister, the florist, the organist. He tells her they should wait before speaking with the funeral home and the cemetery. She nods, but he isn't sure she's listening.

Mrs. Finnegan, a neighbor and member of their church, brings supper over one night, a casserole and a pie, and Aiken's mother dishes out big servings, barely touching her own plate.

After dinner, she settles into the living room. She turns on the television, and her eyes are on the screen, but Aiken knows that his mother's mind is elsewhere. He tries to sit with her and watch, but he can't. He goes out to the barn and examines the birdhouse that looks like the saltbox cottage, but there's nothing more he can do with it, and it only makes him ache for Henry, so he returns to the house. He stands just inside the door, truck keys in hand.

"I think I'll go out," he says. "Okay?"

His mother looks at him. "You don't need my permission, son."

"But you'll be all right?"

"Of course," she says and turns back to the television.

He hears disapproval in her voice, but it doesn't stop him. He had asked her if she wanted to go back to the hospital and she'd said no. Even she's given up now. What more does she expect from him? She's waiting for the end. He can't wait with her.

He drives into Stillwater, to the Turtle Tavern, which he'd first visited as a high-schooler. He'd been cocky enough, despite his height and age, to avoid questions, although Lionel, the owner and bartender, a nervous sort who was called "Rabbit," seemed to know everyone in town and was surely aware of which kids weren't yet legal. Aiken had carried Hank's license, but at the Turtle he never needed it, and everyone there would have known it belonged to his dead brother. The Turtle had been the scene of Aiken's going-away bash when he enlisted, with Jeannette—the Dolly Parton lookalike who'd taken over behind the bar when Rabbit got too sick to work—making sure Aiken's glass was never empty. That night he'd puked in his dad's truck, now his truck, and has no memory of how he got home, but he thinks he surely owes Billy Crawford for that.

When he came back from Korea with Soon-hee, they'd sometimes gone to the Turtle together. It wasn't much different from the Itaewon dive where they'd met, so it was one of the few places in town where she felt comfortable and didn't seem to mind the stares she attracted. So he'd take her along and let her sit in a booth sipping a Coke while he drank at the bar, or circled the room, beer in hand, connecting with old buddies. He guessed from Soon-hee's cheerless expression that she didn't love being there, but she never complained. For his part, he took pleasure in showing off his pretty, pregnant bride.

When Henry came, when he was no bigger than a football and all during his first year, Aiken went out by himself. Soon-hee didn't object. She had the baby for company, and she was busy and tired. Sometimes Tammy came over to help, which puzzled Aiken—no more than anything else his cousin did—but freed him from guilt. Then Henry was walking and babbling and saying his first words, and Aiken had stayed in.

Tonight when he walks into the Turtle, it feels like coming home. Cigarette smoke drifts above the familiar chatter and the rattle of silverware and glasses. He hears snippets of talk about the coming election, and how the Republicans are sure to throw Slick Willie out on his ass—they've just held their convention and nominated a feisty war hero everyone here seems to like. The light is dim, but his eyes adjust to the glow of the neon Coors and Bud signs in the window. He knows Jeannette is gone, and there's a new guy behind the bar, but that's all that appears to have changed. Aiken climbs onto a stool. The bartender throws down a coaster and waits for the order. He pulls a draft with authority and sets it in front of Aiken, then moves on to another customer.

The only woman at the bar is a blond he recognizes, although he isn't sure from where. Maybe she's the mother of one of the kids where he works. Used to work, he remembers and feels a momentary pang of guilt. Her full lips match her scarlet nails, and he imagines the color extending to her toes. He'd bet on it, in fact.

He has a second beer. There's a guy seated at a table who looks familiar, Stu, maybe, or Stan. Kind of a shy guy, they were in high school together, on the baseball team. He's with a pretty redhead and they're holding hands. Good for you, Stu, Aiken thinks. He wonders where Soon-Hee and Henry are, if they're all right. He has a third beer. The bartender comes by and smokes a cigarette at Aiken's end of the bar. His name is Rick, he says, and he's new in town, been working a couple of months. Jeannette left, moved to Wheeling with some trucker who used to stop by the bar just to see her. Rabbit's real sick. No one knows what's going to happen to the Turtle if he dies. When he dies. Rick pours him a fourth beer. Aiken makes his way along the bar to the restroom in the rear, sticks a quarter in the pinball machine on the way back, and slams the side so hard on the second ball that the machine tilts and dies. He gives it a satisfying kick and, as he heads back to his stool, nods to Stu and the redhead. Nods to the blond, whoever she is. He takes his seat, drinks a fifth, last beer.

The blond comes over and sits next to him. Maybe it wasn't at the school where he'd seen her. She looks like Hank's old girlfriend, but is that possible? Dark hair back then, such a long time ago. A sister, maybe? He buys another beer, and a shot. He knows it's a mistake, but he drinks. She smokes with her left hand, drops her right into his lap. He's lonely, but not that lonely, and he removes her hand. Another beer, another shot, he's lost count. Rick winks at him, or did Aiken imagine it? Stu and his redhead are gone.

Almost everyone is gone. Rick wipes down the bar with a rag, unplugs the pinball machine, upends chairs on tables. Aiken isn't sure if the woman has told him her name, can't remember anything they've talked about all night. He thinks her name is Charlotte. She looks like a Charlotte. Was Hank's girlfriend named Charlotte? He and Charlotte slip off their stools, hold each other up. It's comical, and Aiken even in his advanced drunkenness can see that. But all he wants is to get home to bed. He laughs, salutes Rick. He heads for the truck. Charlotte follows.

He drops the keys once, then a second time.

"Shit," he says. Charlotte laughs. He wishes she were gone.

He climbs, stumbles inside. She knocks on the window. He hesitates, knows that he should wave goodbye and leave Charlotte behind. He sees Soon-Hee and Henry, but then they vanish.

Charlotte opens the door. "Lover, you're in no shape to drive," she says, sounding as sober as a judge.

He nods, his eyes struggling to stay open. When she holds out her hand, palm up, he surrenders his keys.

He wakes when the truck stops just outside the barn. How did she know? He wants to ask about Hank. Was it her all those years ago in the barn? Posing for pictures before the prom? What happened to those pictures?

She helps him out of the truck, and with her support he staggers to the barn and falls into bed. She leans over, kisses his forehead, and slips away.

37

It is a healing art, but anything is possible in order to ward off evil. From my shrine on the mountain, where I watch and wait, I see Ay-ken and the fat, yellow-haired woman enter the barn. It is not the woman Ta-mee speaks of, the woman Ay-ken sees when he goes to the wine house, but it does not matter. It is the same. She is a demon, like Little Mother, the cause of our pain.

I tend the fire, watch it feed and grow, inhale the scent of the mountain pine as it sizzles and cracks into flame. The gray smoke rises, forms itself first into a cloud and then into a giant cat. The tiger growls, baring its yellow fangs, eyes burning bright, angry to have been awoken.

I call upon the tiger spirit to inflame the demon. I call upon the messenger of Sansin to fill her bowels with fire, and to burn any man who enters her poisoned chamber. It is a healing art, but she must pay. Like Ay-ken pays with pain.

* * *

A wife in Pae-tu pleads with the *mudang* to cast out her husband's mistress, to end the power that the concubine has over the man. So: the *mudang* captures a brown snake and with the needle of the Household God punctures both eyes; the snake writhes in misery. With the help of the wife and the apprentice *mudang*, the snake is buried. The man's mistress stumbles sightless through the village streets.

Ha-neul and I must go. To do that, we must do what Jay-ke asks. And for that, we must return to the big house. The *mudang*'s art is for healing, but anything is possible.

38

He spends the morning cutting pieces for a new birdhouse.
With the first houses, the hardest part had been the roof, but
for this one he has an idea for a simpler structure, one that
looks like Turtle Tavern, with an angled flat roof, higher in
front where the hole would be. He plans to paint the name
on the front windows, in some fluorescent color to make it
look like the neon signs at the bar. A cosy perch for a couple
of night owls, like him and Charlotte. He shudders at the
thought. He's sure nothing happened with Charlotte—he
was in no shape for that—although he's *not* sure how he got
home or what became of her. He remembers handing her
the keys and nothing after that.

His head pounds, but the coffee helps, and the work
keeps his mind off the pain and that damn sensation in
his back. It's an annoyance that won't go away, even worse
this morning than it's been, but his hands are busy, and his
thoughts travel far.

The birdhouse reminds him not just of the Turtle, but
also of the White Horse in Seoul. He conjures an image of

Soon-hee, laughing her crooked laugh, speaking her fractured English, country music twanging above their heads. And now they're in each others' arms, in the *yogwan*, kissing urgently as they rush down that inevitable path.

On one of their excursions from the room, she took him to a tiny restaurant far from the base. Along one wall were rooms enclosed by sliding paper doors where patrons sat on the floor at long, low tables. A cloud of smoke from the table-top grills hovered over the main room, filled with the sweet smell of sizzling marinated beef, the clink of metal chopsticks on rice bowls, the chatter of diners—an incomprehensible buzz to him. He followed her to a vacant table. The chatter stopped. She ignored the angry stares, already hardened to the names her countrymen called her, names she would not translate for him. But he seethed on her behalf, and when a woman rose from a nearby table, spoke loudly and spat at Soon-hee's feet, Aiken jumped up, tipping his chair to the cement floor.

"What the fuck do you want, lady?"

The woman took a step back, looked at Aiken, and then continued her retreat.

"We're just here for a meal, okay?" To Soon-hee he said, "What did she say to you?" His voice was loud, and the doors to the private rooms opened, like gaping mouths.

Soon-hee shook her head, stood, and left the restaurant. He followed, wishing he could make the people understand that they were wrong about her. How did they get from there to here?

Now she's gone from the memory, and it's Hank he sees. They are wrestling in the yard, the puppy Ralph nipping at their hands, their mother capturing the boys' play with a camera. Except it isn't play. Hank is angry with Aiken, who has been following him, spying when he is with the girl. Hank twists an arm, drives a knuckle into Aiken's back, covers Aiken's mouth until their mother is back inside. Jake is in this memory, too, arms across his chest, laughing, goading Hank, taunting Aiken.

And now, another time, Hank is tucking his long hair into his helmet and speeding away on the Triumph, the sun glinting off the big cat's chrome.

Charlotte was a mistake he was lucky to avoid. He likes the Turtle, though, and the new bartender seems like a good sort, so Aiken pokes his head in from time to time. If Charlotte is in her place at the bar, he ducks out again. If not, he can have a quick beer, catch up with Rick on the latest Stillwater news, and hope that Charlotte doesn't show up with expectations. The urgency makes the visits short and sweet, and Aiken figures that's all to the good.

As he comes out of the tavern one night, the heat of the day still on the pavement and the glow of a late-summer evening lighting the village rooftops, he sees Kelly. Or at least he thinks it's Kelly. She's strolling alone on the opposite sidewalk, gazing in the shop windows. She looks at the junk in the gift shop display, then at the antiques next door, then at the florist's wilting arrangement of roses in a glass vase. He's sure it's Kelly, back from Roanoke for a visit, he supposes. She keeps strolling, in no apparent hurry, and Aiken wonders if he should run after her.

Instead, he climbs into his truck and watches her cross the street. She turns a corner and disappears, and Aiken now doubts that it's Kelly after all. This woman's hair is longer and lighter than Kelly's was, and he doesn't remember Kelly ever wearing a dress. Of course, she'd be older now, grown up, and people change. In his rear-view mirror he catches sight of Charlotte coming toward the Turtle—she's limping, almost as if she were wearing only one shoe, and looks even more bloated than ever—and he knows that he can't stay where he is, so he starts the engine and crawls forward. He turns where Kelly—or whoever she is—had turned, and sees that the woman is making her way uphill, toward the old stone church. She turns again, and Aiken does, too.

He recognizes this street. Kelly's mother lives around here on a pretty tree-lined drive with small yards and white fences and garages out back on an alley. He's nearly caught up to her now and there's no more doubt: it's Kelly. Her stride is long, and she swings her purse as she walks. He watches her turn into the yard, check the mailbox by the front door, and disappear inside. This is definitely the house, a tidy Cape Cod, with blue shutters and twin dormers. The oak in the front is bigger than he remembers, but everything else is the same. It takes him back. He sits in the truck for a few minutes, gazing at the house.

He begins work on a new birdhouse the next morning. The shapes are easy to draw, with no odd angles like the steep roof of the saltbox. The dormers are a puzzle, though, and he wastes a foot of pine boards until he realizes he can get the shape he wants by gluing lengths of 1 x 4s together and cutting that into blocks to be fastened to the roof later. He thinks Henry would enjoy this, like the crafts projects he did in pre-school at the church, with all the Elmer's stuck to his hands and hair. Using a glue gun, which he has discovered among his father's jumble of treasures in the cellar, he covers the joining surfaces of the three strips, then clamps the stack together and watches the extra glue ooze out along the joints. Pleased with himself—pleased that he's working, that he's not polishing school floors or scrubbing toilets—he lets the glue dry while he cuts the other pieces. If Henry were there to help, it would be perfect.

The house is ready for painting by the time he goes to the hospital to pick up his mother, but he'll save that. He likes having a plan for the work to come. It's satisfying, gives purpose to his days. He's never had a real plan before, no structure or meaning to his life at all. He'd been too young and preoccupied to think about such things in high school, and, if he had, it would have been about sneaking Kelly into his room, or finding ways to get his hands on pot or beer. Joining the Army wasn't something he'd planned, either; it was the last of the bad options. During his stint in Kuwait, the plans were entirely up to someone else, of course, usually someone he didn't know and never saw. He needed to think about staying alive, but that wasn't the same as having a purpose. That was instinct. A silent voice. Now, though, he knows exactly what he's going to do tomorrow, and has a pretty good idea of what he's doing the day after that.

And yet, he can't stop thinking about Henry. He should be doing more to find him, but he doesn't know what that would be. Billy Crawford has had no luck, and he's the expert. They can't find her. And there's his father, too, who has slipped deeper into his own dark world. Aiken's mother has insisted on bringing him home. If the end is near, she argued, let it come in familiar surroundings. Dr. Patel has agreed, offering no reasons for optimism, and so Aiken doesn't object.

* * *

He visits the Turtle Tavern. As he sips his beer, he thinks more about Soon-hee. She could not have evaded him all this time without help. They had searched everywhere, up and down the county. It all comes back to Tammy. Somehow, she used Tammy's car. Somehow, Tammy kept her hidden in that trailer—Soon-hee and Henry both—and they'd managed to fool everyone. It had to be Tammy.

He runs to his truck, thinking how foolish he was to believe his cousin. Now he speeds out of town and pulls off the Pike onto a network of back roads toward the trailer park. He takes corners too fast and spins his wheels on Tammy's gravel track. He's focused solely on Henry and what Soon-hee must be intending to do. If she takes him to Pae-tu, he'll never get the boy back, and he can't let that happen. He slides to a stop. The Civic isn't there, but he jumps out and pounds on the door anyway.

"Tammy, you'd better not be hiding that crazy woman," he shouts. He runs to the rear of the trailer and peers in the windows, but the light is all wrong and he can't see anything except his own angry reflection. "Tammy, you hear me?" He comes back around to the door.

The screen comes free easily, its cheap latch surrendering to a firm tug. He rattles the knob of the inner door, twists, pushes and pulls, but this lock is stronger. He steps back and in one motion lifts his leg and kicks the door with the heel of his boot. It flies open and bangs against the tiny kitchen table, shattering the window glass. There's no sign of Henry, though, or Soon-hee for that matter. There's only Tammy's cheap guitar, which he grabs by the neck and swings against the wall, shattering the body in a jangling, harsh chord. The neck and strings hang limp in his hand. He picks up the phone. Tammy could be taking them to an airport, or they could be driving cross-country. All the possibilities rush at him at once. He'll call home first to get the numbers, then he'll call the sheriff and the lawyer, the FBI if he has to. He'll stop them and he'll make sure Soon-hee never sees Henry again.

"We've got to stop Soon-hee," he says when his mother picks up. "I need—"

"They got here a little bit ago," she says. "Tammy and that poor girl, looking like she could use a bath. And a good meal. Where have you been, Aiken?"

Sure enough, there's Tammy's car in the driveway, next to his father's pickup, and his fury floods back. And there's Tammy, smoking a cigarette on the porch, Ralph enjoying Henry's attentions, his mother sipping a glass of iced tea.

"Henry," Aiken calls as he jumps from the truck.

"Daddy!" Henry runs to him and leaps into his arms.

Aiken pulls his son close and kisses the top of his head. All the anxiety of the past weeks has vanished, his concern for his father, and his guilt, forgotten. He tightens his grip, feels tears well in his eyes, and kisses the boy again. Ralph is prancing at his feet.

"Daddy, you're hurting me," Henry says.

"Sorry, buddy," Aiken says, and ever-so-slightly loosens his hold. He isn't ready to let go of the boy just yet, or to share him, and so he carries him away from the porch, toward the fence post where he has mounted the first birdhouse.

"Made this for you, sport," he manages to say, although tears are now streaming down his cheeks.

Henry's eyes are wide, and Aiken leans forward so he can get a closer look. Henry tries to see inside the dark hole.

"Where's the bird?" he asks.

Aiken is pleased that Henry knows what the thing is. "I guess they're not home right now, but I bet if we go back to the porch we'll see them."

They return to Tammy and his mother, Aiken reluctantly lets go, and Henry and Ralph resume their own reunion.

"Where is she?" Aiken asks Tammy. His voice is too loud, and his heart is thumping in his chest, as it did in combat, as it did when he heard about his brother's accident, but he has a right to be angry, doesn't he? Where the hell have they been all this time? But he sees that Henry is fine, playing with Ralph, apparently content, not aware that anything is amiss, and Aiken feels the anger fade like a spent match.

"Where is she?" he asks again, but he's calm now, his voice softer.

Tammy looks to Aiken's mother, as if she's afraid to answer the question.

"I told you on the phone she looked like she needed a bath, so that's what she's doing. We fed her and now she's in the tub. I've never known a woman so happy to see hot water."

He remembers how perplexed Soon-hee was by American bathrooms, where people bathed privately. She'd been used to Korean bathhouses and the self-effacing practice of communal bathing in steamy pools.

Soon-hee doesn't come downstairs. Instead, Aiken's mother goes to check on her and reports to Aiken that Soon-hee will be spending the night in the sewing room that doubles as a guest room. When she says that Soon-hee wants to see Henry, the boy jumps to his feet and runs up the stairs. Aiken is left on the porch with Tammy.

"Are you going to tell me what this is all about? Like why she ran in the first place and why she's come back now?"

"You'll have to ask your wife, Cousin."

"I'm asking you."

"Can't say I really understand it, her English being cracked the way it is. You know, like a mirror? Like you could be looking at it one way, but seeing something else altogether? So she's talking about mountains and rivers and tigers one minute and then starts talking about rape like it's all one subject. I'm not sure what to make of it."

"She was raped?"

"I think that's what she was saying, yeah."

"Who raped her? When?"

"You, apparently. Back in Korea."

He looks at Tammy, then stands and gazes through the screen door into the house. He'd known she was too young, or at least he'd suspected it. In the past four years, almost five, he's been able to think about what happened. He made a terrible mistake. He didn't ask the right questions because he didn't want to know the truth. She told him she was in college. He chose to believe her. But it wasn't rape. The first few weeks were romantic, almost a courtship, respectful. Mutual infatuation. When the time came, she went with him willingly. After that they were together. Happy. A couple. And then her father gave her to him, and he didn't have a choice. She was his. There was no rape.

"She said that?"

"Like I say, it's hard to tell. But I can count, you know. If she's only twenty-one now, and the kid is four, at the very least you robbed the cradle, if you know what I mean."

"So you put this idea in her head?"

"I might have said a thing or two about what men do to young girls, what is and is not acceptable behavior. We women have to stick together, you know."

"I don't know why I'm even talking to you about this. She was a school girl, but I didn't *know* that. At least not at first. I thought—"

"You don't need to explain anything to me. In fact, I wish you wouldn't."

"Seems like I do, though, with you judging me."

"Not me. I know all about mistakes and regret, especially when it comes to sex." Tammy stands to leave, stretches, and lights a cigarette.

"The point is, Tammy, I thought she was happy. She *said* she was happy."

Tammy raises her hand to stop him. "Save it." She starts down the steps, but pauses at the bottom when he continues.

"Tammy, I didn't know she was pregnant, I swear."

"Why are you telling me this, Aiken? I don't want to know. It's high school all over again. You remember Mike? The slob from New Jersey who came down here and no one bothered to tell us he'd been kicked out of three schools up north? I'm in tenth grade and he's a senior and I let *him* do whatever he wanted, too. That's what pathetic, needy girls do. Girls who need a ticket out. I wanted him in the worst way, and I mean that. She wanted you the same way, for all the wrong reasons. And when the inevitable happens, the girl has to take care of it. I wanted to kill Mike, but instead my folks made me disappear until the problem went away."

"I didn't know that. Jesus, I was stupid."

"Yes, you were. To put it mildly. And don't get me started on your brother. Another first-class bastard. And I know the rest of this story with Soon-hee anyway—you track her down, her father hands her over to you like she's a diseased pig, you're out of there as soon the Army finds out what you did, and bang, here's Henry."

"Henry."

"And then your baby wife goes nuts. Is there another word for it? Talks about ghosts and spirits, waves a big-ass kitchen knife in the air like it's some kind of flag."

"Exactly."

"Not too hard to figure out why, though, is it? Don't you feel like this is all pretty much your doing? Bastard. Just like every man I've ever known—thinking only about himself."

The screen door squeaks, and Aiken's mother comes out of the house. Tammy crushes her cigarette in the gravel and gets into her car, waving as she hits the road.

"She should stay here, don't you think," his mother says.

"For a little while?"

"Tammy?"

"Your wife."

"Here?"

"Yes, here. You can't be looking after Henry all the time. You could even go back to work. God knows they've been patient at that school."

"I don't know," he says. He considers telling her about the school. It's one more failure, one more disappointment. But having Soon-hee in the house is inviting trouble. Isn't it? Or maybe it's a chance to make things right.

"And I could use the help with your father when we bring him home."

"You've always hated her."

"Hate's a strong word, Aiken. I'm set in my ways. You should have seen her with the boy just now. With a meal in her, fresh from the bath, and a big grin on her face while he combed her beautiful hair, she's happier tonight than I've ever seen her. And little Henry—he's probably already in dreamland, at the foot of her bed. He's got both his Mommy and Daddy again."

"You know she won't be much help. You've said so yourself."

"She needs to be taught, is all. We all have to learn. I might turn out to be a good teacher."

39

In the hospital, at the old man's bedside, the nurse stopped me before I could chase the demons away. It is not finished, and for now I have come back to this house. I will do what I can for the father of Ay-ken before I return to Pae-tu with Ha-neul. When I first came here, he treated me like his own daughter. He comforted me with his arms. He brought tea to my room when I could not eat. In his eyes I saw his love for this land, these mountains. If I can help him, I will.

The mother of Ay-ken sees I have the power. She has it, too, and she sees that I do what she cannot. She welcomes me. Not like before. The old man's gentle spirit is quiet now, but the house still is angry. There is not much time.

I lie in bed and listen to the ghosts. I am stronger now, and they do not frighten me. The brother, so restless, the grandfather and *his* brother. It is not clear what they want with us, but I must speak to them. We must have the *kut*, or they will take the father before his time. The mother and I will do this together. I will teach her. Together our power is enough.

I sleep, and they will come to me. They will reveal the secrets of this house.

When it is done, I will find money, and Ha-neul and I will go to Pae-tu.

Ta-mee tells me I do not understand the ways of America, but she is wrong. I understand. I don't belong here. This isn't my home and I will never belong. I understand that I was a mistake. Ay-ken's mistake.

Ta-mee is maybe not so wise. I want to tell her that Jay-ke is not her friend. But I think she will not listen to me. She believes I am a child, but I am no longer a child.

40

Jake dropped her off at my trailer. I couldn't believe it. I heard the truck and opened the door of my place, and that scumbag winked at me while Soon-hee and the boy got out, looking like they'd been through hell. Jake was responsible for it, I was certain. But when I asked, she had no answers. Just, "He helps me," and "We want to go home." So, all right, I figured I'd get it out of Jake later, one way or another. Exactly what kind of help, I wanted to know.

Then the next bombshell. She wanted to go to the farm.

"Jake's idea?" I asked, because that would be his kind of fun, sending the lamb to slaughter.

"No," she said. "The father needs us."

That was the last thing I expected to hear. But off we went, across the county to the Alexander farm, and Aunt Ruth welcomed her with open arms, fed them, drew a bath for her, and it was like old home week, the strangest thing I've ever seen. What happened to "She's a witch" and "She doesn't belong here?"

When Aiken showed up finally and finished his teary little reunion with the boy, I laid it out for him. What he did to her in Korea was inexcusable. I know. Soon-hee knows. He knows. It was time for him to settle accounts. As simple as that.

Jake would have been proud.

41

Aiken knocks on Soon-hee's door, remembering the days in Seoul when he would come to her in the *yogwan*. So much has changed.

"*Oseyo*," she says. He remembers the invitation to come in.

He opens the door to find her brushing her long, lustrous hair. There's even a smile on her face, the anger of recent months gone.

"How are you feeling?" he asks.

"Good," she says.

He sits on the edge of the bed. "Thank you for bringing Henry back," he says. "I think he likes it here. He's on the porch playing with Ralph."

She begins to braid her hair, building a single, thick weave that cascades over her shoulder.

"You had me worried," he says.

She continues to braid and doesn't look at him.

"You should have let me know where you were going. I was really worried about Henry." She won't look at him, and he feels his frustration growing. Is she even listening to him?

"Would you look at me, please?"

She does.

"Thank you. I'm not sure how to ask this, but . . . what do you want? What are your plans?"

"Your father."

"He's coming home. But then what?"

She shakes her head. "I help."

"Yes, but then?"

He thinks he hears her say, "Pae-tu," but when he asks again she only shakes her head.

Aiken doesn't want to be separated from his son for even a minute, so he arranges for Henry to sleep with him in the barn, taking the bed, while Aiken rolls out a sleeping bag on the floor. With Soon-hee on the property, he remains wary. He still doesn't know why she has returned or what her plans are, but he won't let her take Henry from him again.

When he tells Henry they're going to build a birdhouse together, the boy's eyes open wide and his mouth forms a joyful o. Henry's job is to line up the finishing nails and screws on the workbench so Aiken can reach them easily. He keeps his line straight, laboriously counts the nails and then the screws, and then the nails again, announcing each number as he points with his finger. Mostly he watches Aiken work. When the frame of the house is done, Aiken balances the roof on top and traces the edges of the sides onto it. They sandpaper the roof and walls. Then they open the cans of all-weather exterior paint Aiken has bought—blue for the roof this time, yellow for the sides. Aiken paints the chimney red, then glues the pieces together.

The shape is right, just like their saltbox cottage, although the angle of the roof is off by maybe ten degrees and the colors are brighter than any house he's ever seen that people might want to occupy. But it doesn't look right. "Something's wrong," Aiken says.

They gaze at their creation.

"There's no windows," says Henry, pointing to the blank walls. "The birds won't be able to see outside."

"By golly, you're right. That's exactly what's missing."

When the paint is dry, Aiken pencils in small rectangles on the sides of the house, and a taller one on the front, then paints them blue to match the roof, and outlines the boxes in black. Up close they don't look much like windows, but when he pulls Henry away from the workbench, Aiken can imagine the sky reflected in the glass, a happy family looking out.

He gets the reaction he was hoping for.

"It looks like our house!" says Henry.

At dinner, Henry tells his mother and grandmother about the birdhouse he and his father have built that looks like the house where they used to live in town. Aiken's mother doesn't seem to hear.

"And it has a blue roof," he says. "And a chimney, and windows, and everything." He's careful with his pronunciation of the word "chimney," which Aiken has taught him.

He knows Henry expects more of a reaction, and the boy watches his grandmother. He looks at Aiken, as if asking what he should do. Should he tell her more? Is she all right? With a wink, Aiken releases him, and Henry flees to Ralph's company. Briefly, Aiken worries that Soon-hee might take Henry and run, but she stays by his mother's side. And, anyway, how could they get far? The notion is absurd, but it nags at him like the ache in his back, and so he excuses himself from the table to join his son outside.

Aiken is reluctant to part from Henry even for a few hours, but he'll know if Soon-hee leaves the farm in one of the trucks, so surely it's safe to re-enroll the boy in his pre-school at the church. He takes Henry to school the next morning to get him settled, grateful that there are no tears—Henry actually seems happy to rejoin his friends—then heads into the house for coffee before starting to work on a new birdhouse. He hears voices as he approaches the kitchen, but the women stop talking as soon as he steps inside. They stand at the sink, washing dishes together, Soon-hee with a towel and a plate in her hands, his mother up to her elbows in soapy water. Soon-hee doesn't look at him. His mother watches as he crosses the room and pours the coffee, and then he pushes open the screen to make his way out to the barn. The voices begin again. He can't imagine what they have to talk about, or what language they might be using. He's never heard Soon-hee so voluble.

In the barn, he realizes the building will move faster if he cuts the pieces for several new houses at once. That way he can clean up the sawdust and scraps and move on to the painting-and-assembly phase. It's efficient, like a factory, like the way his father used to run the farm. It makes sense, even if the houses will lose the individuality that the first models had. But that uniqueness doesn't feel so important anymore. He estimates he'll be able to make three houses in the time it's been taking him to make just one, and that surely is a positive development. Up to this point, his process, if there was a process, has been haphazard, inventing everything as he goes. He's learned what kind of nails to use, the best hinges, how to paint window trim so it looks as if there's a shadow on the side of the house.

It occurs to him that he needs to write down what he's learned, so he can remember what works and what doesn't. He wants to be able to teach Henry, to somehow pass along what he's discovered, so it won't be forgotten.

He studies the saltbox house, the first real creation after the crude early effort that now sits outside on the fence post. He lists all the pieces that went into it—the two ends, a divider in the middle, the floor, front, back, roof pieces and chimney, plus the nails and screws—and he recreates the measurements. He does the same with the Cape Cod house and the tavern. He spends the rest of the morning tracing the pieces on plywood, cutting them out on the table saw, and then begins the process of assembly.

He's nearly completed a new house, envisioning its future inhabitants, feeling a little godlike in his control over this tiny world, when there is a knock on the door.

"Come on in," he calls, reluctant to move his eyes from the work.

Soon-hee pushes the door open and enters, balancing a tray on which she carries a towel-covered plate and a can of Coke.

"Your mother," she says while surveying the barn. She sets the tray on the workbench, lifts the dishtowel to reveal a sandwich and potato chips.

"Hey, thanks. Sometimes I forget and do without."

"I remember," she says. Her eyes stop on the saltbox and she lifts her hand to it, not quite touching it but following the contours of the steep roof. She leans over, as if to look in the painted-on windows. "Our house."

"That's right. Our house. About the same size, too." He's not sure she understands the joke. She doesn't laugh.

"House for spirits?" she asks.

After he nods, thinking she's said "birds," he realizes what she's asked. "I mean, no," he says. "Not spirits."

Next to the saltbox is the Cape Cod. "This?"

"Just a house," he says. Kelly's house, but he doesn't know how to explain that to Soon-hee.

She nods. "Working," she says, and backs away.

As she slips out of the barn, the bright noon light dapples her hair. Aiken watches the dust swirl at her feet and is still watching long after she's gone.

The process of moving his father home is excruciating. His mother doesn't want a hospital bed in the dining room, which is what the doctors have suggested, so Aiken carries his father upstairs to his parents' bedroom. The old man, barely conscious, moans in Aiken's arms as they climb the stairs. If he speaks words, Aiken cannot understand them. He hopes they're doing the right thing.

With Soon-hee's help, he gets his father settled. He wants to stay, to speak with him, to ask him what he was trying to say, but Soon-hee shakes her head, and pushes Aiken out. She closes the door.

42

The mother of Ay-ken knows what I have done. The nurse
gives her the *pujok* she takes from trash. She says nothing,
but she knows, and without words asks for my help.

When Ay-ken is away to pick up Ha-neul from school, we
come to the father of Ay-ken in the bedroom of his ancestors.
We undress him and settle the yellow *pujok* over his heart.
We have no incense, but we burn candles and smoke fills the
room, stealing the air from the spirits. I sing, I call on Sansin,
I call the household gods to protect the father of Ay-ken, to
send away the hungry ghosts. We have no millet, the rough
grain of my people, but I tell the mother of Ay-ken to touch
a handful of barley to her husband's stomach. It will do. The
imps that infect him eat the barley and when she throws the
grain out the window they follow. The father of Ay-ken lies
still, eyes open wide when I come to him with the squawking
chicken. I grasp the chicken by its feet and it sleeps like the
dead. I rub her across his chest and she stirs, beginning to
struggle. She draws from him the last evil spirits, and I hold
her legs tight, swinging her in circles above my head as I

have seen the *mudang* of Pae-tu do many times. I release the chicken, aiming for the open window, but its neck slams into the frame and snaps, and I must run to finish the job. The chicken sails, like a tumbling cloud, to the garden below.

And now the knife. I touch the blade to the gray skin of his chest and chant, slashing at the air. I am stronger now and do not fear the house. I feel the ancestors enter my body and then depart. I feel the evil spirits flee, but I do not know if it is enough.

The *kut* is over and I fall at the old man's feet.

The mother of Ay-ken understands. She tells me about her people, the secrets of these mountains. I am *kangshinmu*, one with the mountain spirit, but she is *sessumu*, from a long line of women with wisdom. I sense it. She has no *kut* to perform, no ceremony, and she does not speak to the spirits as I do. But she knows they are here. She honors them and studies their ways.

Together we work in the kitchen. I was weak when I first arrived in this country, but she saw who I was. She saw *mudang* and I frightened her. But I have grown as the spirit filled me. As the pain filled me. Now I am strong. She has seen my power, and she welcomes me. She makes a cleansing tea from the herbs in her garden, and we drink together. It makes the air clear between us. It is how we speak.

"I like the tea," I say. She smiles and nods. "At home we make a tea with ginseng. It is powerful, like this."

"The sang," she says. "When I was a girl we hunted for the wild sang in the woods. My daddy loved it." Now it is my turn to smile and nod.

"My father also," I say.

I am thinking that we are alike. She is thinking the same, and I can see it in her eyes, in the creases in her brow. But we say nothing.

We work together in the garden. When I feel the warm earth between my fingers I understand her connection to the house and the old man's ties to this land, all the gifts it has given.

"The land speaks," I say. She looks at me, her eyes narrow, questioning. "I mean, there is a history here. Many lives. Many riches."

At this she laughs. "I don't know about riches," she says, "but the history part is right." She tells me about Ay-ken's ancestors who came to this Valley, building this house, the farm. "Henry loves to tell stories about the first Alexander in these parts, old Dermot," she says. "But riches? No, I don't think so."

"Ta-mee says—"

"She's a sweet girl," she says, "but don't believe everything you hear."

But when I see Ay-ken's tiny buildings, I think Ta-mee is right about the woman. There is our house, the little house with the roof like a mountain, a house for Sansin that Ay-ken says is not for Sansin. And the other house, I have seen that house in Ay-ken's eyes. I feel Ay-ken in that house, drawn to that house. If Ta-mee is right about the woman, maybe she is also right about treasure?

Sansin tells me it is time. We have held on to the old man's spirit too long. No more *kut*, no more prayers will keep him with us. Our *kut* prepared him to cross, released him from the demons who held him here, allowed him to say goodbye, but now it is time. I sleep, and in my sleep I feel him go to join his ancestors.

There is no wailing as there should be, as there would be at home in Pae-tu, as there was when my mother's spirit left us. The mother of Ay-ken cries, but silently, without tears. She swallows her grief and keeps it where it will only grow inside her. Ay-ken, too. He will let no one see. And Ha-neul is too young to know.

I think of my own poor father, struggling in his fields, and long for him.

TURTLE VALLEY, VIRGINIA

SEPTEMBER-OCTOBER 1996

43

Aiken can scarcely believe his father is gone. He knew it was coming, he thought he'd accepted it, and yet the reality is a shock. He isn't sure how he feels, exactly. It isn't grief, but he does mourn for the bond that never existed. And he worries about his mother.

The funeral arrangements absorb them all for a time. His father is to be buried in the cemetery at Tangled Root Creek, where Aiken's grandparents and great-grandparents are and also Hank, with the service at the old stone church there. Aiken owns one suit, the one he wore for Henry's christening, dark blue, now a little snug at the waist. Aiken's mother buys a clip-on tie for Henry. Aiken isn't sure Soon-hee will want to attend the funeral—Henry's christening was the only time in her life, as far as he knows, that she's set foot in a church—but she says she will be there. She even finds an old dress of his mother's that she takes in, and it looks fine, although somewhat disorienting for Aiken. For the first time since they've come back from Korea, she's making an effort to fit in. He's not sure what that means, but it gives him hope.

As they prepare to go to the church, he hears Soon-hee in the kitchen. He enters and clears his throat, not wanting to startle her. She is at the sink washing dishes, but her head turns slightly, acknowledging him.

It is too soon, he knows, and yet he has to ask.

"I was wondering if you'd given any more thought to what we talked about?" When she doesn't answer, he goes on. "About the future, I mean. What you're going to do."

He thinks he sees her shake her head, but then his mother enters.

"Are we ready?" she asks. "It's time to go."

It is only when Aiken sees the open casket that he loses control. The wood is burnished, the brass ornaments and handles gleaming. As he approaches, carrying Henry, his father's face comes into view, nested in the taffeta bedding. The old man is rosy-cheeked now, not the pale ghost he had become in life. Where was the warmth? Why had there been such a gulf between them? Aiken feels the tears well in his eyes. He wants to explain to Henry what's happening, but he can't make the words come.

He's written a eulogy. After the pastor has spoken about his father's strong Christian character, after he's called on the congregation not to mourn the death of Henry Alexander but to celebrate his life, and after the hymns have been sung, Aiken approaches the pulpit. He pulls a folded page from his suit jacket, sees before him the words he has written. He had agonized over them most of the night, searching for just the right way to honor his father, to acknowledge the old man's strength and goodness, to admit regret that in this life they had not been closer. And as he looks at those words on the page, he knows he won't be able to say them.

The little church is packed, as Aiken knew it would be. His father had been well known and liked, not much of a churchgoer, but a leader in other ways—president of the district Ruritans for a long stint when Aiken was growing up, sat on the county Agricultural Commission at the request of the local representative on the Board of Supervisors, never ran for office but showed up at school board meetings as regularly as anyone else all the years Hank and Aiken were students. And there are a lot of folks in the Valley who were his contemporaries, men who'd been raised on the shrinking farms in the county, many who'd known each other since childhood. They've all come. Kelly is there, too. That's a surprise. He'd been thinking about his father that day when he followed Kelly home from downtown, how his dad had liked her when Aiken and Kelly dated in high school, had ribbed him about how it wouldn't be long before they got married and had kids. She's alone, in a black suit, hair tied back.

But Aiken can't speak, not without causing a flood of tears, and so he hands the page to the pastor who reads the words aloud while Aiken stands silently by, head bowed, barely able to breathe.

There's a final hymn, and Aiken looks up, pushes back the tears, and watches everyone go.

He thinks Kelly will come say something to him, but she remains at the edge of the crowd, even when it's all over and the mourners stream by to whisper comfort to his mother, touch their fingers to her arm, shake his hand, pat Henry on the head. Soon-hee seems lost, but stays by his mother's side, like a shadow.

*   *   *

At the house, after the burial, the churchwomen spread the dining table with casseroles and platters of meat. Aiken wants a beer, but he knows there aren't any in the house. He does go out to the barn for a while, to be alone, but also to take advantage of a pint bottle he's hidden for the occasion. He lifts the roof off a half-finished birdhouse, a version of the Cape Cod—he's pleased with the tiny black shutters he's glued next to the painted windows of this one—and pulls out the bottle. He hears footsteps on the gravel outside and drops the flask into the pocket of his suit coat just as Jake walks in.

"Sorry about Uncle Henry," Jake says, looking around the barn. "Say, you live out here now, or what?"

"It's more private." He hopes Jake will take the hint.

"I see what you mean," Jake says, eyeing the bed, "but I thought you and the chink split up."

"Still an asshole, aren't you, Jake?" Aiken pulls out the bottle and takes a long drink, then sets it on the workbench where Jake can come and take a swig if he wants. Aiken doesn't care and isn't offering.

"You saw Kelly at the cemetery, right? Man, she looks good. Still have the hots for her, I bet." Jake grabs the flask and takes a short swallow, followed by a long one. "Very convenient that you're both divorced, or good as."

Kelly's divorced? How did he not know that? Surely his mother knew. "Was there something you wanted, Jake?"

"Now that you mention it, seeing as how we're cousins and old pals, brothers practically, and because your father screwed my father out of his share of this place, I was wondering if good old Uncle Henry left you any money. Money you could loan me."

"You're asking me this at his fucking funeral?" Not that the question, coming from Jake, isn't predictable, but Aiken hasn't thought about inheritance, or money, or what his father's death means for the family financially. He doubts there's any good news. He does know that he won't be lending anything to his cousin.

"No time like the present," says Jake. He's examining the Triumph, and squats to take a look at the twisted front fork. Aiken covers the workbench and the birdhouses with a tarp. He'd rather not have Jake asking questions about what he's been doing.

"What do you need money for anyway? I heard you were back working for Dave."

Jake stands, brushes his hand over the seat of the motorcycle, and leans against it. "I thought I'd go into business for myself. Just need some cash for a truck and mowers, so I can tell my brother-in-law to go fuck himself."

Aiken shakes his head. Jake folds his arms across his chest.

"I don't think there's any money, Jake. And it would go to Ma if there was. It's going to be tough for her to hang onto this place as it is. You know how things are. Besides, your dad sold out to mine a long time ago. He knew what he was doing. They made a deal." Jake's father, Archie, after he sold his share in the farm, became a long-haul trucker, divorced Jake's mother, had frequent scrapes with the law—public drunkenness, assault, a drug charge. When Jake was still in high school, Archie set off in his rig and never came back.

"Now, see, that's not the way I heard it. What I heard was your old man had it in for mine. Stabbed him in the back. I just want what's due."

"He wasn't like that, Jake. And besides, there's no money. How many times do I have to say it?"

"Aiken." Jake pushes off the bike, picks up the bottle and takes another drink. "Don't give me that bullshit. Before he ran off, my old man told me Uncle Henry was loaded. Maybe there's something hidden away that you don't know about, Cousin. You never were the sharpest knife in the drawer. Or maybe you're just not telling."

"You don't get rich from farming, Jake. Not doing it the old way like folks around here. You know that. Your dad knew it, too, which was why he was happy enough to take the money and run. They get by, some of 'em, if they work damned hard, and the rest of 'em sell." And now that Jake's brought it up, Aiken realizes, with a twinge of regret, it's only a matter of time before they'll have to do just that.

"The thing is, Cousin, a little birdie tells me you've got a secret or two you might not want everybody in Stillwater to hear."

"What are you talking about?"

"I think you know. For starters, there's some less-than-honorable behavior in the Army. I bet the brass would be real unhappy to find out about that. Then something about a certain child bride? A child bride who happened to be pregnant? And how you've been sneaking around on her from the get go?"

"You're out of your mind."

"Although I don't know why you'd want to cheat on that sweet piece. A fine little woman."

"Are you threatening me?"

"I wouldn't call it that. Just being persuasive is all. Negotiating."

Aiken takes a step toward Jake, who raises his hands, palms out. "Bring it on, little man. You're not going to catch me off guard this time."

"Get the fuck out of here, Jake. Or I'll throw you out."

"I'm going, Cousin. Out of respect for your dear, departed daddy. But think about what I said. You hear? See you around."

Back at the house, the visitors are leaving. The casseroles have been wrapped and put away. Soon-hee is clearing dishes and glasses and cups that have landed on side tables and windowsills, while Aiken's mother stands on the porch accepting condolences. She's wearing a black suit that Aiken remembers from Hank's funeral, and clutches a white handkerchief.

Aiken watches Jake bend over to talk to Henry. His cousin pulls a piece of paper from his jacket and shows it to the boy, who laughs. Jake folds it and slips it into Henry's shirt pocket, glances over at Aiken, then tousles Henry's hair before saying his goodbyes to Aiken's mother. With a last glance at Aiken, he leaves.

Aiken sits with Henry on the porch swing.

"What's that you got from Cousin Jake?" he asks.

Henry pulls the paper from his pocket and opens it. "It's a picture of Mommy," he says, laughing.

"Why is that funny?" Aiken asks.

"Because Cousin Jake said she's pretty."

"She *is* pretty, don't you think?"

"I guess so," Henry says.

Tammy emerges from the house—she's been with Soon-hee in the kitchen, Aiken guesses—then she's gone, too.

The last guest remaining is Sam Carpenter. Sam limps onto the porch with the aid of his walking stick and settles into the rocker. His pinstriped suit droops, red suspenders peeking out from his jacket. His shirt is frayed at the cuffs and collar. A crumb of yellow cake floats in his white beard.

"Your mother tells me you're out of work, son." Sam rocks a little and strokes his beard.

"Yes, sir. That work wasn't right for me."

"I can understand that. Takes a while to find what suits a man. Don't fault you for calling it quits."

"Truth is, Sam, they fired me." Aiken sits on the porch swing, looks up to see if his mother is in earshot, but she's gone inside. The quiet is broken by a screeching crow. "Can't say I blame them. With everything that was going on, my wife and me, Pop being sick and everything, I wasn't doing too good a job there, I guess."

Sam nods and rocks. "What do you plan to do now?"

Aiken doesn't have a plan. At least not one that he's thought of until that very minute. It isn't so much what he's going to do, but what he's already doing.

"You mean to farm this place?"

He searches for an answer to that question. He hasn't thought it through, not the way his father probably had when he was Aiken's age. He only knows one thing. "I'm going to make a home for my son," he says.

That seems enough for now. He's happy to be alive, to have survived a war, to have a son who's healthy. He's even happy that Soon-hee is safe and keeping his mother company, although he wonders how long their peace will last.

"Take your time, son," Sam says. "And remember, you can't grow if you don't stretch."

His father's words, exactly.

After Sam hoists himself out of the rocker, hobbles down the steps, and drives off in his pickup, Aiken heads to work in the barn, still in the tight suit.

There's a new design he wants to try. He's been thinking about an Army buddy who died in Korea. Tony had gone into the mountains with his Korean girlfriend to a famous Buddhist temple, Beopjusa, and stayed in a cheap *yogwan*, but they never made it back. Carbon monoxide, leaking from the under-floor heating system killed them both. Aiken and Soon-hee made the same trip a few weeks later to see where Tony had died. They visited the temple, with its towering pagoda and massive Buddha statue. A rocky stream chattered all night, magpies all morning. He'd been hoping to feel Tony's presence as he strolled the temple grounds. But there was only emptiness and stony silence.

He sketches first, although this design is a challenge to his limited skill, and drawing the pagoda from memory doesn't make it easier. He knows he should find a picture, so it will look right, but he wants to do this now. It seems urgent. When he's finished the sketch, he begins cutting out pieces—the front and back, the sides and floor, the tiers of the roof, and ribs to hold them in place. He looks at the sketch again, realizes that something is missing, and adds a spire to the picture, nodding at the memory it brings back, the peaceful temple on the mountain. He isn't sure how he'll make the spire, but he's confident that something will come to him.

Henry enters the barn, his clip-on tie askew, and Aiken is glad to see him. He isn't sure Henry understands where his Grandpa is, why the old man had been sleeping in a box in the church, or what the day has been about. They sit together on the bed.

"Do you know where Grandpa is?" Aiken asks.

Henry shakes his head.

"He's in heaven," Aiken says, hesitant to mislead the boy, no matter how comforting the lie. "Do you know what that means?"

Henry nods. "It means he's dead."

"That's right. But he's not gone. Not really. He's up in the sky, watching over us."

"Like the birds?"

"No," Aiken says, choking back laughter. "Well, sort of. Sure. Like the birds." Is that really what he believes? Or is he just handing down yet another story?

Aiken returns to work, sunlight fading and the barn lights burning, and Henry watches closely. He sits on the bench and props his elbows on his knees, rests his chin in his hands.

"Is that house for Grandpa?"

Aiken had thought he was building it for his friend Tony, but Henry's right. It does feel like a tribute to his father. "Sure," he says. "Do you think he'll like it?"

Henry nods, a big exaggerated nod.

"Good. I think so, too."

Aiken enlists Henry's help to glue the ribs and roof pieces to the basic nesting box and attaches the spire—a piece of coiled fence wire.

"There," Aiken says. "A new house for Grandpa."

As they're admiring their creation, the barn lights flicker and go out.

44

I look out the window and watch the women with wet eyes force smiles, embrace. The men nod and look serious. But there is no real grief. It is not like at home, where the whole village comes and there is wailing and mourning, and the *mudang* presides, dancing and shrieking her song while the fires burn.

I see the man, Jay-ke, who speaks to Ay-ken. I do not want him to see me. I cannot look in his eyes.

The people are gone now and the old woman sleeps. I work in the kitchen. I clean. It is too quiet, but the ritual is not finished.

I send Ha-neul to his father in the barn, and I go in search of Sansin. Up the mountain.

At the shrine I have built from stones, I prepare. I set out the wine and cakes. I have made a doll from straw, like a basket, and lay him on the stones. I shut my eyes and let the cool stream wash over me in the dark. I let the clouds lift me. I hear the beating wings of the rising white crane. I smell the pine and feel the rumble of the tiger at the heart of the mountain, and I am not Lee Soon-hee, I am Sansin.

The mountain spins and shakes.

The old man appears. The father. He stands straight and tall, his face glowing, with his son, the brother of Ay-ken, at his side.

45

Weeks go by. Aiken has come to realize that he *does* have a plan, a notion that began to grow on the day of the funeral when he replaced the faulty light fixture in the barn. The lights came back on, and he saw clearly: he'd build birdhouses. No mopping floors and emptying trash cans and cleaning up the messes a few hundred kids left behind in toilets and sinks. He'd build birdhouses.

He rises early and cuts pieces for whichever design he'll make that day and then assembles and paints. At first, the finished birdhouses sit on the workbench, partly as models for new houses but mostly because there's nowhere else to put them. But he needs the work space, so he rigs a series of knotted ropes that drop from the barn's overhead beams, and he hangs the finished birdhouses on the knots, like enormous Christmas ornaments. When the ropes are full, he builds high shelves along the barn walls and starts filling those.

The saltbox and the Cape Cod are his staples—he barely needs to measure the pieces anymore, they've become so familiar—but he works on new designs, too. He adds a covered porch to the basic model and it becomes a farmhouse. By modifying the chimney, notching the sides and adding a cupola roof, it becomes the bell tower of a schoolhouse. Tapering the chimney and adding a cross turns it into a church, and he begins to pay more attention to religious buildings as he drives around the county, noting how he might add details to distinguish a Catholic church from a Baptist, or a Methodist from a Presbyterian. He even studies the county's only synagogue.

The collection grows. Henry has them all memorized, so he notices whenever a new one goes up on the shelves, and he never fails to comment on the changes. He even suggests a variation, one that looks like the barn itself, and Aiken builds a series of them in different sizes and colors, some with a gambrel roof and some gabled to match the styles favored by their neighbors. Soon-hee is less observant than Henry, but she surely does see, when she brings Aiken his lunch each day, that the barn is beginning to feel crowded with the houses themselves and with the supplies that Aiken has accumulated. There are stacks of plywood and pine boards, boxes of nails and screws, cans and cans of paint. Not to mention the tools he's bought on credit to replace his father's decades-old equipment—a new table saw, drills and bits, clamps and a miter box.

"Don't be mad, son," his mother says at dinner one evening, "but I have a suggestion."

The meal is steamed fish with soy sauce and ginger, vaguely Asian, something his mother would never have thought to make if Soon-hee hadn't been helping in the kitchen. His mother glances at Soon-hee across the table, and Aiken settles his fork onto his plate. His father's place at the table is vacant.

"What exactly should I not be mad about?"

"I've been thinking it might be a good idea, what with all the work you're doing out in the barn, if Henry moved into the house." She drops her hands into her lap, looks again to Soon-hee, and waits for Aiken's answer.

He figures the move, like the dinner, is probably Soon-hee's idea, since his mother never comes out to the barn. It's true that the place has become cramped, what with the growing collection of birdhouses, the hardware and tools—a potentially dangerous spot for a little boy. Not to mention that the nights are beginning to get cold and, for Henry, the novelty of sleeping in the uninsulated barn has probably worn thin. But he's not sure he's ready to let him out of his sight. Soon-hee has been fine these last few weeks and an enormous help to his mother, but can he trust her? He looks at Soon-hee, then his mother, sees their resolve, and then he turns to Henry.

"What do you think, sport?"

Henry's mouth is full of white rice, another dish that his mother would not have thought to make on her own, potatoes being her starch of choice. His eyes shift from his mother to Aiken. He nods.

"Well, then," Aiken says, "I guess that's settled."

During the day, he sees his mother and Soon-hee coming and going, tending the garden or hanging wash on the line, sweeping the porch. If he needs to go into the house he might hear them chatting in the pidgin they've developed, washing dishes, vacuuming, baking, stirring some rank concoction on the stove. He frequently notices that Soon-hee leaves the house by the back door and heads uphill. He doesn't know where she goes. To gaze at Brother Mountain? To think of home?

Most days, Soon-hee brings lunch out to the barn for him, but sometimes he joins his wife and mother on the porch or in the kitchen. The table is set with the red and white checked tablecloth and straw placemats and tall glasses brimming with iced tea, or milk, or lemonade. One day, when the sandwiches are finished, and Soon-hee has cleared the table, Aiken's mother puts a plate of oatmeal raisin cookies in front of him.

"She made them," his mother says. "Have one."

Soon-hee had swung around to look when Aiken's mother mentioned her accomplishment, but now turns her back to him, making herself busy at the sink, running water and wiping dishes. He knows she's dying to look while he tastes, to gauge his reaction. He takes a bite of one and knows there's something wrong. They're salty, and dry, more like crackers than any cookie he's ever eaten. His mother holds a finger to her lips.

"They're good," he says. He can't bring himself to lie any more than that, and he suspects Soon-hee will be satisfied with it. Surely his mother will be able to diagnose the problem and get it fixed before any more cookies are attempted, before Soon-hee does any more damage in the kitchen.

One Saturday, Aiken, Henry, and Ralph explore the forest adjacent to the farm and the creek that runs through it. Although only the leaves of the dogwood trees show any signs of color, and the undergrowth is still dry and brittle with drought, it's September now and the air smells clean. The sky is a deep blue. As they enter the woods, Aiken spots a brilliant flash of red, then another following it, like two bursts of flame. But these flames are chattering at each other high in the trees, a pair of enormous woodpeckers, hopping up tree trunks, chasing each other, piercing the serenity of the late summer morning with their brash calls.

He begins work that afternoon on a new house, a much bigger birdhouse for much bigger birds. He doesn't even know if woodpeckers will occupy a birdhouse, but it's the idea that attracts him more than the practical application, and he wants to use as his model the most impressive building the county has to offer: the cathedral. As he conceives it, most of the house is the same as the other birdhouses but on a grander scale. What will distinguish the cathedral—apart from the larger opening for the larger birds—will be the ornate buttresses and massive façade to simulate the bell towers. For the entry hole, right where the rose window would be, he draws a circle with a compass and uses the jigsaw to cut it out. To make the buttresses, he cuts ten pieces of plywood and traces identical patterns on them, in what he imagines is a gothic design, although he's doing it from memory of the big church in Stillwater, and what he knows about cathedrals is limited to a documentary he once saw on television. Then he uses a band saw to cut away the ends, and a jigsaw to carve the interior sections of the design. When he's cut and fastened the sides of the cathedral, he paints the buttresses and attaches them, first with glue and then permanently with screws.

The result is an imposing birdhouse that covers his entire workbench.

On Sunday, he takes his mother, Soon-hee, and Henry to church. He's surprised that Soon-hee is going—she's wearing another of his mother's dresses that she's altered to fit—but supposes this is more evidence that she's at last trying to fit in. He knows she hasn't abandoned her own faith—he's seen the tiny shrine she erected in the kitchen, with a drawing of Buddha, another of an old man with a tiger, her yellow and red hand-drawn signs, and an offering of fruit—but if she's only going to church to please his mother, that's all right with Aiken. It's a tight fit in the truck, but for the first time in months his body is close to Soon-hee's. Her leg presses against his. It's intentional. He's sure of it. But what does it mean for the future? Is she saying she wants them to try again? Is that what *he* wants?

Henry announces that he'll stay with his father while his mother and grandmother are in church, and normally Aiken would be sympathetic since he isn't the least bit interested in church himself, but this morning he has something he needs to do. Henry's protest is a short-lived tantrum that ends when he sees he won't get his way. Aiken waves without looking back.

He travels the rest of the way into Stillwater and up into Kelly's hillside neighborhood. He drives slowly, conscious of the growls his truck spits into the early quiet, and, as he approaches her house, he cuts off the engine and coasts to a stop.

It's a brisk morning, with portents of fall. The dense maples on this street have begun to turn: gold leaves adorn the treetops like crowns. He gets out of the truck, closing the door softly, and lifts a Cape Cod birdhouse out of the back. He checks his hair in the side mirror, remembers teen dates when he did the same, and follows the snaking brick walk up to Kelly's front door. He rings the bell. He doesn't hear movement inside and begins to feel foolish, standing there on the front stoop with the birdhouse balanced clumsily on one palm. He knocks, there's still no answer, and he's about to leave when he hears footsteps inside. The heavy oak door swings open, and there's Kelly.

He's startled because Kelly is every bit as pretty as he remembers. He's seen her twice in recent months—once walking down the street and once at his father's funeral—but both glimpses were from some distance. The last time he *really* saw her, seven years ago, she'd been sleek, with long brown hair, blushing cheeks. She's grown a little heavier now, and it looks good on her. Her hair is short, the sign of a busy woman, he thinks. Professional. She's not a kid anymore. It makes him self-conscious of his own long hair, which suddenly feels childish.

"Aiken," she says. She steps onto the porch and crosses her arms over her chest.

He wants to kiss her. Just a hello kiss, as he's seen people do, but it feels awkward, and he's got the birdhouse in his hands. He doesn't move.

"How've you been, Kelly," he says. "Been back long?"

"A year," she says. "Since Mom died."

"I'm sorry. I didn't know." He wonders why his mother hasn't told him, because surely *she* knows. And he *is* sorry, although Kelly's mother had hated him, or hated what she suspected he was doing with her daughter. Probably both. Kelly was the smartest girl in their high school class, and one of the most attractive. Her father had been a professor at the women's college in Stillwater and his sudden death hadn't left the family with much money. But they did have culture, books, music. They traveled. School was important.

Her mother insisted Aiken wasn't a good match for Kelly. He was the best athlete in the county, or at least the best second baseman, a good-looking kid, and a middling student who did well enough when he tried. The difference was that he grew up on a farm, had no interest in college, and no ambition. Kelly's mother had been polite whenever he came to the house, but icy. It was clear she wanted better for Kelly.

When it became evident that they had grown extremely close—no amount of track-covering can hide such things from a watchful parent—Kelly's mother did what she could to break them up. She introduced Kelly to other boys, the sons of college faculty she was still in touch with, even the boys who were themselves in college somewhere, despite the inherent risk in that tactic. She sent Kelly away on vacations to relatives, in Richmond or Atlanta, always far enough that it wouldn't have been easy for Aiken to follow. She offered Aiken money once—to stay away, to promise never to call—which had infuriated Kelly but made Aiken laugh hysterically. When that didn't work, she arranged for a friend to hire Aiken to do odd jobs on weekends. Aiken found out later that she'd been responsible, but at the time he'd welcomed the extra cash, even if it did eat into the time available to spend with Kelly—her objective all along. But nothing she tried was effective, and it was only Aiken's decision to enlist that finally drove them apart. He left, and then Kelly left, and they were finished.

"Why didn't you call?" Aiken asks.

"Because . . . I didn't know I was going to stay. Because you were married and I'd only just been divorced. And because I wasn't sure I wanted to see you again anyway."

"That's a lot of reasons." A car whizzes by on the street and has to swerve around Aiken's truck.

"You aren't supposed to park there, Aiken."

He hadn't expected this to be so awkward. He thought they'd connect, have a lot to talk about, years to catch up on. He thought she'd ask him in and serve him coffee. As an old friend. He didn't think they'd be able to recover what they'd once shared. That's not what he wants. In fact, he's not sure now why he came at all. He remembers the birdhouse in his hands.

"I brought you this," he says, and gives her the Cape Cod.

"It's beautiful," she says, and even twists to look at her own house, to compare. The details are exact. The shutters, the dormers, the windows, even the red door. "Where did you get this?"

"I saw you, Kelly," he says. "One day on the street. You were window shopping, I guess. I followed you here. I thought you were just visiting. But I remembered your house, picking you up here, sneaking you back after curfew. How hard it was to get past your mother. She'd have made a good drill sergeant. Anyway. Seeing you and the house reminded me. So I made this."

"You made it? I guess you learned all sorts of interesting skills in the Army." Another car swerves around the truck and they both turn to watch it pass. "You'd better go," she says.

Not, "You'd better move the truck," but "You'd better go." He nods, tips an imaginary cap, and backs toward the pickup. He's sure she'll say something to stop him, invite him to park in the alley behind the house or to return in the afternoon. But she doesn't. Without looking at him, she opens her door and slips inside. As he climbs into the truck he sees that the drapes are closed. She's gone back to whatever he'd interrupted, and she isn't watching him.

It's too soon to go back to the church to pick up the family. And he doesn't know if the Turtle is open so early on a Sunday. Instead, he goes to the lumberyard and buys a stack of plywood sheets and pine boards. The hardware store isn't open but he heads to the Lowes out by the highway and stocks up on finishing nails and screws, looks at the paint he might use for the various new designs he has in mind, buys small brushes for the increasingly intricate detail he wants to try. He's late getting to the church, and his mother glares at him briefly, but it's evident from the load in the truck where he's been. At first Soon-hee won't get in, and stands at the door, studying the truck from bumper to bumper, muttering something Aiken can't make out. He remembers the ride into town and the closeness of their bodies, and he can't imagine what's changed.

"Let's go, Mom," says Henry. Only then does Soon-hee climb in, with Aiken's mother and Henry between them.

Starting the next day, he's more systematic about building the houses. By working on one variety at a time, he makes himself into a one-man factory, an assembly line of floors, sides, roofs, chimneys, or even window trim, cupolas, steeples, and flying buttresses. He can make five or six of the simpler houses in a single morning that way, maybe more in the afternoon. Soon, all the shelf space in the barn is taken, the ropes are full, and he's started stacking the houses in the barn's empty stalls, dark caves that he's not yet renovated, that still smell of hay and manure.

Henry watches him while he works on the weekends, and since Aiken goes back out to the barn each day after picking Henry up from school, the boy joins him then, too. One afternoon, while Aiken replicates the cathedral birdhouse, Henry sits at the bench by the barn door and eats the homemade cookies that Soon-hee has brought out for them both—much improved from her earlier attempts after his mother's persistent instruction.

"How come no birds live in the houses, Daddy?"

Aiken looks up from the work he's doing on the rose window, sanding the entrance smooth. "There are birds in that one out on the fence post. Remember?"

"What about all the other ones?" Henry's eyes take in the whole collection, the houses hanging from the rafters, those piled on the shelves, the full caverns in back. "Nobody lives in them."

Aiken looks around the barn at the tiny taverns, saltboxes and Cape Cods, the schools, the farmhouses. "What should we do about that?"

"We could put them in the field and watch all the birds go in and out."

It strikes him, with the jolt of a gunshot, that he's been foolish. No doubt seeing Kelly contributes to the realization, but it occurs to him that all this time, the energy poured into building the birdhouses, has been a monumental waste. A childish hobby, no more useful than the models of cars and planes he'd assembled as a kid. Originally he'd wanted to build them for Henry, but he's lost sight of that. He's been single-minded and driven, but to what end? It had made sense to give one to Kelly. But now he's got dozens of the things. And he doesn't know why. It seems crazy. As crazy as anything Soon-hee has done. Crazier.

"Or maybe," Henry says, cautiously, as if he sees the doubt that has clouded his father's face, "we could sell them to somebody."

He looks at Henry. The feeling of foolishness evaporates, and he laughs. It's obvious, and yet he'd missed it. Just as a moment earlier he'd felt completely insane for wasting his time on this outlandish venture that had no rational purpose, he now realizes that selling the birdhouses is what he's meant to do all along.

But how?

46

Have I mentioned how I met Henry? I'm not proud of what happened, but I did what I had to do. I must have told Aiken, but I don't remember. Probably I told Hank, and some days I forget that he's gone, or that I ever had two sons, as if Aiken and Hank are the same boy.

I was young, younger than . . . Aiken's wife. It was after the war, of course. I was in high school, and lucky for that, with no prospects. Home was all I knew, nowhere to go, no one to talk to except my brother Johnny, who'd listen but never say anything back. And of course I could only talk to him when I was alone, or people would have thought I was plumb tetched for talking to a ghost.

The town back then—Typton, I mean, not Stillwater, a big city by comparison—was just a filling station, a wide spot in the road where folks would come down from the hills and gather, swap stories, trade goods. Helen and I made lace, not like the delicate machined patterns you see in the store nowadays but still it was pretty, hand-stitched, no two pieces the same, like snowflakes. We brought our lace down to the road and waited, and talked to the other folks, with their wood-carvings and baskets and canned goods and such, and I don't think I knew it at the time but we were really waiting for the tourists, the people with money who might want to buy. The little cash we took in was a help around the house. I remember that much.

Anyway, we were down at the road on one of those days, and along came a truck that I didn't think looked too promising. It was the color of manure and had wooden sides in the back, something like a split-rail fence. And the back of that truck was filled with young men who spilled out fast when the truck came to a stop. Some kind of work crew, as it turned out. Most headed over to the filling station to buy sodas or whatever, but a few wandered around amongst us inspecting the wares, although they sure didn't look like they had money to spend.

I was mostly looking at feet, seeing what kind of shoes people wore, boots and such. It's not that I was barefoot, but we didn't have much and my shoes were pitiful. I suppose they'd been Helen's before coming to me. I hated them—brown as mud, all scuffed and patched. So I liked to see what other folks wore on their feet, and I remember these boots like they're sitting right here beside me. Black as can be, hobnail boots that made me think of Johnny, because they were like the ones he wore. These were shiny, too, under a fine layer of dust, like the owner took pains to make them nice even if they were just going to get messed up in the dirt. I wondered where those boots had been.

When I looked up to see the face of the man in those boots, I saw him gazing into Helen's eyes like he'd been bewitched. I think I probably laughed because it was the funniest thing, the kind of lost expression I'd read about in stories. She was gaping right back at him in the same way, and now I'm sure I laughed out loud because they both looked down at me, and they laughed, too.

"I'm Henry Alexander," he said, "from up in Turtle Valley."

"I'm Helen," my sister said.

"And I'm Ruth," I said, chirping like some baby bird who wants to be fed, but I knew Henry wasn't listening to me.

He and Helen were about the same age, so it shouldn't have bothered me that they were making eyes at each other. I didn't think of her as ever having a beau, because she helped Momma so much and looked after us little ones. So I thought maybe I could be the one this Henry was interested in, and I studied on ways to make that happen.

Sure enough, Henry came back, claimed his work crew had another job in Typton, which I didn't believe for a minute, and he located our cabin in the hollow by asking folks about that pretty girl who sold lace by the side of the road. He meant Helen, of course. But by that time I had a plan.

I'd found what I needed up in the hills, a secret Momma taught me. There's a root, I don't even know the real name of it, but Momma called it "man root." It's not that wild sang that everybody hunts and that my daddy liked so much, but it's shaped like a man just the same, and the leaves are dark green with a soft velvety underside. What you do is you boil a sliver of that root in a little bit of water and honey to hide the bitter taste, and then you add that to a person's tea or whatever they're drinking. It doesn't cause any harm, really, makes a person act a little crazy is all. I meant for Henry to drink it, I'm ashamed to say. I hope he'll forgive me. I thought if he behaved badly Helen would lose interest in him and I'd have him all to myself.

Except that somehow the concoction ended up in Helen's tea instead of Henry's. There we were, sitting on the porch sipping the tea and Helen's face went white as the snow up on Brother Mountain. She bent over double and was sick right on Henry's shiny black boots. I felt terribly guilty, but I also had to hide my laugh behind my hands. She ran off into the woods, embarrassed, I guess, and Henry wanted to chase after her, but Momma told him he'd best stay put. Momma looked right at me when she said that, and I think she knew what I'd done.

After that, whenever Henry came by, Helen hid somewhere so she wouldn't have to see him, and I kept him company on the porch. I thought he was so handsome. Better looking than any boy in Typton, by a mile, at least. One thing led to another after that, even though I was so young.

I never should have told him what I'd done. Never should have. But I was so young, you see. I didn't know it was wrong. To have that power, I mean.

And so when I saw Aiken's . . . Soon-hee, so young, with such wise, black eyes, I knew. One hill woman to another, I knew.

This morning, as Soon-hee and I weeded the garden, I thought of my Henry, and how much I missed him. There was a bond between us, and I am sorry that the bond between Aiken and this girl is broken. It's a shame, but I think there is nothing to be done. Is there a potion that will mend a marriage? I don't think so. I listened to her hum a lovely tune—a Korean love song she told me—and prayed that they might rediscover each other.

Soon-hee stopped her humming, and I wondered why. Just then Jake appeared. I hadn't heard his truck or footsteps on the gravel, but then maybe I'd been distracted by the lilting tune. Soon-hee stood, bowed to me—I'd asked her not to do that, but she said it was her duty—and hurried into the house. Both Jake and I watched her go.

Maybe I shouldn't say this, but it looked like he'd been drinking, and it was well before noon.

"Morning, Jake," I said. "What brings you out our way?"

"I wanted to talk to the girl," he said.

"Soon-hee?" I guess I was surprised, especially because it appeared she didn't want to talk to him. "Is everything okay at home?" I asked.

"Everything's fine, Ma'am. I just need to talk to her."

Jake followed Soon-hee into the house. I caught a glimpse of him through the window, and I heard his voice, shouting as he was. I don't think she said a word, or at least I couldn't hear. I thought of moving closer to the back door, not that I approve of eavesdropping, you understand, but there was something going on in my own kitchen and surely I needed to know what it was.

But then Jake came out, rushed past me, and a few minutes later Soon-hee was back by my side, her hands in the dirt as if nothing had happened.

Maybe it was none of my business, but I couldn't help myself.

"What did Jake want," I asked.

She looked at me like I was crazy, like she'd never heard of a soul named Jake, and then she went right back to her work. Didn't say another word the whole morning. Stopped her humming, too.

47

On Friday night, Aiken loads birdhouses into the back of the pickup and covers them with a tarp. Before sunrise the next morning, he rouses Henry, fixes him cereal and toast, and carries the sleepy boy to the truck. By six, in the thin early light, they're at the farmers' market in Stillwater's main parking lot. Aiken watches Charlie Doak, a friend of his father's, unload bushels of tomatoes and squash and corn at his stand. A young woman in a long flowered dress, her hair covered by a lacy bonnet, sets loaves of bread and trays of pastries and cookies on a crisp, white tablecloth. Another woman arranges bouquets of flowers—tall sunflowers and yellow foxglove, and smaller bundles of daisies, black-eyed Susans, and purple blooms Aiken doesn't recognize. One woman has a banner strung behind her stall that says "Herbs," and she displays baskets of leafy green sprays— basil, rosemary, sage, mint—on varnished plywood risers. He takes note of the risers. He resolves to build a set for next time; it'll be a great way to show off the houses.

He backs the truck into an empty stall some distance from Charlie Doak. He has no idea how the market works, or how to sell anything, or how much to charge for the houses. And he doesn't know if he needs permission to do what he's doing. He's never thought about any of this before. His father would have known—it wasn't that long ago that he'd operated a stand at the market himself and sold all manner of produce—but that's one more question it's too late to ask. So he's picked a spot where he can be out of the way and watch what's happening.

The first thing he discovers is that he doesn't have anything to put the houses on. The other vendors all have folding tables they've pulled off their trucks, and the herb lady has her risers on top of that. And they all have chairs, too, a place to sit and be comfortable while shoppers stroll from stand to stand. He should have thought of that. Henry's still asleep in the truck, but, once he's awake, Aiken can't expect him to stand up all day. He'll give it a try for a while. They can sit on the tailgate, display a few houses there and on the sidewalk, and see what happens.

He lifts the tarp and takes out three houses—a saltbox, a Cape Cod, and a school. He sets the two cottages on the truck and the school on the ground. And then he waits.

In a few minutes, a man strolls their way, and Aiken girds himself for his first customer. The sales pitch he'd practiced on the drive into town vanishes from his head. But he notices the man is carrying a clipboard, and his bright yellow T-shirt says "Farmers' Market" across the chest, above the man's ample stomach. A red splotch covers the man's cheek and spills down his neck; Aiken finds it hard not to stare.

"You got a license?" asks the man. "You got to have a license."

He pulls out his wallet, removes his driver's license, and hands it to the man, who doesn't even look at it, wrinkles his brow, and hands it back.

"Not that kind of license. I mean a market license. We rent space to vendors and I'm pretty sure I didn't issue you a license."

"Guess I didn't know I needed one just to park my truck," says Aiken.

"It's not the parking, friend. We've got our administrative costs, advertising, that sort of thing. All these folks pay a fee to sell here all summer and fall." He turns and with a sweep of his arm takes in all the other vendors, who are now beginning to attract the early shoppers.

"Didn't know how it worked," Aiken says, although he'd suspected there had to be something like this. He'd even helped his father in the market from time to time years ago, although of course he hadn't paid attention to such details. He pulls his wallet out again and this time removes the only cash he has, a twenty. "Is this enough?"

The man's expression turns from stern to agitated. He rips a form from his clipboard and thrusts it at Aiken.

"Tell you what. You're okay where you are for today, unless John Worley shows up with his pumpkins, but it's still early in the season for him. You fill out this form and bring me a check next week. Everything you need to know is right there on the back." The man moves on, chats with Charlie Doak for a minute, and Aiken watches him stop at every stall in the market, shaking hands, sampling the goods, and generally making his official presence known.

Aiken goes around to the front of the truck and sees that Henry is awake. He carries him to the back and the two of them sit next to the birdhouses and wait together.

The last few months have been rough on them, but right now, sitting there on the back of his truck with his son, he's content. He's not worried about his family or work. He's got what he wants and, with any luck, this birdhouse venture will take off.

"You're going to help me, right?" He settles a hand on his son's shoulder.

"Yessir," says Henry, and he seems happy, too.

The market isn't quite awake yet, only a few customers getting a crack at the best produce, and vendors are still setting up. A siren erupts in the distance, then in an instant a fire engine appears, races along Central, whining and honking its way through the sparse Saturday traffic. Henry covers his ears, but he watches the big red truck until it's out of sight. The siren fades away. Aiken wonders if he could build a birdhouse to look like a fire station.

More shoppers trickle into the market after seven. A teenager wearing an apron comes by, pushing a cart with drinks and pastries, and Aiken gets coffee for himself and a donut for Henry. A couple approaches the truck, well-dressed and, Aiken guesses, because the locals all wear jeans and work boots, from out of town. This woman is in a pink pantsuit and the guy sports shiny loafers and a blue blazer.

"Look, Ed, folk art," says the woman. Her voice is high-pitched, nasal.

"It's a birdhouse," says Henry.

"I see that," says the man.

"My dad makes 'em."

Aiken says nothing because Henry seems to be doing fine on his own, although the couple moves on without buying.

A teacher from Aiken's school, Mrs. Rutledge, strolls past. She carries a wicker basket over her arm and already has a bundle of greens and one big beefsteak tomato. She doesn't stop to look at the birdhouses and doesn't appear to see Aiken, much less recognize him. She smiles at Henry, but keeps walking.

For an hour no one even comes near. People meander by with bags or baskets full of purchases, but the birdhouses attract no attention. Henry swings his legs under the tailgate, and then he discovers he can bounce the truck by hopping up and down, even making the birdhouses jump.

"Boy, stop that," says Aiken. He says it sharply, the way he talks to the dog when Ralph's digging in the garden. Henry stops jumping, but soon he's seated again, swinging his legs and finding new ways to make the truck shake. "Stop," says Aiken.

"I want to go home," says Henry.

"We need to stay a little longer, son."

The man with the clipboard stops by again, an insipid smile on his face. "How's it going?"

"Not too good," Aiken says, struggling to keep his eyes off the mark on the man's cheek. "Haven't sold a damn thing."

Mid-morning, Aiken is about ready to call it quits. He has to find Henry a toilet and take him there, leaving his birdhouses sitting on the back of the truck, and doesn't expect to see them there when he returns. But they are—even that's a disappointment—and he resumes his spot on the tailgate.

"Can't even give the damn things away," he mutters. "This was a stupid idea."

Charlie Doak wanders over. Aiken has been watching how he works with the customers—joking and urging them to buy four tomatoes when maybe they only ask for two, a bag of peppers when all they want is one. All the produce he'd brought in is gone.

"Aiken, ain't you?" Doak asks.

"Yessir, Mr. Doak. How you doing?"

"I was real sorry to hear about your dad, Aiken."

"Thank you, sir."

"You going to be here next week? Seems like you could set up next to me over there. Folks'd see your stuff that way."

"That sounds fine, sir." Since no one has shown interest in the birdhouses, he's begun to think they're crap and that probably there won't be a next week. But Charlie Doak doesn't say they're crap, and that gives Aiken a glimmer of hope. Maybe he needs to do a better job of selling, like Charlie, or like the shopkeepers and vendors in Korea who stood in front of their stores and invited customers in, or lured them inside with tea and sweets.

When he's thinking about heading home, Jake strolls up to the truck.

"Howdy, Cousin," says Jake.

"Jake," says Aiken.

"So this is what you've been up to? Birdhouses?" Jake winks at Henry, who laughs.

Aiken crosses his arms over his chest. "What can I do for you, Jake?"

"Don't be like that, man. I wanted to apologize. About the funeral. We're family, after all."

"Family. Right."

"Okay, I get it. You're pissed. Don't blame you." Jake lights a cigarette, chucks Henry under the chin. "See you around, Cousin." And he moves on.

Aiken watches Jake leave, wondering what his cousin is up to. He surely didn't come into town just to apologize. Aiken puts the three birdhouses back under the tarp, gets Henry settled up front, and drives home. He moves the whole load of birdhouses back into the barn and joins his mother and Soon-hee in the house for lunch.

"Henry says you went to the market," his mother says. "He says you sold birdhouses."

"Tried to sell. Didn't have any takers."

"I'm sure you did your best, son."

"And Uncle Jake was there," Henry says.

"Up to no good, I'm guessing," says Aiken.

That afternoon he stays away from the barn. Until today all he could think about was building more and better birdhouses, and recently the notion of turning them into cash had given his work real purpose. Now the thought of a couple hundred empty wooden boxes with holes in them makes him sick to his stomach, evidence of his supreme idiocy, proof that Kelly was right to leave him way back when and that Soon-hee had good reason to cut her losses and kick him out. What a fool he's been. His back aches, and his throat feels dry and rough. He should call that Mr. Keeler from the school and see if he can get his old job back. The birdhouses don't make sense anymore, if ever they did. He'll call on Monday. And he'll talk to his mother about moving into the house, where any sensible person would live. Maybe Soon-hee is willing to try again. Maybe life can return to something resembling normal.

Instead of building more birdhouses, he does chores around the house. There's that porch step that needs mending, and the wobbly banister and loose stair runner inside. God knows he has the lumber and tools to make the repairs. With his mother's attentions elsewhere, weeds have overrun the garden, even in the drought. A screen on the back porch has a tear, thanks to Ralph. He has to go into town to get the mesh for that, but at least the errand takes his mind off his market embarrassment.

The family sits down to supper together, the first that Soon-hee has made on her own since moving into the house. Aiken's mother says grace, Aiken carves slices of ham for each of them, and Soon-hee serves an extra spoonful of glazed carrots onto Henry's plate—it's his new favorite because his grandmother calls them candied carrots.

They're eating in silence. Aiken doesn't want to talk about the market, but there isn't much else to say.

"You did great," Aiken finally says to Soon-hee, nodding at the table. She lowers her eyes, but he can see her proud smile.

"She did a fine job," says Aiken's mother.

Soon-hee clears the dishes and won't let Aiken help when he offers. Henry plops in front of the television. Aiken's mother knits. Aiken sits to watch TV, but he can't follow what's happening. Some men in uniform are talking to creatures Aiken guesses are aliens, but they're also in uniform. Aiken stands, looks toward the kitchen and its sounds of running water and clanking dishes.

"I think I'll go out to the barn for a while," he says, but gets no reaction.

Halfway to the barn, he stops. He doesn't want to watch TV, but he doesn't want to sit in the barn either, not with all the damn birdhouses and their gaping holes, like so many one-eyed aliens staring at him, mocking. He looks back at the house, and doesn't feel that he'll be missed. He won't be gone long. Surely Henry will be okay for a couple of hours. He gets in the truck and heads for town.

The Turtle is lively, as is to be expected on a Saturday night. He doesn't care anymore if he runs into Charlotte. It's been long enough, and the embarrassment has faded. He doesn't owe her anything except thanks for getting him home. In fact, as restless as he's feeling, he might be willing to maneuver himself back into her good graces. One more mistake to add to the list, and what's the difference? He's not married anymore, not really. The divorce is inevitable. It could be awkward, with Soon-hee staying out at the farm now, but at least Henry is settled into Aiken's old room in the main house, and he might be able to slip Charlotte into the barn and then out again in the morning without anyone seeing. And if not Charlotte, maybe someone else. He laughs at himself, thinking about sneaking a girl into his bed, as if it were high school all over again. And that makes him think of Kelly.

The memory of her is so vivid, her sweet lemony scent, her soft hair, that he expects her to be standing behind him. If he turned around now she'd apologize for not inviting him in that day when he stood awkwardly on her front stoop. He even looks, but all he sees is the window, its bright neon signs, and the empty street.

He takes up his place at the bar and keeps an eye out for Charlotte. Rick brings him a beer.

"Haven't seen you in a while. Working hard?"

"Hardly working."

Rick laughs at the old joke and Aiken sips his beer.

"That Charlotte been in here lately?"

"Who?"

"You know, that blond I was here with awhile back."

Rick looks puzzled, but his attention is grabbed by noisy customers at the other end of the bar, and Aiken is left alone.

Which is too bad, because he's in the mood to talk, and just now there's no one at hand. He wants to tell Rick that he's lost and lonely. And confused. His old optimism has vanished. He'd thought the birdhouse scheme would work, although even if he had managed to sell a few of the damned things it wouldn't amount to much, certainly not enough to support him and Henry. And he doesn't understand Soon-hee, doesn't really trust her. One minute she's coming on to him in the truck, as if she wants to go back in time, and the next she doesn't want to be near him. And then there's Kelly, who obviously wants nothing to do with him.

He'd finally given in to his father, signed up for the Army, had the physical, got papers. And only then did he tell Kelly what he was up to. He explained that he did it for them. That he was thinking about their future. But she didn't see it that way. It's not that she was angry. She just sat there, in the truck, hands in her lap. They'd been making out, headed toward the main event, and for some reason he chose right then to tell her. That stopped her dead. She pulled away, wouldn't look at him. She started straightening herself up, checking her hair in the mirror, and it was clear nothing was going to happen. She wouldn't even talk to him, except to say, "Take me home."

She avoided him at school after that, wouldn't take his calls. Not that it had ever been easy to get past her mother when he called there, but now the old biddy said, "She doesn't want to talk to you, young man," like he was some stranger. He never had a chance to explain.

When he came home on leave after Basic, he'd called all her friends. The ones who would talk to him wouldn't say anything about where she was. A letter came. Her mother had mailed it to the farm, but it was from Kelly. "Don't try to find me. It's better this way. There's no future for us." The thing was, though, he couldn't try to find her. He didn't have a choice. His leave was short and he had to get back. Later, his buddy Alec said he'd heard from his girlfriend that Kelly was down in Roanoke, in nursing school. But by then he'd gotten the hint and was angry that she'd dumped him that way. He didn't try to find her. He started going out and living it up. Then he was sent overseas, the war, and that was that.

But now, maybe it's not too late. Because Kelly's back.

Rick brings him another beer and Aiken drinks. When he looks up, he sees Hank, sitting at the other end of the bar. There's his long hair, the reason Aiken wears his long now, and his brave, square jaw. Hank winks at him, but when Aiken looks again, his brother's gone.

48

Ay-ken goes to her. She has come back for him, and she's the reason for his restless spirit. I have seen her house. I saw the spirit-house he made for her. I will pray to the Mountain God.

In the high land, on the mountain behind the house, Sansin shows me many things that remind me of home. There is the pine forest, where I collect seeds from the cones, and a thick grove of whispering *dae-namu*, bamboo, along the trickling stream. The meadow where the deer make their beds of straw. The desolate, round tree, bare of leaves, the orange balls, the *gam* fruit, that hang, like ornaments. The *gam* is bitter, not sweet, like poison.

In my country, I showed Ay-ken this tree. We rode a train from Seoul and I ignored the stares of the old woman with her long skirts and bundles. She muttered and I did not tell Ay-ken what she said, although he could hear the meaning in her voice. He could read it in her scowl. It was what they all said, and I did not listen.

The train emptied at Honnung, a village just outside the haze of Seoul. We strolled into the countryside, past blooming fields of melon and squash. A vendor shouted at us, "Come in, eat the apples!" I told Ay-ken what the old man had said, and he laughed. "Eat the apples!" he said, over and over, and we both laughed. Under a bright sky—blue, and vast like the ocean of my childhood memory—we rested at a shop along the path. We joined others sitting on a wide, low platform under the persimmon tree. The bright fruit, like planets orbiting our heads, hung ripe and heavy. "*Gam*," I said, teaching Ay-ken, and showing him how to slurp the wet meat from the skin. He drank the white liquor men drink, and let me taste. The *so-ju* reminded me of my father, the wine on his dark breath.

We continued up the hill to the tombs of the Yi kings, the Honinnung, perfect mounds guarded by the stone animals. As we circled the tombs, Ay-ken leaned over and whispered, "Eat the apples!" It is a serious place, visited by many who honor the kings, and I slapped at his arm. But I laughed, too.

The tree on the hill behind Ay-ken's house makes me think of that time. It was a happy day, the day I first knew about Ha-neul, although I didn't know his name then, before I was afraid.

I collect the fruit in a basket, so bright, like suns, glowing all together. I recall the tale of the old monk who wanted to keep all the persimmons for himself. He told his young disciple that the fruit was poisonous so the boy would not touch them while his elder was away. But the boy could not resist and ate them all. As he heard his master return he broke the monk's precious inkstone and fell to the floor of their hut moaning and groaning as if he might die. "What's wrong?" asked the old monk. "I broke your inkstone, Master, and could not live with the shame. So I ate the poisonous fruit and am waiting now to die." The tale makes me think of home, the stories of my father. My mother.

The fruit is not poison, but not everything in the forest is so innocent. I search for what I need to stop her.

49

How things have changed! I drive out to the farm to visit with Soon-hee and Aunt Ruth, to see where I fit in now that they're pals. I figure Aiken is in the barn, working at whatever it is he's been doing out there—making birdhouses, Jake says, but that can't be true—so I park, slip into the house, and don't see him, which is fine with me. I'm not too happy with my cousin, even if he did replace the guitar he smashed up at my place.

The two women are in the kitchen, Soon-hee stirring something on the stove and Aunt Ruth chopping and slicing. They even get me into the act, peeling potatoes and carrots. They're carrying on a conversation and I bob my head from one to the other, but I'll be damned if I know what they're talking about. My job done, I lean over the pot on the stove to see what's brewing but Soon-hee pulls me back. She says something in Korean. What an ugly language it is. I don't know the words, but I get her drift: stay away.

I think back to Aunt Ruth's pronouncement not so long ago, that the girl is a witch. Well, sure, why not? Fortune teller, witch, gypsy, whatever. And it occurs to me she might be better equipped to protect herself than I thought. Maybe she isn't the weak little girl who got herself trapped in a bad marriage. Maybe she knows what she's doing. Maybe she knows how to handle Jake.

Maybe it's something I need to learn.

50

Although the first attempt at the farmers' market had been a failure, he resolves to give it another try the following weekend. He's got nothing to lose, and lots of birdhouses to unload. He's better prepared this time, at least, and knows what to expect. He tries to convince Henry that he'll be bored, that there isn't anything for him to do at the market, but Henry throws a spectacular tantrum, one that sends Ralph cowering under the sofa, and Aiken gives in. Henry probably *will* be bored and miserable, but at least Aiken won't have to worry about Soon-hee, and, besides, he'll be grateful for the company.

As he did the previous week, Aiken loads the back of the pickup, but this time he takes only a few houses, ones that he's bubble-wrapped and boxed, plus the few that he'll use for the display. He's found a folding table at the thrift shop in Stillwater and that's in the back, too. And he's built risers like the ones the herb lady has, except he's covered them with scraps of carpeting that he convinced Mr. Miley at the rug store to give him. The risers are in the back, also, everything under the tarp.

And he's filled out the paperwork for the license but hasn't mailed it to the guy with the clipboard. The form says there's a fee of $100, and he doesn't have more than $50 left in his checking account. Aiken hopes a discount might be available because the season is almost over, and maybe he can pay in installments, once he starts selling the birdhouses. That's what he plans to ask for, anyway, and if that doesn't work then maybe he can pay Charlie Doak a commission to let him sell the things right at his spot, instead of taking up a whole space of his own.

When he pulls the truck into the market, Charlie waves to him and directs him to the parking spot next to his own pickup. Charlie has already laid out his produce, the bushels of tomatoes, the beans, gourds, and squash. But he's blocked off a spot with orange traffic cones, and now he moves them out of the way so Aiken can set up there.

"I told you we need to work together, Aiken. This is the spot for you." Charlie even helps Aiken and Henry with the folding table and the risers. He whistles when he sees those.

"That's one fine idea, boy. Mighty impressive."

Charlie has surely seen the herb lady's display and knows exactly where he got the idea, but the compliment feels good. He doesn't know what to say, but nods his appreciation.

He arranges a couple of the Cape Cods, a saltbox, the little Turtle Tavern that he's begun replicating, a schoolhouse, and a church on the risers. Charlie pours him coffee out of his thermos and digs into a paper bag for a homemade donut he hands to Henry. Aiken has taken his cue from Charlie and brought folding chairs this time, so the three of them sit down and wait for the market to open and the selling to begin.

"Daddy, it's raining," says Henry.

He hadn't counted on that, although he'd noticed the overcast sky on the way into town. It's drizzling before he's taken two sips of his coffee.

"Just a little mist," he says. But he cocks his eye skyward, sees the clouds churning and growing darker, and has a good notion that they're in for some serious, possibly drought-ending rain. As the drizzle turns into a steady patter, Charlie secures two tent poles to a tarp from his truck, and Aiken moves his and Henry's chairs under it with him. Because there aren't any customers in the rain anyway, Aiken puts the birdhouses back under cover in his truck bed, and they sit to wait it out. But the patter becomes a downpour, swirling creeks materialize in the gutters, and vendors pack up their wares.

"Damn rain," Aiken says. All year long, farmers have been praying for an end to the drought. Aiken's seen the parched crops, the mountain brushfires. He's heard the complaints in the hardware store and the farm co-op, predictions of disaster. He knows that the rain is welcome to most, although it's likely too late to do much good for the corn. Still, he curses his own luck.

"It happens sometimes," says Charlie, who drains the last of his coffee. "There's always next week."

Soon Charlie announces that he's calling it quits, which means that Aiken is done, too. He carries Henry to the cab of the pickup, and gets himself soaked helping Charlie load his vegetables back onto his truck, and then thoroughly drenched as he deals with his own table and chairs, and the carpeted risers, which he figures have been ruined by the rain.

"You're all wet, Daddy," says Henry when Aiken finally climbs inside. Henry is laughing, and that makes Aiken laugh, too.

"I guess I am." He shakes his head the way Ralph does when he's wet, spraying water on Henry and everywhere else, and that makes both of them laugh more.

He follows several other trucks out of the market parking lot and heads south on the Pike in the direction of the farm. Another week has passed without a single birdhouse sold. He's beginning to believe this was not meant to be.

The rain lasts all afternoon and into the evening. He'd thought about making another visit to the Turtle, but then he'd also counted on having money in his pocket from selling birdhouses, and that didn't happen. So he stays home, watches TV with Henry in the house, and then with Soon-hee and his mother after they put Henry to bed. The show is the nighttime soap opera that his mother likes about a winery in California, but he can't figure out what's going on, who's scheming against whom, or who's sleeping with someone else's wife. He finds it hard to believe that Soon-hee is getting much out of it, either, since the dialogue rushes by so fast, but maybe *not* listening to something like that is the key to understanding. Or maybe she's making up her own narrative to match what she sees—the story she needs to hear. He watches her, notices that she's intent, even gasps when the field hand pulls out a gun and laughs when the angry wife pushes her husband in the pool.

Then the program is over and his mother says goodnight, but Soon-hee stays in front of the television. Now there's another drama, a hospital show with beautiful nurses and handsome doctors, and Soon-hee is just as engrossed in this one. Aiken finds himself aroused by the thought of all these characters sleeping with each other, which appears to be where the story is headed. He clears his throat, wondering how to suggest that he might not go out to the barn tonight. Do they have a future together, or don't they?

Soon-hee's eyes remain on the flickering screen. He clears his throat again. She looks at him but then looks back at the program.

"Soonie," he says.

She looks at him again, and stands. She bows slightly, says something in Korean that he recognizes from hearing her say it to Henry every night. He wouldn't be able to repeat the mish-mash of sounds, but he knows what she's saying: "Sleep well."

In the morning when he comes in from the barn, he sees that his mother is on the couch in the darkened living room, a shawl draped over her shoulders. Henry and Soon-hee sit morosely at the kitchen table. A kettle whistles on the stove.

"Grandma's sick," Henry says before Aiken has a chance to ask. Soon-hee makes tea and carries it into the living room. He follows with his coffee and sits opposite his mother.

"You okay, Ma?"

"It's starting, Aiken."

"What's starting?" In the darkness he can't see her face, only the black outline of her shape. Soon-hee enters. Aiken's mother sips her tea.

"I might lie down for a bit," she says.

"Sure, Ma. That's probably best."

Soon-hee helps her up the stairs, and Aiken watches them go.

* * *

He starts working on a new project. It's something he's seen pictures of, although he's never been to New York City himself. As with his other designs, he sketches it first, all from memory, and then identifies the individual pieces he'll need. This one seems like a series of arches, each narrower than the last, with a spire on top. He uses heavy paper folded in half to make patterns for the arches, and then cuts. When he has all the pieces, he bevels the edges and assembles the top arch into a square tube. He carves a piece of pine that barely slides into the tube and traces the spire shape on two sides of the pine, cuts them away, and then cuts the other two sides before planing all four sides smooth. It doesn't look right squared off like that, so with a chisel he bevels the corners, turning it into an octagon, then planes it again, and finishes by sanding all the sides. He attaches the spire to the top tube of arches with glue and clamps the whole thing to dry while he turns to the rest of the tower. Since the other arches are already cut, he keeps adding layers around the top section. He drills and cuts the entrance hole, then adds the last of the arches. He cuts the floor, attaches it with hinges, and assembles a pedestal on which the house will sit. He sets the tower aside, but his eyes are drawn to it whenever he sets foot in the barn.

On Saturday, he rises in the dark and is relieved to see a starry sky. Whatever else happens, at least the day won't be a washout. He worries about his mother, but he and Henry leave for the market before she's up. Soon-hee is already in the kitchen, though, and she fixes breakfast for them, promises to look after his mother, and they set off. Charlie Doak has again saved them a spot next to his stand, and

Aiken arranges his creations. The carpeted risers are musty from the drenching they took the week before, but they'll do. He puts out two Cape Cods and two saltboxes plus a Turtle Tavern, and he and Henry sit back to wait.

The man with the clipboard, who had not shown up in the rain the week before, comes by. With Charlie's help and encouragement, a deal is struck. Since the market season is nearly finished, the license fee is cut in half, and the town council will accept installments, which is exactly what Aiken wanted. He hands the man a ten-dollar bill, the very last of his cash, and the man writes out a receipt. They shake hands.

As soon as the market man is gone, a woman in a short leather jacket, a gleaming coat that Aiken knows has never been near a motorcycle, sidles up to the risers and studies the birdhouses.

"My dad made 'em," Henry says.

"He did? They're beautiful." The woman picks up a Cape Cod, looks in the hole, and examines the house from all angles.

"You can't see in the windows," Henry says. "They're not real."

"Hush, Henry. The lady's thinking." Aiken is proud of Henry's efforts, but this would be his first sale, and he doesn't want to blow it.

"How much is it?" Before Aiken can answer, the woman sets the birdhouse down and rushes to the herb lady's stall. She pulls a man by his elbow back over to Aiken. The man is wearing a matching leather jacket, equally pristine. "Sorry," she says to Aiken. "He's got the money. How much did you say?"

He's given this some thought by now. He has to start making money, so he needs the houses to sell. But he doesn't want to price them so low that folks will think they aren't any good. He doesn't know much about money—his only previous sales experience is from his black market days in Korea—and wishes he had asked Charlie for advice.

"That one's ten dollars," he says. The man has his wallet out and hands Aiken two fives almost before the words have left his mouth. Ten dollars. He's broken even on the day so far. When the couple leaves, he replaces the Cape Cod with another from the pickup. By the end of the morning he's sold three more houses, another Cape Cod and two saltboxes, and has treated Henry to a donut. He has money in his pocket.

When they get home, Soon-hee tells them his mother has been up, but has gone back to bed. He sticks his head in her room, but the curtains are closed and the room is dark, the air stale. He hears his mother breathing steadily and believes she's asleep, so he begins to back out, until he hears her feeble voice.

"Aiken, is that you?"

"You need anything, Ma?"

"I'll be down in a little while."

He pulls the door, leaves it open a crack, and retreats.

He goes out to the barn to work, satisfied that he'll be able to make money selling the birdhouses. Now he needs to keep making them. And maybe, he realizes, he needs to charge more, especially for some of the houses, like his new tower, that take so much extra work and materials.

The glue on the tower has dried, and he's ready for paint. He uses aluminum-colored spray paint, in multiple coats, to build a smooth surface. He shakes the can, hears the ball rattle inside, and sprays, up and down the tower on each side. While the paint is drying, he trims the patterns he already has, and cuts triangular windows in each one. The last step is to paint black windows on each arch, using the patterns. He steps back to admire his work.

He hears a rustling behind him and turns, expecting to see that Henry has slipped into the barn. No one's there. And yet, he feels he's being watched. That he's not alone. He's felt this more and more lately, but he sees nothing. Only the array of birdhouses on the shelves and hanging from the rafters. His bed and the bench by the door. And Hank's motorcycle, gleaming in the light of the afternoon sun.

51

Have I ever told Aiken about my brother John?

I imagine I haven't. He knows about Samuel. Tammy's stepfather, another hard-luck story. But I don't believe I've talked much about John. Too painful, I suppose. To Henry, years ago, when we were first married, but just a little. We gave Aiken his middle name, of course. I even think of John when I see Aiken. Looks just like him.

When I was a little girl, John was already a man, old enough to join the Army. I remember how handsome he was in his uniform, his hair cut short like there was a girl he wanted to impress. Oh, I know that's normal for the Army, Aiken looked the same when he joined, but I didn't know that at the time. It seemed funny to me. That's the last real image I have of him, waving goodbye as he walked down the porch steps.

My mother cried, I remember that. And because she was sad, all the rest of us were sad, too, including me, even though I didn't understand what was happening. Johnny had given me a present, a little toy soldier he said would help me remember him, and I carried that around. I loved that soldier. And he kissed me on the lips. I remember that, too, because it was so odd. He hugged me often, even kissed me on the cheek or the top of my head sometimes when we were horsing around. But that day he kissed me on the lips.

After he left, the family talked about him all the time, as if he'd just gone down the hill to visit his girlfriend. "Oh, let's wait till Johnny gets back," someone would say. "Be sure to tell Johnny about that when he gets here," as if Johnny would be home in a few minutes. There were letters from him now and then. I didn't really understand letters, I think, since I couldn't read yet, or not much anyway. But everyone treated those letters so special, as if Johnny himself had walked through the door instead of a scrap of paper delivered by the mailman. Momma would carry the letter into the house, open the curtains because it was usually so dark in there, and she'd plop down in her sewing chair. Then she'd fix her glasses on her nose while everyone else got settled, the little ones on the floor, the rest of us on the benches around the dining table.

Where's Poppa in this picture? He must be there. Momma would have waited for him to come home to read the letter, so he must be there. Maybe he's leaning against the door, behind us all, so I can't see him. No, there he is: I can smell his pipe, that sweet ginger smell that swirled around his head.

"Dear Momma and Daddy and everybody," Johnny would usually start. Then the letter would say something like, "it's cold here, not like home," or "the rain here turns everything to mud, not like home." He compared everything to home. I guess that's the only way he could make any sense out of it. They were in Italy, I think, and he got hold of some cheese and bread, and he didn't like it much because it wasn't like the kind we could get right in our own Valley. And the people were different, friendly enough he said, but he couldn't get over not being able to speak to them, since all he ever did at home was talk. We loved to hear Momma read those letters. It was better than listening to the radio, which was full of bad news.

I remember that the letters stopped. Then there was talk about why we hadn't heard from Johnny in a while. The weather had been bad, someone said, so probably the mail was slow. Or they were real busy with the fighting, although I didn't understand about the fighting. Or ... and no one would ever finish the thought. What was the one other reason Johnny might have for not writing? And then the grownups stopped talking about him completely. If I mentioned something about Johnny, to Momma or my sister, they'd say, "Hush, Ruth, you don't know what you're talking about."

I found out later—much later—that they'd had a telegram from the Army. Johnny had been killed. Shot in the head by a sniper. And that's why they stopped talking about him. They didn't tell me, though. They didn't think I'd understand, so they just didn't tell me.

When Aiken went off to his war, I remembered Johnny. When we'd get a letter and we'd sit in the living room reading it out loud to each other, I remembered.

But Johnny never came home. Except my memories of him don't stop. I see him as clear as Brother Mountain on a winter's morning in my remembrance of the day I graduated high school. He's beaming his proud smile, standing erect in his pretty uniform, trousers flapping in the breeze, cap in hand. And when Hank was born, and especially when Aiken came. When I needed him, he was there. When Hank died, Johnny was here.

* * *

Just now there were loud voices downstairs. I thought it might be Aiken and Soon-hee, but I listened and heard Jake. He was asking for money. As if the poor girl had any money! Where would she get money?

52

The mother of Ay-ken is sick. But I think it is not her body
that ails. She is lonely for her husband. I have seen this
before in Pae-tu. I have the power to heal her body, if she
will let me, but I do not know if I can ease her true pain. I
can chase away the spirits that afflict her. But I cannot make
her forget. I cannot erase the memories.

I will do what I can do.

Either the ghosts will come to her, or she must go to the
ghosts.

When Jay-ke comes, he is drunk. Ha-neul is with Ay-ken,
building the spirit houses. I look toward the barn, but Jay-ke
pushes me inside.

"We had a deal," he says.

"Deal?" I ask.

"Here's what I think," he says. "You're holding out on
me. You moved in here and you got the old biddy to tell you
where it is."

"Jake? Is that you?" It is the mother of Ay-ken calling from upstairs.

"She is too sick," I say.

"Don't give me that crap," he says.

"Is that you, Jake?" The mother of Ay-ken stands at the top of the stairs.

"How are you feeling, Aunt Ruth? I just stopped by to see if you needed anything."

"I thought I heard shouting," she says. "Is there something wrong?"

"Nothing wrong," he says. "I just couldn't find her, is all."

"He is going," I say. And I open the door, looking out toward the barn, hoping Ay-ken will see.

53

I'm so tired all the time now. But it seems important for me to finish these stories. If I don't tell them, they will be lost forever. I will be lost forever.

So here's something else I want to say.

I had hoped to go to college. This was the fifties and some girls went to college, Sweetbriar or Hollins or Randolph-Macon, but not so many from around Typton. I don't think they prepared us for it in high school. They should have. I remember the boys had math and science, but we took sewing and cooking. I think I took typing, too, although I never thought I'd be a good secretary. Typing was just something they thought the girls needed to know.

I thought I might write. You know, novels and such. And not just trash. Good stuff. Not that I read any of the good books these days. I don't know who I thought I was. But even if they'd prepared us, even if I'd been smart enough, there was no money. I couldn't have gone to college.

When Johnny didn't come home from the war, the family spun apart, slowly at first and then all at once. Momma and

Poppa were still there, but it seemed like they didn't speak to each other much. I think Momma blamed him for Johnny going off to the Army, but that wasn't a choice anyone could make, was it? Not then. Not in those times. And maybe she blamed the rest of us, too. My brother Robert, he passed away when Aiken was in high school. The second son, he had so many expectations heaped upon him when John died. Poppa's business was ailing, always on the brink of disaster, and Robert was stuck in it, no options there at all unless he ran away or defied Poppa somehow. So he couldn't leave and instead sulked. He married that fool Lettie, just to get out of the house, but his life didn't get any better.

And there was Helen. She didn't have it any better than Robert, I'm afraid. She was stuck, too, taking care of us younger ones, and the house, and seemed little more than a maid. Nanny to me and Joseph, cook and laundress. I don't know if Momma resented her, or was just training her for the future, or what. But by the time I'd finished high school and was already engaged to Henry, it was clear that Helen was never leaving, would never have a house of her own to care for. When I think of Helen now, and how I took Henry away from her, there's a shiver that runs up and down my spine.

I sometimes think she's standing right behind, watching, as if waiting for me to stumble. She learned what I learned from the old women in the hills. She had the power to seek revenge, if that's what she wanted. I feel her here now. But surely that's just a draft, the wind swirling through these old, cracked walls.

The middle boys, Samuel and Benjamin, always managed to find trouble. And when they did, usually one blamed the other. After a while they left home and took off in opposite directions. To this day they don't speak.

I wonder what would have become of Hank if he'd lived. Aiken admired him so, but there were seeds of resentment even then, and signs that history would be repeated. Would they have feuded, like brothers seem to do?

But no, that isn't what I wanted to say. What I wanted to say was about Archie, Henry's brother. Jake's daddy. I remember him from the wedding, a handsome, strong man. They were rivals. I could see that. In the games they played, in the household. Sometimes Archie came to me when Henry was away, and I would barricade the door, not trusting him, not trusting myself. When their father passed on, the boys fought endlessly and finally Archie disappeared. Henry thought he never came back.

But that isn't what I wanted to say, either.

It makes me tired, just to think about it.

54

Aiken listens outside his mother's door while she speaks into her recorder. He can't make out everything, but he hears her say, "tired," and soon the voice stops as she drifts off to sleep. He's known for some time that she'd embarked on this storytelling project, another of Tammy's silly notions, but he can't imagine why. Hasn't he lived with these stories his entire life? Hasn't he seen the photo albums, and listened to her as she pointed at the faces and remembered who this gaunt uncle was, which homely aunt stayed home and never married? What more could she possibly have to say?

He returns to work in the barn. He sold more birdhouses at the market that weekend and is encouraged to create more designs. One idea in particular seems promising, since two have sold, despite their higher price. There used to be an old shed up on the hill above the farmhouse. He isn't sure what the shed was used for originally, since even when he was in high school it stood empty. But he remembers, or thinks he remembers, years earlier it had held tools for the timber work—saws and ropes, a ladder, a sled for hauling logs—that once was a part of the farm's operation. It had collapsed, finally, from neglect and weather, and he saw an opportunity. He'd pulled out of the wreckage the weathered boards and the twisted tin roof, and he'd cut them into pieces following a new pattern. Assembly was simple—he even used the rusted nails he'd salvaged—and he knew the houses would sell, even though they looked more like outhouses than homes for birds. He plans to make more of these, and then when the shed debris is gone he'll track down another source of weathered lumber. With all of the run-down farms in the county, that shouldn't be hard.

After he's finished working for the day, and has had supper with Henry—Soon-hee fixed soup for his mother and sits with her while she eats in her room—he goes down to the Turtle. He has cash, for a change, and he can pay off his bar tab, with a little something for Rick besides. But it's a weeknight, and the Turtle is quiet. After a couple of beers, his solitary celebration over, he heads for his truck.

"Aiken?"

He turns to the voice behind him and stops. "Kelly," he says as she approaches.

They walk together, neither speaking, until they come to his pickup. He has his keys in his hand and expects Kelly to keep walking, to end their awkward silence by disappearing into the night. But she doesn't leave. She stands next to him, even moving closer on the sidewalk to let a young couple pass.

"I put the birdhouse in the front yard," Kelly says. "I couldn't believe it, but a pair of bluebirds moved in almost immediately, even though it's so late in the season. I know it's my imagination, but I can't help thinking they like it because it looks just like the big house. That sounds crazy, doesn't it?"

"I don't think that's crazy. That's why we make birdhouses in the first place, right? If you leave it up to the birds, they'll build their nest in some hole in a tree, or your gutter. My dad every year had to clean out the tractor because a bird had built a nest in it. But we know if we build a house that looks like a house, the crazy things will love it. And if it looks like the big house, so much the better. I think it's the house they like."

"You've been thinking about this, Aiken? Birdhouses?" She's grinning now, but she's still standing close.

"What's wrong with that?" He doesn't mean to be defensive, but he knows that's how he sounds.

"I didn't say there was anything wrong with it. It's just a funny topic of conversation, is all."

"What should we talk about then?"

Common Grounds is right across the street. He points to the coffee house.

"You want to go in and talk about something other than birdhouses?" He knows his tone is sharp, and it's a dumb way to ask for a date, if that's what he's doing. And if it is, does that mean he's given up on Soon-hee?

Kelly lowers her eyes, and now she does step away. "I didn't mean to make you mad, Aiken. I think it's fine. Really, I do."

She hasn't said yes to his invitation, but she hasn't left yet, either. He smiles, to tell her he's not angry, to apologize if that's how he sounded. She follows him to the corner and across the street. And now she passes through the door he holds open.

They sit at the table by the window, and he buys coffee for them both. The table, with a chessboard painted in the center, wobbles, and he avoids leaning toward her, although he wants to. She's wearing the perfume she always used to wear that smells vaguely of lemon and cinnamon. He never asked the name when they were dating, but now he wishes he had.

"What shall we talk about?" he asks. It's been so long since they spoke. So much has happened. He's not able to talk about the war, even all these years later. What then?

"I want you to tell me about your little boy," Kelly says. "He looked so cute holding your hand, wearing that little red tie."

He isn't sure when she's seen them together, but then remembers his father's funeral, where Kelly had stood at the back of the crowd of mourners.

"He's a great kid. I don't think he understood what was happening that day, but he figures most stuff out fast. He knows that his mom and I don't talk much." He doesn't want to talk about Soon-hee, and he senses Kelly stiffen at the mention of her. "I think he has a good idea why. But it's a little better for him now, even though it's plain weird for me—me living in the barn and his mom living in the house. My folks' house."

Kelly arches her eyebrows at that and he has to explain how the living arrangements came to be.

"And, to tell the truth, it's been a big help. With my father ... and Ma being sick lately, she needs help with the cleaning and whatnot, not to mention someone to take care of her. She won't go to the doctor, no matter how much I wheedle at her, so the best option we've got is my ... Henry's mom." He lifts his coffee cup and sets the table wobbling. He grips the leg with one hand to keep it steady.

"I could come out and talk to your mother," Kelly says. "It wouldn't be the first house call this nurse has made."

"As I recall, you used to make a lot of house calls."

Kelly's face turns a deep red and she sips from her coffee, letting the cup linger at her lips as if she's hiding from him.

He wishes he'd kept his mouth shut. He'll only make matters worse if he says more.

They agree that Kelly will come to the farm the next day. It will be awkward for him, having Kelly and Soon-hee meet, but it's what his mother needs. He drives her home and starts to get out of the truck, but she puts her hand on his arm to stop him. It's like their school days, when he couldn't walk her to the door because of her mother, except that now she's the one who seems hard, distant. He wonders what's waiting inside for her, what's stopping her from opening up to him.

The next day, a chilly, overcast afternoon, he's working in the barn. Perched on a stool, he's finishing one of the weathered-wood houses, applying glue to the tin roof. He hears the rattling of the door as it's pushed open, feels the rush of cooler air, but he's concentrating on the work and doesn't look up.

"Aiken," says a woman's voice.

The voice is Kelly's, and he recognizes her scent. He wants to welcome her, to try to get past the wall that seems to have grown between them, but he's at a critical juncture in the assembly and can't stop. He presses the roof firmly onto the frame.

"This is amazing. How many are there?"

He's fixing clamps to the house now, still unable to look away. "How many what?"

"Birdhouses. There must be a hundred."

"More like three." He tightens the last clamp, then climbs off the stool. He takes her by the hand and leads her to the rear stalls. He's finally put in light fixtures back there, and now he throws the switch, illuminating shelves that line two of the stalls, all stacked with houses. In the center of one stall is a table holding his woodpecker cathedral. He's rigged a spotlight to show off the massive church. In the next stall, another spotlight shines on his Chrysler Tower.

"They're beautiful. I had no idea. I thought . . . I guess I thought you'd made just the one. Silly of me. Why would you make a house just for me?"

They've now come back to the workbench and he's cleaning up before he takes Kelly to see his mother.

"But I did, in a way. Honestly, the first house I made was that ugly one on the fence post." He points out the window. "And then I made this one." He lays his hand on the original saltbox, mounted on the wall just above the bench. "That was when I moved out of our little house and was . . . confused. I missed Henry, I think, and made it to remind me. And then I saw you and your house, and to tell the truth it brought back a lot of good memories, so I had to make that one. All the others just spilled out after that. I'm not sure why, or how. Something about being back here after so many years, I guess. More often than not, I don't know where the ideas come from."

They close up the barn and cross the drive to the house. As they enter, Soon-hee is coming out of the kitchen and stops. The two women watch each other. Aiken looks from Soon-hee to Kelly and back. He never thought this moment would happen, and he doesn't know what to say.

"This is Kelly," he says to Soon-hee. "She's a nurse. She's going to take a look at Ma."

Soon-hee says nothing. Kelly offers her hand and Soon-hee takes it, limply. They stand together that way for a moment, touching, until Soon-hee withdraws her hand. She leads the way upstairs, knocks on his mother's door, and pushes it open. She crosses to the window, pulls the curtain wide, and light fills the room.

His mother squints and turns away from the light. "Who's that?" she says.

"You remember Kelly, Ma? From school? I told her you weren't feeling well so she wanted to come by and see how you're doing." He's decided not to remind her that Kelly's a nurse, in case his mother's distrust of doctors extends to everyone in the medical profession.

"Aiken, I'm not a dunce, you know. Of course I remember Kelly. It was me who caught you two after all."

At that, Kelly blushes. Aiken glances at Soon-hee, standing in the doorway, to see if she's heard, but there is no change in her expression. She shuffles into the room, places a small bundle on the nightstand, and then returns to her place by the door. It looks like some kind of doll made of straw, but it fills the room with a sweet fragrance.

"And don't you think I don't know what you're doing. I knew before you did when Kelly went away to nursing school, so I'm perfectly aware why she's here. Hello, dear. Come sit beside me." She pats the bed covers and Kelly sits, taking the old woman's hand.

Soon-hee bows slightly and backs into the hall. He hears her footsteps on the stairs.

"That's Aiken's wife, you know," his mother says. "She's a shy thing."

"Leave us now, Aiken," Kelly says as she wraps her hand around his mother's wrist and studies her watch. The command is a surprise, not an unwelcome one. He leaves and closes the door.

In the kitchen, Soon-hee doesn't look at him. A tea kettle is already steaming on the stove; she pulls a tray from the cupboard, takes out cups and saucers. Without a word she carries the tray upstairs.

* * *

Kelly rejoins him in the barn. This time he stops working the moment she opens the door. The overhead lamps aren't on and the barn is dim.

"There's only so much I can say without having tests done." She stands near the door, her hands folded in front of her. "You need to convince her to see a doctor."

"I don't think she will," he says.

"She has a growth in her abdomen. I can tell that much. It could be harmless. But it's making her uncomfortable, at the very least, and should be treated. And if it's *not* harmless, then . . ."

He waits for her to say more and looks into her eyes. She turns away. She didn't say "cancer," but he assumes that's what she means, and he doesn't want to talk about it any more than she does. It's so soon after his father's death that he doesn't even want to think about it. He picks up the birdhouse trim he'd been sanding when she came in and turns it over in his hand. As a cloud moves on, light streams through the window and stretches to Kelly's feet.

"Why did you leave?" he asks.

"I told you. There's nothing more I can do without tests. And she was tired."

"I mean before."

Kelly moves a few more feet into the barn, moving out of the light. There's still a gulf between them.

"I knew what you meant, Aiken," she says. "You left first."

"But you knew I was coming back."

"I knew you wanted me to follow you. I also knew that if I didn't, you might drag me wherever it was you were going. I didn't think you'd let me be the one to decide for myself."

"Was I that horrible?"

"Honestly? At times, you could be smothering. And other times . . ."

He sets the trim on the workbench. "I would have treated you good, Kel."

"Did you treat me that way when we were kids? You don't remember, do you? It wasn't always good." Kelly pulls the door open. "Get your mother to see a doctor." The door closes behind her.

He picks Henry up from school and they enter the house together. Soon-hee is upstairs with Aiken's mother, so he pours milk for the boy and himself, gets them both a couple of Soon-hee's new and improved oatmeal cookies, and they sit together at the kitchen table.

"Bobby Barker ate paste today," Henry says.

"You wouldn't do that, would you, son?"

Henry shakes his head. "That's gross. Bobby Barker is a booger."

He conceals his laughter by biting into a cookie.

Soon-hee joins them and listens to Henry talk about his day at school. When Henry has gone up to his room, Aiken says, "Kelly—the nurse—thinks Ma needs to see a doctor." He's never sure if Soon-hee understands him. Her head is bowed now and he can't see her eyes. "But she doesn't want to go. And she won't listen to me. It would be great if you could convince her. I think she might listen to you."

Soon-hee's head bobs and she leaves him.

* * *

He's in the barn when he hears a car pull into the drive, along with Ralph's urgent barking. He comes out to investigate, and a man wearing a checked sport coat and bow tie is standing next to a black Expedition. The massive Ford makes the man look like a child, despite his gray hair and paunch.

"Are you Aiken Alexander?" The man sticks out his hand. "Virgil McNeal." They shake, and McNeal thrusts a business card at Aiken, which he takes.

"Wife's got a place in town you probably heard of. The Stillwater Shop?" Aiken shakes his head, but the man goes on. "I'm in insurance myself," he says, pointing to the card in Aiken's hand, "but I help out at the store."

"I don't think we need any insurance, Mr. McNeal," Aiken says.

The man laughs. "I could probably convince you otherwise, Aiken, but that's not why I'm here. We heard folks talk about your birdhouses. Seems you've been selling 'em at the Saturday market, and Alice, that's my wife, she thought they might move real well at our place. You sell more birdhouses, we take a little cut, everybody's happy." The proposition is something Aiken never dreamed of, but then he hadn't thought about selling the birdhouses at all until a few weeks ago.

"That's kind of you, Mr. McNeal. Mind if I think about it some? Right now I don't mind just selling at the market, you know?"

"Market closes come winter, Aiken. Then what?"

"Hadn't thought about that yet. But I will."

"Going to wait for some kind of sign? Don't wait too long, young man. Opportunities don't last forever."

55

Aiken's mother still has not agreed to see a doctor, although it's obvious how uncomfortable she is. When she tries to move, she is nearly doubled over, hands clutching her stomach, and pain constricts her face. Soon-hee does every-thing for her now: helps her to the bathroom, bathes her, cooks for him and Henry, cleans. Drifting in and out of sleep most of the day, she doesn't seem to be aware of his presence even if he sits in her room, breathing the sour air, peering at her in the darkness, and yet he doesn't want to be far away. So, on Friday night, he decides to skip the Saturday market. Henry whines when Aiken tells him, and Soon-hee insists that they go.

"No fun for Ha-neul in the house now, bad for health," she says. "Go to market."

"We shouldn't leave Ma," Aiken says.

"I am here," Soon-hee says. "I will take care."

Reluctantly, Aiken loads the truck. This time he takes the cathedral birdhouse with him along with dozens of the smaller houses. He covers them all with the tarp, and before dawn on Saturday he and Henry head into Stillwater. While Aiken is setting up, the man with the clipboard comes by. He doesn't say anything. He stands in front of the display, waiting. Aiken pulls a ten-dollar bill from his wallet, pleased that it's like plucking one leaf from a full bush.

There's no room on the table for the cathedral, so Aiken balances it on the gate of the truck and angles the two risers to funnel attention toward the big bird church. He goes around to the front to look at the arrangement from the customer's point of view and can't help but grin when he sees it.

"What are you smiling about there, Aiken?" Charlie Doak asks as he sets up his vegetable stand. Charlie comes around his table to join Aiken. "My Lord. I've never in all my days seen such a thing. No wonder you're grinning like a fat cat. I'm going to have to get me some fancier tomatoes to compete with that!"

The cathedral attracts a steady flow of gawkers all morning. Although Aiken had decided he wasn't charging enough for the birdhouses, and has raised the price to fifteen dollars, he sells so many he loses count. While he digs under the tarp for more houses to replenish the riser display, or counts out change, or packs purchases in bubble wrap, Henry occupies himself with buyers.

"My dad makes 'em in our barn," he says to a woman waiting to pay for a Cape Cod. He points to a saltbox. "These ones look just like our old house. We got one at home that looks like a spaceship."

Aiken hears that and laughs, because it does look like a spaceship. "It's a skyscraper, Henry."

"Looks like a spaceship to me. And we got a . . . a dapoga."

"A pagoda, Henry."

"My grandpa lives in it," Henry says.

The woman leans forward, a puzzled expression clouding her face.

"It's Korean," he says, realizing it explains nothing.

"I love the church," the woman says.

Another couple is standing at the table, examining a new Cape Cod he's added to the display. The woman picks it up and they study the hinges on the floor, the black shutters, the perfect joints. "Nice work," the man says.

"It's so big, though," says the woman looking at the church.

"It's for woodpeckers," Henry says.

Another man asks, "How do you make those buttresses?" He points to the cathedral.

"It's not so hard, really, I start—"

"You could sell tickets to people. To watch. I've seen something like it up in Richmond. I bet you could do it."

Henry falls asleep on the ride home. Aiken's worn out, too, but he's amused by how much his son seems to love talking to people, as though it's his job to chat with the customers. They make a good team. His wallet is so full of fives and tens that he'd barely been able to fold it into his pocket at the end of the morning.

Soon-hee comes down as soon as they enter the house. Aiken is scrounging in the refrigerator, but he stops when he sees Soon-hee's wide eyes.

"Bring the nurse?" she asks.

He runs to his mother's room. She's white, ghostly in the darkened room, and clutches her abdomen.

"Let me take you to the hospital, Ma. You've got to get this looked at."

"People die in that hospital, Aiken. If I'm going to die, I want to do it right here."

He dials Kelly's phone number. The phone rings three times, four, five. Where is she? Six, seven. He's thinking of getting in his truck and going to look for her when she picks up. "Hello?"

"Can you come see her?" he asks, without a greeting. "Can you get a doctor to come out here?"

Kelly goes directly into his mother's room. By the time the doctor arrives, she has made it clear to her that there's no choice, that they need to know what's causing so much pain. Maybe they can take care of it at home without going to the hospital. But they need to know. His mother's head moves. She may be saying no, or yes.

When Dr. Solomon comes, she lies quietly, lets him probe, answers his questions. He's distinguished looking, tall, with gray-flecked black hair and dark-rimmed glasses. She swallows the medication he offers, but when he says they need to move her to the hospital, she shakes her head.

"I'm not going," she says.

"It would be best," says the doctor.

"No," she says.

On the way into the kitchen, Dr. Solomon whispers in Kelly's ear and she blushes. Aiken looks from her face to the doctor's and back, wondering if this is Kelly's secret, the reason she's so distant. He pours coffee for them both. Whatever the doctor's relationship with Kelly, having him in the house makes Aiken feel better. Kelly trusts him. Even if his mother won't budge, Aiken knows he's done what he can.

"I've never seen such a stubborn old woman," he says.

"Then you haven't seen very many old women," the doctor says. "It's understandable. She's home here. She's in her own bed, with family to care for her. Why would she want to go to a hospital where the mattresses are too hard, the sheets chafe, and the food alone is enough to kill you. I don't blame her."

Solomon explains that she probably needs surgery, but until he takes blood tests and x-rays and an ultrasound, he can't be sure what the problem is.

"My guess is it's a tumor. And if it's malignant we need to act fast. If it's not malignant we need to figure out what caused it and prevent it from recurring. We can't do any of that here. But if she won't go, she won't go, and the best I can do is give her something for the pain."

Although his mother remains in bed, her pain is gone. Or, at least, she's hiding it better to avoid being forced into the hospital. She's sitting up. She's reading. She asks to have new batteries installed in her tape recorder. It seems as if the crisis has passed, but she still depends on Soon-hee for everything. Aiken, though, is able to return to work in the barn, despite lingering concern.

On Wednesday, when he comes back from picking Henry up at school, there's a car in the driveway. The barn door is open. He tells Henry to run inside the house. He's thinking of the coffee can full of cash that he's stuck under the workbench, wondering if someone who planned to steal from him would park out front like this. He slips into the barn.

A man and a woman are standing at the workbench, each with a birdhouse in hand, their backs to him. The man is holding a Cape Cod; the woman is admiring a new model, a townhouse with maroon and gold awnings over the windows—colors he thought might appeal to all the Virginia Tech fans in the area and possibly the start of a whole new collegiate line of houses.

"Can I help you?" Aiken asks. The woman nearly drops the house.

"You startled me," she says.

The man says, "We were told there was a shop here that sells these birdhouses."

"Just my workshop is all," Aiken says. "But I'm happy to sell those, if you're here to buy." It occurs to him that if people are willing to drive ten miles out into the country to buy his birdhouses he's still not charging enough. "Those are twenty dollars each."

The man pulls two twenties from his wallet and hands them to Aiken, who folds the bills and slips them into his shirt pocket. He switches on all the lights and shows them the collection that has been growing in the stalls—a virtual museum now with the spot-lit displays. He appreciates the man's whistle at the sight of the cathedral.

"I'm about to get back to work, if you want to stay and watch," he says, and he means it as a way of getting these people out of his hair. But the woman nods enthusiastically, so he sets up the rough-hewn bench at a spot near the table saw where they'll have a good view of the next step in his process. He's working on another new design, this time a purple martin house in the style of a southern plantation. He's sketched the house on a wide sheet of paper and taped that to the barn wall. He points out the tall columns and series of dormers on both sides of the roof and finds that he appreciates having an audience to explain things to. He's already cut all the pieces and he's now at the stage of assembling the house, from the inside out, since, unlike the other styles he's built, this one has many separate nesting boxes inside.

The couple settles onto the bench. The woman holds her purse in her lap and the man shifts his bulk from side to side. He tugs at the crotch of his pants, loosens his jacket, lifts his foot to examine the sole of his shoe.

"We're the Rowleys. I'm Amy and this is my husband Mark. We're from Maryland."

"Is that right?" Aiken concentrates on attaching the dormers to the roof. It doesn't take much thought, and it won't matter if these folks distract him, but it still makes him uncomfortable. It shouldn't be any different from when Henry watches him, but it is.

"This is what you do?" the man asks. "I mean, the birdhouses aren't just a hobby?"

Aiken draws a line across each roof, to mark where the bottom edge of the dormers will go. "There's the farm," he says, checking that he's drawn the line straight. This guy doesn't need to know that he and the family haven't worked the farm for years, that the tractors and the animals are long gone, that most of the land they have left is leased out for pasture. The lease provides his mother with some income, so it isn't a complete lie.

"Oh," says the man, his voice falling, so that Aiken understands that he hadn't really been interested in the first place. "I run a little copy shop over in Annapolis. It's no Kinko's, of course."

Aiken doesn't know what a Kinko's is, but he doesn't care enough to ask, and he doesn't want to keep the man talking, particularly. He marks the location of each dormer on the roof, four on each side, and then begins to glue them, one at a time. He looks over at the couple, sees the man has turned red, as if he might be offended that Aiken hasn't asked him about his business. They did buy two birdhouses, after all, at jacked-up prices.

"Coffee shop, huh?" Aiken asks.

"*Copy*," the man says loudly, and now the offense is clear. "I've got four machines. Of course, only one of them is your big full-function model, collates and staples and all that. High speed. Cost a fortune. The others are the coin-box type for do-it-yourselfers." Aiken nods. He's heard all he needed and didn't understand a word.

"See," Aiken says, "what I'm doing here is simple." He glues in the next piece and presses it to the roof. "I just have to hold these dormer windows in place until the glue dries. When I've done all eight of 'em I can set the roof sections aside and put the columns together with the nesting boxes. Later on I'll drill pilot holes through the roof and fix these dormers permanently in place with screws."

"Looks like a lot of extra work for a damn bird," the man says.

"Hush, Mark," the woman says.

"Seems to me everybody deserves a nice, solid roof over his head," Aiken says. "Even a bird."

The Rowleys soon leave, each carrying one of the bird-houses. But the next day he has more visitors. First is a little sports car, a model Aiken's never seen before although he recognizes the BMW medallion on the front. It's parked in the drive when he comes out of the house after breakfast. A young couple peers through the window into the barn. The woman wears a tight T-shirt with a scoop neck, and jeans slung low on her narrow hips. Her red hair frizzes out in all directions, and makes Aiken think of a circus clown. But her skin is pale and smooth. The guy is bearded, broad shouldered, about Aiken's age.

They sit and watch him work, less talkative than the Rowleys had been. After a few minutes there's a knock on the barn door and another couple enters, this one holding the hands of a little girl in pigtails. The younger man stands from the bench to make room for the new woman, a large gal in stretch pants and a bulky sweatshirt. The girl sits on her ample lap. The two men stand behind the bench.

"Sorry that we've only got standing room there, gentlemen," he says, and waits for the men to shrug in reply. He begins his show by pointing to the drawing on the wall, the southern plantation purple martin house, offering the same explanation he'd made the day before. That house still lies on the workbench with the roof, now painted a sky blue with the dormer windows white, yet to be attached. But he stops in mid-sentence when he notices the little girl yawn. "I'll be right back," he says, and jogs to the back of the barn.

He returns with two birdhouses, a new design he's been working on that he thinks the child might like better than the plantation house. Her eyes open wide when she sees it. He calls it his gingerbread house. He's borrowed some of the details from a cottage in the old part of Stillwater, lacy scrolls along the edge of the roof, trim over the windows. And, remembering the gingerbread houses his mother had made when he was a boy, Aiken has painted candy canes on each side of the door. To Aiken they look a little too much like barber poles, but the girl doesn't seem to care.

"Look, Mommy, candy canes," she says.

The other house is plain wood, still unpainted, not even fully assembled. Aiken lifts off the roof. "What colors should we paint this one?" he asks the girl.

"Pink," she says, without hesitation.

"Is that your favorite color?"

She nods. He doesn't have pink paint, but he opens a can of red, mixes it with white, and does the first coat on the house. He paints the dormers pink, too, but the rest of the roof he does in slate, with the scroll and window trim a bright white. When the paint has dried—he's set up a fan to speed the process—he attaches the roof to the walls. The girl's parents buy the pink house, the model with the candy canes, plus a Cape Cod.

The young couple tours the stalls in back and the man lingers over the cathedral and the skyscraper.

"It's too big for the car," he says. Then he comes to the pagoda, which Aiken has put in its own stall, with its own spotlight. "But this one is perfect. We're going for an Asian theme in our house. How much for this temple thing?"

The pagoda is one of his favorites, the one Henry call's "Grandpa's house." He isn't sure Soon-hee has seen it yet and he's wanted to give it to her, a reminder of home and their trip to Beopjusa. But he's got a willing buyer, a bird in the hand, so to speak, and he can always make a new one. He looks at the tall birdhouse, remembers those happy early days with Soon-hee in Seoul.

"It's not for sale," he says.

In the afternoon, he devotes time to building bleachers. If he's going to keep having visitors, he can't expect them to sit on the little bench, or just stand. So he copies the design for the display risers he made and builds a larger-scale platform, with three benches. He braces the risers along the back wall of the barn and tests their sturdiness by jumping from one level to the next. Now he's ready for a show.

His mother is awake and reading, with the curtains open and the room bright and airy. He calls Kelly to tell her that his mother seems to be doing much better. But there's more he wants to say.

"Last time at the coffee shop didn't go so well," he says.

"All things considered, I thought it was okay," she says.

"Still, I'd like to try again, if you're willing."

"What's the point, Aiken?"

"Old times," he says.

"I'm seeing someone, you know."

"So I gathered," he says.

"And you're married."

Yes, he's married. For now. "Still. I'd like to talk."

They meet the next morning at Common Grounds, after he's dropped Henry at school. They get coffee, they sit at the same wobbly table.

"It would mean a lot to me if you could come visit her again," he says. "The pills have helped, but I know it's not solving the real problem."

"I don't think it will do any good, Aiken. She's made up her mind. But I'll be happy to try."

"Henry wants you to come, too. He likes you."

"Could that have anything to do with the sucker I gave him?"

"It might. But he really wants you to see the show. In the barn." He explains that the business is taking off and that customers now are coming to him. He might even stop going to the farmers' market on Saturdays, although he and Henry both enjoy the outing.

"So, you're doing well?"

"I am. It's a little lonely out in the barn, though."

They haven't talked about her divorce, and they haven't really talked about Soon-hee, either, about the fact that her presence out at the farm is a temporary arrangement, to help his mother. For that matter, he hasn't spoken to Soon-hee about it. He knows he's never been good at communicating, not with Hank, not with his father, but especially not with women. Soon-hee can't read his mind. Neither can Kelly.

"You know we're not together, right? She's in the house to take care of Henry and Ma. But that's it."

"She's young, isn't she? Barely twenty, from the looks of her, and she's got a five-year-old boy. That doesn't look very good, Aiken." She stares directly at him.

He looks away. This was a mistake. He can't fix what he's done. He can't go back. He's close to standing up, walking away, saying goodbye forever. She's moved on; he should do the same. But he doesn't do that.

"He's only four," Aiken says. "But no, it doesn't look good. I don't know what to say, Kelly. It happened, that's all. I was in the Army. I missed you. She was there. It happened."

"That's the thing, Aiken. It doesn't just 'happen.' There's no mysterious force that drives people. Things like that happen because you want them to happen, regardless of what anyone else wants. Your problem is you don't think about anyone but yourself and you don't think about the consequences of what you do."

He doesn't know how to respond. She's right. She never said anything like that to him when they were younger, but she's right. He sips his coffee. He notices that the crazy paintings are gone from the walls of the shop, replaced by somber photographs of homeless people. He doesn't want to talk about Soon-hee anymore, or anything else that happened in the past. He has no excuses for his behavior. He's truly sorry for what he did, but there's nothing he can do to change anything. Is sorry enough? He watches an old couple, both gray and slightly stooped, stroll by on the sidewalk outside. How long have they been together? Forty years? Fifty? How did they manage it?

"I wasn't completely honest with you about why I left," Kelly says. Now he looks at her. "I loved you. I really did. As much as a teenager can love someone. I thought we'd spend our lives together. But that time, in that cabin, you were wild."

The cabin. He'd forgotten about the cabin. Uncle Sam's place at the lake. It was supposed to be special. A celebration. He'd explain everything to her, about the Army and their future together, and they'd make love and it would be like they were the only people in the world. But she didn't want to go. She told him to take her home. He couldn't do that. He needed to make her see.

"You forced me . . . and I didn't want it. All the other times, sure. Just not that time." Her voice is low. He can barely hear over the clanking of dishes at the counter, the whoosh of the steamer. "Nobody would have listened to me if I'd accused you of . . . that, but that's what it was."

"Kelly—"

"You know it was. Don't look so shocked, Aiken. It's not like I was a virgin. But you forced me when I didn't want to. What you did was wrong. I hated you after that."

"That's not what happened. I explained it all to you. The Army. Our future. We were celebrating. Don't you remember? It was a good night."

"No, Aiken, it wasn't. You're fooling yourself if that's what you think. It was a nightmare. Is that what you did to that girl? Your wife? Kidnap her and force her to have sex?"

His hands tremble, and he sets the coffee cup on the table between them. He's thought of that night, when Kelly had been so distant at first, angry about the Army. But she'd given herself freely, just like all the other nights. Hadn't she? How could that have been wrong? The image he's had in his head for so long, once so clear, blurs. Isn't that how it happened? Isn't it?

"Soon-hee was too young," he says, nearly whispering. "Seventeen, as it turned out. I should have known better. But I didn't rape Soon-hee, and I sure as hell didn't rape you."

"Saying so doesn't make it true, Aiken. I know what happened. I was there, too."

Can he apologize for something he doesn't think he did? Will it help? What can he do to make it right? He's aware of people watching them, the teenagers at the table next to them, the old couple out on the street peering in through the window, the guy behind the counter. Their eyes spin around him, accusing him. But now he sees the cabin, sees Kelly huddled under a blanket, as far away from him as she could get. And there's something else about that night.

"Kelly . . ." he says. He isn't sure how to ask. "When you left . . . were you pregnant?"

She stands. He can't look at her, doesn't want to see the hatred in her eyes. Because she must still hate him for what he did, and he still loves her.

"Yes," she says. And leaves.

56

Aiken sits with his mother. He's troubled by what Kelly said, and even more troubled that he doesn't know what happened to the baby, or why she's never told him. He loved her and would never have done anything to hurt her. But he's no longer sure what really happened that night. How could he be the person Kelly remembers? Or the one that Soon-hee remembers? He made mistakes, he knows that, but that's not who he is. He's never been that man.

The sky outside his mother's window is hazy and soft. There's a splash of color on the hillside, red and gold among the evergreens. Every year when he sees this change, the last turning of the wheel before it all begins again, the death followed by rebirth, it's as if he's seeing it for the first time. He watches as the trees sway, like resilient, waving hands.

"Aiken?" His mother has been sleeping, and her voice is raspy and low. "I want to tell you about Hank," she says.

She's been telling stories lately. About her childhood, about her brother Johnny, about school, courtship, the early days of her marriage. He knows it's because she doesn't want the stories to be forgotten, and so he listens. He knows, too, that she's been telling the same stories to her tape recorder, preserving them. It's her gift to him, but he's afraid it means it will be easier for her to leave.

"You should rest, Ma."

"It's the worst thing that could happen to a mother. The worst thing." She closes her eyes, and Aiken imagines her traveling back to the day it happened. He closes his eyes, too. "You probably don't remember this, because you were so young, but your father and I were separated at the time of Hank's accident."

His eyes spring open. "No," he says. He not only doesn't remember, he finds it hard to believe.

"We hadn't decided to make it permanent, and I honestly don't think we would have. We were just angry about something, or your father was angry, and so he was staying over at Sam's, on the other side of the mountain. He came every day to see you boys and do the chores and work the farm, take care of the animals. Everything. He just didn't sleep here. You asked him where he was going and he told you something about needing to take care of Sam."

"I remember that. Uncle Sam was sick."

"That's what we told you."

"You lied to us?"

"Hank knew the truth, and he was upset. With me, mostly, because he blamed me. Whoever he was angry with, I suppose that's the reason he was going too fast on that motorcycle." She stops, and looks surprised that the tears still come after so many years. "When the sheriff called, he wouldn't tell me on the phone what had happened, just that he wanted me to come down to the hospital. I thought it was about your father, at first. I think I even said something like, 'What's the old fool done now,' but the sheriff said, 'No, ma'am, it's not Mr. Alexander.' Well, right then I knew it was Hank. I called your father at Sam's and he went down to the hospital. I couldn't go. I just sat there by the phone. You were asleep and I sat there alone, waiting for your father to call to tell me that Hank was gone."

He's heard part of this story, the version his parents had told him for years. Hank was riding the motorcycle he'd bought with the money from his part-time job at the farm co-op. He swerved to avoid a pickup that had turned into the road but lost control, spinning and sliding along the pavement like a boulder crashing down the mountain.

"He didn't call, and he didn't call, and as time passed I allowed myself to hope. I thought if the worst had happened, I would already know. He wouldn't have waited to tell me. So I looked out the window, imagining I heard your father's truck coming up the road. You remember this was a long time ago, when he had that old Dodge? It made such a ruckus. So I knew it was my imagination because I thought I heard the truck wheeze and rattle, but then it was quiet. Or I'd see headlights on the hill and I'd wonder what he was doing up there. But of course it wasn't him, it was Liza Coffey, who worked the nightshift over at the hospital and was leaving for work. And I very nearly ran out into the road to catch her, to ask for a ride up there so I could find your father.

"It didn't do any good to keep on worrying like that, but I couldn't help myself. I went upstairs and peeked in on you. The light from the hallway sliced across your bed and your arms were twisted, one above your head, one under the covers. Then I put my hand on the knob to Hank's door and prayed that he'd be lying in his bed when I looked in, that it was all a bad dream, or a mistake, that it was some other woman's child who was dead. I really thought that, you know. I didn't reproach myself for a second. I wanted what I was feeling to somehow leave me and go into the heart of someone else.

"I pushed open the door, and of course he wasn't there. The bed was mussed, as it always was unless your father and I got after him, or I just went in there and made it myself. I almost did it right then. But seeing it that way, the quilt turned back and the white sheets kind of glowing in the dim light, made him seem alive, somehow. If I made it, if I even fluffed the pillows and squared the corners on the quilt, if I tucked the blanket under the mattress, was I giving up on him? As I wondered what I should do I caught sight of his motorcycle helmet sitting on the floor of his closet. That made me gasp. I closed the door.

"I boiled water for tea. I sat at the kitchen table with a cup in front of me and heard the kettle whistle, like a train that was bearing down on me. I didn't move a muscle. I was still sitting there when your father opened the door, this heavy, sagging expression on his face, like all the juice had been sucked out of him. He had his cap in his hand. I remember he stood there just inside the door and looked at me without saying a word, turning that cap over and over and over. I think he couldn't say it. But of course he didn't need to. He went over to the stove and took the kettle off. The whistling stopped, but I could still hear it.

"I was the one who had to tell you. Do you remember? The next morning I went in to wake you, to let you know that you wouldn't be going to school that day. I sat on the edge of your bed and sobbed. I took your little hand and sobbed, and you started crying, too, not because you knew yet but because your mother was so terribly unhappy about something, and that's the way you were. The way you are.

'There's been an accident,' I managed to say. I think you said, 'Daddy?' because that's who you'd been missing. I shook my head. I don't remember if I was able to say it then. Did I say, 'Hank'?"

She hadn't. He remembers asking if it was his father, but even when she shook her head, he wasn't sure what it meant. She'd left his bedside, and he felt the bed rise when she stood up, a silly rocking sensation, like a boat on the water, that always made him laugh and did then, too. But she hadn't ever said what had happened, and so he didn't know. What was he supposed to do? How was he supposed to feel? He'd wiped away his tears and got ready for school, even though she'd told him he wasn't going. When he went downstairs his father was at the kitchen table, his head bowed as if in prayer. It was his father who told him Hank was dead.

57

The mother of Ay-ken is almost gone. It will take strong *kut*
to hold her here. She is fading, like fog in the morning sun.
I sense that she does not want to leave. That she is not ready,
that she has more to say. And so I will try. I will summon
Sansin. The Mountain God will come to us and he will give
her strength. The nurse, the woman Ta-mee tells me about,
tries to help. She is a good woman, with her own medicine.
I do not give her the dark tea that I brewed for her. I see now
she means us no harm. She too feels pain. But she cannot
help the mother of Ay-ken. And when the mother of Ay-ken
is at peace, Ha-neul and I can go home.

She is sleeping. Ha-neul is in school, and Ay-ken works in
the barn. I step onto the porch with my cloth bag, and Ralph
raises his head to look at me. He asks where I am going and
I tell him, "To the mountain."

There is a path behind the house that follows the edge of
the woods, where the forest was cleared long ago for fields.
The deer have made this path over many years, wearing the
earth smooth, and I follow. Ralph is with me, some distance

behind. I tell him to go home, but he doesn't listen. When I stop, he stops. When I go, he moves also.

We turn into the pine forest where the deer path is not so clear, and tread softly on the dry needles. I find a fungus growing on the side of a thick tree, cut it away from the bark and place it in my bag. I find pine cones—closed, like the buds of flowers, and put them in the bag. I find a piece of the antler of a deer. It is enough for my purpose, and I pick it up. I climb through the trees, higher and higher, and pass into woods that are thick with undergrowth, thorn bushes and sweetbriar. I take a walnut for the bag, green and pungent and solid, like the flesh of a horse.

I rise higher, Ralph lagging behind, and gather more of the mountain's bounty to offer Sansin: hickory nuts, with their rich brown shells and the smell of ginger and earth; tiny pink wildflowers; and bold yellow blossoms that stain my hands with gold. I am content when I reach the shrine of stones, and I turn, gazing out on the Valley. The clear sky stretches, soaring and endless, and the rolling hills try to follow. Below me, our house stands at the base of the mountain. Next to it, where Ay-ken works, the barn sleeps like a wintering beast.

In the distance, a plume of black smoke stains the horizon. It is the earth's angry breath, summoned by demons with their fires and siren shrieking. It must be stopped, this breath, before it reaches the mother of Ay-ken, or it will be too late.

I pour the contents of my bag on the sun-baked ground and arrange my offerings on the shrine. I whisper my prayer to Sansin, to come to our aid.

Ralph barks, and I look up from my devotions to see the old man, with his flowing white beard and the hickory cane.

58

When Jake comes, I tell him to stop. No more with Soon-hee.
Things have changed. With Aunt Ruth the way she is, we
can't go on.

"Let's just leave," I say. "We don't need their money. We'll
start over."

"It's not fair," he says.

"Life's not fair. Don't you know that by now?"

We're sitting out in front of my trailer, watching the sunset,
smoking a joint. He puts his arm around me, as gentle as he's
ever been, and I think if I can get him to do this one thing, to
give up his crazy notion about hidden treasure on the farm,
our future is bright. Just this one thing.

59

Why do secrets escape our lips? Why do we cling to them? I tried to tell Aiken about Hank, and I ended up speaking a half-truth. I felt—I feel—as though I'd killed Hank, had ripped him from my body and thrown him away.

Yes, Hank flew into a rage when he discovered that his father was staying up at Sam's place. He shouted terrible things at me. He blamed me for that, and for his girl going away, too, that Charlotte. It hurt me to hear these words from him, my beautiful boy who was our future, so much stronger than little Aiken, so much promise. Who would bring us grandchildren, who would fill the house with joy? He was right, though. It *was* my fault. It was *my* fault. Even the girl, who wasn't good enough, and drank the tea I gave her.

When he told us about the girl, about the baby, I raged. It was what I wanted, but too soon. Too young, both of them, and the girl wasn't right for my Hank. Not strong, like him. Not smart. I went up the mountain, found the root, invited her to visit. Henry was furious with me, the baby went away, and the girl. I suppose Hank knew. He had to know.

And so when he slapped me, when my beautiful, strong boy slapped his mother, it was my shame that brought tears to my eyes. Not the sting, not the shock of the explosion—his hand against my face. Not the look of horror in his own eyes. But the guilt. Because he was right.

He ran from the house. And I think I knew then what would happen. I saw, with the treasured vision that had faded long ago, exactly what would happen. And I could do nothing to stop it. The sad truth is that you can't change the future.

But that isn't the whole truth either.

Hank took after his granddaddy. A moody, dour man he was, always seeing the dark side, as if the shadows spoke to him, wouldn't let him see the light. As a child, Hank sulked when he didn't get his way, stormed out of the house and tramped the hills, disappearing for long dark hours. I didn't know sometimes if he was ever coming home, but what could I do? Henry wouldn't say anything to the boy.

"He'll find his way back at supper time," he'd say. "Black clouds have a way of lifting when a boy gets hungry enough."

And he always did come back. Cold and shivering, or covered with mud, he'd appear on the porch, like an apparition. Didn't say a word, and I never knew what he did up in those hills. The moods would pass, eventually, and we'd carry on.

Aiken doesn't remember, but I suspect that jealousy played a part in Hank's moods. It's not as if we treated Aiken any better. If anything, the opposite was true. We hadn't counted on Aiken, and sometimes it seemed like he might not ever grow up. A sickly child—he doesn't seem to remember that either—he drained attention from Hank. Older children always resent the younger ones, probably since the beginning of time. Like Helen resented me, I suppose.

Could we have done anything to reassure him? To let him know we still loved him? A farm is like … I don't know, like a magnet. It grabs onto everything—time, energy, money—and there's nothing left. There was nothing left for Hank, I'm afraid. At least, that's how he felt. And when children, especially moody boys haunted by so many grievances, get to feeling they can't win, that there will never be enough for them, they lash out. That's the way it was with Hank. He'd get angry with his father, or me, or his little brother. He'd shout things. He'd twist Aiken's arm until the shrieks could be heard from here to Roanoke. When that happened, Henry had to exact a price. We didn't spare the rod. But it only made things worse.

I never did find out where he got it, but once I discovered Hank sitting on his bed, cross-legged, staring at a gun, some kind of pistol, that lay on the bedspread a few inches from his feet. At first I thought it was a toy, although neither one of the boys had ever shown much interest in such things. We own a shotgun and a hunting rifle that Henry keeps under lock and key, and we'd taught Hank how to use those and take care of them, something most boys in the country learn. I looked more closely, and I could see the pistol was no toy.

"What's that?" I asked.

Hank glared at me, as he sometimes did.

"Where did you get it, Hank? Whose is it?"

"Found it," he said, and he looked away, back toward the gun.

"I guess we better put it in the gun box, then. Okay? That's how we take care of the guns, remember?"

"It's mine," he said. "I found it."

"Okay, honey, it's yours. But let's put it away."

He didn't answer, and I didn't know what to do. I wanted to get Henry, so that he could take the gun and lock it away.

But I didn't want to leave Hank. I didn't think he would hurt himself, but I didn't know what might happen when he got into one of his moods, and . . . I was afraid. So I stood there with him, listening for Aiken so I could send him out to the barn to find his father. I wasn't going to leave Hank alone.

"How was school today?" I asked.

He didn't answer. He stared at the gun.

"I baked an apple pie this morning," I said. "And we have ice cream. Doesn't that sound good?" I heard the tractor start up outside and knew that Henry wouldn't be coming in anytime soon. Hank only stared at the gun.

"We could have some now," I said. "Won't that be fun? Dessert before dinner, just this once?"

The screen door slammed downstairs, and Hank and I both turned our heads toward the sound of Aiken tramping up the steps. Hank grabbed a pillow and set it on top of the pistol, and we waited for Aiken's arrival.

While the boys ate pie and ice cream, I went back upstairs, retrieved the gun, and hid it. Later, Henry locked it with the others, and Hank never mentioned it again.

The night Hank ran from the house, after he'd slapped me and shouted those awful things at me, I thought of that gun.

60

To streamline production, Aiken fastens two sheets of plywood together. That way he can cut the pieces for two birdhouses at once. He uses patterns over and over again. He has orders for two more cathedrals and three skyscrapers and he's able to assemble these complex houses faster than it used to take to build the simple saltbox. He collects one hundred dollars in advance for each of these orders and adds that to the considerable wad hidden in the coffee can under the workbench.

He still goes into the farmers' market to sell on Saturday mornings. He and Henry are fixtures now. Once they get set up and Henry has had his donut, the boy makes the rounds. Aiken watches him chat with the herb lady, the woman who sells bread—he sometimes comes back chewing a sample she's given him—the apple pickers, now that autumn is upon them. He worries about Henry's explorations because he isn't always able to keep an eye on him. Business is brisk.

He pays off his license fee earlier than he and the clipboard man had agreed, which pleases them both. It turns out that the man is the town's director of tourism—it's news to Aiken that the town has, or needs, such a thing. He mentions the bleachers he's installed in his barn, and the man asks for a full description and a brochure.

"Tourists will flock to an artisan's studio. I'll put that in the next newsletter."

He doesn't think of himself as an artisan, and there's no brochure, but he posts a hand-lettered sign at his table in the market, letting people know they're welcome to come watch the birdhouses being made. He can't bring himself to use the word "studio." He has business cards printed with directions to the farm and sets those out on the risers. At least once, sometimes twice a week, the curious pull into the driveway, some of them locals who want to see what it's all about, but mostly tourists who've heard about the birdhouses at the visitors' center in Stillwater. And almost no one leaves without buying one or two. He has to laugh when the bleachers are full, as if he were an actor on a stage. In some ways, though, that's what he's become. What can these people possibly see in a young vet, a man who can't seem to shake the horror of war, who can't keep a janitor's job, who's got a lousy history with women, who's only trying to make some kind of life for him and his son, gluing plywood together for a bunch of birds? He isn't sure who's crazier.

Emerging from the barn late one cloudy afternoon, content with his day's productivity, Aiken knows instantly that something is wrong. All the windows in the house are wide open, curtains flapping out of the upstairs bedrooms in a stiff, hot breeze. From the front porch he sees Soon-hee running across the pasture, her thick black hair streaming behind like a cape. He calls to her, but she doesn't stop, and he loses sight of her in the tall grass.

He hurries inside. The lights are burning, music blares from the kitchen radio, and the television in the living room shouts a commercial for some indispensible gadget.

"What's going on?" he yells over the din.

A lamp has toppled, and magazines that had been stacked on the coffee table lie scattered across the carpet. He punches the off button on the television, and in the kitchen he fiddles with the knobs on the radio but only manages to make the music louder, so he yanks the plug from the socket. Another radio somewhere on the second floor is blasting the same station, a Springsteen song that Hank used to listen to all the time. He runs up the stairs to Hank's room, grabs the old transistor set, turns the volume down, then fumbles for the off switch. Across the hall, in *his* old room, he finds Henry curled on the bed.

He peels the boy's hands from his ears. "What's up, buddy?"

"It's too loud in here," Henry says. He tilts his head, listening. The noise has stopped. "Mommy turned it on."

"Why?"

Henry shrugs. Aiken has given up trying to understand his wife; he can't very well expect Henry to succeed where he has failed.

The house is quieter now, but the wind still rushes through the open windows, and there is distant thunder.

He looks in on his ailing mother.

He takes one cautious step into her bedroom, then another. She's nestled under the fraying patchwork quilt, her thin white hair nearly invisible against the pillow. On the side table are her medicines, the ones she concocts from herbs and flowers and tree bark, and the pills the doctor prescribed. It had been a struggle to get her to see the doctor; he wonders if she's been taking the pills. "Ma?"

She opens her eyes. "It's quiet," she says. "Where's the girl?"

"What happened here?"

"Might be something I said." Now she closes her eyes, as if the effort to speak has been too much.

Aiken crosses the room to the windows. He pulls the curtains back inside, fighting the wind, and wrestles the window shut. He gazes across the meadow but sees no sign of Soon-hee.

"You got her wound up?"

"All I said was how quiet it was in the house," his mother says. "That it sounded like death. And she threw up her hands and started shouting. Of course it made no sense to me. She yanked the windows open, stomped up and down the hall making noise, yelling in her language. Pretty soon she was thrashing around downstairs, turning on radios and whatnot—I never heard such a commotion. Then just now it got quiet again, except for the wind whistling through here and the curtains flapping, like the house had wings."

She gasps, clutches her side, and squeezes her eyes tight. She groans his name, and he rushes to her side.

"Ma," he says, taking her hand, hoping that whatever it is will pass, that the dreaded day has not yet come.

"Aiken," she says again. Her breath is labored, coming in deep, rasping wheezes; yellow bubbles erupt between her lips. She jerks upright and doubles over, vomits on her legs and his.

61

Such a powerful woman in this life, a powerful spirit in the next. I will not be allowed to touch her, to be with her, to prepare her body for its journey, but her spirit is here now. It is strong, although her blood and bones are not.

I make the straw figure with its arms and legs, I lay it in the bed, on her chest, to take up her strength, the vessel, as our *mudang* did with my mother. And when she has faded, when I see in her eyes that the spirit has abandoned her, I begin to chase the ghosts who would lead her on the wrong path.

I scream and whirl and dance. I bang on walls. I turn on music and voices and open the windows so the ghosts, afraid of the mother's powerful spirit, will flee. Too late, but the noise does what it is meant to do, the television and the radio, the voices of the ghost, the wind swirling through the house chasing death from the mother of Ay-ken.

But too late, I am afraid, and I run to find the old man with the cane, to summon Sansin to protect her, and pray the ghosts will follow me. I hear Ay-ken call my name as I run, but I must not let him stop me. There is no time. I take the straw figure, the spirit of the mother of Ay-ken, and I run with it up the mountain, to the home of Sansin.

62

So loud!

But it was quiet before. Terribly quiet. The girl came into my room with the little doll.

"What's that?" I asked, but she didn't say anything, like she was in a trance.

She put it on my chest and began to chant, some kind of prayer, and then she seemed angry, grabbed the doll and ran from my room, turning everything on.

I hear Aiken shouting, and then the noise stops, bit by bit, as if I am floating from it, until all is quiet again.

The wind rushes in and waits to carry me away.

63

Against his mother's wishes, he does what he should have done long ago and hopes it's not too late. He slides his arms under her and braces for her weight as he lifts, surprised at how light she has become. She weighs nothing, little more than air inside her nightgown.

"Daddy?" Henry stands in the hall, eyes wide. "Is Grandma okay?"

Henry. Aiken stops, clutching his mother to his chest. He had wanted to shield the boy from this, but it's too late. And now what can he do? With his mother barely conscious, there won't be room for Henry in the truck, but he shouldn't leave him alone, either. Not with Soon-hee acting crazy again. There's no telling what she'll do. What if she comes back? What if she doesn't?

"I'm taking Grandma to the doctor. I'll be back as soon as I can. Will you be all right by yourself for a little while? Everything's fine, so don't worry. Okay?"

Henry nods slowly, uncertain, and Aiken doesn't know what he should do.

He rushes downstairs with his mother, backs through the door and out to the truck. Black clouds boil over the ridge and the wind is screaming through the treetops. There's no sign of Soon-hee. Henry and Ralph watch through the screen as he settles his mother in the truck. Then he's gone, racing out to the Pike, and, as fast as he dares, north toward the hospital. Aiken forces himself to imagine the good that will surely come of this—the tests they'll finally be able to do, the cure for whatever ails her—but the foul smell of her fills the truck as she vomits again, and the vision disappears.

"Aiken." Her voice is barely audible, and Aiken thinks she might have said more, but he can't hear her over the engine and the rushing wind.

"It'll be okay, Ma," he says. "We're almost there."

He's barely stopped when he flings the door open and carries her into the emergency room, a gurney thrust in front of him the moment he sets foot inside. He lays his mother on the ghostly sheet.

He asks to stay with her, but the nurses won't let him. He feels relieved. Guilty, but relieved. He asks for Kelly, and a nurse says she'll page her. There are forms to fill out. The nurses ask a flood of questions about his mother's medical history, symptoms, insurance. He can't answer most of them. He can't remember the name of the young Indian doctor who treated his father. He can't even remember the name of Kelly's friend, the doctor who came to the house, who prescribed pain medicine.

"I need to talk to Kelly," he says.

He sits in the waiting lounge and is drinking weak machine coffee when Kelly finds him. She's already looked in on his mother. Jonathan—Dr. Solomon—is on his way, she says. She sits beside him. He can't stay, he has to get back to Henry, but he can't leave, either, and so he doesn't move. He barely breathes.

"I've got to get back to work, Aiken. I'll check with you in a while. Or have them page me if you need me."

"Kelly..." He wants to ask if she's happy with Dr. Solomon. Has she found what she's looking for?

"What?"

She must hate him for what he did. How can he make her understand that he didn't mean to hurt her? He thought they belonged together, that's all. He wanted to be with her and thought she wanted the same thing. But after what she's told him, he can't trust his own memories, and now everything is spinning apart. He doesn't know how to make it stop.

"Nothing," he says. She turns, begins to leave. Nothing now, but he has to say something. He has to make her understand that it was a different time. Whatever happened, it was a different world, and he is a different man. And suddenly he has to know. "The baby?"

She stops. She looks at her feet, the shadows that vanish in the bright corridor. "There was no baby, Aiken." And then she's gone.

He waits. Outside, the sky darkens, and he thinks of Henry and the open windows at the house. He'd closed some, he remembers, but not all. He hopes that Soon-hee has returned and come to her senses, but he doubts it, and he realizes, in fact, the way she's behaving again, she could be a danger to Henry. She wouldn't hurt him, not intentionally, but she might take him and leave again. He should never have left the boy alone. Is there anything he can do here? Or could he go? He considers calling Tammy, even Jake, but they're both unreliable and angry. He waits. He calls home, but there's no answer, and he wonders if Henry would pick up. He would, because that's what he's been taught, and so now Aiken's sure something else is wrong at the house, that Soon-hee has returned to make matters worse.

But there's been no word from the doctors and he shouldn't leave until he knows something. He goes to the nurses' station to ask for news, expecting to be rebuffed and told he must wait for the doctor, but the nurse's head is down, eyes on paperwork, and he walks past, unseen. He looks in each room as he moves down the hall, pushes in and takes three steps to see an empty bed, or an old man, or a pretty little girl with a cast on her leg. Until finally, there she is, looking tiny, pale, and dead. But the monitors click and beep and hum, and the tubes flow, and the room seems alive, even if she isn't.

"Ma?" Did he say that out loud? He isn't sure.

"Ma?" No reply, no fluttering eyelids. The machines beep. Of course he thinks of his father, so recently in the same place, the same limbo from which Aiken was sure he would not return. And yet he did, for a time. He should be hopeful now. The hospital isn't the death house they all imagine.

Lightning flashes outside. He has to go.

He retraces his steps down the hall and out to his truck. Driving fast—a downpour beginning, exploding in huge drops against the dusty windshield, the sky black, thunder rumbling—he hydroplanes through the curve at Poplar Spring but manages to keep control. Their rutted road is already turning to mud. At home, he skids to a stop on the gravel and runs into the house just as lightning flashes and cracks nearby, rattling the windows. The rumble echoes inside. The lights flicker—they're all on, table lamps, ceiling fixtures, everything—and Henry runs to him, jumping into his arms. There's no sign of Soon-hee.

They discover napkins littering the kitchen, liberated by the wind from the holder on the countertop, taking his mother's porcelain salt and pepper shakers with them. He picks up the larger shards, momentarily ponders whether repair is possible, whether his mother will ever return home to see what has happened.

He assigns Henry the job of picking up all the napkins while Aiken runs from room to room closing windows, assessing damage. There's a puddle in the dining room, with its west-facing windows. He grabs a towel from his mother's linen closet and spreads it to soak up the mess. The windowsills in the living room are damp, but no worse than that. He runs upstairs to the room Soon-hee has been using, his mother's sewing room. The carpet is soaked where the rain still streams in, the curtains hanging drenched and heavy beside the open window.

He comes back downstairs and finds Henry in the kitchen sniffling, staring at his finger, which sports a red gash.

"Where's Mommy?" Henry asks.

Aiken examines the cut for the porcelain that caused it, part of the broken salt shaker, and then finds a Band-Aid, settling Henry into a kitchen chair while he sweeps up the remaining pieces and the spilled salt and pepper.

"Where's Mommy?" Henry asks again.

He doesn't answer, but peers out the window toward the mountain. It's still pouring. He hears water running fast in the creek that's prone to flooding. There's no telling where she might be. He can't leave her out there, but he doesn't want to leave Henry alone in the storm.

He crouches by Henry's chair. "Will you and Ralph be okay by yourselves for a few more minutes while I go look for your mother?" Henry nods, but Aiken sees that the boy isn't sure. He wishes he didn't have to leave. He grabs a slicker from the hall closet and runs out.

The deluge has formed muddy pools in the uneven gravel of the drive. He jogs to the stock gate, which stands partly open. A trail weaves through the tall grass, but he can't tell if that might be Soon-hee's course, or a deer path, or just the route Ralph takes on his daily explorations. He follows the trail.

The pasture slopes down toward the creek before rising sharply on the opposite side, and the trees and shrubs are thicker as he gets closer to the water. There's a cataract here, and the swollen creek blasts through the rocky course. If he calls her name, she won't hear, but he shouts anyway. The only answer is the din of rushing water. His jacket snags on the brambles, dense and thorny and impenetrable. He doesn't see how she could have passed this way. Even the animals too large to crawl under find an easier route. He backtracks and heads farther west, above the falls. He's still near the water, but in a pine grove. Here he finds traces. Muddy footprints. A sandal. He pushes on, searching for signs along the edge of the creek. The water is slower at this point, quieter, with pools that form in its twists and turns. He calls her name again and listens, but the rain and nearby rapids still consume all other sound.

"Soon-hee," he shouts again. But there's no reply, and he follows the creek upstream. He's near the head of it now and the terrain is marshy. Only fallen trees here, and dense grasses, soft wet earth. This is where the creek bubbles up from the limestone spring and assembles for the journey downhill where it will join the mountain stream for the long trek to the sea. There's no shelter for her here, but she could be anywhere in the grasses, in the shallow pools. Or higher up the mountain. He calls her name again.

An answer. Or a voice. He hears something—a whimper. He runs, pushing aside the low shrubs and thick grass and nearly trips over Soon-hee, huddled in a ball, on her side, arms around her knees. She's smeared with mud. She shivers and chatters and speaks words he doesn't understand. She flinches when he touches her, but then lets him carry her out of the marsh. She wraps her arms around his neck, hides her face in his shoulder. His own relief at having found her is swamped by new fears. What's happened to her? What can he do to help her?

He climbs the hill as best he can, avoiding the brambles. Soon-hee's face and arms are already covered with oozing scrapes, and he doesn't want Henry to see her like this, so he takes her into the barn and settles her on his bed in a nest of blankets.

Then he runs back into the house, sees the blood on his hands and wonders whether it's his own, or Soon-hee's, or both. He finds Henry, sitting stiffly in the kitchen where Aiken had left him, Ralph at his feet. Aiken's return frees Henry from the command to stay put and he slips off the chair, but Aiken can see in his son's knotted face that he's frightened by his appearance.

"Look at me, will you?" He laughs and hopes Henry won't detect that it's a forced, false laugh. "What a mess I am!"

There's a half grin on Henry's lips, the expression of a boy who is amused, but thinks maybe he should not be. "Did you find Mommy?"

"I did. She's out in the barn. I'm going to go get her now. Go up to your room, please. You can see her after she's had a rest."

Henry whines, but trudges up the stairs. Then Aiken carries Soon-hee into the house and up to the bathroom. He runs a bath and gently lays her in the water even before the tub is full. She looks blankly into his eyes through the limp strands of her hair, as if he is a stranger, but still she lets him wash her.

"I'm so sorry," he says.

There's a knock on the door.

"Is Mommy okay?"

"She's just having a bath, son," he says, and he sees recognition in Soon-hee's eyes. "Then she's going to bed. You can talk to her tomorrow."

He wraps Soon-hee in a towel and carries her to her room. He puts her on the bed, covers her, and lies down next to her.

Mrs. McGrady comes as soon as he calls. She'd been one of the first to bring a casserole when his father died—something he remembers all the neighbors doing after Hank's accident. Now he doesn't know where else to turn. He needs help with Henry and with Soon-hee, and he needs to get back to his mother in the hospital. And he needs to see Kelly, because his remorse is swelling inside him, malignant, and he can't leave things the way they are.

At the hospital there's no improvement in his mother's condition. She's barely breathing on her own, the pain medication now comes intravenously, and she's mostly incoherent when she stirs at all. Kelly comes by while he's in the room. They exchange only a glance before she rushes off. She won't look at him. He can't look at her.

When she's gone, he sits next to his mother's bed. Her eyes are closed, breathing labored. He can't tell if she's awake, or even aware that he's in the room, holding her hand. The hand feels lifeless and empty.

He needs to talk to someone about Kelly, about what she's told him. He'd been so sure about their future, sure they were meant to be together. But he blew it. She left and it was his fault. Their lives would have been so different. There'd have been no Soon-hee.

"Soon-hee," he says aloud. He realizes, again, that no Soon-hee means no Henry, and that's not something he wishes for. But Soon-hee is acting crazy again. He's ruined her life, too. Now he doesn't know what he wants, he doesn't know what to do, and he doesn't know what else to say.

He sits with his mother silently. He's tired and he lays his head on the bed. He closes his eyes. He feels her fingers on his cheek and looks up at her.

"Bring the girl to me," she says.

He sits up. Has she spoken? Her eyes are still closed. She doesn't appear to have moved.

When he gets home, Mrs. McGrady has bathed Henry and put him to bed. Soon-hee has not stirred. He stays in the house, sleeping on the sofa, and he's still there the next morning when Mrs. McGrady returns before dawn. She makes breakfast for Henry. And she keeps her distance as Aiken leads Soon-hee to the truck. He's certain this is a bad idea, but he can't deny his mother's request. In the past weeks the two women have grown close. It might be that they both need this.

The nurses stiffen when they see him and Soon-hee. Her hair is wild, her eyes vacant. He's told her that they're coming to see his mother and, although he thought she'd protest, she hasn't reacted at all. Now, as they pass the nurses' station, she leans heavily on him, pliantly moving with him, steered by him.

"She's been here before," says one of the nurses, someone he doesn't recognize.

Aiken stops. "Years ago. When our son was born."

"No," she says. "Recently. She visited an old man."

"I'm sure you're mistaken," he says. But he *isn't* sure. Anything is possible. He'd found the yellow and red paper in his father's room, and had had no idea how it got there. What if it was Soon-hee? Had she come?

His mother is awake when they enter, which should surprise him but doesn't. He greets her with a kiss on her cool, pale brow and settles Soon-hee into the bedside chair. He takes his mother's hand.

"Leave us," she says to him. Her voice is weak, barely audible.

"I don't think that's a good idea."

"Please," she says.

He looks from mother to wife and back, and then goes. They have secrets between them, he supposes, about the house, about their lives. In Soon-hee's nearly catatonic state she seems harmless, but still he worries.

He waits in the lounge. He considers returning to the room, troubled by what might happen in his absence, but ... he doesn't. He recalls his childhood and his mother when she was much younger, vibrant and full of energy. He thinks of his father, working in the fields and the barn, always working, always distant. He remembers Hank. He prays. No, he doesn't pray. He wishes, as he did when he was a boy, for a miracle.

"Mr. Alexander?"

He looks up. He's not sure how much time has passed. An hour? More? He's been lost in his memories and barely knows where he is. A nurse, the one who recognized Soon-hee, beckons. Her expression is grim.

"You'd better come."

When he enters the room, Soon-hee is still sitting next to the bed, holding his mother's hand. The machines are silent. His mother's eyes are closed.

"I'm so sorry," says the nurse, and leaves.

There will be no miracles. He knew it was coming, but he didn't think it would be now. He thought there was still time. Why did no one tell him it would be so soon?

He goes to the bedside, rests his hand on his mother's forehead and says a silent goodbye, fighting the tears. If he had to speak now, he couldn't. But there are things he wishes he'd done differently, things he wishes he'd said. A lifetime comes to him all at once, not a single memory but all of them, a collage of his mother's journey, his own. He wishes he could tell her about it. The tears flow now. They aren't enough, but they're a relief.

Soon-hee won't let go of his mother's hand. He tries to pull it away, but she slaps at him with her free hand, and scoots the chair even closer to the bed. She buries her face in the bedding, her wild hair shrouding his mother's arm. When he'd brought Soon-hee home from Korea, he'd hoped his mother would help her, that she could relate to a young country girl in a strange world. And he'd hoped Soon-hee would learn from her, that she'd think of her as her own mother. It hadn't happened that way, but Aiken can see that a genuine bond did finally grow between them. He doesn't know why or how, but it's something to be grateful for.

And now he's afraid for Soon-hee. She'd made so much progress staying at the farm, but in her current state she doesn't seem capable of running the household by herself. And Aiken won't ever be able to leave Henry with her now. Can he even let her stay in the house? It doesn't seem possible.

He approaches her and wraps his arms around her, pries her hand from his mother's and pulls her away. He rests her head against his shoulders, and for an instant he remembers their carefree life in Seoul. Her feet move, her head droops, her black hair falls across her eyes like a veil. She lets herself be lifted into the truck. She stares straight ahead as he drives, slowly, thinking, lost, down the Pike toward the farm.

He'll have to move into the house. He has to let Soon-hee stay, if she wants to—where else could she go?—but he can't leave her alone with Henry. He'll do what he's always done and take the boy to school in the morning and pick him up in the afternoon. When he's not in school they'll stick together. Henry likes working with Aiken in the barn. He can read, or play, or help. The situation may only be temporary, anyway. It isn't clear that he'll be able to hang on to the farm, and if they have to move then he'll figure something else out, find help for Soon-hee, somewhere for her to go.

She doesn't move when they stop in the driveway, but he helps her out of the truck, past Mrs. McGrady's gaze, and up to her room.

"Do you want something to eat?" he asks, but she doesn't answer. "Should I make tea? Are you okay?" No answer. He pushes her shoulders gently so she'll sit on the edge of the bed. He removes her shoes. He pushes again so she'll lie down. He lifts her feet, settles her head on the pillow.

When he's thanked Mrs. McGrady and told her about his mother, when he's accepted her teary condolences and a brief, awkward embrace, and when he's watched her climb into her station wagon and disappear into the night, he pours Jack Daniels into a glass and goes back upstairs. He looks in on Henry. He stands at the foot of the bed, sipping the whiskey, listens to his son's steady breathing, and retreats.

At the end of the hall, light pours from his mother's room, and he goes there now. The lamp by the bedside glows as if expecting her imminent return. The sheet and quilt are tossed back, fouled by her vomit. On the nightstand is her tape recorder. Aiken sets his drink on the table and reaches for the machine.

64

It's time. Time to tell the rest of the story.

Henry moved home after Hank's funeral. I asked him to, standing next to him at the cemetery, both of us holding back tears, but I believe he'd already decided. Aiken needed him, and our differences were small. I don't even remember what they were.

That's a lie, of course. I remember, but they don't matter. It was so long ago, and none of it matters. I told him about the girl, Charlotte, what I'd done to her. That was the heart of it. How I'd invited her to the house to talk. How she fidgeted on the sofa in the living room, so out of place, so uncomfortable. How I served the tea, watched the fire rise in her pale cheeks. How she ran to the bathroom clutching her belly and afterward fled the house.

"How could you?" Henry had asked.

And when I reminded him of Helen, her wild behavior all those years ago when he was courting, that's when he left, as if I suddenly frightened him.

But how, after all those years together, could he not know? Could he be so blind that he did not see me? What I can do?

But there's something else.

After Hank was born, I wanted another child. More children. But Henry had seen the pain that two brothers can cause one another, the grief that shared blood brings. Without asking me, he had an operation, a vasectomy. And then, years later, came Aiken. A miracle, I told him. I had wanted another child so badly, and my prayers were answered. Henry knew he wasn't responsible. He just didn't know who was. But he didn't leave, not then. He stayed, angry, and he was a good father to Aiken.

You'll think I'm crazy, but I talk to Henry all the time. It's as if he's sitting in this room with me. He's forgiven me. He knows I did what I thought was best for our family. He's asking me to come home with him now, and I surely know what he means. I ask if Hank is with him, but there's no answer. He only says, "Come home."

TURTLE VALLEY, VIRGINIA

NOVEMBER-DECEMBER 1996

65

I hear her voice. She is dead but she is not gone. She is beginning her journey.

I knew where I was, in the hospital, with its clamoring spirits. She knows I have taken hers and given it to the mountain. She touches my head, smoothes my hair as if I am a child. I am still a child. She tells me she knows. She is at peace. She has taken off her secrets, like stones that weighed her down. She is ready for the journey.

As I am ready for mine.

It is time to leave this place and return to Pae-tu.

66

That last tape of his mother's—can it be true? All this time, years and years, and she never said anything. She lied to him and to his father. His father—Henry—never said a word. Did he really know? Or was that another lie? And if Henry Alexander wasn't his father, who was? He searches his mother's room for answers. He doesn't know what he's looking for and finds nothing—no letters, no photo albums, nothing. He listens to the tape again and again, the gentle rasp of his mother's voice, keeping her alive this way or, at least, keeping her near.

There is a funeral to plan, relatives to notify, arrangements to be made, but he can't bring himself to begin. He's not ready.

All he can do is work. In the barn, instead, he starts a new design. As he sketches, he isn't sure what it will be. He'd built the purple martin house in a southern colonial style that he liked—he's made several more of those since and sold them all—but this will be a bird community of a different sort. He draws an octagonal tower, with a pointed, conical roof, and two holes on each side, with perches in front of the holes. Drawing patterns takes him most of the morning, but he's cut their pieces and planned their assembly, so he'll be ready to get back to it when he returns from picking up Henry at the church.

He goes into the house to check on Soon-hee. Upstairs, light streams from her open door. She isn't there.

He calls her name. He looks in Henry's room and in Hank's room, where he's been sleeping since he moved back into the house. He rushes down the hall and stops in front of his mother's closed door.

"Soon-hee? Are you in there?" He knocks. He turns the knob, but the door is locked. He doesn't like the idea of Soon-hee being locked in his mother's room, but at least he knows where she is. "I'm going to go get Henry now," he says through the door. "We'll be back in a little while. Okay?" Still no answer. He wonders if he should ask Mrs. McGrady to come over. But maybe Soon-hee just wants to stay close to his mother, he thinks, and he understands that, so he doesn't call. As Aiken drives away, Ralph watches from the porch.

When Aiken comes back with Henry, the dog is gone.

They enter the house, and Aiken sits Henry down at the kitchen table with milk and cookies while he checks on Soon-hee. Now his mother's door is open. The fouled sheets have been stripped from the bed, but there's a depression in the pillows, as though Soon-hee has been lying there. The room smells of the sweet bath powder his mother liked. He searches for Soon-hee again, but she's not in any of the upstairs rooms. She's not in the living room or the dining room. He makes a quick check of the cellar, and she's not there either.

He tells Henry to stay put in the kitchen, and he goes out onto the porch. He whistles for the dog and calls his name. Unless Ralph has wandered far away, which he rarely does, he comes when he's called. But there's no sign of him. Soon-hee has run into the woods again, Aiken thinks, and smart, old Ralph has followed to keep an eye on her. He heads down to the barn, but Soon-hee doesn't appear to have been there. Nothing has been disturbed. The pieces of the new octagon birdhouse are just where he'd left them.

He calls for Ralph again as he heads back to the house. He listens for the jangling of the dog tags, or a barking in the distance, but there's nothing. At the kitchen table, he breaks off a piece of his son's oatmeal cookie—Henry laughs—and takes a sip of his milk. He sets Henry up in front of the TV and goes back outside. No Soon-hee. No Ralph.

The phone rings and he runs inside to get it.

"I'm so sorry about your mother, Aiken," says Kelly.

"It's hard to believe she went so soon after Pop." He considers telling her what he's learned about his father, but he's still not sure how he feels about it, or if it's even true. And if it is, what does it mean?

"I know it's small comfort, but it often happens that way," Kelly says. "Is there anything you and Henry need?"

"I don't think so," he says. "But maybe you could come visit us anyway? I'd cook dinner."

"Aiken."

"I could use a friend, is all."

"Where's your wife?"

"That's a real good question," he says.

*   *   *

On the porch, Aiken rattles kibble in Ralph's bowl, the fail-safe summons no dog in earshot can resist, but there's still no sign of him. Darkness comes, along with an evening chill, and Aiken sits on the porch steps. He should have gone out looking before now, for both dog and wife, but he thought they'd be back. He listens to the night, and hears nothing but frogs, katydids, and owls. He puts Henry to bed, deflecting questions about his mother, and lies awake, unable to sleep in Hank's room. He feels Hank's presence here, but maybe that's because it has changed so little. It takes no effort to see Hank sitting at the desk, gazing dreamily out the window toward the mountain. Soon-hee is out there, somewhere.

While Henry is in school the next day, Aiken hangs a "Closed" sign on the barn door and tramps through the pasture to the woods, then to the marsh where he'd found Soon-hee before. He searches with more dread than urgency, as if he already knows what he'll find.

This time he sees no signs of her. No scraps of clothing, no dropped sandals or muddy prints. He lurches through the tall grass and hopes to see her nestled in the mud or curled under a tree with Ralph keeping watch. That's what he hopes to find, but not what he expects. He continues his search.

Instead of Soon-hee, he comes upon Ralph. The old dog lies stiff and still, on his side, a gaping, bloody wound in his chest. The matted grass around him is soaked with blood. Aiken drops to his knees, the breath torn from him. He wipes away tears, but they return. He strokes Ralph's flank, digging his knees deeper into the soft, wet earth. Ralph has been shot, he can see that much. At close range. Aiken lifts his head, turns, aware how vulnerable he is, sensing that he isn't alone. If Soon-hee is responsible for this, it's best that he not be the one to find her. Alert, eyes scanning the trees and tall grass, transported to the danger of desert warfare, he lifts Ralph's cold body and holds it close, filled with a fog of wet-fur scent.

He carries the old dog to the barn and retrieves the shovel. He knows he should wait; a crime has been committed and the body is evidence. But he doesn't want Henry to see Ralph this way. His father—the man he thought was his father—buried another dog when Aiken was a boy. He hasn't thought of King in a long time, but he was hit by a car and left to die along the side of the road, until Hank found him and brought him home. He digs a hole behind the barn. He makes it deep and wide. He removes the collar and tags, and he buries Ralph. For a few moments he stands over the new grave and remembers the dog's long life.

His jacket is covered with blood. He wonders how and why Soon-hee has done this. Ralph would only have wanted to protect her, and didn't deserve this. How could she do it? And where did she find a gun? It comes to him. He returns to the house and opens the cellar door again. He'd looked here before, cursorily, but he already knows what he'll see. He has to be sure. He pulls the light cord on the bulb over the stairs.

"Soonie? Are you down there?" He scans the basement—the washtub, the furnace. The washing machine. Boxes of Christmas ornaments on shelves. The gun cabinet, door closed, but the key, which ordinarily is hidden inside the kitchen pantry, sits in the lock. His father's rifle is there, but the shotgun is missing, Hank's pistol gone, too. How the hell did she learn to use guns?

The one thing he understands is that he can't count on Soon-hee to do anything rational, and that means, no matter how much she loves their son, she might be a danger to Henry. Aiken doesn't know what's causing her behavior, but his mother's illness may have hit her harder than he realized. Still, he feels responsible. Kelly's right about that much. He hadn't meant to hurt her, but he ruined her life just the same and brought her here, and now he realizes that he has to get her home. There is no atonement for what he's done, but maybe he can bring her peace. And until he can get Soon-hee back to Korea—or any place far away—Henry won't be safe.

First he calls the sheriff. Aiken would like to think he can handle the problem himself—she's his wife, he's a soldier and can defend himself and his house—but there's too much at stake. The sheriff can hunt for her. He needs to stay with Henry.

"She's got a gun, Billy," Aiken says. "She found the key to the gun cabinet and she took a pistol and the shotgun."

"Does she know how to use it?" Billy asks.

"My dog's dead."

"We'll find her, Aiken."

Aiken calls Kelly next. He's on hold a long time while the hospital locates her. He gives up, dials her home number, and she answers.

"I need a favor," he says. "Can I bring Henry to stay with you for a while? Maybe just tonight?"

"I have to be at work early," she says.

"I promise I'll come for him first thing. It's just I don't want him to be out here." He doesn't want to explain, but he also doesn't want Kelly to get the wrong idea. He tells her about Ralph.

"Surely she wouldn't hurt Henry?"

"I didn't think she'd hurt the dog."

"What about you?"

"I need to find her."

* * *

He picks Henry up at school and heads into Stillwater.

"Where are we going, Daddy? Home's the other way."

"You're going to spend the night at Miss Kelly's house."

Henry whines. He wants to go home and see his mother and play with Ralph.

Aiken doesn't answer. If he speaks, he'll sound angry, and he doesn't want to frighten the boy. He grips the steering wheel, feels the ache in his back grow and burn. But he concentrates on driving, and by the time they arrive at Kelly's, he's calmer. Now he can explain.

"Your mother's not feeling well. I don't want you around her until she gets better. That's the truth. I hope you can come home tomorrow, but I don't know. Okay? Please be good at Miss Kelly's."

Henry drags his feet on the walk to the door. Aiken is sympathetic, and knows Henry can't be happy about being left with a stranger, but there aren't any other options. Henry hasn't asked about his grandmother, and Aiken isn't ready to tell him.

When he rings the bell, he wonders what—or who—he'll find inside. Is that doctor—Solomon, he remembers—part of her life now? But the living room is dark and dour, not Kelly at all. And he knows she hasn't changed a thing since her mother's death.

She has a snack ready for Henry in the kitchen, and he eats a cookie, kicking his heels on his chair. He doesn't look up when his father kisses the top of his head and leaves.

Kelly stands with Aiken on the front stoop.

"Why don't you stay and have supper with us," Kelly says. "He'll feel more comfortable if you're here awhile."

The air is cold and smells of a nearby wood fire. He imagines how nice it would be to stay, to build a fire in the fireplace, to begin, somehow, to apologize for what he did. If she'll let him.

"I can't do that. She's still out there somewhere, and I need to find her."

He remembers his search for Soon-hee in Korea. It had taken him across an alien landscape, full of smells that made him gag and people who spoke a language he couldn't have mastered even if he'd tried. He'd been on his own then, taking trains and buses, depending on strangers for help. He'd felt alone and lost, but he'd been determined to find her. He felt responsible for her then. He's still responsible.

"I'd like to," he says. "But I can't."

Driving south on the Pike, he has to pull onto the shoulder as a sheriff's car flies by, siren wailing, then a fire truck, and then a second. It's as if he's racing them, falling farther behind, and he accelerates to close the gap. They turn on his road, and he does, too, skidding on loose gravel, and then he knows. In his gut he understands, even before he sees the smoke, or smells it. And then he does see smoke rising above the trees, black and churning. As he gets closer, he spots three pickups pulled to the side, and men he recognizes from the farmers' market leaning against their bumpers, watching the flames lick through the roof of his barn. The fire trucks block the driveway, and he pulls into a ditch. He jumps out and into the yard. The barn is engulfed, lighting the night sky. He moves closer, but even if Billy hadn't pulled him back the angry blaze would have prevented him from getting anywhere near the barn door.

The building burns like dry grass. The windows explode. Now flames are leaping through the roof, and then the roof collapses in a gusher of sparks and cinders. Paint cans erupt inside, each a dull burst, like the echo of a distant gun. Aiken drops onto the steps of the porch, eyes tethered to the unfolding catastrophe.

"Got to ask you some questions, Aiken," Billy says, his leg propped on the step.

"Why would she do it?" Aiken asks. Just then the back wall of the barn collapses, and the two men watch the structure cave in on itself.

"Now, see, that's just what I was going to ask you," says the deputy. "We can't get too near the place yet, of course, but there's a gas can out in the yard that somebody didn't bother to hide. I was wondering if you knew anything about that."

"Me? You think I had something to do with this?"

"I didn't say that, Aiken. I've got to ask. So you think your wife did it?"

"Who else? She wants to hurt me. To punish me. She wants to go home to Korea. Maybe this is her way."

"Punish you? For what?"

"Damned if I know." But he does know, and he wishes he could tell her he's sorry. It's long overdue

There's nothing the firemen can do for the barn, but they stand by in case the flames spread. Billy and Aiken go through the house, room by room, to be absolutely certain she isn't there. Aiken tells Billy about Ralph and shows him the gun cabinet. He assures himself and Billy that she's taken only the shotgun and Hank's pistol.

"How'd that little girl learn to use a shotgun, Aiken?"

He has no idea. Ordinary people in Korea didn't own guns, although her father had fought in the Korean War and no doubt knew something about weapons. Maybe she learned from him. But that's unlikely, from what little he knows about the family, and there has to be another explanation.

It comes to him.

"Tammy's a crack shot. She's been hunting since she was a kid. Damn. We've got to call Tammy."

He dials Tammy's number, but there's no answer. It hardly matters. He already knows what she'd say.

"Jesus, Tammy, what have you done?"

Billy promises to send someone to Tammy's in case Soon-hee shows up there. He posts a man at the Alexander place in case she comes back, and then the two of them go to look for the spot where Aiken found Ralph. Billy finds no trace of her but says they'll keep looking.

He returns to the empty house and reflects on the changes of these last few months. The house is still there, the house he'd grown up in that had been in the family for generations, dating back to old Dermot Alexander, with the views of Brother Mountain. But it's not the same. It will never be the same. Hank gone. Both his parents gone. His father not his father. Soon-hee disturbed and dangerous. Poor old Ralph.

He calls Kelly and talks to Henry, to touch base with the one thing left in his life that makes sense. And then he returns to the porch.

The barn is gone. He hasn't thought of this until now, until this very instant when he stands on the porch in the chilly night, but gone, too, are hundreds of birdhouses, the Cape Cods, saltboxes, taverns, schools, churches, Soon-hee's pagoda that he never got a chance to give her, even the skyscraper and cathedral—all his work from these past months. Along with a small fortune in tools and the money in the coffee can—thousands of dollars he'd managed to save. All gone. Insurance? He has no idea. He hadn't bothered with renter's insurance at the house in town because they couldn't afford it, and anyway he'd never owned anything worth insuring. He vaguely remembers his father dealing with an insurance agent after Hank's accident. His mother must have done the same when his father died, but she hadn't talked to him about it, and he hadn't thought to ask. He has no idea what the agent's name is, or where his mother's records might be. He's meant to look for them. That's something he'll certainly have to do now.

In the looming darkness, looking out into the night, he can imagine that the barn is still there, although his imagination also fabricates an impossible glow and burning embers. If the barn is still there, then why not his mother, and Hank, and the man he thought was his father?

He sits on the porch as the fire trucks leave and most of the sheriff's cars follow. He hears voices in the woods, Billy and another deputy still searching. Their flashlights dance in the darkness, heading toward the house like wild night eyes. And soon they, too, have given up, get in their cars, and leave. There is more work to be done in the morning, an investigation, sifting through the rubble. They'll find the truth. An explanation will be harder to come by.

All that remains is the acrid smell that hangs everywhere. The night seems darker than usual, and then he remembers the floodlight attached to the barn. It used to come on at dusk, but that's gone now. The darkness is complete. He watches the stars emerge. The moon rises, the constellations twirl across the sky. Cars pass occasionally, and when they do the darkness lifts briefly, the smoke appears in the headlights, drifting, and a breeze brings the sour smell freshly to him. Then the darkness returns. The McGradys' donkey brays, a cow lows. Owls call from the woods. There's a rustling in the bushes, and then silence. He closes his eyes to hear better, but still there's nothing.

He thinks Soon-hee might want to kill him. She thought he was in the barn, since that's where he spent most of his time, and she set it on fire to kill him. Because of what he did in Korea, maybe, or because he took his mother to the hospital against her wishes. Because he would never let Henry go. Had she searched the house, hunting him with the shotgun? And what then? With him gone, would she live there with Henry, go on as they had before? Or would she take Henry back to Korea, to the little farm in Pae-tu? Would she take up that old life, that old language? Become the ghost of herself?

Aiken goes inside and, for the first time he can remember, locks the door. There's no longer a dog to warn of intruders, and there's someone out there who wishes him harm. He hasn't felt this way since the war, and now that floods back, the sense that he's a target. He retrieves the gun cabinet key from its new hiding place in the living room and heads down to the cellar. The shotgun is gone, but he takes his father's rifle and loads a cartridge. He can't imagine using it on Soon-hee, but he's not sure he'll have a choice.

In the living room he turns on the TV for company, but he needs quiet, so he turns it off. He wants a drink, but he needs to stay alert, to hear her approach. He's waiting for the enemy to come to him, and he wonders how she became the enemy. He'd loved her, in his way. He still loves her.

He calls Kelly again. Henry is asleep. He'd refused to eat, then cried for a while after dinner. He'd asked for his mother and grandmother, then for Aiken. He'd accepted ice cream, and they ate it together on the floor while the TV blared a cartoon, and then he nodded off.

He tells Kelly about the barn.

"Maybe you should come here," Kelly says. Her voice is soft and inviting. It's a relief to him. Is he forgiven?

"I think she'll come back."

"That's my point. The woman's obviously dangerous."

"I can handle her."

"Aiken, I need to tell you something," she says. "About the baby."

He hears the wind whistling outside, the creaking of the porch swing's chains. He presses the receiver to his ear. He thinks the line has gone dead, but then he hears Kelly's sharp breath, as if she's holding back tears.

"I had a miscarriage, Aiken. I went away because I was going to give the baby up for adoption. I had a friend in Roanoke and it was all arranged. It was the hardest decision I've ever made in my life and I was all alone."

"Your mother didn't know?"

"No. I didn't tell anyone. If people had known . . . it was a story that would never die. I thought I could forget and go on, and no one would have to know."

"Not even me." Of course she wouldn't tell him. Not after what he'd done.

"But then I got sick, and it was gone."

"I'm sorry, Kel."

"And it turns out you can't forget. I met someone and got married, but it didn't work because I couldn't forget. You don't ever forget."

"I'm truly sorry. About . . . everything."

*   *   *

He sits in the darkened living room. Kelly is on his mind, what he did to her, what she went through. But he also has to think about Soon-hee.

Soon-hee. Enemy. Yes, he supposes they were headed for divorce, if that's what she wanted, and he'd deluded himself into thinking that they might reconcile. She apparently didn't want to be the woman he'd tried to make her. And yet, as his mother had declined, Soon-hee had grown stronger. More capable around the house, more confident, more flexible. They'd all grown to depend on her, the way he'd once envisioned. She was blossoming. Until his mother's death changed everything, sent her sprawling back into madness.

The rifle lies on the table next to him. He'd been holding it in his hand, but his palm grew sweaty as he remembered the fighting in Kuwait, huddled in the shell of someone's home, waiting. So he has laid it down and dried his hands on his jeans. He focuses on staying vigilant, ready. He listens. The wind has stopped. There's nothing. It's as if the desert has buried him in sand, where the world cannot reach.

Hank is at his side. The patrol leaves Wadi al-Batin and resistance is light, at first. The Iraqis respond with mortar rounds and tanks, trenches of flaming oil sending black smoke skyward. The patrol moves forward, pressing into a dusty hamlet. They exchange fire. A shell finds its target and a Bradley explodes nearby. Hank needs to see this, he thinks. Shots come from a sandy compound, or the house next to it. Aiken fires, advances, fires, watches as a grenade arcs into the compound and the building erupts, a wall collapsing into rubble. The guns have ceased. Arms raised, two Iraqis emerge from the smoke and flames. More gunshots. Hank, did you see? The men fall.

He jerks awake. Rosy light filters into the room. He gets up and checks the doors and windows. He makes coffee. He looks into the yard, sees deer grazing on the hillside, a doe and a yearling. He hears a car on the road and the deer bolt into the woods. He takes his coffee out on the porch. Smoke still hangs over the remains of the barn, but for the first time he can see into the field beyond. The landscape has changed.

Kelly calls. "Everything okay?" she asks.

"I don't know what I'm going to do," he says.

"Don't worry about Henry. He's eating cereal now, and I can drop him at his school on the way to the hospital, if you like."

"I mean, I don't know what I'm going to do about *anything*. About Soon-hee, about making a living, about *anything*. I thought I had it all figured out. I really did. I must have been dreaming."

"You sound tired. Did you sleep at all? Why don't you pick up Henry from school later and bring him here. Leave . . . your wife to the sheriff to worry about. The three of us can have dinner and we'll all try to relax a little. You can stay on the couch."

It doesn't seem possible that he can escape from this trouble, even for one night, but that's what he wants.

"Yes," he says. "Thanks."

He hears a car in the driveway and looks out. Billy is back. Aiken takes a position on the porch, gripping the railing with both hands, and watches while Billy and his investigators pick through the rubble. He sees them concentrating on the gas can, and to Aiken it doesn't look as though there could be any doubt about what she's done, or how. Now they're poking around the back of the barn, or where the barn used to be, where he'd moved Hank's motorcycle when he began filling up the place with birdhouses. The bike is surely just a molten lump now. After a while, Billy saunters up to the porch, but stays at the bottom of the steps.

"There's something we'd like you to see."

Aiken follows Billy around the blackened edges of the ruin, toward the back, where the rear wall had been the first to go.

"This looks like where it started. Probably gas poured all along the outside there, judging by the burn pattern. But we found another gas can inside. Next to the body."

"Body?"

Billy stands beside the charred remains that must surely be Soon-hee.

67

He lies in Hank's bed, longing for sleep. But the hubbub outside continues, and he knows sleep won't come. The coroner, the sheriff, the fire department investigators, even a reporter from the newspaper. They don't need to tell him what happened. It will be awhile before they can positively identify that body, so burned and black, but it has to be Soon-hee, doesn't it? She'd done the only thing she knew she could, the only thing she thought was in her control. She was never going to get home to Korea. That was impossible, even if her family would have her, and he would never have allowed her to take Henry. She had to know that. Maybe her death was an accident. Maybe she only meant to hurt Aiken, or maybe not even that. Maybe she was just trying to damage the barn, to send a message.

It was Soon-hee, he was reasonably sure, but that didn't answer all the questions. He had never understood why she'd rebelled against her father—a high school runaway, basically, in a country where kids didn't do that. She'd fled something then, and he'd been her refuge. Why had she been in that bar in Itaewon that day? Why was he so drawn to her, and why had she agreed to dance with him? Why had she let him do what he did? And when the inevitable happened, when she discovered she was pregnant, why did she keep it from him? Why did she leave him, when she had to know what would happen in her father's house? Why was it home she went to, if that's what she was rebelling against in the first place? Somehow it was all connected to home—running away, running back. That much, at least, he understood. He'd been there himself.

Does Billy really think he had something to do with her death? He didn't say as much, but there'd been so many questions. How long had they been separated? Where had he been that day? Isn't it true he was angry that she killed his dog?

"When did you last see her?" Billy had asked.

"You can't believe I killed her."

"Aiken, I'm just trying to find out what happened."

"Because I'd never hurt her. Ever."

"I believe you, son. But that may not be how it looks to everyone. People saw you arguing in your old neighborhood. George McCormack said it happened all the time. A lot of yelling and whatnot, from what he tells us."

"You talked to our old neighbors?"

"Doing our jobs, Aiken. So you fought?"

"Just yelling, Billy."

"And you considered her a threat to your son, isn't that what you told me? You thought she might try to take him away?"

"I'd protect my son, sure. But not like this."

"And you were pretty mad about the dog, weren't you?"

"I didn't kill her."

"Maybe you'd been drinking? Like that night we brought you home from Turtle Tavern when you were in no shape to drive?"

"When?"

"A month or so back. Babbling about ghosts and someone named Charlotte, passed out in the squad car. I've been worried about you."

"I didn't hurt her."

These past months she's been no end of trouble, a danger to them all. She'd threatened to take Henry away from him. She killed Ralph. Now that's all over, she can't bother them anymore, and Aiken can't say he'd blame anyone for thinking he did it. He'd do anything to stop her from taking Henry away, but he'd never hurt her. Never.

He manages to doze, then wakes. It's time to get Henry. When he steps inside the classroom in the church basement, his son runs to him and grabs his leg. It's going to be so hard to explain to him what happened. A child can only take so much loss.

"We're going to Miss Kelly's for supper, pal," Aiken says.

"Do I have to stay there again?"

"I heard you had ice cream. You like ice cream, don't you?" Aiken does at least get a grin out of him for this. "But, no, we'll go home after supper."

"Will Mommy be there?"

"No. Your Mommy went away. We'll talk about that later. Okay?"

"Where is she?"

"I'll explain later," he says, and immediately hears the echo of his parents. He doesn't want to be like this, because he remembers being aware that they were keeping things from him. He knew then, and Henry knows now, and he'll remember.

Kelly's waiting for them, with a snack for Henry and a beer for Aiken. While Henry is occupied by the TV, they speak softly in the kitchen.

"What will you do?"

He knows she means everything. What work, what about Soon-hee, what would he tell Henry?

"I honestly don't know," he says. "We've lost so much."

He's thinking of the house in Iraq that he reduced to rubble and the family left with nothing. "I think I was on to something with the birdhouses. First thing I've ever really been good at, you know? It's hard to believe I could make a living building birdhouses, but that's the way it was beginning to look. But now? I don't think I can start over."

How do you build a life? How do you put all the pieces together—a family, shelter, a job. How do you decide one day that the thing you're doing is what you're meant to do? You *don't* decide. A life just happens, it grows over time. One day you wake up, and there it is. Your life. Your home.

And then, in an instant, it's gone.

"Thanks for taking care of Henry yesterday. It seemed like things were crashing down around me, and the only thing I needed to be sure of was that he was out of harm's way. This was the only place I could think of. Thanks."

"You're welcome, Aiken," Kelly says. "You know, I didn't think so at first, but you've changed since we were together. I see it now. You've grown up."

"Is that a good thing?"

"Very good."

When supper is over—Kelly makes meatloaf because Henry had said that's what he liked—Aiken takes Henry home, back to the house.

He wants to tell him what happened. He doesn't want to wait too long because he's afraid if he doesn't get it all out, he won't be able to do it at all.

They're getting close to the turnoff toward the farm.

"I have something to tell you, pal." Aiken glances over at Henry, who looks back, expectantly. "The reason I wanted you to stay at Miss Kelly's yesterday was we had a fire at the farm and I thought it might be dangerous." He's bending the truth. He can't tell it straight, after all.

"You mean like a campfire?" Henry knows what a campfire is. Last year Aiken and Henry had pitched a tent up in the farm's high pasture, to watch the stars. They'd built a fire and roasted hot dogs and marshmallows. Henry had fed Ralph a melted marshmallow and they had both laughed to watch the dog struggle with the gooey mess.

"Not a campfire, no. This was an accident, and the barn caught on fire. Remember we saw that house one time and all that was left of it was the chimney? That's because the house was all wood and wood burns. Except for the chimney because that's brick. That's what happened to the barn. It was all wood, so it all burned."

"The barn's gone?"

"That's right. It's gone." They pull into the driveway and Henry stares out the window at the spot where the barn used to be. The headlights shine on the charred rubble.

"Wow."

"'Wow' is right. Pretty unbelievable, huh?"

"The birdhouses." Henry seems to be fighting tears, and Aiken drapes an arm over his shoulders.

"Yep. The birdhouses. I'm afraid they're all gone, too. Except for the ones in the truck. Guess we can take those to the market this weekend, huh?"

"Are we going to make some more?"

His eyes follow the beams of the headlights over the debris of the barn and on to the hillside beyond. He imagines that house in Iraq, the dead men, a family in despair.

"No, buddy, I don't think so," he says.

68

Aiken and Henry are sitting on the porch. It's a warm November day; the breeze carries the sweet smell of apples, which makes Aiken think of the old orchard that used to be in Kelly's family. Henry tells him about the Bell girl in his class at school, something about how she'd wet her pants and everybody laughed at her, but Henry felt sad because he thought she was going to cry. He says he's glad it wasn't him, though. Aiken tousles Henry's hair.

"That kind of thing happens, now and then. It was nice of you not to laugh at her."

A dog barks somewhere down the road, a high-pitched, cheerful bark, and Aiken thinks about Ralph. He misses the old guy. He'll never be able to forgive Soon-hee for that. When Henry asked about the dog, Aiken told him he'd gone with his mother, to take care of her.

He'd explained to Henry about Soon-hee. That she'd been lost in the woods and when she came back the barn was on fire, she tried to put it out, and it fell on her. He needs to know that his mother's dead, but what's the point in telling him more truth than that? That she was trying to kill him is something Aiken will do his best to forget, a secret just between him and Soon-hee. Let time and Henry's imagination turn her into a hero.

But Henry's reaction to her death has been a surprise. He didn't cry. He shrugged, said he was glad she'd be watching over them now, and that she'd come back some day, that they should make a birdhouse for her in the meantime, and one for his grandmother, too, like the pagoda house for his grandfather. Aiken didn't try to explain that it could never happen. If the fantasy helped him cope, what was the harm?

As for building more birdhouses, he can't do it. What kind of future is that? What kind of legacy for his son? If it weren't for Henry, he would probably sell the farm and leave town, maybe even go back into the Army. He's been out awhile, but he's still young and it could work. He could see more of the world, learn a skill that will last. It was his way forward once.

But he can't do that, and he puts it out of his mind. He'll find another solution. He's had a call from the school, and they'll take him back. Mr. Keeler had heard about all the problems, how Soon-hee had gone wild, his parents being sick, and he figured that had been the reason for Aiken's poor performance during the summer. Aiken's grateful, but he doesn't see how he can go back to that either. His mother had always told him the job was a dead end, and she was right. He's heard about a warehouse job over in Parkersville, a big distribution center where it seems half the men in Turtle Valley have worked at one time or another, and a lot of the women, too. Some of his buddies from high school went to work there after graduation and are still at it. He can probably sign on, but for the first few years it would likely be the night shift for him, and what would that do to Henry?

He's been considering police work. He likes that deputy Billy, and he thinks the guys who'd tried to find Soon-hee, and then investigated the fire, had done a fine job, an important job. That's a career, not just work, and he could be proud of it. Dangerous, though, and would that be the right thing to do? What would become of Henry if something happened to Aiken on the job? The boy has no other family except Tammy and Jake, and Aiken can't stand the thought of Henry living with either one, assuming they would have him. Still, he plans to talk to Billy about it next time he sees him, find out what's involved.

In the meantime—the remaining birdhouses. He and Henry go back to the farmers' market, one of the last of the year now that the days are chilly and growing short. When he parks his truck in their usual space and lifts Henry off the seat, Charlie Doak is there with a grin and warm hug for both of them.

It seems as though everyone in town has heard what happened. All the vendors come over as Aiken gets set up. He shakes a lot of hands while Henry eats his donut, courtesy of Charlie. And all morning there's a steady stream of buyers. Long before noon, Aiken sells the last birdhouse he has. He knows there will be no more, but it feels good to have the money in his pocket. He packs up the table and risers and throws the tarp in the back of the truck. He and Henry wave goodbye to Charlie.

They drive over to Kelly's house. As they pull up in front, Henry points to the gangly, bare tree in the yard.

"Look, Daddy, it's one of our birdhouses." Apparently noticing it for the first time, he looks from the birdhouse to the big house and back. "It looks just like Miss Kelly's house. Isn't that funny?"

The three of them eat a picnic lunch on the front lawn where they can see the birdhouse. It's too cold for it, and they're all wearing jackets, but Henry insists. Two bluebirds emerge from the house and fly to the yard's other tree, and then come back. They leave again and come back.

"Why do they keep coming and going?" Henry asks.

"I bet they have a baby inside the house, and they're bringing him food," Kelly says. "Usually they have babies in the spring, but if they've got a nice safe place, like a fine birdhouse, sometimes babies come in the fall."

"Can I see?"

"I don't think so, buddy." Aiken says. "That might get the parents upset if they think we're trying to hurt their baby."

"But I won't hurt him."

"I know that. But let's just leave the little family be."

The next morning, while Henry eats his breakfast and Aiken sits with him drinking coffee, a truck pulls into the driveway. He looks out and sees Charlie Doak and his son Matt walking toward the house across the gravel. Another truck turns in behind the Doaks' Ford and there's another one pulling to the side of the road. Aiken recognizes the Campbells, Bill and his two sons Kerry and Terry, and Rafe McBryde with his boy Cal.

"Morning, Charlie," says Aiken when he comes out to the porch. "What's going on here?"

Charlie's wearing jeans and a field jacket. His son's dressed just the same and stands a few feet behind his father at the base of the stairs, greeting the others as they approach.

"It's a real shame what happened to your barn," Charlie says. "A damn shame. We all knew your dad and he was always there when we needed help. We figured you might need a little of that right now. We don't have much to give but sweat and lumber. So we're here to rebuild your barn."

Aiken doesn't know what to say, so he gazes at the swelling crowd and says nothing. He's always known people in the area to be generous and helpful, but this is far beyond anything he's imagined. He comes down from the porch to shake hands.

Rick the bartender comes, too. "The Turtle will get by without me for one day," he says.

Mrs. McGrady comes, on her way home from church.

"I'm not planning on hammering any nails, boys," she says, "but I thought y'all might get hungry at some point." She moves into the kitchen with a bag of groceries.

Kelly arrives. "Heard there was a barn-raising," she says, and lifts a box off the front seat of her car, like it might have a cake in it, and takes it up on the porch. She sets it in front of Henry.

"Daddy, come look!" Henry pulls a puppy out of the box, a little yellow lab.

By the end of the morning, the men have cleared the debris from the old barn, including a couple of charred but intact birdhouses, and have unloaded the lumber for the new structure. Aiken had gone directly to the workbench, now a charcoal ruin, and finds little he could salvage: a few of the tools, loose nails and screws, hinges.

Kelly and Mrs. McGrady bring out broad trays of sandwiches and fruit, and set up two card tables on the porch along with pitchers of sweet tea. While Henry plays with his new puppy, whom he's christened "Ralphy," the crew eats.

They're about to return to work when a figure approaches, striding down the hillside through the pasture. Aiken can't make out who it is, at first, but then he spots the gray beard and the walking stick, and he knows it's Sam Carpenter. The table is cleared and the workers move toward the trucks to unload lumber and tools. No one else seems to have noticed Sam, as if he's visible only to Aiken. Even when Sam passes through the stock gate and limps to the house, the team pays him no mind, although the striped tomcat, missing since the fire, appears out of nowhere and follows him to the house.

"Heard about your troubles, son," says Sam as he climbs the porch steps. His boots make a reassuring thump, punctuated by the whack of the walking stick. "I came to say how sorry I am for your loss."

"Thank you," Aiken says. "It's good of you to come, Sam. It means a lot to us."

He looks at Sam and his long white beard, the broad shoulders. Sam. Could it be? Sam had known Aiken's parents forever and he'd always been around, watching over him, like a protective uncle. Like a father. He wanted to find a way to ask. Are you . . . ? But not here. Not now.

Sam reaches into his pocket and pulls out a package. It's wrapped in yellow paper, and he holds it up for Aiken to see. "I've got something for little Henry," he says. Henry turns away from his new puppy when he hears his name.

"What is it?" Henry asks, reaching for the bundle.

"What do you say, Henry," says Aiken.

"Thank you."

"No need to thank me, son. I believe it's your mother's. I used to see her sometimes up in the hills. She built a little . . . altar, I guess you'd call it. Used to come upon her while she was praying, or some such. Singing. Found this up there yesterday, the paper, too. Shiny thing, caught my eye the way the sun came out as I was walking past. Thought she might want you to have it."

Henry holds the gift in both hands and gazes at it. His eyes are wide, as if he can't believe the riches of the day. First the puppy, and now a present from his mother. He holds his hands up to his father, an offering, and Aiken bends to untie the twine that holds the paper in place.

"I don't know what it is," says Sam. "But I saw her work with it, hold it close to her chest, lift it up to the sky, kind of like you're doing right now. I guess maybe it's some kind of good luck charm."

Aiken recognizes the tiny doll he'd seen in his mother's room, woven from straw and dried flowers. And the yellow paper, like the sign he'd found in his father's hospital room. He picks it up, feels that it still holds the warmth of Sam's pocket, and returns it to Henry's hands.

"That's a nice thing to remember your mother by," he says, and kisses his son's head.

In the afternoon, the new barn rises from the ashes.

69

A light snow is falling, but Aiken doesn't expect it to amount to much. It's been a dry summer and fall, and no one predicts the drought will break soon. It's peaceful while it lasts, though, and he remembers that Soon-hee liked the snow. When the ground and the trees were covered in white, all the harsh edges softened, she could pretend she was home. He sips his coffee, and gazes at the dusting on the roof of the new barn.

It really is a shame about the old building, a handsome relic of the way things used to be. The new shed is functional, and it has everything he needs, but it's not much to look at. He's not ungrateful to his friends and neighbors, but there's something missing. He hasn't spent much time inside the place, and maybe that's the problem. He has to get used to it, make it comfortable. That might take some doing. He recalls that house in Iraq, nothing more than a gutted shell, thanks to him, until one day when the family erected a simple wooden frame and covered that with a tarp. It wasn't much, but it was shelter.

As he's thinking about whether today might be the day when he'll get back to work—despite the new barn, he's not sure he's ready—Deputy Crawford pulls into the driveway. He can't imagine what else there is to talk about. Billy had called the fire an arson, which plainly it was, and seemed satisfied with Aiken's story of what must have happened. There'd been no official word on the death, though, and so he girds himself for that news.

Billy nods as he approaches the porch. He brushes the snow off his jacket. The men shake hands and move inside, where Billy accepts a mug of coffee.

"I've got some news," Billy says.

"I figured that's why you came out. We knew it was her, though."

"Yeah, we did." Billy blows on his coffee and takes a sip. "Except it's not. Not your wife, I mean."

Aiken looks at Billy, wondering if he's heard right. He'd been so sure. And although it was sad and terrible, he'd been relieved, in a way, because that nightmare was over. She was no longer a threat to him and Henry. They could move on with their lives. But now?

"Who is it, then?"

"You seen Tammy lately?"

"Tammy?"

Billy nods.

He'd wondered why, since she and his mother had been on good terms, Tammy hadn't come to the funeral, hadn't even come to the house to pay her respects. He'd called and called looking for Soon-hee, left countless messages, and she never answered. And then, after they'd found the body, there seemed to be no point. What was Tammy doing in the barn?

"But there's something else you need to see," Billy says. He unbuttons the flap on his shirt pocket and pulls out a wad of cash wrapped in a familiar rubber band. "I expect this is yours."

His birdhouse earnings. Aiken takes the money, feels its heft, and looks at Billy. "But how?"

"Your cousin Jake has got to be the dumbest crook in the country."

"*Jake* did this?"

"One and the same. Said you'd loaned him the money."

"Not a chance." He remembered Jake asking for money to start a business, landscaping, he'd claimed. Jesus. What was he thinking? And how did he know where the money was? Jake had been snooping around the barn the day of his father's funeral, but Aiken had been with him the whole time. Had someone tipped him off? Soon-hee knew. Had she told Tammy?

"And the barn fire?"

"Covering up the robbery, most likely. As much as confessed to the trooper who pulled him over in South Carolina doing about ninety. A lot of unexplained fires around here we want to talk to Jake about. Similar M.O.—stolen equipment and a fire so people don't hunt too hard for what's missing. And now this one looks to be murder. Plus, when he skipped town he left behind one pissed-off wife who's happy to tell us everything she knows. Robberies. Drug dealing. A con game he ran down in Florida. A string of girlfriends, according to the wife. Apparently Jake and Tammy were kissing cousins, if you know what I mean."

"Son of a bitch."

"Yep."

Aiken is looking at the new barn through a scrim of snow, seeing it differently now.

"If that's Tammy," he says, "then where the hell is Soon-hee?"

70

I lie on the old woman's bed and remember the poems from my childhood. The shrine on the mountain. The descent of the Mountain God. I see the swirling clouds, the swaying bamboo. I watch the white crane leap into the sky.

There is pounding on the front door. I know the mother of Ay-ken is gone, her spirit is finally free, but for a moment I think it must be her. There is more she must teach me, and so she has come back. I rise, drift down the stairs as if in a dream. But it is not the old woman, it is not a dream. It is Jay-ke, the cousin of Ay-ken, and he is shouting. He says "parents" and "money." He says "bastard." He says "we had a deal."

He would help me, if I helped him.

He pushes inside. I am afraid. He shouts, "Henry," and I know—from the way he growls the name, from the twisted expression on his red face—that he means to do Ha-neul harm, he would hold him until he gets what he wants. He grabs my wrist and pulls me to the kitchen. He demands keys. He says, "Hank's guns." I search the kitchen and give him keys. We go down the stairs into the cellar. He opens the cabinet. He takes guns. I try to run but he squeezes my arm and I cannot move. I hear Ta-mee outside; she calls my name.

"Shit," he says, and pulls me up the stairs, one gun in his belt, the other in his hand. "What's she doing here?"

71

"Don't hurt her," I shout. I was afraid of this. I never should have trusted Jake. "You lying bastard, you said you wouldn't hurt her."

"I just want the money," Jake says. "*We* want the money. Remember? Wasn't the whole fortune telling thing your idea? The old woman's tapes?"

I look at Soon-hee, and suddenly I'm sorry for everything. What I told her about Aiken. What I told Jake. It's just that I have my dreams. This was my chance.

"I'm so sorry," I say.

Jake yanks her by the arm. "Tell me where it is," he shouts.

"Don't hurt her, Jake," I say again. "There's another way. We don't have to do this." I haven't told him yet what Aunt Ruth told me, about her affair with his father, Archie. How he and Aiken are brothers.

"What?" he says.

I grab for the gun.

72

He lets go of me to hit Ta-mee. Blood spurts from her face and she is on her knees, her head in her hands. He kicks her. "Stupid bitch," he says, and kicks her again. She falls and lies still. I run.

It is not the *chom*, the fortune telling, but I see fire. There are no flames yet, but I see fire.

I am in the field, running as fast as I can, as far as I can. The golden dog follows, running, barking. And Jay-ke. He catches me. He grabs me by the shoulders and shakes. We are hidden, in soft earth by the creek. "Money," he says again. The dog growls and barks. He is warning Jay-ke. He is protecting me, like the Mountain God. "Where's the money?" Jay-ke says, and now the dog is fierce, his teeth bared, he is coiled, like a snake, ready to strike. And Jay-ke shoots.

The shot rings in my ears, and I am afraid he will hurt Ha-neul the way he has hurt Ta-mee and the dog. So I say, "Barn," when he turns the gun on me.

73

Where is Soon-hee? Billy Crawford and his people have searched every inch of the farm, and Aiken has done the same with the aid of Charlie Doak and his son. They came across the family burial plot, a tiny, overgrown cemetery that had fallen out of use more than a century ago. But no sign of Soon-hee.

One morning, searching on a high slope above the property, Aiken stumbles over a rock and falls into a tangle of sweetbriar. As Charlie helps him up, his eyes are drawn to a shadow behind the bush. It's the mouth of a narrow cave. His father had said there were caves on the mountain, and when Aiken was a boy Hank had warned him that old Dermot dragged his victims into those caves, but Aiken had never found one until now. They cut the bramble away and Aiken, whispering Soon-hee's name, crawls inside.

Near the entrance of the cave he finds a mound of small, smooth stones, glittering in the daylight like jewels. Deeper, there's a candle stub and one of those yellow papers of Soon-hee's with the red writing. And deeper still he finds a pile of bones—human or animal, he can't tell—that must have been there for years, maybe a great many years.

The police have kept an eye on Tammy's empty trailer. They've alerted law enforcement in adjacent counties to be on the lookout for Soon-hee and for Tammy's car, which, as near as anyone can figure, is how Soon-hee managed to vanish so thoroughly. Because except for what they found in the cave, there's no trace of her. Nothing. Aiken knows some people still suspect he had something to do with her disappearance. Billy's boss, Sheriff Hale, even had Billy bring Aiken in for a new round of questioning. He seemed satisfied with what he heard, but Aiken supposes he won't really be free of suspicion until Soon-hee is found. Jake claims he didn't touch her. So where is she?

Mrs. McGrady now comes once a week to clean. Aiken and Henry did all right without her for a while, using Sunday mornings to sweep and scrub and vacuum, but he knows they were doing a poor job of it, and Mrs. McGrady is only too glad to help out and earn a little extra money. Most weeks she brings over an apple pie or one of her ham and cornbread casseroles. Aiken isn't a terrible cook, but the nights when Mrs. McGrady has visited are definitely the dining highlight of the week for the Alexander men. It becomes something of a ritual on Wednesdays when he picks up Henry from school.

"What did Miss Emily bring us?" Henry asks.

"She said she wasn't going to cook for us ingrates anymore. Said we didn't seem to appreciate what she brought us last week."

"But it had *eggplant* in it," Henry protests. "I bet she brought us something anyway, though. What did she bring?"

"I believe she said it was a chocolate cake, and for dessert there's a hamburger and noodle casserole."

"Daddy, that's backwards!"

"Don't tell me, tell Mrs. McGrady."

Kelly's a frequent visitor. She almost always brings something for Henry, usually a book. As soon as she pulls it out of her bag Henry wants to sit with her and read, and she seems happy to oblige. While Aiken finishes cooking dinner—hamburgers on the grill or his new specialty, spaghetti—the two of them squeeze into the armchair that Aiken's father had always occupied in the living room. Seeing them together, he's reminded of what might have been, but he's pleased to see their growing love.

After dinner, Kelly and Aiken stand at the sink and wash dishes and then watch TV with Henry until it's time for Henry to go to bed. And then Kelly picks up her purse, says goodnight to Aiken, and heads home. He'd like to ask her to stay, but worries that it's too soon for that. This time, he won't rush.

Aiken applies for a job with the sheriff's department, after asking Billy about his chances.

"I don't see why not," Billy says. "Being in the Army is great experience for the job."

"And it doesn't matter that I got into a little trouble way back when?"

"Not since it was way back when it doesn't. Hell, some of these boys were in trouble last week." Billy slaps his knee and laughs so hard he spills the Coke he's drinking.

But there are no openings just now, and Aiken's application is in limbo. Billy promises to let him know if something comes up. He applies for a job at the Wal-Mart. He even starts working there, since they seem to be hiring just about anyone with a heartbeat. He gets his hair cut short, back to his Army buzz, and makes arrangements for Henry to join the before-school care group at the church so he can drop him off early on his way across the county to the store, then pick him up on the way home. Henry doesn't like the extra hours at the church, and Aiken doesn't like what the whole situation does to him either, turning him cranky and likely to snap at every little thing. Plus, he feels silly stocking shelves with plastic junk in his ridiculous red vest. It doesn't seem like a real job. Doesn't seem like it can ever feel like a real job. But what choice does he have?

He's barely set foot in the new barn. It's not quite what the old barn had been. Where that was a cavernous, working mountain of a structure, with a hayloft and the horse stalls, a relic of another time, this one is more utilitarian. It rises only one story, so the landscape is considerably different than it had been; from the porch he can see the stony crest of the hill, which gives him the feeling that the farm has sunk into the earth. Instead of the big double doors of the old barn, this one has a simple aluminum door that he picked up at Lowe's.

One night, after a frustrating shift at the Wal-Mart, after yelling at Henry for being too slow to feed the puppy, he examines the new barn. He recalls that house in Iraq, the rubble where the family first erected a tent and then gradually rebuilt their home. They found the strength to start again. Could he? He walks the length of the barn, bangs his head on a low, unfamiliar beam, scatters sawdust on the plywood floor. He paces off the area where he might put a workbench, eyes walls for possible shelving and the low rafters for storage. It could work, he thinks. But is he ready?

That night he lies awake. He wonders about his real father, whoever he was, and what advice that man might have for him. He'll probably never know the man's identity, but in truth he doesn't much care. His mother's revelation had changed nothing. Henry Alexander was his father. They'd loved each other in their own ways. And his father had said, "If you don't stretch, you can't grow." The old man was right.

In the morning he takes more precise measurements and, after dropping Henry off at school, visits the lumberyard. He builds a crude bench that afternoon, good enough to get started. He has some ideas for the perfect workshop, with a sturdy table, shelves and baskets for storage and racks for tools, but that will come in time. He needs tools, too, and his credit is shot. He's already spent most of the money the sheriff recovered from Jake, and it will be awhile before he sees a check from Wal-Mart.

He contemplates going to see to Jake, to find out just what his cousin was thinking. Did he hate Aiken and his family that much? Jake and Tammy both had loved Hank. Did that have something to do with it? Were they still angry about his death? Did they blame him for some reason? And if Jake and Tammy had been having an affair, as Jake's wife claimed, was Tammy in on the scheme? Aiken imagines that they plotted it together, a fire to hide the robbery, and Tammy simply got in Jake's way, or she was baggage he didn't want to take with him. Or maybe, he'd like to think, Tammy was only trying to help Soon-hee get the money she needed to go back to Korea, and the fire was all Jake's idea. But he'll never know. According to Billy, the case against Jake is solid: prints on the gas can, his own confession to the robbery and a couple of other arsons, evidence that Tammy was beaten before she died in the fire, testimony from the wife. And if Jake was capable of doing that to Tammy, Aiken wonders what he might have done to Soon-hee.

He circles back to that question: where is Soon-hee? If she's dead, if Jake killed her, then why hasn't Billy found the body? Jake still had both the stolen guns when the cops in South Carolina pulled him over, so Aiken's satisfied that it was Jake, and not Soon-hee, who shot Ralph. But Billy said they didn't find blood in Jake's truck, no proof that Soon-hee had ever been in it. They've got every cop in the state on alert. If she's alive, where is she?

Aiken has a theory, one that he hasn't shared with anyone but Kelly. He figures Soon-hee saw Jake set the barn on fire and drive away in his truck. Then she got in Tammy's car and drove after him, and just kept going. What he doesn't understand is why.

Tammy had said Soon-hee wanted to take the boy back to Korea with her. So, does she still pose a danger to him and Henry?

He rarely lets Henry out of his sight, except when the boy is in school. If Soon-hee turns up there, the teachers understand that she's not allowed anywhere near him. They're supposed to call the police and Aiken, but keep her away from Henry. At home, when Aiken's working in the barn, Henry is with him, or with Kelly. Otherwise they're together in the house, or tramping through the woods.

Aiken feels some regret that he was quick to blame Soon-hee for the fire and Ralph's death, but since she hasn't turned up, and Jake isn't talking now that he's got a lawyer, it isn't clear what role she played. Aiken will never understand Tammy's involvement, either, but he wants to believe, now, that Soon-hee wasn't willingly part of Jake's treachery. He doesn't know what, if anything, to tell Henry.

Some days he imagines—it's the only answer to the puzzle that gives him real comfort—that she's managed to return to Pae-tu. In a few years, when Henry is older, maybe they'll go look for her there and, if nothing else, meet Henry's grandfather.

On an unseasonably warm late autumn day, he's on the porch with Henry and Ralphy. They've just eaten a heavy lunch—Mrs. McGrady brought lasagna this week, and there are leftovers—and Aiken, at least, is content to sit and enjoy a peaceful moment before going back to work in the barn. He's reading a book that Kelly gave him about the history of settlers in the Valley, and he's pleased and surprised to discover references to his ancestor Dermot. It makes him wonder whatever happened to that family tree his father and Hank used to work on, the one Aiken never cared about. Of course now he isn't sure whether he has a place on that tree, and may never know. Even so, he's intrigued. And then there is the family cemetery they discovered and those bones he found in that cave. Is that what happened to Dermot? Not a ghost, after all, but a hermit who met his lonely end on the mountain?

At his feet, Henry plays with Ralphy, seeking to pull from the puppy's mouth the straw doll that Soon-hee made and that Sam brought down from the mountain shrine. The dog clamps his jaw on the doll, and Henry tugs, twisting one way and then the other. Happy growls pour from the dog, and Henry answers with his own childish laughter. Now Ralphy has one leg, Henry has the other, and there is a ripping sound. Aiken looks up from his book. Both boy and dog appear startled that the doll has come apart, and neither seems to have noticed the roll of money that has dropped to the floor.

Aiken pushes himself out of the porch swing and stoops to pick up the bills. As he does so, he realizes that his back doesn't hurt, and, now that he thinks about it, hasn't hurt in some time. The ache, which on most days had been debilitating, has gone away as mysteriously as it arrived. He unrolls the money. There's close to a thousand dollars.

"What's this?" Aiken asks.

"Mommy's money," says Henry. "She saved it for us."

"For us?

"Uh-huh."

"How do you know that, Henry?"

"She told me."

"When?"

"Just now."

"Now? Where is she?"

Henry shrugs.

Aiken scans the yard and the hillside beyond, but there's no sign of Soon-hee. The boy hasn't been out of his sight all day.

With the windfall, which he decides to simply accept without further questions—Tammy had mentioned once that Soon-hee had been saving money out of her allowance for years, and she must have made some more when she sold the furniture from the cottage, and probably she told Henry about it before she disappeared—he buys a used table saw and new tools and a supply of plywood, pine, and paint. He buys stiff paper for patterns and stencils. He buys a drill and jigsaw and a bevel and a set of clamps. He buys hardware for shelves and wire for hanging from the ceiling and beams. He buys finishing nails and screws and hinges. He buys a barstool with a swivel seat. He buys a lamp to hang over the workbench. He buys thick planks and carriage bolts to build new bleacher seats. He buys a fire extinguisher and a fireproof safe. He quits the job at Wal-Mart.

Kelly joins them most nights for supper now—she's made no further mention of her relationship with Dr. Solomon, and Aiken doesn't ask. He wants to, but he's pressured her before, and he doesn't want to repeat that mistake. One night, they're standing at the sink washing dishes after dinner while Henry finishes his apple pie and Ralphy gnaws on a rubber bone beneath the table. Aiken leans over and kisses her, just once, lightly, on the lips. Her face reddens, but when he backs away, she's smiling. Kelly has told him that she likes his hair short, and she now caresses his head, the way Henry softly strokes the puppy. Her touch is warm and gentle, and, whether he deserves it or not, he feels forgiven.

Working in the barn, he makes a list of all the birdhouses he's built over the last few months. The basic birdhouse, the one that still sits on the fence post. The saltbox, the Cape Cod. The tavern, the school, the church, the synagogue. The cathedral, the pagoda, the skyscraper. The farmhouse. It's a long list and he thinks he's even forgotten one or two. He's sure he can build all those again, but he has an idea for a new kind of birdhouse, and he sets to work that afternoon.

The frame is simple, but he chooses beveled edges so the shape will be more of a diamond than a square box. He cuts the hole with the Forstner bit he's bought, and fixes a perch in front. He drills a small hole in the top and sets in an eye screw so the house can be easily hung. And then he makes five more, exactly the same. He sits on the stool and picks up the first house. He paints it white, with a slate roof. Then he paints in windows and a door. He paints a mailbox by the front stoop, with the red flag up. He paints a cat in one of the windows with a paw poised to swat the lace curtains. He paints a geranium in a pot on the other window. He paints a bush next to the door.

He picks up the next house and repeats the process, but instead of making it look like a cottage, he turns it into a post office, with a blue box in front, a sign in the window announcing its business hours. A man with a green eyeshade is visible through the window. The next one is a barber shop, with the red and white totem out front and the white-coated barber in the window. The fourth is a dress shop, with a mannequin in the window and a seamstress kneeling by its side. The last is a pet store, with puppies napping in the sunlit window. He's surprised by his own artistry. Maybe he has more in common with Jake than he thought.

Aiken goes to work inside the farmhouse, too. Mrs. McGrady is a great help, but he decides that his life there with Henry needs a new beginning, and bigger changes than just clean toilets and the new barn. He tackles his parents' bedroom first, removing all of their clothing. He enlists Kelly in the effort and they pack boxes to give to Goodwill. Kelly takes some of his mother's clothes for herself. It's hard to imagine any similarity in the two women's tastes, but Kelly assures him she knows how to adapt and update. She finds a hat she likes, one that had been in style years ago and seems to be again. They find costume jewelry and shoes and underwear and socks and souvenirs and church programs and a box of romance novels that his mother had bought at an auction and never got around to unpacking. In the sewing room they find old photo albums filled with snapshots of people Aiken can't identify—aunts and uncles, he supposes, but there's nothing written on the backs and he has no way of knowing who they are. Maybe one of the men is his father, but it no longer matters to him to know the truth, and so he doesn't dwell on them. Several pages are devoted to him and Hank. There are pictures of the two of them wrestling in the grass. One picture has been torn in half leaving only Hank looking handsome and happy in a dark suit with a boutonniere in his lapel. There's a picture of Aiken and Kelly at their senior prom. When they see that, they look at each other.

"How young we were," Kelly says.

"You're even more beautiful today," Aiken says. He leans toward her and kisses her. She squeezes his hand.

He gives Mrs. McGrady the lamp that, for as long as he can remember, rested on the dresser in the exact center of a lace doily. He gives her the doily, too. He finds a pocket watch that might have been his grandfather's, and he keeps that, but there's a cheaper watch he remembers his father wearing, and he gives that to Henry. They make up a box of shoes—his mother's practical shoes, with one or two nicer styles she wore for church and the occasional celebration, along with his father's workboots and his church shoes—and begin to build a pile on the porch. He fills two boxes with old sheets and blankets. He folds his mother's quilt into a box that he sets on top of the others.

When he loads the truck to haul it all to the thrift shop in Stillwater, he notices that the quilt is gone. Kelly helps him search for it among the other boxes, chiding him for giving away an heirloom that had probably been in the family for generations, but it's nowhere to be found, and they're too busy to keep looking.

"Maybe old Dermot took it," he jokes. "Mr. Bones."

"Or some other restless spirit?" Kelly says.

Aiken stops his work and gazes out toward the mountain. He sees only the brown pasture and the leafless trees, the rocky hillside. Wherever Soon-hee is, he hopes she's at peace.

74

When Aiken asked me to help clean up his house, I hesitated. What would it lead to, I wondered. It felt as though we were moving too fast again, the very thing that had derailed us once before. I had to admit that these weeks of spending time with him and his son had stirred feelings I thought were long dead. But was I ready to trust him again? I wasn't sure.

One night when I stayed at the house for supper after a day of sorting and packing his parents' things, I helped him get Henry ready for bed. Henry raised his arms and let me slip his red pajama top over his head, and Aiken attacked the boy's exposed belly with a barrage of tickling, sending them both to the floor in laughter. Before he climbed into bed, Henry came to me and hugged me tight, whispering "Good night," into my ear when I bent down to him. While Aiken read him a story, I watched from the doorway and listened. He's a devoted father, and the realization brought tears to my eyes. Henry's a lucky boy.

I slipped downstairs, put on my coat, and went out to the porch. The night air was sharp, and the sky was a comforting blanket of stars.

Aiken joined me. "What's the matter?" he asked.

I shook my head, unable to speak. I felt his arms wrap around me. He held me, and neither of us said a word. Finally, I pulled away. It was too soon.

"Maybe I was wrong," I said.

"About what?" He took my hand and we walked to my car.

"About a lot of things," I said. "Everything."

I saw Dr. Solomon at the hospital the next morning. I could barely look him in the eye because I knew he'd see how confused I was. Jonathan's been good to me. He was there for me when my mother died and he's been generous and patient. He asked if we were having dinner that night—something we've been doing most Fridays since we started seeing each other—and I couldn't lie.

"I can't see you," I said.

"It's Aiken, isn't it?" he asked.

I looked away. It wasn't just Aiken. It was Henry and the farm and Aiken's parents and my miscarriage. I'd made a mistake before, and I didn't want to make another. I needed time.

"You told me that was all in the past, that you didn't have feelings for him anymore. You told me—"

"I know what I told you," I said.

Instead of having dinner with Jonathan, I picked up a pizza in Stillwater on my way out to Aiken's farm. In the day's last light, Brother Mountain looked blue and inviting, as if it were calling me home. For the first time since I came back from Roanoke—really, for the first time since my miscarriage—I felt hopeful. And yet, I knew the mountain held secrets, a past. I knew what Aiken was capable of, the pain he could cause. Still, I went.

And then, as I walked from my car to Aiken's porch steps, Henry ran to me, shouting, "Miss Kelly's here, Miss Kelly's here!" He hugged my legs so hard I could barely walk.

"I'm happy to see you, too, Henry," I said. "Are you ready for pizza?"

"Pizza!" he shouted, and ran back inside the house.

After dinner, after the dishes were washed and put away, after Henry was asleep, Aiken and I sat on the couch. He put his arm around me.

"What are we doing, Aiken?" I asked.

"I don't know," he said. "But it feels right. Doesn't it? Us?"

"Does it? Then why I am I so unsure?"

"Kelly—"

"No, listen to me, Aiken. I think you're doing a wonderful job with Henry. I do. But you can't just expect me to forget about what happened between us. We can't go back to the way things were before."

"I know that." He lifted his arm off my shoulder and leaned forward, elbows on his knees. "And I've said I was sorry. I truly *am* sorry. What else do you want me to say, Kel? I've changed."

"How can I be sure?"

He looked at me. "Henry. Henry is how you can be sure."

"What about Soon-hee?"

He didn't answer. We listened to the wind in the trees. He took my hand.

"You know what Henry said to me today? He said, 'I'm glad Mommy chased away all the bad ghosts.' I asked him what he meant, of course. Apparently, according to Henry, his mother is some kind of good spirit watching over us and has managed to frighten away whatever—or whoever—was haunting this house."

"Do you believe that?"

"No. Of course not. But who knows? Maybe he's right. She used to talk all the time about destiny, about becoming the person she was meant to be. Right now, today, is the first time in a long time I've felt at home in my own skin, like this is who I was meant to be. So maybe, just maybe, Henry's on to something. And then I asked him how he would feel if Miss Kelly came to live with us."

"You asked him that?"

"I did. And you know what he said?"

"What?"

He said, "That would be perfect."

75

Aiken's parents had slept on the same mattress and box spring forever. With Charlie Doak's help, he drags those down the stairs and carts them to the county dump. He buys a new set, and Kelly helps him pick out linens at Belk, because what does he know about buying sheets, and, besides, he hopes it will soon be her bed, too. He strips off two layers of densely patterned, dark wallpaper and finds traces of the log cabin that is the house's core. He takes down the old curtains in the room and installs mini-blinds. He paints.

In Henry's room, his own boyhood room, he removes all the old trophies and briefly relives glory days while Kelly helps him pack the little statues in boxes. Henry wants to keep one, so they leave a single baseball trophy on the shelf, and Aiken tells the story of how he'd won it in Little League one year for being the most valuable player. Kelly sits next to Henry on the bed. The springs creak, and Aiken winks at Kelly.

He even starts on Hank's room. His mother had never been able to do anything to it, and Aiken is tempted to leave it alone, too. But he wants everything to be fresh as he and Henry start their new lives together. He doesn't need a shrine to remember Hank. On the shelf over Hank's desk he finds a tiny toy soldier. His mother had mentioned a toy soldier on her tapes, a gift from her brother John, so Aiken leaves the soldier on the shelf.

The downstairs is a bigger job, and takes longer. He'll save the kitchen for last, since the appliances will be expensive. But he removes all the old curtains and that makes the dining and living rooms instantly brighter. There'd been worn carpet tacked down in the living room, and he rips that up, discovering dull pine boards beneath. It will take awhile to get those refinished, but he'll do it.

He's found a place in his bedroom—his parents' room—to store his mother's tapes. He's listened to them again and again, startled by how little he knew about her and her family, their life up in the hills. He's hoping for another clue about who his real father is, and he pauses when his mother mentions Uncle Archie, Jake's father, making unwelcome advances. But that was years before he was born, and he dismisses it. At first he is bothered by his mother's deceptions—the lies and half-truths, the manipulation, the secrets—but he knows she thought she was protecting her family. Hasn't he done the same? Wouldn't anyone? He's puzzled by the references to her powers, though, and to Soon-hee's powers. These are only superstitions, after all, hillbilly make-believe, and he gives them no credence. And yet it seems that the bond between his mother and Soon-hee grew out of their shared beliefs, no matter how backward and absurd. He loves listening to the tapes, although he can hear his mother fading, her voice becoming weaker over time. He looks forward to one day sharing them with Henry.

It's the end of the year, one that has brought Aiken more change than he thought possible. Although he feels a dark sadness when he dwells on all that has happened, and he still worries about what happened to Soon-hee, he accepts that nothing is out of place. Kelly has come back to him. Henry is happy and safe. What more could he ask for?

He doesn't admit this to Kelly, but he is sometimes visited by Hank, who guides his hand while he works, urges him on when he's tired, reminds him of all that he's built. Aiken even feels Soon-hee's presence, although that is more removed, as if she's still torn between the farm and her own mountain home, or some other place he can't imagine. He knows it's all ridiculous, that what he senses are just lingering memories that will fade in time, but still they comfort him.

On a cold afternoon in late December, he feels the need to celebrate the coming of the new year, not in the way he might have when he was younger, with a raucous visit to Turtle Tavern, but by getting to know his land. He bundles Henry into a parka and snug cap, and, with Kelly at his side and Ralphy sometimes romping behind, sometimes riding in Aiken's arms, they traipse up the hill behind the house. Henry stops every few yards to explore, which Aiken is content to let him do. There are sweetbriars that prick Henry's hand, producing a sharp squeal of pain and a valuable lesson; there are gnarled vines that twist around the trunks of trees, drawing Henry's gaze into their leafless reach; there are glittering stones that Henry collects along the way, now and then dropping one in favor of a newer, shinier find. The rocks put Aiken in mind of the smooth stones he'd found in the cave, perhaps the collection of some other child, from long ago.

When they reach the high pasture and come upon a mound of larger stones, Aiken knows that Soon-hee has been here. How recently, he can't say. Henry and Ralphy nose along the edge of the woods, while Aiken examines what he takes to be an altar. The stones are worn and flat, of the sort he's seen at the bottom of the hill, in the creek, and he wonders if Soon-hee carried them up the mountain just to build this shrine. The view from here, of rolling hills and stony peaks with their caps of snow, reminds him of Korea, as it must have reminded Soon-hee. She would have found solace here. It's a peaceful place. He runs his hand along the surface of the stones.

Aiken turns when he hears the excited shouts of Henry and sees the boy striding across the field hand-in-hand with old Sam, Ralphy bounding alongside.

"You found her shrine, I see," says Sam.

"It's a fine spot," says Aiken. "You've been here?"

"This is where I picked up that little doll of hers. Saw her here, too, once or twice."

"You've seen her here?"

"Some time ago. Before."

Aiken wonders if there's more that Sam isn't telling him. They're both watching Henry, who has emptied the shiny rocks from his pockets and added to them several that he's picked up in the pasture. He brushes dirt away from a spot next to the altar and firmly places one of the rocks, flat and round, pushing it into the hard earth. He takes a second rock and places that one on top of the first, and he keeps doing this with his rocks until he's built a small pyramid of seven or eight stones.

"What've you got there, Henry?" Kelly asks.

"It's a present," says Henry.

"A present?" Aiken looks at Sam and grins, amused, like all fathers, at the peculiar things his child comes up with. "Who's it for?"

The top stone of Henry's pyramid has fallen and he replaces it with a pebble that stays. He backs away cautiously, tugging at Ralphy's collar when the puppy wanders too close to the tower.

"It's for Sansin," Henry says. "He's the man who lives in the mountain."

"Who told you that, son?"

"Mommy. She tells me lots of things."

"When did she tell you this?"

Henry shrugs.

Aiken takes Kelly's hand. The wind picks up, carrying the pine scent of the forest, and stony clouds bunch over the humps of Brother Mountain, bearing the promise of snow. A hawk soars high above the altar, its shadow brushing Aiken's shoulder, then disappears, riding the windy currents down in broad rings, into the depths of Turtle Valley.

THE END

AUTHOR'S NOTE

Over the long road that led, finally, to the publication of this novel, many people and organizations provided help and encouragement.

Thank you first to Jeffrey Condran and Robert Peluso of Braddock Avenue Books for believing in the book and bringing it to life. I'm grateful.

Thank you to Fred Leebron, Director of the Queens University of Charlotte Creative Writing MFA Program, whose encouragement means everything.

Thank you to Kevin Morgan Watson for all of our literary collaborations and friendship.

Thank you to Kimmel Harding Nelson Center for the Arts and the Virginia Center for the Creative Arts for providing the time and space that allowed me to write much of this book.

Thank you to the Sewanee Writers' Conference for providing me with a fellowship while I was still finding my way with this story.

Thank you to some of the best writing teachers anyone could wish for, including Russell Banks, Richard Bausch, Charles Baxter, Pinckney Benedict, Amy Bloom, John

Casey, Peter Ho Davies, Robin Hemley, Bret Anthony Johnston, Fred Leebron, Kevin McIlvoy, Tim O'Brien, Patricia Powell, Elizabeth Strout, Chuck Wachtel, and the late, great Grace Paley.

Thank you to a host of friends who have read and commented on portions of the book, but especially to Mary Akers, who read early drafts, and to Leona Sevick, who read a near-final draft.

And, finally, thank you to readers. Without you, this would all be pretty pointless.

What I know about building birdhouses I learned from the following works: *Architectural Birdhouses*, Thomas Stender (Lark Books, 2001); *65 Birdhouses and Bird Feeders*, Ronald D. Tarjany (Tarjany Publications, 2001); *Building Birdhouses*, Don Vandervort, Editor (Sunset Books, 2002); and *The Complete Book of Birdhouse Construction for Woodworkers*, Scott D. Campbell (Dover Publications, 1984).

Although I first learned about Korean Shamanism through direct observation when I lived in South Korea in the mid-1970s, the following works greatly contributed to my understanding: *Shamans, Housewives, and Other Restless Spirits*, Laurel Kendall (University of Hawaii Press, 1985); *The Life and Hard Times of a Korean Shaman*, Laurel Kendall (University of Hawaii Press, 1988); *Shamanism: The Spirit World of Korea*, Chai-shin Yu and R. Guisso, Editors (Asian Humanities Press, 1988); and *Six Korean Women: The Socialization of Shamans*, Youngsook Kim Harvey (West Publishing Co., 1979).

Clifford Garstang is the author of the novel in stories, *What the Zhang Boys Know*, winner of the Library of Virginia Literary Award for Fiction, and the short story collection *In an Uncharted Country*. He is also the editor of *Everywhere Stories: Short Fiction from a Small Planet*, a three-volume anthology of stories set around the world. A former Peace Corps Volunteer in South Korea and an international lawyer, Garstang lives in the Shenandoah Valley of Virginia.